# SHOPPING LIST

# 4

## 18 Terrifying Tales of Horror

## Compiled & Edited by
## Xtina Marie

A HellBound Books Publishing LLC Book
Houston TX

# CONTENTS

# SHOPPING LIST 4

# Kenneth Bykerk's
# Shopping List

Needles

Thread

Buttons, small bag

Thimble

Frozen burritos (important)

Kerosene

# Necessary Arrangements
# A Tale of the Bajazid
*Kenneth Bykerk*

This place stank. It reeked with an undercurrent of evil, a taint Jonathon Kearns could well discern. There were spices and herbs and plant smells amid musty deterioration and rot. There were stenches foul he could not place, and each disturbed his senses. There was no disguising his disgust.

"Does my house offend your nose, Mister Kearns?" The crone before him spoke. Her voice was meant to be harsh, sharp and cruel, but the deformities which afflicted the woman had affected her speech rendering that effect through the mumble of a soft mouth.

"You know damn well that it does." There was no need with this woman for pleasantries. That he was here conversing with her at all was a test of his faith.

"I am what I am, Mister Kearns, and my preparations can be a bit overwhelming for those unaccustomed. Still, if your child is sick, who are you going to ask for? The healing woman or the learned physician?" Certain consonants and sounds were muffled, swallowed in the impediment that ruined her voice, the reason for her shawl and veil.

"I would summon a respected doctor for the elixir needed and tend the rest through prayer. I would not stain my soul with the counsel of witches."

"Yet here you are, in my parlor. Mister Kearns, before you turn, listen to what I have to say."

Kearns' intent was in his eyes. He had no desire to be here but here he needed to be. There were necessary arrangements that must be made and only here could they safely meet. Satan's spies in this town werc thick as flics on a corpse in summertime. Restraining his deepest inclination, he drew breath and hissed out tersely, "Speak your peace."

"Don't be temperamental with me, Mister Kearns. Mind your manners if you want my help."

"You want them gone as well..."

"Tut!"

The crone raised her hand, a mitten of patchwork cloth caked and stained with dirt and grime. The hag raised her foul hand, crusted burlap finger waving, and shut him off with a *tut*! Rage, deep and righteous began to boil in his depths. A woman should not speak to a man such, let alone a degenerate pythoness such as the Widow Weaver to a man of his status, of his sanctified and venerable importance in God's plan. Scripture and Revelation were quite clear on that. Still, he reminded himself with a deeper breath and an admonishment that whilst resorting to sorcery challenged his resolve, God reveals his plans at his own choosing and uses what vessels he needs. He held his tongue through clamped jaw.

"Good, I was wondering if you had any self-control."

"It would be better if you arrived at the point of this meeting without further testing my patience. I follow scripture and it is only through the grace of the Heavenly Father that I do not tear you asunder this very moment."

"Which is why you need to listen to me. Now sit down, Mister Kearns, and please pretend to be civil. I do not get many visitors."

Jonathon Kearns honestly did not know if she was teasing him. Who would visit her in this rank dump? No sooner had the thought crossed his mind than he shied at his own whimsy. He was here, was he not?

The Widow Weaver chuckled a soft, muffled laugh. "Yes, Mister Kearns, you are here, are you not?"

Sorcery! Jonathon Kearns once had a very serious poker-face, back some years before when he still played poker. Now he did not play such games, nor, when confronted with Satan's power direct, could he not keep incredulity and shock from his face. The sorceress had read his...

Her laughter rose as a prayer formed on his lips. "Oh, do stop, Mister Kearns. Not all my seams are strong! If you make me laugh further,

"You're a wicked, evil bitch."

"And you are not making this easy. Are you always this obstinate, Mister Kearns?"

"Yes." Jonathon Kearns took great pleasure in that response. He could not see the face of the woman before him, the dim light of the single lantern hanging and her concealing veil made it seem he was talking to a lampshade in the dark. The response of that lampshade, a complete cessation of movement and sound for a full fifteen seconds, was rewarding.

"Well then, Mister Kearns, I guess we should call this council off then and each continue our paths to damnation separate. You can sit back and watch your prophesy come true down to the consumption of your last heir by this demon that is not Satan and I will continue to suffer as I have these many years until whatever becomes of me..." The draped shadow shrugged softly.

Jonathon Kearns knew a bluff, but he also knew the dance involved. It grated on his nerves that he was forced to play this absurd game with this vile woman, but he was set back by her words. Yes, in their first talks, when the Lord brought him to this witch to seek help destroying that den of serpents, he had told her his reason, his need to leave the valley. He had told her of prophecy, but no specifics. He did not tell her the Beast ate his seed. He sat silent, his face exposing only his hatred and the open truth he was revealed in whole.

"You aren't the only one with prophecy, John Kearns. Are we witches not soothsayers? What do your storybooks and the tales parents tell their children say about us? Shall I produce for you a crystal for us to gaze at?" Then, with tone dropping to a disgusted sneer, "Grow up, Jonathon Kearns. You're an embarrassment to men."

That was enough! Jonathon Kearns rose before he thought to stand, his chest puffed and proud, the anger volcanic in his eyes.

"Damn you, witch! I will kill you now! Dare mock me again, and I will smite you down!"

The damned witch was unruffled. She simply lifted her teacup beneath her veil. This casual dismissal infuriated Kearns even more. He was unused to women speaking to him in any way but adoration or servility. Be they after his money as all the whores of his past or his blessing and grace as they flocked now, that was their place yet here this slurping pox of Babylon dared pretend to ignore him.

"Speak, witch! I have accused you! In the name of Jesus Christ, our Father in Heaven, you have been declared a witch. How do you plea?"

"I plea that you are tedious. Shut the door when you leave."

The slurp was wet and loud, as if sucked through cloth without care to manners. It was enough, this disrespect shown him, to cast verdict and know it divine. Mockery of the Host was blasphemy and that alone deserved the judgment coming and who was he if not the Viceroy of the Christ, the representation in flesh of the Sinful Man Redeemed.

In one motion, the Bowie cleared his belt. With force, he grabbed the cursed little witch by the neck with his other hand and lifted her back up against the wall. She weighed a feather, no more than a child. Her resistance was futile as he braced her against the wall, her feet kicking feebly. She was chuckling hoarsely from beneath her veil as one damp, gloved finger jabbed ineffectively at his face. He squeezed hard at her throat, his fingers clenching tight on what felt nothing like it should. It yielded, the vital substance within cushioned as if not by meat but padding stolen from the flesh of a child's cloth doll.

She chuckled. Gasping and wheezing, she continued smearing her finger over his nose. His incredulity was clear on his face.

"What are you?" The words came out mixed with disgust and fear but his grip did not slacken.

Her response was a choked whisper, "Put...down..."

He did just that, without any hint of gentleness at all. That was more than she deserved. Kearns, his hand before him as if it needed cleansing itself, backed up a pace with knife ready. "What are you?"

"Get out!" She sagged against the wall, one hand pressed back for support and the other beneath her veil. "Get out! We are done here. May your children feed that thing you bring forth for generations!"

"What are you, woman? I need to know! You are not of flesh, not of Adam born! What are you?"

"You have no right to ask! You have only to leave before you suffer far worse than what you felt. We are done, Mister Kearns."

"Done? And what of you? You bluff!"

"What do you care? You are ready to skin me alive! Your knife is in your hand! Begone!"

"You need me. Like I need you. Now tell me what you are!"

"I don't need you, John Kearns. Ha! Look at me like that! You are a fool, a weak and stupid fool. Look at you! You quake from my touch. Me! And still, that is all you have to say? That you need me in exchange for holding that on me, threatening my life?"

"The Lord stayed my hand for he knows what must be done." Kearns was forthwith in every word. No lie, no falsehood ever escaped his lips, not since he was reborn to the Light four years prior. Everything he said became truth. Her sharp, short laugh did little to drain the bile from his gall.

"You are a fool and a liar. You need me. I don't need you. My punishment is already upon me. Yours is coming. Now leave!"

"If yours is upon you, then why did you need me in the first place? Did you just lure me here to taunt me, to tease me? Is that your game, witch?"

"My game, Preacher Kearns, is that my doom is here. I just wanted to see my revenge before it is complete. You?" She jabbed that damp, wet finger back at his chest. "Your doom is coming."

Kearns was a fighting man, always had been. He was quick, faster than his gangly appearance let on. He snatched her again, this time pulling her close and placing the tip of his knife to her gut. "Then I guess I might as well kill you."

Her soft gasp showed her surprise at his speed, at how fast she was disassembled before him. Her words though, were perverse—mockery with a harlot's intent. "Darling," she cooed, "I wish you would. I wish you would slide that into me and end this for me. Oh, darling, I know my fate and you would do me a mercy but...do you smell that?"

Damn her! She was confusion. Her body was loathsome in his arms. It had no substance, no weight behind it. Even her bones felt frail and in his rage and hate, he felt his grip loosen in unconscious deferential disgust.

"What? This whole place stinks, you crazy bitch!" He had but to slip the knife forward, jab in and up against where she was pressing herself right then. That's all he had to do.

"This?" She quipped, a lilt to her voice as she poked his nose with her soft, damp finger.

The bile rose in his throat, his stomach clenching in disgust at what distinguished itself above the many odors of the room. He shoved her back and fought to keep his stomach as she laughed from the floor where she landed.

"You've bewitched me! What have you done?" Kearns could feel his head swimming. He was no stranger to intoxicants of diverse nature. He knew, from personal experience in selfish pursuit what it felt like to be poisoned.

"I ain't done nothing, John Kearns. I ain't done nothing but made fool of you!" The perverse hag cackled her response as she climbed to her feet.

"Damn you, woman! You will..."

"TUT!"

Jonathon Kearns' words leaked soundlessly away and he stared at her in disbelief. How dare she! He stared with open hatred at her, the knife forgotten in his hand. The witch before him was gaining substance. She remained small, frail and bent under her shawl and veil, but her presence gained strength and force as she pointed her damp glove at him.

"Mister Kearns, I invited you here so we might conclude our business. You seek to flee this place, to run like the coward you are from the fate you think you can avoid. You need me to accomplish this. Tut! You listen now. You listen and you listen good for this is your doom, Jonathon Kearns. You walk out that door now, your prophesies come true. It's that simple, John Kearns. Now, you have made it clear that you do not want my help so please, leave."

"And what of you? You will still be damned."

"What care you? I am already damned. I simply want payment for the flesh they stole, the marks they cast upon me."

"What? You blame them for...?"

"Leave, John Kearns."

"Ha!"

"You are not welcome here."

Jonathon Kearns was incredulous. Was he really afraid of this woman? He knew what she looked like, or what she did before she hid herself under her shawl. She was horse-faced and ugly and her face was marred by birthmarks. As he remembered her for who she was before she hid herself under these capes, the power of that figure before him waned to the diminutive, ridiculous thing it was.

"You are a fraud." The words came with determination. "You are nothing but a fraud. You pretend at this game, hiding behind your widow weeds to cover your stained face." Yes, that damp glove withdrew. "You know nothing. I am wasting my time here."

"Get out!"

Jonathon Kearns could feel the Spirit descending, that light warmth that began from above and seeped like sacred oil into his skin. The glow of holy sight teased at the edges of his vision. "Forgive me, Lord, but this well is dry. What you sought is not here."

"Aw, shit!"

"No, Father, she is an empty vessel." Before the Lord first descended upon him in the hour of his greatest peril, he had only thought he'd known ecstasy. The depths of decrepitude to which his wealth and license had allowed his soul to sink was deserving of the damnation he had faced. It was the divine intervention, this glorious anointing of spirit and soul that deterred the Devil that day and showed him redemption. The knife in his hand returned to his mind. "Yes, Father, your glory is divine."

"Mister Kearns, I warn you..."

Jonathon Kearns' attention sprang direct from his celestial dialogue, his focus burning sharp onto the Widow Weaver, who now was backed against the wall once again. The air burned red around the black flames that traced her soul. "You warn me? Witch! You dare speak another word and your death shall endure the night! Now hold still and know mercy!"

Jonathon Kearns stepped forward, the Bowie blade rising up for a sacrificial plunge. His sight was full upon him, the world blurring to indistinct fractures excerpt what mattered. Here, all that mattered was the Widow Weaver, a witch admitted impotent before the power of the Host and thus condemned. She stood out in full brilliance, her aura distinct in coruscating corruption, and removed her veil.

The power of the Beast is great. Jonathon Kearns knew it was a fool who believed otherwise. That of the Lord is ever greater and so the weakness must be his. What was revealed behind that veil and beneath that shawl stopped his sight complete, knocking the air from his breast and staggering his step back in surprise. The witch had not lied. Her damnation was already full upon her.

"What is the matter, Mister Kearns? Does my face offend your sight?"

"Holy God! What damns you?"

"TUT! You are in my house, John Kearns. You wanted to know why I want them gone? This is why! This is why, John Kearns! Because of this! Look! Look at me! Look at my stitches and my scars!"

Jonathon Kearns had no choice. The horror before him demanded his attention. It was perverse mockery that forced horror but abandoned the possibility of pity. The slurp of disgusting proportions was explained.

"This is what they have done to me, John Kearns. We, those cunts in their little coven and

I, we wage war with each other in ways little men like you will never understand. We transcend your laws and replace with our own the laws we see fit. Sometimes things get complicated. For all I have done to them, they have caught me in one way my wards did not defend."

"Evil woman," all he had left was a whisper, "what are you?"

"I don't know, foolish man, neither what I am nor what I'm becoming. It is interesting, is it not?" With this, the Widow Weaver let slip the whole of her dress from shoulders short and loose, her naked form in perverse glory before him exposed.

"This is damnation!" Kearns backed up, his knife again a forgotten relic in his grip.

"Yes, this is my damnation, John Kearns. Would you like to share it? Would you like this visited upon you? Look at me! Look!"

"Cover yourself!"

"Look!"

There was no refusal possible. The horror that was before him could not be ignored. The Widow Weaver stood naked, exposed complete to his sight. The lusts of Man were not possible from the mockery that was her skin, the revelation of her curse. No less than half her flesh exposed was replaced by scraps of rag sewn crudely into her very form. The fabrics were diverse and chaotic in their patchwork placement. One rough trapezoid covering half her left breast was of a pattern he recognized from the chair on which he'd sat.

"Is this how you remember me? What? You don't remember, John Kearns? You didn't mind my face that night. What vexes you now? Oh, you were quite the tippler, then, weren't you though?"

The night in question he remembered, ever so vague. His years in hedonistic excess left some memories best forgotten, but they were also the basis of his soul redeemed. He could not escape his past sins and here one stood before him to remind him that he too has slept with the Beast, that his soul too was hostage to his redemption. He remembered her birthmarks clear. He had stared at them as he raced his way to his own satisfaction.

Those marks were not what he remembered. Where a strawberry stain ran a scythe from her left eye to beneath her nostril, now a jagged cut of scarlet extended that length and more. That strip of felt arced back from her eye and over her ear, ending at the base of her neck. Over her left eye, where a port-stained crescent hung upside down, a piece of burgundy silk in the same pattern remained. The ruination, the reason for the veil, was expressed in further alterations, pieces of her face replaced with patterned scraps of fabric. Half of her upper lip and parts of her lower were no longer flesh but cotton stained to colors vile. Where patches of her scalp announced their absence, her remaining hair did little to conceal her pains.

"Do you see why I want my revenge, Mister Kearns? Do you see now? You are not my only hope. There are other means, ones which may prove less than satisfactory for they are, combined, much stronger than me, but I do not need you. You do need me though. You know that, don't you? Answer me, Mister Kearns."

"I will take my chances."

"You are a prideful fool, John Kearns. You will survive the last of your seed. That is your prophecy, is it not?"

"You seem to know, Mrs. Weaver, so why should I answer?"

"Ha! So you recognize me by name now, do you? Mister Kearns, you are shameless and deserve what is coming. You will suffer your doom realized unless you escape this place, but That Which Damns needs distraction. That is why you came to see me, but you aren't man enough to treat me as worthy of anything but contempt. You are on your own. Go die, John Kearns. Go await your doom."

"And that is it? You surrender?"

"How can I treat with a bared knife in my room? How? You expect me to deal under threat? Have I so harmed you?"

"What was that you put on my face?"

"Tea, you oaf. You spilled my tea. Do you feel the fool yet?"

Jonathon Kearns did feel the fool. It was discomforting, a sensation he was unused to but one here he could not escape. "You tricked me, witch."

"Of course I did. Don't you know what witches do? When we are not healing the children of ungrateful fools like you, we are tricksters. You act surprised. Ah! Be careful, John Kearns. If you harm me, you will take my curse on yourself. Do you want to piss the rest of your days through a besotted sock while your generations corrupt before your eyes?"

Kearns had nothing to say in response. With her exposed before him, seeing her own dilemma revealed, he shuddered at the thought suggested.

"You need to leave now, John Kearns. Our dealings are done. I will tell you what you came to hear, what you've refused to hear so far this night. Your arrogance does not deserve this revelation, but I want my last years with some flesh of my own. This is my mercy to you. Five nights hence, John Kearns, the moon will eclipse. That is the hour to act. That is when you must distract the demon that holds us both."

"You portend this moon? How can I trust your divination?"

"You can't, but you can trust an almanac, right?"

This night was humiliation. Following the Widow Weaver's glance, Kearns looked down to see the dramatically illustrated, well-worn cover of *The Family Christian Almanac of the United States*, 1884 edition, on the table he'd abandoned.

"What should I do?"

"You don't know? Ha! What do you do with witches, stupid man? You burn them! Burn all of them! They will be there, all of them together under that roof."

"How do you know?"

"I'm a witch. It is an eclipse. I know what witches do in covens on eclipses. Burn them!"

"And what will you do?"

"Me? I've given you the night of success. You do this while your people escape through the tunnel to Pitt's Junction. Then you'll be free. When you light the flames to their house, I will toss their dolls into my stove. The Beast of the Bajazid will devour their souls as the flames eat their bodies. Isn't that enough?"

"And then we will be done, witch?"

"Then we shall be done, Preacher."

A sense of finality came over Jonathon Kearns, a surety he knew was acknowledgement divine. The knife with unseen ease slipped back into its sheath as Kearns turned without further word and stepped to the door. Not another second need he remain.

"Five days, John Kearns! You have five days to prepare. If you fail, it is on you!" Her words followed him, devolving to laughter as the door swung shut. Let her laugh. Let her cackle at his back. He had what he needed. In five days, it would all be over.

*M U Nib's*

*Shopping List*

*Corvid's beak and virgin's blood*
*Mixed in with some graveyard mud*
*Werewolf's tooth and*
*Vampire's ire*
*Ashes from a funeral pyre*
*Mixed up by some leprous hand*
*By imps living in strange lands*
*Glass bottles both strong and true to hold onto the Zombie Brew*

# The Exercist
## *M U Nib*

**Exercist** n. *Yorkshire, UK*. Dialect word for an exercise instructor.
**Were** *Northern England, UK*. Local dialect, singular form of **was**.

#

"I'm afraid there appears to have been some sort of misunderstanding."

And *that*, if you really want to know, is how it started off with me and Hugo. I suppose you could say that it were a right inauspicious start, but then ain't that how these things *always* are before getting to the *best of times worst of times* part?

There I were—in his hoity-toity antique-ridden study, in his huge hotel—stood up, with the door at my back, and him, sat facing me, on the other side of his desk. A grandfather clock—still stuck on Greenwich Mean Time, like a set-in-its-ways doddery old soak—broke the silence with its repetitive *tick-tick-tick.*

Despite the inclement weather, I wore a little black number: not too showy or revealing, professional, smart, serious, sassy and with enough shoulder musculature on display to show that if a top-flight exercist were needed, I could do the *rugger-bugger* stuff as well as any bloke, even if I were just a young Yorkshire lass straight out of Leeds University, and with a broad northern accent to boot.

"Look, *Miss*," said Hugo, tapping the desk with his finger-tips. He wore a black three-piece suit and an equally black shirt. Dark he were, top to bottom—including his demeanour, and with such a beaky nose that he looked like a po-faced raven. "Unfortunately, you've had a wasted trip. I was expecting a *Mr.* James for interview. You *Misss*, clearly are no Mr. James."

I laughed, there were no missing his hissing emphasis of the Miss, and my laugh got him frowning—as if he weren't used to having underlings, or even wannabe-underlings, laughing at him.

"I'm sorry," I said, stifling my outburst. "But I can see how the error occurred. There's no mystery! M'name is Mary Roget James. *I'm* M R James! But don't worry, it happens all the time. I even get confused with some don down in Cambridge who came up with these scary short stories."

"I see," he said, turning to stare up at an oil painting of an equally snobby-looking ancestor which hung over the mantlepiece. A polite cough from myself made him turn back and look at me.

"Look, I know I'm not a mister, but I'm perfectly capable of being a right good exercist. I've got a first-class honours degree in exercise physiology, I've a black belt in taekwondo, I've been a personal trainer for two years and–"

"How many ghosts have you gotten rid of?" he said, cutting me off.

"Sorry?"

"How many spooks have you spooked?"

"Is that like some sorta trick question?"

"No," he said. "It's the sort of straightforward thing one asks a filly who's applying to be my hotel exorcist."

"Ex*orcist*?" I said. "Ex*orcist*! I thought the newspaper ad said ex*ercist*."

He shook his head. "Like I said. There's clearly been a misunderstanding or  . . . two. Clearly, they come in pairs, like socks."

"Darn," I said, trying to sound jokey.

"Ahem . . . Quite. Now, if you'll allow me to call you a taxi, we can stop wasting each other's time."

I stared down at my feet. My black brogues were still damp from the drizzle *and* the walk up the long winding driveway; and I'd had nowt to eat since yesterday. I could just accept my bad luck, or I could try to make the most of whatever fate had slung at me.

"Well, no, I'm not an exorcist, but don't you need an exercist also? Someone to run the gym? I mean, you do have a gym, don't you? A big place like this, an' all."

Hugo, who at the time were just as he's shown in his portraits, stared up from his desk and looked at me with his dark, soulful eyes. "I think that would be a wretched idea," he spat.

"But why? It'd help attract guests."

"Guests!" he cried. "Guests! Damnit, that's the last thing this place needs, even more guests! More people turning up and for you to get them pumping weights, so they collapse on the gym floor with a heart attack!"

If the sinister shape and name of DeVille Hall hadn't done the trick, if the cacophony of cawing from the crows on the hotel heights hadn't pecked worry into my head over why the heck I were trying to get a job in a joint like that, then I suppose that nothing, not even those words, straight from the horse's mouth, would have done the trick.

"Ah," I said. "Ah, but I'm sure you need more guests. An injection of cash would definitely help give this place some life, make it feel less knackered . . . and anyways, if you've someone as highly trained as me, you won't have folk falling flat on their faces in the gym—or anywhere else. Did I mention that I used to work for the St. John's Ambulance Service and am trained in advanced adult and child life-support? I'm even a dead good lifeguard for Godssake."

"Oh," he said, sitting back in his big armchair, steepling his fingers, and staring at me intently. "Oh, sit down then, would you? Maybe your coming here wasn't a total waste of time."

#

So, from thereon the interview were dead easy. There were one or two tricky moments. You know, *left-field* questions. Like when he asked me if I minded tying-up people, and I had to tell him that though I might be a broad-minded lass from the wuthering heights of Haworth, I drew a line at that sort of stuff. I were MR not EL James!

"Well maybe you can be prevailed upon to do it in extremis," he said, with a tense stare directed towards the study window and the waning day.

I shrugged. There were no point in trying to debate what-ifs—hypotheticals—and I suspected it were a trick question, and he were trying to give me rope to hang myself with. So, all I said were that it were a knotty question, and that I believed that *no meant no*, and if he were a good Christian boy there should be no shades of grey in stuff like that.

At the end, he looked up at me and said, "Are there any questions you have for me?"

"Yeah," I said. "When do you want me to start?"

"Would tomorrow be an inconvenience?" he asked politely.

"No. As you can see, I've brought my suitcase; not quite all my worldly belongings, but I try to prepare for all eventualities. My dad were a boy scout, so I supposed he rubbed off on me."

"And I suppose you want to know about renumeration, too?"

"Too right," I said. "Not to sound like a tight Yorkshireman, but a lass wants to know she's not getting nowt for the effort."

He smiled and wrote down something on a pad before pushing it my way. I stared down at the number.

"Cor blimey! As much as that!" I said. It were like a small fortune in them days, believe you me.

"Well yes. And I'll increase it by ten percent after two years, if you stay."

"Alright then!"

"Also," he said. "I'll provide a small pension, board and lodgings, four weeks holiday per year and funeral expenses should the need arise."

"Funeral expenses?" I said, raising an eyebrow.

"Funeral expenses *or* cremation . . . burial at sea, whatever you prefer."

I didn't let my heart sink, but I could tell he'd thought long and hard about that sort of stuff.

#

After the interview he took me on a grand tour of the hotel, which you may not know—being new around here—were once an estate owned by Hugo's Norman ancestors. After the First World War they'd fallen on hard times and had turned one of the wings into an hotel. Slowly, the entire estate had turned towards hospitality, and for a period of time it were right successful; but then on Halloween, nineteen thirty-nine, the writer Donald Measham, a guest at the time, had gone on a killing spree after his latest novel had been rubbished in The Times Literary Supplement.

Hugo and I were standing in a dark corridor on the first floor, a naked lightbulb flickered overhead as he told me about the history of the house—and the Measham episode, in particular. As he reached and grasped hold of the door handle, I felt a chill come all over me.

"…and ever since that Halloween night, Donald's presence has remained in this room—Room 121—the room where he finally turned his axe upon himself."

"Upon himself?" I said.

"Yes," said Hugo. "One obituary writer said that only in death had he managed a novel ending worth talking about."

I watched as the door were flung wide open. There were a loud creak, a bang as the door found the farthest reaches of its arc and then silence. Silence. Darkness. It were like waves of darkness flowing towards me. I watched as Hugo stepped inside and flicked on a light.

I followed in his footsteps.

Blood. Dried blood, but blood it were. Blood on the carpet; not the red from a freshly aired artery, but the dull rust of a tetanus infested tin you don't want to slit your hand with. Spatter, spray, smears . . . it carpeted the carpet and the yellow wallpaper; and though the room had a musty, empty air, I could feel the tang of metal on the tip of my tongue. That and the sharp edge of stomach acid. I leaned over a little, with my hands on my hips, and that were the first time he touched me. Brushed my shoulder with a fingertip.

"I'm fine," I said, standing up straight. "I can see it's right old."

"Very. We have tried getting rid of the stains, but they refuse to budge, much like Donald's presence."

I tried to take my eyes off the obvious. Tried to stare at the curtains and the furniture, but there too, there were the unmistakeable hue of blood.

I shivered, as another chill swept through me. My eyes swivelled towards the desk, and then something strange happened. Out of the dimness, maybe just in my mind, or maybe leaping out of my mind, flashed a vision of a gleaming axe-head arcing down. It were held by a man, wrists bared, teeth bared. He were hacking his hand off . . . off . . . off.

The first cut were the deepest, the most savage, the one infused with all his strength and madness. His crazed cry full blooded. The spurt, the vigour of red rushing forth, like a river. His lips flecked and frothed. His eyes grew madder, tighter, blacker as he hacked a second, a third time. Each successful swipe were weaker, less potent; but with blow after blow, there were less sinew, less tissue, less tendon, less cartilage, less to hack through, and then I watched as he screamed jubilantly as the bloody stump fell with a thump to the floor. And then he turned, turned my way and whispered . . . whispered my name!

*MARY!*

"Mary? Mary? Are you okay?" It were Hugo! Hugo's hand were on my shoulder again, and the vision were gone.

"Oh," I said, feeling confused, dazed.

"You went a bit strange there. Your eyelids were flickering, it was like you were having a seizure."

"Seizure?"

"Yes. Come on let's go. This room has an unwholesome atmosphere. I'm sorry, I just wanted to show you how gruesome it can get. Prepare you."

"Wait," I said, standing my ground. Not yet ready to budge. An enforced bravado building in me. "Is this as bad as it gets?"

"No," he said, shaking his head. "No."

He said that if I wanted to know everything then he'd be happy to tell me, but that he needed a good stiff drink first.

"Where there's stiffs there's spirits," I said.

"If only you knew," he said.

Then he led me back the way we had come, down the corridor along the winding staircase and into the back of the North Wing.

#

The bar were just the same as it is now. Down a few steps, on the lower ground floor. It had a big unpolished counter, beer stains despite the beer mats, and a big mirror that stretched the width of the bar and added depth to the dinginess. It were empty.

I sat down on a stool facing him. He stood behind the counter. Over his shoulder, I could see my face reflected in the mirror. It were pale, and the distortions on the surface of the mirror made me look disfigured and ugly.

"Would you like some red rum?" he asked, his eyes shining.

"Red rum?" I asked.

"*Red* rum, yes."

I nodded. "Aye, I could murder a red rum, and I ain't being backwards about saying so, even if my boss is overlooking me."

He poured us both a shot and then, after taking a sip of his drink, began to speak. "The problem isn't just that we don't have enough guests, it's also that we have far too many ghosts. They're out of control, and they do as they please. That's why I wanted a resident exorcist. Not only to get rid of *some* of the ghosts—not all of them, mind you, there's money in haunted property—but also to stop us from *acquiring* more ghosts. You can't help guests dropping dead occasionally, but this place seems to have some sort of psychic energy that coerces dead people, their spirits, to linger longer than they ought to."

"Dead people . . . I see." I said.

"You do?" he asked.

"I do what?"

"See dead people?"

"Not at the moment, why?"

"You said you saw dead people."

"No, I said: dead people . . . I see!"

"Oh good. I was worried for a second that you might have had some sort of sixth sense kind of thing going on. That would only attract more of the blighters, and we don't need that.

Don't worry you will see them soon enough. They're just a little quiet. It's always quieter in the off season. I think they feed off mental energy."

"Well, if you must know. I don't spook easily. So, if it's just ghosts, then I don't think I'm too worried."

He nodded, too polite to mention that back in Measham's room I had seemed to spook very easily. I watched as he slung back another sip.

"There's more," he said, finally.

"You mean like non-ghost stuff."

"Yes . . . For starters there are the neighbours."

"Oh, I didn't realise there were neighbours. There were only empty fields as far as my eye could see."

"No. Carry on down the lane that leads to the entrance, you'll come eventually to the last house on the left."

"And what's wrong with the last house on the left?"

"The house is fine, but the neighbours from Hell live there."

"Why, what's wrong with them?"

"I just told you! The neighbours are from Hell."

"You mean they're *really* from . . . "

"Yes . . . Hell."

"So basically, no trick or treating, eh?"

"Are you finding this amusing?"

"No! But . . . well you have to laugh, right?"

Hugo shook his head and wiped his mouth on his forearm. "I suppose so."

I thought back to the taxi journey from the train station. How several minutes before we'd arrived, we had passed through the dark shadows of a little village.

"What about the village?" I asked. "There must be quite a few people who live there."

"Yes. Quite a few of the staff are from there. That's where you need to go if you need to see a doctor."

"Oh good. I were going to ask about that."

"It's easy to find the surgery: it's just next to the florist and the undertaker, on Elm Street."

"Oh, it sounds like a one-stop shop," I joked. "Is the cemetery next door too?"

"As a matter of fact, it is. Dr. Johnson's wife is the florist and his brother is the undertaker. Mrs. Johnson's uncle is the vicar."

"Sounds like a bit of a conflict of interest, don't it? A monopoly."

"No. It's just that this is a close community, people like to keep things in the family. It's not Mayfair or Park Lane with their multitudes. But don't worry. You'll eventually fit in, and hopefully get to like it. The same goes for this place too."

"Oh yes," I said, looking around me. "I like it already. It's right grand! Well not that it couldn't use a lick of paint and some bang-up carpentry; it's a bit of a hammer horror in here if I'm honest."

Hugo shrugged. "Yes, well, it's the last time I use *Cushing, Lee, Price and John Carpenters.* The thing is, it's hard to find a good handyman who is what he appears to be. Too many charlatans. Might as well be living in

Antarctica. Oh, well! Next time, I'll go out of town, but I'm glad you approve of DeVille Hall in general."

"I do. It's possessed with many fine features, but if I'm honest, I really can't wait to go see the gym."

"Yes," he said, glancing at his watch. "I think there is just enough time for that but–"

Before he could say more, there came the sound of a far-off crash, and this were followed by footsteps on the staircase leading into the bar. A tiny girl in a smart maid's uniform appeared. She stood gawping at me for a second, then seemed to remember why she were there and turned to Hugo.

"Sir! There's trouble. It's Lady Daphne. She's complaining that some of the spooks are in high spirits."

"Oh hell! Which ones? The usual suspects?"

"Yes, sir! The children of the Korn's."

"Oh, for God's sake! Which one's? Not at all of them surely?"

"Afraid so, sir. All three: Jason, Freddy and Michael. There's no stopping them, there's ectoplasm all over the floor, and if we don't get them under control then Mrs. Korn is going to turn up and start doing them in all over again."

At this, Hugo threw up his hands and turned to look at me. "This is why I wanted an exorcist! I mean, I've tried the Vatican but they're so useless they might as well be called the Vat-I-can't."

"How old are these boys?" I asked, as a thought sprang up in my mind.

"Well, their mum poisoned them with prussic acid when they were pre-teens, before she leapt out of room 322. That was twenty years ago, but they're in a state of permanently arrested development."

"I think I've had an idea," I said. "Do you mind if we go see them?"

"Be my guest," said Hugo.

"I just need to go and get my whistle out of my bag," I said.

#

*Weeeeeeeeeeeeeeeeeeeeee!*
*Weeeeeeeeeeeeeeeeeee!*

I suppose it were that moment when I came into my own. With my swimming instructor's whistle at my lips, the sound more screechingly savage than that of a wailing banshee, it were then that Hugo saw that I could stop three stroppy little poltergeists in their tracks.

There they stood, in the hallway—amongst overturned flowerpots and armchairs—three pasty-faced little muckers in seventies flairs, fly-away collars and basin-haircuts—all looking guilty as sin.

"Right, boys!" I said, sternly. "You've got thirty seconds to tidy up this shite and ship out of here before I start to get really stroppy!"

Jason, Freddy and Michael nodded violently at me, and then dashed madly around the hall picking up the pots, cupping the earth back in amongst the flowers, and all the while Hugo stood back and stared in amazement. When they were done, they came and stood facing me.

"This house is clean," squeaked the tallest poltergeist—that were Jason.

"Yes," said the second—the one called Freddy. "I've clawed all the earth into the pots. It were a right nightmare!"

I looked to the third, Michael, who, mired in silence, stared at me with a blank expression. I suppose it were better than dagger looks, eh?

"Well then, lads," I said. "You'd better run along then, and I want no more noise out of you when there are guests around, understood?"

"Ugh, Miss!" two of them said, trying to remonstrate, before a quick flash of my whistle shut them up.

"We'll disappear now," said the eldest, and they did. Disappear. Literally.

"Bravo!" I turned to see Hugo clapping as he came forwards. "Well, well, well. I have never seen anything like that before. Are you sure you don't have exorcist blood in you?"

"I don't know that I do," I said. "But I have trained some right nasty little shites at the swimming baths in Toddy; they were always interrupting the rest of the class; and I guess all kids, even ghosts are the same."

"I see," said Hugo. "Well we'll have to see who else you can work your magic on. I suspect your methods may meet with some success around here. Something tells me you might be a natural."

I shrugged my shoulders and turned to the maid, who throughout the palaver had parked herself silently in the corner of the hall.

"What's your moniker?" I asked.

"Monica."

"Yes, your moniker! Your name!"

"Monica! My name *is* Monica," she said.

"Well, Monica, I think you can go and tell Lady Daphne that the coast is clear."

I waited 'til Monica disappeared round a corridor and then turned to speak to Hugo. "So, who is this Lady Daphne, anyway?"

"Lady Daphne Hitchcock was a famous belle in the forties. She's harmless enough, although she might come across as a bit of a psycho. She comes for breakfast, though as soon as that's done the lady vanishes back into her suite. She spends time up on her balcony, or at her rear window, looking at the birds. She's up on the third floor, but she still manages to trek up and down those thirty-nine steps despite her dodgy hip and her vertigo."

"She sounds like the mad woman in the attic. Are you sure she ain't going to cause some sort of con-flag-ration, set the Hall on fire?"

"*Mad* woman in the attic!" said Hugo, with a look of irritation. "Why, whatever makes you say such a thing? No! She's harmless. She just hates the boys. Really, please put such notions out of your mind!"

"Righty-Oh then."

He seemed to ease at that, and the smile returned. "Thank you once again for doing that. I truly appreciate it. In fact, I think you could easily be more than the exercist, you might one day end up being the hotel manager."

"I'm just glad I could help."

Hugo seemed genuinely pleased at his idea, but, as I looked closely, I noted that he seemed a little different to how he had looked back in the bar. It were hard to say exactly what it were, except for maybe a sheen of sweat glazing his forehead—his less prominent forehead. That were it! He looked hairier than he had a little while back. It weren't just his head, either. His eyebrows too.

"Well, look," said Hugo. "There's just time to show you the gym, and then I'll leave you in the staff lounge. There's not much staff around, but I'm sure we can find someone to show you the rest of the place. I'm going to be locked away for the rest of the evening with something important."

"Course," I said. "I understand."

But I didn't understand, how could I?

#

And so, we went to the gym. Back then, before benefitting from my touch, the gym were a right dump. Who'd want to come and work-out there? If you got landed in a place like that, the only thing you wanted to work out, were to work out how to get out as fast as possible. The punch bag had literally had the stuffing pummelled out of it, the pommel horse were slipshod, and you had to tread carefully over wires just to get to the treadmill—which had no plug. It smelled of stale sweat and rat piss. And as I stood looking, I saw them. By gum! Dozens of the scurrying sods. Rats! This were their lair, their shrine. It weren't no gym.

"Gordon Bennett!" I said. "As my uncle Henry Herbert James would say, it definitely needs more than a lick of paint, and a simple turn of the screws. You need a rat-catcher and a bob or two to be spent on the equipment if you want this place to be a stellar example of a gym."

"Well I'm sure you can whip it into shape, can't you?"

I scanned Hugo's face. It seemed deadpan, but his words worried me. You see, I'd studied Freud, I'd learnt enough about the Id and stuff to know that Hugo were hiding something; that he were trying to repress some sort of latent urge, but that with all this talk of whipping and tying up, it were leaking out into the open. At the time I thought it were maybe just some strange kink or fetish. I didn't think he were a tosser, or anything. I just thought he needed to get a right good grip on himself. Once I knew him better, perhaps we could thrash it out together. But not now. It would have to wait.

"Yes," I said. "I'll have a go. The rats go first, then we'll see to the rest."

He smiled, nodded. His eyes crow-footed as I spoke, and my mind took to the air in these sudden wild flights of fancy: I thought of this right swanky looking palatial thing. Then all my fancies came crashing down to earth, like a brick with paper wings flown by a rat-arsed pilot.

"Ughhhh" he gasped, bending over at the waist.

"Are you alright?" I said, reaching over to touch his arm. He shrugged me away.

"Yes . . . No."

"Well which is it? Yes or no?"

He shook his head violently, as if trying to shake off something inside it. "I'll . . . be . . . fine." He tried to stand and wobbled before falling to the ground.

"Blimey!" I cried, falling beside him and feeling his brow. It were dead clammy.

"I don't understand," he cried, lifting his arm with great effort to look at his watch. "It's too early!"

"Too early?"

"The transformation. I don't know what it is … but it's not 'til five."

"It's five to five," I said, checking my watch.

"No." He said, panting, gesturing to his watch. "It's not quite four."

"Oh!" I said. "That's yesterday's time. We went forward an hour today." I lifted my wrist to his face.

"Oh!" Clocking my watch, his face looked like it had been struck hard. He glanced at me with a rigid stare, a face fixed with dread. "Oh, God! You've got to help me get to the room before – ughhhh!"

No. No. What I'm telling you about were no sort of lycanthropic transformation. We don't do werewolves here. It were the family secret. The curse on his family line, at least on his grandmother's side of the family—the Jekyll secret that they all wanted to hide. It infected the male descendants who, just after teatime, at a certain time of the month all went a wee bit lunatic. And by lunatic, I'm not talking about some sort of aristocratic period-drama: like being slightly irked at discovering that the sandwiches don't have enough cucumber in them. No, I mean a full-Monty, stark raving, nut-job episode.

#

Heavy. Oh, he were dead heavy, and seemed to grow heavier with each step of the descent, which were the black hole leading to the basement. It were as if his limbs were steadily giving up the connection to the rest of his body. His breath were raspy, his stubble coarse; I felt the scrape of his fingernails on my skin. 'Course, I didn't know what were happening.

It were dark. So dark that he were guiding me by memory, rather than eyesight. Then a light bulb moment occurred—something dangled in my face and, thinking it were a web, I flicked at it and it caught in my hand. It were a cord. I pulled, and light streamed meekly from a bulb overhead, like a child wary about coming out among the playground bullies.

Hugo's eyelids seemed to snap open like a coffin lid. His voice came out as a series of gasps. "The door ... on the left. Pocket ... key. Once I'm in, lock me. Leave me. Don't open the door. No matter what."

I heaved us over to the door, afraid that if I let him drop, I wouldn't be able to help lift him again. I pushed him up against the door, kept him erect, and, despite my reservations, despite my upbringing, fumbled in his pocket for the key.

"Quick," he mouthed. "On the left."

*There, there it is!* I told myself as my clammy fingers closed around the hard, steely body. As I drew it out, clasped it tightly in my fingers, his voice roared out.

"Faster! Faster! For God's sake, faster! Open it up and let me in!"

I could feel his body making jerky movements, shuddering against the door as I located that tiny, tight opening within and pushed his key deep inside. Despite the hammering of my heart, the click came hard, and when I turned the handle, the door swung open before us with a groan; we both collapsed onto the ground, one upon the other.

Panting, both of us out of breath, I peeled myself off his exhausted body. His sweat drenched me. He'd stopped moving. For a second, I worried he were dead. I placed my hand against his back and felt the sporadic rise and fall that told me, no, he were alive.

I looked up; his heels were in the doorway. I couldn't close the door without pulling him further into the room. The light from the corridor were faint. It were like being in a pit, like being imprisoned with the darkness itself; darkness whose own cold shoulders and heavy breath reached out towards me from every direction.

I bent and grasped Hugo's hands. They were unresponsive; I gripped him hard and tugged. Groaned with all my might to move him, move him even an inch.

"Come on, you sod!" I cried. "Come on!"

"Coming!" he cried, with a note of glee and madness in his voice. Suddenly his hands were alive and gripped me with the force of a wolf's maws.

I screamed as he pounced upon me, dragging me to the floor, dragging me to hell. His weakness had ebbed; he flowed with strength in the dark. His hands pinned me to the floor as I struggled to free myself.

"Scream all you like girl!" he cried, "Hugo won't hear you! He's out for the night."

I did scream. But it were to no avail. We were deep underground, and my voice, even if it did take flight up the stairs, would only emerge feeble, strained, a whisper at best.

He were all over me, straddling me, pushing out all the air from my lungs with his body, even as his hands about my throat denied me another easy breath. I could feel his nails gouging, his foetid breath upon my cheek, his lips smacking. No longer gentle; maybe no longer a man. He were a monster, and I knew if I lay there, I'd be giving up the ghost very soon.

No! No! I thought. No! This weren't what I came for. I weren't going to be another ghost. NOT ME TOO!

I summoned what strength I could, tried to will what wouldn't stir easily, clenched a fist and hit out ...

The first punch were on target. It found his nose, it were big enough I suppose not to miss in the dark, and I felt the crunch of cartilage beneath my knuckles, felt the pressure on my throat fall away.

"Stupid bint! ... You've broken my nose!" he roared, falling off me. I heard him rolling away on the floor.

I shifted, sharp-like. I knew I had to get off the ground if I stood a chance.

"My nose! I'll gut you for that!" his voice spluttered, and as I looked into the shadows and the dark, I could see his form start to take shape, rise up.

"Don't worry." I said, "It weren't like you were some sort of oil painting!"

He roared and charged at me like a rhino. I let him come at me, waited 'til he were a little more than kissing distance away, 'til I knew that this Miss wouldn't miss. Grabbing him by the shoulders for traction, I drove up with my hip, kneed him in the bollocks. A right good blow it were too!

He dropped like a stone; lay there, silent as one too. I went and stood over his still form. The only movement were that of his breathing. But there were something else. It were like a thrum in the air. Like energy, like power. I didn't know what it were, just that it were there.

I stepped around Hugo and went to the doorway. Reaching out with my hands I found a light switch and turned to watch as a low-watt bulb shed light on the carnage around me.

Well that explained the musty smell: Damp walls. I saw the peeling period paper; cobwebs that had trapped the dust of ages and had no room left for flies; a soiled mattress pushed into the corner of the tennis-court sized room. To my side there were a bundle of clothes, ladies' clothes. I stepped closer. Scooped up stuff with one hand and then the other. Dresses, a pleated skirt, stockings, a maid's uniform: all different sizes, all of them bloodied. Clearly, I weren't the first to have been brought down there, by Hugo, or at least his alter ego. I wondered how the others had been tempted, fooled, cajoled, coerced down there. I wondered for how long Hugo's Hyde side had been in control.

I felt this anger welling up inside me, taking hold of me.

Then I saw it. Lined up against the wall there were a spade. I were drawn towards it. As I reached out to clasp it, I heard a groan behind me. Turning I saw Hugo, on his hands and knees, slowly trying to rise.

I know he were a monster in this form, even though he weren't always a monster, and though I knew he had to be stopped I didn't know what came over me.

Striding to where he stood, I raised the spade high over my head.

He turned to look at me. Fixed me with his bloodied face.

"Go on!" He spat. "I dare you. You haven't got the ball-"

The spade cut off his words with the first blow. I raised it high up again and screamed as I brought it smashing down in a violent arc, which spattered blood all over the surroundings.

*Again.*

*Again.*

*Again.*

I watched his body jerking on the floor, and a puddle of piss spreading in a halo of liquid gold. And then, just to be sure, I bashed his brains in.

When it were over, when the adrenaline began to let go, when the pain began to take hold, I slumped down in the corner of the room with the spade cradled in my arms and passed out.

#

"Is she alive?"

"Well that's what I'm waiting to find out! Have some patience for God's sake, it's not like you have some other urgent business to attend to … not like me. I've a damned hotel to run!"

The first thing I remember were the voices, a man's and a woman's.

I opened my lids slowly, but still almost defenestrated my eyeballs. There, clustered around me on the floor sat Hugo and three women. Well, their pasty faced and not very attractive ghosts, at least.

"Oh, don't look so shocked!" said Hugo with a frown. "I told you this place attracted ghosts, didn't I? Did you really have to go and kill me?"

"Well," I said. "I were defending myself."

"Come off it!" said Hugo. "You could have knocked me out once and called the police."

"I-I'm sorry, I don't know what came over me!"

"It's this place," said the woman who had spoken earlier. "The energy is uncontrollable. It's because there's too many of us! We wind people up!"

I looked at her and the other women who sat at my sides. Their faces were disfigured to the point that their mothers would not have recognised them. From their bloody and bedraggled appearances, it were clear that their phantom forms wore the same garments they had died in.

"Who are you ladies?" I asked.

"We're the girls who weren't as lucky as you were with Hugo," they chorused.

"Well …" I said, slowly inching myself onto my feet. "I intend to make the most of my luck and get the f**k out of here!"

"You're not going anywhere!" said Hugo.

"What?" I said.

"That's right! You've signed a contract."

"Well I'm quitting!"

"You can't! You have a three-month notice period."

"Notice period? Have you noticed you're dead? Period. Try to stop me!"

"You're also a murderer," said Hugo.

"It were self-defence!"

"You can tell that to the judge."

"You can't tell anyone anything different!" I countered. "You're dead too."

Yes. It were like a Mexican stand-off, and then I watched Hugo's shoulders slump.

"Okay," he said with a resigned look. "If that's what you want, then go! But just remember. I gave you a chance. I took you on. And look around you! Look at it! It needs a woman's touch … no! It needs the touch of someone who has a touch of class! And a certain something else. That's why I picked you. And I think maybe this place has picked you too! Look, can't you stay? Give it a bash? I mean, someone is going to have to run the place and I'd rather hand it all to you."

"I don't know." I said. "It looks like a tall order."

"No. I'm around to do what I can. And besides, now that I'm a ghost, I can maybe help calm the spirits too. Though I think you'll be good there also. But look, someone needs to sort out the living as well as the dead. Please? Won't you stay?"

I looked at the women. They were nodding and smiling.

"I'd like to," I said. "But … I don't know that I want to be meddling with forces beyond my control."

"Well, look," said Hugo. "Try your whistle again. See who comes calling, and let's see how the troops take to you. Give it a bash! Go on, be a sport! Otherwise … you'll never know."

I reached slowly into one of my pockets. There it were: the whistle. I drew it out and stared at it. "I suppose I have a job to do and I were always one for doing a job right, even if it killed me."

Hugo nodded.

I lifted the whistle to my lips and paused to speak. "This is Yorkshire grit for you! You take the shite, and you polish that turd 'til it shines."

I blew six times.

There were no human ears to hear it. But soon, I heard plodding feet, and one by one a whole host of ghosts appeared. One after the other they trudged in to meet the newcomer.

They stood there: the pale, the frail, the impaled, the nailed; all dead to a man, woman and child. I surmised how everyone's demise happened—it were writ upon face and body. They packed the surroundings, jostled impatiently like hyperactive rabbits with no sense of personal space; I were hemmed in on all sides, stifled. I stared at them all. The whistle had silenced them, but with so many jostling ghosts in one hall—I imagined the chaos they could cause when it weren't the off-season. I looked at them, and they looked at me. I felt like I were holding Gabriel's silver trumpet or something.

"See?" said Hugo, standing to my side and staring out at the sea of faces. "Didn't I tell you? You're a natural with the supernatural. Born to lead the dead. You called; they came. What a calling!"

"We'll see." I said. "Oh … and by the way, before I forget, I'm sorry I said you were no oil painting."

"Well, you can't get it right all the time: my oil painting hangs in the dining room. But forget about that."

So, I turned back to all the ghosts and tried to frame my thoughts before speaking.

"Well, let's see … Hugo here, thought I were going to be an exorcist …"

Ghostly gasps. Everyone took a step back.

"Relax! Chill! No, don't chill, it's bloody freezing in here! Just keep still. I'm not … I thought I were going to be the exercist. But I see that that's not going to happen now. But I can see that you lot need a good sorting out. All you ghasts and poltergeists and ghouls with all your free kinetic energy, it has a bad effect on the living, real estate prices and hotel bookings. So that's what I'm here for…to get you into proper shape, make sure you're fit to be ghosts! Exercise you! Got that? So, when I blow this whistle, I want dead silence …

"Oh! By the way I'm Mary. I'm not the madwoman in the attic, or even the madwoman in the cellar; I'm the new hotel manager; and I can tell you lot have been dying to meet me!"

# A.K. McCarthy's
# Shopping List

Ramen noodles (at least four or five packets, usually chicken)
Peanut butter
Kodiak wheat bread (made in Alaska)
A can of Mountain Dew Kickstart, energizing mango lime flavor
A six-pack of Midnight Sun Brewing Co. Sockeye Red IPA
Vitamin D supplements
Garlic
Extra garlic in the winter

# Beneath the Ice
## *A.K. McCarthy*

It was almost time to go when the dogs started barking.

Tarkik and his fellow hunters had been in their igloo for much of the afternoon, waiting for the tide to go out.

The three hunters had taken dogsleds out to the sea this year instead of the customary snowmobiles, which had been acting up recently. For Tarkik, now on his 24th mussel hunt, this was the first time he'd come with dogs.

And now they were barking, some of them howling, as the tide began to go out.

Anik, the leader of the party, cocked an ear with some concern at the cacophony outside the igloo.

"Not normal," he muttered, his dark eyes darting back and forth as he pondered what the problem could be.

"Probably just scared that the ice is moving and cracking beneath their feet," Ila croaked as she chewed a piece of seal meat.

Tarkik had always had a bit of an overactive imagination and pictured a far more dire scene developing outside the igloo. A polar bear, maybe.

These trips had always amazed Tarkik. For just minutes on this day every year, he and his fellow tribesmen were hunters of the frozen sea. The spring equinox brought the most volatile tides of the season, causing the sea to drop 40 feet at low tide.

This tidal shift would reveal a large area of the sea floor, which was dotted with various sea creatures. Most notably, mussels.

At the lowest point of the tide, the hunters would cut through the thick layer of sea ice—for this, they used large metal poles and even chainsaws to get through—in order to get to the sea floor. Once they were underneath the ice, they had 30 minutes or so to gather as many of the mussels as they could before scurrying back out.

It was a risky endeavor, as the ice would constantly be shifting and moving as the tide came back in. There was no telling how hard or easy it would be to get back up.

Tarkik had been part of one expedition where the hole they had cut in the ice had nearly closed up when they returned. The last man out, a man called Aguta, had almost drowned as the water level rose.

Aguta was never the same after that. The water, the cold, the darkness, all of it had nearly consumed him. Being in that frigid dark space felt like a tomb sometimes.

"Well," Anik said, "it's about that time."

Tarkik took one last sip of the coffee, holding it in his mouth and exhaling through his nose as he closed his eyes and tried to savor the warmth for a few extra moments. He placed it back on the snow near the fire and stood.

Anik grabbed hold of the block of ice that enclosed the entrance and wiggled it until it slid out of its spot with a scraping sound. Immediately, wind swept through the igloo with enough ferocity to take Tarkik's breath for a moment. He grabbed a metal pole and a basket, and moved toward the bright open space in the igloo's wall.

As they stepped out of the dark and into the blinding light, their eyes slowly adjusted and found that there were no bears or predators there to scare the dogs. Despite the wind, the howling and baying of the dogs was still audible.

"Good omen," Ila said sarcastically as she walked by and revved the chainsaw for emphasis.

Tarkik smiled, always calmed by the old woman's well-timed cynicism. Wearing his dark, thick coat with the fur-lined hood pulled as tightly over his head as possible, Tarkik followed Anik and Ila to the place where the ice had dipped. Anik quickly identified a flat place in the sunken ice where they could cut.

Anik's first hunt came long before Tarkik's, perhaps as many as 15 years earlier. Anik was approaching 60, which was incredibly old for this kind of trip. Tarkik was a little older than 40. Tarkik felt as if he didn't have many left in him and was amazed that Anik was still going.

Ila brought her chainsaw to life and dipped it into the ice, as she briefly disappeared into a cloud of spraying ice. When she had made a square of cuts in the ice, Ila stepped aside for Tarkik to finish the job. He took the short, wide metal pole and thrust it into the middle of the cut-out square. After a couple dozen hard impacts, the pole knocked the square of ice down into the darkness. It landed with a thud on the sea floor, about 10 feet under the sea ice.

All of their interior clocks began running.

Anik wasted no time, tossing his basket down into the opening and lowering himself into the entryway. He stepped onto the block of ice they had just cut out, and almost glowed for a moment as the light from above spotlighted him in the darkness. He crouched, looking first to his right and then to his left, hopping off the ice to the left. Tarkik quickly followed, landing on the block of ice and jumping to the right.

Immediately Tarkik and Anik felt that something was different. A smell quickly enveloped them in the darkness, one that stunk of rotting flesh, not of musky sea life.

"Tarkik, do you smell that?" Anik asked.

Tarkik, gagging, could hardly make a sound. He coughed and doubled over, nearly falling to his knees.

As Ila lowered their lanterns down onto the block of ice, the sea floor was illuminated, and the two men saw … nothing. No mussels. No sea life of any kind, in fact.

The sea floor looked as if it had been dragged clean in some artificial manner, as if large ropes had been pulled in one direction. Long grooves ran across the floor, a difficult feat to do on this rock-hard surface.

These were clearly man-made, Tarkik immediately thought, his nostrils becoming a bit more used to the stench and the shock of the sight wearing off. Anik had made his way over to Tarkik, carrying both of their lanterns.

"What kind of machinery could do this?" Anik asked, setting Tarkik's lantern down next to him and kneeling.

With better light on the floor, the men saw the grooves were remarkably smooth. They were also greased with something, some kind of slick substance. Whoever had done this, they had wanted to move quickly across the sea floor.

"Maybe these are for some kind of machine to move across the floor and pick up mussels," Tarkik theorized aloud, running his mittened fingers along one of the grooves. The grooves were about the width of his hand, and Tarkik lifted his lantern up and saw that the grooves extended as far as the light shone.

Above, Ila had noticed that the men had hardly moved.

"Time's running out!" her scratchy voice belched at them. "Get moving!"

She hadn't looked closely into the opening to see the grooves in the floor, as she'd been looking back at the dogs, which were beginning to fight with each other. It was a snarling, foaming mess.

"Well, let's have a look around," Anik said calmly as he stood up.

Anik began walking slowly in the other direction, lantern still aloft as he reached down and grabbed his basket.

*I have a feeling that basket will remain empty,* Tarkik thought.

But he did the same, picking up his basket and turning to walk in his own direction. The first few times he'd been under the ice, Tarkik had felt a mix of fear and excitement. Over time, that changed into just excitement. Now, it was as if he were back on his first expedition, as he once again felt like a stranger in the cold darkness.

Tarkik's hand trembled slightly as he held his lantern in front of him, around the level of his hip. The sea floor was slick and totally cleared of anything—except those damn grooves. And what was that rotting smell? He wasn't sure if he wanted to find out, but whatever it was, it was getting stronger with every step.

His lantern cast a circle of dim light around him, and soon the edge of that circle illuminated a white figure in front of Tarkik. As he moved closer, he saw what it was and felt his breath catch in his throat. He couldn't scream and couldn't breathe as he stared.

He dropped his basket and turned to run. The opening was now maybe 50 yards away from him. He slipped in the ooze and his legs went out from under him.

The lantern fell as he put his hands out in front of him to catch himself. He heard a loud clatter and a low hiss as the light in the lantern was apparently extinguished by the layer of ooze. Now the only illumination was the light that came in through the opening in the ice.

"ANIK!" Tarkik screamed as he scrambled to his feet. "ANIK! WE NEED TO GET OUT OF HERE!"

Tarkik was back on his feet and running, gasping for breath to yell out to his mentor again. He was probably halfway back to the opening when he heard Anik start screaming.

"AWAY! AWAY!" Anik screamed, his voice rapidly raising in pitch as he said it.

Tarkik stopped rapidly, slipping again in the ooze and falling on his rear end. He sat paralyzed and breathing heavily as he heard Anik scream again. This time, there were no words. Tarkik was half-surprised the scream didn't crack the ice above them with how shrill and loud it was.

There was a loud pop, then a splashing sound as something wet and heavy splatted on the floor. Then, the worst sound of all, was a loud and wet sucking sound. It was like somebody aggressively sucking the oyster out of its shell, trying to get every drop of juice out of it.

The sucking went on for a few seconds, as Tarkik sat motionless on the ground. Then there was silence for a moment before something came flying out of the darkness.

It looked like a large, furry bird that was dragging its wings behind it as it flew into a brisk breeze. It came forward and landed with a splat on the block of ice that was left from the hole Ila had cut.

It was Anik. Well, sort of. It was what was left of the top half of Anik.

Still wrapped in a parka, Anik's torso was without form. The ribs had been crushed, the arms had been broken and it was clear that he had been drained of all his blood.

Tarkik was maybe 20 yards away from the block by this point, close enough to see that whatever had consumed Anik had also made sure to take his eyes.

Ila's scream took Tarkik out of his trance. She might not have heard the pop or the sucking, but she sure as hell saw Anik's deflated, broken body lying there on the ice.

"TARKIK! TARKIK!" she screamed.

"I'M HERE!" he answered.

"GET OUT OF THERE!" she replied; a rare sense of panic evident in her voice.

Tarkik put a hand out to his side to stand and found that in his shock from all of this, he hadn't realized that the tide was starting to come in. He twisted his body into a standing position, the water dripping off his fur garments into a pool that was a few inches high at this point.

He took a couple uneasy steps forward, toward the discarded body of his friend and mentor. How was he going to climb up on that block of ice and maneuver around Anik's body to get out?

He never got to answer that question.

Tarkik heard the wave before it hit him. The whooshing of approaching water made it sound like a large ship was coming in.

He stopped about 10 yards shy of the block of ice, seeing a wave that was about three feet high strike the bright blue block and send up a splash that might have even gotten Ila wet. The wave kept coming, hitting Tarkik's hips with enough force to push him backward.

Tarkik didn't fall, but he had to take a couple of steps backward as he regained his balance. He planted on one foot, determined to get moving forward to get to the block.

It quickly became clear that whatever was down here, whatever had consumed Anik, was watching Tarkik. Two large, black tentacles twisted their way out of the darkness and wrapped themselves around the block of ice. They dragged it quickly back out of the light, just before Tarkik reached it.

He stopped, standing in the spotlight created by the hole. He looked up in an attempt to see Ila, but the bright sun blinded him.

"I'll cut a new one!" Ila yelled. "Maybe 30 yards back the way that you came!"

He didn't say anything, but nodded and took off back into the darkness. *That's probably the last I'll ever see the sunlight*, he thought to himself.

The tide comes in quickly, and by this point, the frigid water was already up past his knees. He moved as quickly as he could, but his legs moved slowly through the water. The freezing temperature of the water was doing more damage than the height of the water, as he already couldn't feel his feet and his body was starting to shiver.

He felt like every second could be his last. That creature, whatever it was, could lash out one tentacle at any point and drag him into the darkness.

But step after slow step, Tarkik kept surviving. No tentacles came, no waves came and there was no sound from the creature.

He heard a low rumbling from above as Ila began to saw at the ice. A pang of hope throbbed through his shivering body as he allowed himself to think for a second that he might get out.

The water was making its way up to his waist when something hard brushed up against his hip. Tarkik reached his hand down. Even before touching it, he knew what it was.

It was the skeleton of the polar bear he had seen in his lamplight earlier. The sight that made him run screaming back to warn Anik.

From what he had seen, Tarkik recalled the shape of the skeleton was mostly intact, but many of the bones were smashed. This creature in the darkness had apparently done the same thing to this animal as it had done to Anik, crunching its bones prior to feasting.

Tarkik ran his hand over the bear's skeleton until he felt a painful poke. His mind worked quickly, and he grabbed the broken bone that had poked him. He ripped it free of the skeleton.

It might not do much good, but now he had a weapon.

A moment later, he heard another wave approaching. He pushed the skeleton away from him, holding tight to the bone he would use for protection. Tarkik turned and faced the point of the bone toward the wave that was coming.

He braced himself as much as he could for the force and the cold that was about to crash into him, but he proved ill prepared for both factors. The wave smashed into him, taking his breath away with its frigidity and lifting him off his feet.

Tarkik was pulled under the water and for a few moments he was paralyzed with how cold it was. Tarkik couldn't tell if he was vertical or horizontal, if he was still holding the bone or even if he was dead or alive.

For all he knew, this is what drowning felt like: your body and your mind both coming to a complete halt.

Then the wave passed, and Tarkik was back in the air, gasping for breath. He was relieved to find that he was still holding onto the bone, but his body was shaking so severely that he didn't think the bone would be much use. In this weakened state, the creature could easily snag him, snap him and snack on him.

Tarkik looked above him, hoping to see some evidence of Ila's progress. Everything was still dark. He wasn't sure which way he was facing or even if he was in the right place anymore. That wave could have knocked him a couple dozen yards for all he knew.

Then he heard the sounds all around him. Slithering quickly through the water like an army of eels, the tentacles sounded like they were partially above water as they grew rapidly closer to him.

With a right hand that was still shaking violently, Tarkik gripped his bone in a stabbing position and started thrusting the sharp end of the bone downward into the water all around him. He didn't think it would do much good, but it was better than doing nothing.

Before Tarkik could even feel that they were close to him, one tentacle wrapped around his feet and one wrapped around his waist. He let out a cry, as both tentacles squeezed him as if they wanted to break him.

He thrust the sharp end of the bone toward his waist, bringing the point straight toward his pelvis. Had he not been in pure survival mode, he might have been afraid of stabbing himself. But now all he wanted to do was stop the pain that came as his hips were being crushed.

Despite being unable to see and shaking with cold, Tarkik hit his target. He felt the bone puncture some kind of thick skin and descend into a fleshy mass of muscle. First came a kind of hissing pop, then a squelching sound and then a distant squeal.

Tarkik thought quickly enough to pull the bone free as soon as possible, so that if the tentacle let go of him it wouldn't take the bone with it. That's exactly what happened, as the tentacle immediately unfurled and released him.

To Tarkik's delight, the tentacle wrapping around his ankles also let go.

He'd never heard anything like the unearthly howl that came from the creature. It was like it had three or four voices, each at a different pitch and octave. The sound of pain contained all of those voices crying out at once. Part of it even sounded similar to Anik's death scream from earlier, Tarkik thought.

Even if the creature was withdrawing, the water was not. It was now up to his navel, and being in cold water for more than 10 minutes or so would undoubtedly result in hypothermia. Tarkik felt like this ordeal had lasted hours, but in reality Anik had only been dead for a few minutes at this point.

Tarkik again started looking upwards, turning in a circle to see if he could see anything in any direction. The light from the original opening was still visible, but it seemed farther away than 30 yards. He began moving slowly in that direction.

The cavern below the ice had become almost silent now, and he could hear the faint rumbling of Ila's chainsaw echoing through the space.

As he grew closer to the original opening, he saw a thin shaft of light coming from the ceiling between him and the opening. The chainsaw sound was louder, and Tarkik's pace quickened.

Tarkik approached the shaft of light and saw that it was even more than a shaft. Ila had the block cut out and was starting to beat on it with the metal pole, it appeared.

Hope again surged through him. Perhaps he had fended the creature off for long enough to escape. Still, he gripped the bone as firmly as he could and stood near what would be the new opening. He made sure not to stand directly under the spot, as the falling chunk of ice could be heavy enough to knock him unconscious.

The surge of hope quickly came to an end. The sound of another wave was approaching.

"IL-L-L-A!" he screamed, his teeth chattering and mouth shaking. "HUR-R-R-R-Y!"

As if she could hear him.

This wave didn't sound like the others. Tarkik quickly realized that the previous waves were just created by the creature to knock its prey off balance. This wave had a little something more behind it.

First Tarkik saw the tentacles appear under the original opening, and then he caught a glimpse of the creature. It looked like a bullet, smooth and black, that reached almost all the way to the ceiling. In the brief glimpse, Tarkik couldn't make out any eyes. Why would it need eyes, living here in the dark?

Based on the silhouette of the quickly approaching creature, Tarkik could see it had more than just a couple tentacles. At least four or five on each side were visible as they flailed wildly at the creature's side. They looked as if they each had a mind of their own.

*The tentacles certainly aren't propelling the creature*, Tarkik thought. *There must be some kind of tail behind it that's pushing it—and perhaps that's what made the waves too.*

This crossed his mind in just a split second, and he readied himself to again face the creature.

Before Tarkik knew it, four tentacles wrapped him up. The combined impact from the tentacles knocked the bone out of his hand and it fell harmlessly into the freezing water.

*This is it*, Tarkik thought as the tentacles lifted him off his feet. The shaft of light from what was about to be the new opening illuminated the area about 10 feet in front of him.

The creature's face (or at least the front of its bullet-like form) moved underneath the shaft and suddenly everything was in slow-motion for Tarkik. He could make out the grooves that ran vertically up and down the creature. The grooves, of course, were the same width as the grooves on the floor.

Its tentacles wrapping themselves tighter and tighter around its prey, the creature lifted Tarkik quickly upward to slam him against the ice ceiling. Tarkik put his hands above his head to cushion the blow but it didn't help much.

His hands were mostly numb at this point, but he heard a crunch just above his head as his hands were slammed between his head and the ice. He knew the crunch wasn't from the ice.

The impact still sent a shockwave of pain up and down his spine, and an explosion of pain detonated at the top of his head. His hands, dully throbbing with pain, fell back down to his sides and he could feel the slimy surface of the creature that was about to consume him.

His head bobbed woozily as he clung hopelessly to consciousness. His thoughts were as fuzzy as his vision, as he knew somewhere inside that this was where it ended but he couldn't quite put into words how it felt to be within arm's length of death.

More tentacles began to work their way around his top half, preparing to pull him apart just as they had done to Anik a few minutes earlier. Tarkik gazed almost sightlessly at the creature when suddenly something seemed to explode above the menace.

Light flooded Tarkik's eyes as his broken hands tried in vain to cover his face. He could feel the tightness around his body quickly loosen, and the creature again screamed in agony.

This time, maybe the pain was from simply being in the light. Or perhaps it was the large block of ice that crashed down in the middle of its bullet-shaped torso.

A couple tentacles loosely held Tarkik as other ones abandoned him to grab at the chunk of ice that was sliding down the front of the creature's body toward where its mouth was.

Blood quickly returned to Tarkik's extremities and he felt a little closer to consciousness. The block of ice splashed into the water just in front of Tarkik, as the water was now three quarters of the way to the ceiling. Tentacles pushed the block to the side.

The creature ceased its screams for a moment, but then another sound filled the ice cave.

To Tarkik, it sounded like the calving of a glacier, a sound that was so awesome and powerful that it sometimes felt as if the earth was splitting in two. Despite his vision still swimming, he quickly realized what the sound was.

Ila pointed the chainsaw straight down and plunged it into the top of the creature's oblong body. The creature again released its horrible, cursed screech right into Tarkik's face. The scent of rotting flesh and dirty water flooded Tarkik's nostrils.

Black, thick liquid exploded upward as if Ila had struck oil. Fortunately her face was covered and her eyes were closed, as she was bathed in the ghastly, unholy flood.

The screams from below only made her want to plunge the whirring saw deeper into the creature's flesh. She pushed down for a moment and then swung the chainsaw from side to side, opening up a gaping gash in the top of the bullet-shaped body.

The creature began to pull away, retreating back in the direction of Anik's death. As it moved backward, it released Tarkik and he sunk into the freezing water. His body went stiff as the shock of the cold water overtook him.

The creature's retreat took the chainsaw out of Ila's hands, as it hit the edge of the new hole in the ice and went spinning away from her. The creature's movement and the tentacles withdrawing in the water also dragged Tarkik toward the new opening.

Ila wiped some of the black blood from her eyes and opened them just in time to see Tarkik's broken hands appear in the water that was now almost all the way up to the surface. She reached in and grabbed onto his coat, leaning back and using all her remaining strength to pull the wet man up onto the ice.

His body was still in shock and convulsing horribly. He tried to scream Ila's name, but just a garbled yell came out.

The old woman moved as quickly as her aching body allowed, as she grabbed under Tarkik's armpits and dragged him across the ice back toward the igloo. Progress was slow, as Tarkik's body shook and his waterlogged clothing added a couple dozen pounds to him.

Eventually Ila got him back into the igloo. It was immediately clear as she took his wet clothes off that Tarkik would at least lose his feet and probably more from the cold. Still, he was going to live.

And finally, the dogs that were still alive began to settle down.

# Steven Van Patten's
# Shopping List

Chicken
Fish
Steak
Night Vision Goggles
Oil Of Cloves
Rope
Riding Gloves
Baclava
Leather Repair Kit
Batteries
Wizards 22214 Mist-N-Shine

# The Massage
## *Steven Van Patten*

"**D**ude! I feel bad for you, but you're freaking out the other customers. Isn't there someone you can call?" Lance looked over his shoulder to see two of the four hipster types at the bar taking pictures of Henry cowering in the side booth.

"My wife will kill me! You don't understand!" Henry's teeth chattered as he spoke.

"Well, can I call someone other than your wife?"

"I don't have anyone else's number memorized. I left my phone up there."

"Then, I suggest you go back and get these people to give you back your clothes and your phone."

"I'm not going back there! Ever!"

"Then I'm going to call the police."

"NO! Can't I just hang in the back and borrow some clothes from someone? You know I'm good for it and I'll pay you back once I get myself back together. Please, Lance. I just can't go up there."

Lance closed his eyes and sighed. "Okay, I'm going to take you in the back and you're going to explain this to me, once and for all."

Except for the hipsters and Scott—the other bartender—the front of Killington's Irish Pub was empty. The early part of this December had been especially brutal, so the owners spent the first week of the month decorating the place for the holidays before leaving to visit relatives in Ireland for Christmas. This left Lance in charge of everything and everyone else. This included Manuel the cook, Oliver the busboy, Scott, and the waitress, Rachel, who had taken a cigarette break since all of her tables were empty.

It would be a cigarette break interrupted minutes ago as Henry, a regular of Killington's, ran past her and inside, wearing nothing but a towel. Rachel watched from through the glass as Henry and Lance talked, her face as pretty as it was puzzled. She thought about putting her cigarette out before she was done, if only so she could hear whatever Lance was saying to Henry, but remembered that though Henry was a regular, he wasn't that great a tipper. There was no sense in wasting a good cigarette for a story she could just download from Lance later.

"Come on, Henry! Let's go!"

Clinging to his towel, Henry slid out of the booth and followed Lance. His face was filled with shame and trauma as he walked past the sniggering hipsters.

"Knock it off with the pictures, okay boys?" Lance spoke with just enough growl in his voice to intimidate the casually dressed Caucasians. "Guy's having a bad night."

"Is he going to be okay?" Standing behind the bar, Scott was genuinely concerned.

"I'll let you know."

Pushing open the door that led to the kitchen and adjoined storage area, Lance seemed to have interrupted Manuel and Oliver arguing in a broken mix of English and Spanish. It took a second for Lance to see the cause of contention; a soccer game the two men had been watching on a small monitor mounted on the far left wall. The sight of the nearly naked Henry following Lance silenced both the Mexican cook and the Chilean busboy.

Lance knew Manuel, if not checked, would launch into a string of expletives over having a naked man in his clean kitchen. To prevent this, he shot Manuel a look that screamed, *Just give me a minute*, before guiding Henry to an empty chair in the storage area half of the room. "Hey, Oliver, you have any spare clothes here?"

"I'm just supposed to give you my clothes?" Oliver was apparently not feeling very charitable.

"Of course not," Lance answered. "You'd get them back."

"He can have a spare uniform," Manuel volunteered. "It has a bunch of food stains I can't get out anyway."

"Great," Lance said with the tone of someone trying to get something over with before turning back to Henry. "Okay, I'm listening. And this better be good or I am definitely calling the police. Now, where the fuck are your clothes?"

Henry sighed. "They're at this massage place a few blocks away."

While Manuel looked puzzled, Oliver—in Spanish—said, "He went to get his dick yanked and the place got raided."

"You went for a massage? Was this a nice spa with robes and mimosa's and hot rocks, or a rub and tug?"

"I wasn't sure at first."

Lance could see that Henry was avoiding eye contact to the point of mimicking autism. Of course, when you've been a bartender for as long as Lance had, you knew that no eye contact during a story usually meant that the storyteller was full of shit. Lance knew from personal experience what places like the one Henry had gone to were like. He also knew that while men patronized these establishments under the pretense of having the kinks worked out of their necks and backs, the very thorough hand job administered by a pretty, young Asian masseuse at the near end of the massage was the real draw.

"Not judging you, Henry," Lance decided to clarify. "Just trying to understand what happened, is all."

Manuel walked over with his spare chef's uniform and handed it to Henry, then joined Lance as they both averted their eyes to avoid seeing Henry's turtle-headed penis as he dropped the jacket and the towel and scrambled to get the white pants over his legs and butt.

When he could see that Henry was reaching for the jacket, Lance turned back around.

"Okay, we got you some pants. I still need to know what's going on here."

Henry pulled the chef's jacket over his chest and buttoned it. "I was meeting some of my other friends here. You know, Marc and Kirk. They were coming to watch the game. But they both texted me that they were running late. So I just thought I'd have a little harmless fun, you know?"

"And your harmless fun turned not-so-harmless?" Lance speculated.

"It was just like any other time you go to those places," Henry suddenly blurted. "You go up the stairs, you ring the bell, they let you in, they put you in a room, you strip and get a massage. Only there was just one girl there and she told me she had just finished up with a client, so she sat me down in the waiting area. When she went back in the room, I could hear the guy talking. The guy was an idiot. Asking her stupid questions like did she know who Jeremy Lin, was. Like she's supposed to know who Jeremy Lin is because she's Asian."

"That's dumb," Lance agreed. "And racist."

"Well, I guess I fell asleep, because I never saw the guy leave. I remember her shaking my shoulder. 'I'm ready for you now,' she said, with this really big smile. She looked even prettier than when I'd first walked in. She escorted me to the room and left, so I stripped and got face down on the massage table. Had to poke a hole in the paper they put over the face cradle."

"Sounds like business as usual." Lance said with a shrug.

"It was, at first. She asked how much time I wanted, and I said an hour. She asked if I liked it light or strong and I said strong, because what kind of candy ass says 'light', am I right? Anyway, she's going in on me and she had the strongest hands I'd ever felt, man or woman. For a second, I thought I'd fucked up and ended up with a girl that used to be a guy or something. I figured I would enjoy the massage and politely decline the hand-job if it came up."

"No sense getting your meat squeezed off." Lance felt a laugh coming on and repressed it, since Henry still looked traumatized.

Henry stopped to glance at Manuel and Oliver, both of whom were only half listening and really more concerned about the soccer game. "After a while, she stopped with the massage and started with the slow moving fingertips across my back and my inner thighs. Then she told me to turn around."

Lance interrupted. "I'm guessing you didn't say no to the hand job after all."

"You don't understand! She was suddenly the most beautiful woman I'd ever seen. I couldn't even speak. In fact, when she asked if I wanted to fuck her, all I could do was nod."

"Wait. She asked if you wanted to fuck? Did you flash a shit ton of money? I don't understand. I mean, no offense, but you're not that handsome."

"I just figured that this is my lucky day. I couldn't have been more wrong. I could also swear that when I first walked in, she was wearing a t-shirt and jeans, but when I nodded it was like her clothes just melted away, like a magic trick."

"You didn't do anything before you went there, did you? Like have a drink or smoked some weed?"

"No, man! I swear I'm telling the truth and I wasn't hallucinating!"

Lance held his hands up. "Okay, you and the Asian masseuse started fucking or whatever and at some point, she hurt you?"

"You don't understand!" Henry stood up, looking quite ridiculous in the chef's uniform that was at least two sizes too big. "She put me inside and I felt like my soul was being drained."

Manuel's eyes widened and Oliver's head slowly went back to Henry.

"Your soul was being drained?" Lance repeated. "You sure you weren't just panicking? Or maybe just feeling guilty? Again, not judging, but you are married."

"It felt so good, but I threw her off me eventually. It took every bit of strength I had, but I had to throw her off me. I felt like I was dying. Like she was killing me."

"You realize that if you assaulted this woman and she has your wallet, the cops are probably on their way to your house now," Lance theorized. "I can put you in an Uber and you can go face the music."

"Demons don't call the police!" Henry shouted.

Lance looked back to see that Manuel and Oliver had started paying attention to Henry again. "Demon? Come on, dude. She put it on you, and you freaked out." Oliver and Lance began to laugh.

Manuel continued to look on with a look of genuine concern as Henry started to cry and stammer. "When she fell on the floor, sh-sh-she hissed something at me. I think it was Ch-Chi-Chinese. I don't know if she put a curse on me or what, but I think I'm going to die."

"You're going to die because your wife is going to kill you, bro!" Oliver shouted.

Lance might have normally laughed at a quip like that, but the desperation in Henry's face stilled him. "Okay, where did you say this place was?"

"Two blocks away. Ninth and 48$^{th}$. I forget the name."

"I'm sure there's a sign. I'll be back," Lance walked over to the coat rack on his left and grabbed his jacket and wool cap.

As Lance got dressed, Oliver's eyes widened. "Dude! You're going to go try old girl out? You're a wild dude, Lance!"

"Shut up, asshole! I'm just going to see if I can get his stuff back and gauge how much trouble he's in. Then, I'm sending him home."

As Lance turned to leave, Manuel grabbed a silver shaker from a nearby food prep table. Since he had his back turned, Lance failed to notice as Manuel tossed a healthy handful of salt in the air above him. The impromptu baptism of white crystals left the unknowing Lance glistening in the kitchen's spotty lights as he exited.

"What the fuck are you doing?" Oliver asked once Lance was gone.

Manuel knew that if he told Oliver the truth, there would be endless and unwanted commentary from the young and immature busboy. "Nothing."

Oliver rolled his eyes. "You fuckin' people are weird."

#

Lance told Scott and Rachel that he'd be back as he brushed past the hipsters and stepped briskly out of Killington's and into the street. Frustrated with himself, he began muttering under his breath.

"Nice work, dumbass! I guess this is what I get for fucking Henry's wife. She probably hasn't been giving him any, which is why he was compelled to go to the massage parlor. Poor guy is probably backed up as hell. Anyway, no point in her knowing about this if she doesn't have to. She might get mad and tell him about us."

There was snow on the ground from a previous dusting, but the sky was clear and the air was brisk. Despite the clusters of jolly tourists and the occasional slippery spots of sidewalk, Lance was able to navigate his way past Eighth Avenue and 46th to the much less populated Ninth Avenue. Momentarily distracted by the plethora of Christmas displays and the small groups of drunk people stumbling in and out of other restaurants, he almost missed the sign that read, *Massage*. "You forgot the name because there was no name, Henry," Lance sighed.

The street level door was open and led to a dimly lit staircase. As he walked up, he noticed branding for a Miss Yolanda, a psychic who apparently operated out of the second floor. Once on the landing, he peered through the locked glass door only to see that Miss Yolanda had apparently moved on to greener pastures. Outside of a single lamp, the office was devoid of furniture. To his right hung a sign very similar to the one he passed outside. *Massage. 3ʳᵈ Floor*. There was also an arrow pointing up.

About midway through the second staircase, he could faintly hear slow tempo Christmas music being played by on what he speculated might have been a pan flute or some other Asian specific woodwind instrument. *Curse of the Golden Flower meets Frosty the Snowman,* he mused to himself.

Once at the door, he noticed a glowing red button and pressed it. *BING BONG*. After a moment, the woman who Henry had accused of being a soul-snatcher came to the door and opened it.

"Massage?" she asked.

Aside from the warm, inviting tone of her voice, her face was beautiful to the point of hypnotic. Her figure was impressive as well, as her breasts were each roughly the size of a nine-month old's head. Suddenly stuck in 'gaze wantonly' mode, he silently recollected watching a stand-up comedian on HBO talking about the first time he'd met Halle Berry and how that had been what 'looking into the sun is supposed to be like.' He'd always thought that statement more poetic than actually a good joke, but for the first time in his life, he'd understood the sentiment. He had to fight to find his voice.

"Actually, no," Lance said as his eyes involuntarily descending down her body. Under the t-shirt, jeans and sandals, he imagined her naked body was everything Henry had said it would be. "You had a customer about an hour ago. He left his stuff. I think he might have suffered some sort of delusion."

"Yes," she smiled a smile that made all cares melt away. "You forget about him. Get massage, yes?"

Suddenly flustered and feeling his body temperature spiking, he took off his wool cap and held it in front of him. He didn't notice the granules of salt glistening in the dim light and falling on the floor, but he saw the masseuse's face turn to a rictus of anger as she glowered at the hat. She let out a scream that seemed to come from her toes, before saying something in Chinese, the closest English translation being 'how dare you'.

Snatched hard from the lusty mind-fog he'd nearly fallen into, Lance shook his head and jumped back, as the woman ran off behind a curtain. He caught a glimpse of a man lying eerily still on a massage table covered by a towel behind the heavy draping. He involuntarily took a second step back. As desire made way to fear, he faintly contemplated leaving without Henry's things. Just as he turned to exit, the angry masseuse returned.

"Here! Here! Get out! Get out!" She practically threw a black plastic bag at him, presumably containing Henry's things. It occurred to him that he wouldn't know until he'd gotten back to Killington's. "Get out! Now!"

She screamed again as she threw the bag at him.

"Well, goddamn it! Rude ass crazy woman!"

He turned and opened the door and she shoved him so hard that he was nearly thrown into the stairwell wall. He didn't notice the sizzling sound as her hands touched his salted coat, as it was drowned out by yet another anguished, otherworldly cry of agony.

The door slammed shut and locked behind him. Before he could turn around and perhaps hurl an insult or two at the clearly deranged woman, the massage parlor and the entire stairwell went black, as if someone had pulled a master power switch. The Christmas music also cut off abruptly. The only available light in the entire building was the lamp from Miss Yolanda's abandoned psychic business, which he used to slowly descend the stairs as his eyes adjusted. Walking back to the restaurant with the plastic bag swinging in his right hand, he shook his head and hoped that returning Henry's things would get them all back to having a normal evening. As he reentered Killington's, the looks on everyone's faces told him that would not be the case.

The first thing he noticed was that the hipsters were gone. In their place at the bar stood two uniformed policemen and a crying Rachel. Scott also looked pretty upset.

"What the hell?" he asked the room.

Manuel suddenly appeared in front of him. "Are you okay?"

"Yeah. Why?"

"Quick, just between you and me, did you have sex with the masseuse?" Manuel's eyes squinted as he seemed to be bracing himself for bad news.

"What kind of question is that? Of course not!" The fact that he probably would have had the encounter remained friendly seemed a long ago thought.

"Good, because Henry is dead."

"Say what, now?"

"Henry is dead. Slumped down, then fell out of the chair like in *The Godfather,* right after you left. Scott called the police after giving Oliver time to go hide next door at O'Reilly's. Oliver's work visa is expired, by the way, so we didn't want to take the chance."

After a moment, Lance nodded. Instinctively, he felt a wave of gratitude for Manuel, even if he wasn't completely sure why.

"You sure you're okay? Manuel asked.

"Just working out what I'm going to say to Henry's wife," Lance answered.

Behind Lance, Henry's friends, Marc and Kirk, finally entered Killington's. Oblivious, the two men wished everyone a Merry Christmas and asked about Henry. Lance delivered the bad news, while leaving out the more salacious details. It would prove to be good practice for later that night.

# Sinister Sweetheart's
# Shopping List

Bananas

Coca-Cola

Two Huge Bloody Steaks

Fang Cleaner with Whitening

Raven's Eye Nail Polish

Cauldron Spices- Garlic Salt, Paprika, Eye of Newt, Pickling Brine Mix, Cloves

Toilet Chamber Paper

Wolf's Blood Incense

Sinister Seasonings Tea- Scarecrow Blend (Chamomile, Honey, Clove and Vanilla)

Little Demons Brand Diapers- Size 4

A Mini Fan for my writing desk to blow through my fur when I type

Green Giant Brand Baby Corn

Devil's Food Chocolate I'Scream

Black Hole Eyeliner to look good for dates with my Mega Beast

Medusa Brand Hairspray MEGA Hold

A Baby's Head of Lettuce

# Cat Call
## *Sinister Sweetheart*

I n here! I got the door open!" A fellow officer yells as I exit my squad car. The house was derelict, run down would be the generous thing to say. The yard is overgrown and as unloved as the house. The closer I get to the front door, the harder it is not to gag. The overwhelming smell of ammonia and bad meat wafts from within. The wood of the porch is frayed, as if slashed with millions of tiny knives.

We've been getting calls about this lady for weeks now complaining about the cats. They stayed in her yard; she appeared to be taking good care of them. Not much you can do with that really as far as the law is concerned. However, over the past week the calls have rapidly increased; now with reports that the cats were looking sickly.

I hated to be the one to answer this call. My childhood home was overrun with cats. I was the kid at school no one sat near because he smelled like cat piss. My daughter has only one, and she takes care of him very well. I don't have the heart to tell her how much I hate them.

I enter the residence, gun drawn and ready for what awaits me. The inside is an absolute mess of food smears, hair, and animal feces turned white and fuzzed with age. That all too familiar smell hits me with dreadful nostalgia. I don't understand how a house can be so dusty but so oily at the same time. Almost every piece of furniture is frayed like the porch. The sofa's ripped to Hell, the table legs have been clawed so much that I'm surprised it still stands.

There are two officers that arrived on scene before me. The officer's voice that I heard upon arrival belonged to Billy Sarvis. He still looks winded from having to break the door down. His eyes scan the largest room of the house.

We step over various items of neglect and search. Every room is uneventful so far except for a bathroom that contained an overflowing clawfoot tub of gritty cat waste. There's only one more room to go, her basement. The smell increases ever-still. I rub some Vicks under my nose, an old trick I remember from childhood. We start to descend the stairs; hoping not to find much of anything but also knowing that smell has to lead somewhere terrible.

The room is surprisingly clean. I don't see anybody down there; nothing looks disturbed. The light switch isn't working so I have to rely on my flashlight. I do a quick sweep of the room. Just as hoped, I don't see much of anything. Then my light rests on a far corner of the room.

There is a MASS of fur, too large and oddly colored to be any animal that I recognize. It looks like a huge pile of fur coats. Fur coats don't make sound though . . . I hear a sickening cacophony of chews, licks and growls. Coats also don't wriggle around on their own either.

As soon as the beam of light hits, it explodes into a scattering of whites, yellows, oranges, blacks and browns; cats. It's a huge group of huddled up cats. Temporarily distracted, I don't immediately see what they were huddled around. I wish now that I hadn't seen. All these years as an officer and I'd thought I'd seen everything; I was wrong.

The two other officers turn their lights on it as well. With all of the new visibility, we instantly see hundreds, and I mean hundreds, of tiny red footprints. All over the floor, repeating over and over again. They're even on the stairs we have just come down.

There on the floor . . . is a bloody mess that appears to have once been an elderly woman. She's wearing a worn paisley dress that's in bloody tatters. She's been there for quite a while and the cats . . . were eating her. I don't believe that was how she initially died, but they definitely took advantage of the event. There are two left behind, the skinniest of the group, enjoying their dinner too much to be frightened away.

Their mouths gleam with red. Droplets of blood and flesh stick to their whiskers, growling at each other between chews. They seem to lick up the blood as soon as they draw it out. I shudder to think about it.

"Oh God!" Sarvis exclaims, running to the opposite corner to vomit. He's the newest officer here, not to say I don't have a hard time not doing the same thing.

"Have you ever seen anything like this in your life?" the other officer asks me. I shake my head, not being able to take my eyes off the partially consumed body.

I look over and see a book lying next to her; barely affected by the pool of blood that surrounds her. I put on gloves to pick it up. It appears to be a journal of some sort. We call for the coroner, animal control and forensics to arrive. I open the book and begin reading:

**July 10th, 1980**

*I've never been much of a cat person. Honestly I'm not really a pet person at all . . . but especially not cats. Their litter box fumes that take over the entire house, all of the hair left lying around and the constant grooming always grosses me out. Also, why is it that every time a cut jumps and decides they want to cuddle they always present themselves butt first? Is it just me? I don't know . . .*

*I'm not completely heartless, the sad puppy eyes get me just as much as the next gal. I wouldn't wish harm on an animal; I just don't find them necessary as companions. So when I find a strange kitty sitting on my porch steps, I'm a bit confused. I know I'm not going to get any fans here; but I'm sure if I just don't feed it . . . eventually it will go away.*

### July 18th, 1980

*I'm wrong. A week later and still . . . morning after morning on my way out the door there it sits. He . . . she? It's a tuxedo cat with short hair and 1.5 ears. It looks mangy and its feet are stained with dirt. It tries to rub against me. I gently shoo it away with my foot in response. It shakes its rump at me as it saunters away. Yep, the cat's definitely a He.*

### July 24th, 1980

*My roommate, Iris has just come home from vacation a couple of days ago. This is the first chance I had to talk to her. I found her in the kitchen making what smelled like meatballs. It smelled amazing!*

*We got lucky really. We hadn't known each other at all before we moved in together. Our situations had both brought us to the right place at the right time and it worked out. Despite my nervous social tendencies, we got along right away. I was totally comfortable around her.*

### Undated

*I ask Iris where the tuna was, hoping to make sandwiches. Her eyes look to me without lifting her face. She said, "Laurel, there was the cutest little kitty on the porch when I came home. He was just sitting there waiting for me and he looked so hungry." Of course I got onto her about. "Great now he will never go away! Did you give him a name too?" I ask her.*

*Iris is trying hard not to show her excitement! She tells me . . . "YES!" She named him Pepe' after the cartoon character! Said he looked just like him. My annoyance grows more and more at the situation. I tell her we just re-mulched the front yard and it looks nice. How long does she think that's going to last with a cat outside? She lifts a finger as if she's already thought of this. "Welllllll then maybe he could be an..... inside . . cat'; was the suggestion she gave                                me.*

*No way, Iris. I'm sorry. I'm really not comfortable with stray cats hanging around. I tell her if she stops putting food out, he'll move onto someone else. I asked her to please respect me on this. I couldn't believe that we had to have this conversation. It was the first term that we ever had disagreed on and I feel like a total jerk. I know I won't change my mind though and she needs to know how I feel about it. I should have just lied and told her I was deathly allergic . .*

## August 4th, 1980

*I wake up late and have to rush out; there's a lot to do today. I get about 5 miles down the road when something terrible assaults my nostrils. It's honestly one of the worst smells I've ever experienced. My eyes dart around the car to see where it could be coming from.*

*As soon as I get out of my car, I check my patchwork boots. Sure enough, the bottom of my left boot has cat crap all over it. This is why I'll never want a cat. They are all fluff and balls of yarn; just wait 'til you track their shit all over. It's in the grooves of my shoe and also my brake and gas pedals. The shoe I can take to the tub and hose off with the high pressure shower setting. The pedals though, that all has to be cleaned by hand.*

*I pull back into the driveway, trying to put it out of my mind. As I get in front of the porch steps, I find an once steaming, smeared pile; right in the mulch. "Goddammit!" I yell aloud to the sky, as if my voice can be heard in the vastness of the cosmos.*

## September 3rd, 1980

*Iris isn't home. Her boyfriend, Eric, has the weekend off, so she is staying with him tonight. They usually alternate between his place and ours. I don't need to tell you that I prefer it when she stays there, honestly. The house stays cleaner, I get to listen to my music as loud as I want and can eat dinner in my underwear. Oh, and no guttural sex chanting through all hours of that night and sometimes the next morning, that's nice too.*

## Date Illegible

*I walk out to check our mail and 'Pepe' runs towards me; weaving in and out between my feet with a swiftness I can't match. I trip and almost fall right onto an iron rake face first. As I just barely catch myself, I see the cat sitting there staring at me. The look in his eyes is unmistakable, he knows he tripped me. That fucking cat could have killed me!*

*I try to shoo him away with my foot and he hisses at me. He trips me, almost gravely injures me and then has the balls to hiss at ME?!? Fucking cats! And Jesus Christ wouldn't you know, another pile in the mulch. I can't just pick this up or scoop it with a plastic shovel. Whatever this cat's eating clearly isn't working for his stomach. Enough is enough, I call my parents and ask to borrow their cat carrier.*

### Undated

*The next day I take Pepe' for a drive to the next town, find a gas station and drop him off behind it. The gas stations in Florida are loaded with stray cats at night. Surely they'll 'adopt' him and help him find food. Satisfied, I get back in my car and take the hour drive home. I'll tell Iris I found him a good home and he will be happier now. I feel good about what I've done. My mind justifies itself by telling me that I'm helping him but really, I only care about myself and my yard.*

### September 24th, 1980

*A week has gone by and it's been awesome! A totally hair free, poop free, cat free week. Pepe' s probably off having fun with his new merry band of wayward cats. Iris is happy because she thinks the problem was solved without any trips to the humane society. I even tell her he'll be an inside cat, so she won't worry about him getting hit by any cars.*

### October 5th, 1980

*My best friend Jennifer has called to ask if I want to have lunch; I'm happy to accept the invitation. I've just bought a new black and white paisley dress! I go outside and my blood chills to see a familiar sight. I shake my head and re-open my eyes, it's Pepe'.*

*He's come back! They say this happens all the time, pets travel great distances to find their owners. We've been seeing this cat for less than two months though and I have no emotional relationship with him. He sits on his hind legs, sharpening his claws on my tires. "Stop that!" I yell. I know cat claws can't flatten a tire from one time but with over time and repetition, they sure                                    might.*

*I get into my car to leave and turn on the air. My windshield is wet, the wipers smear it in a way that tells me it's not just water. Instantly the smell of ammonia wafts in from my AC vents. The fucking cat! Also, that's another thing, remember when things got weird earlier with me talking about the cat scat?*

*Well, the same also goes for cat urine. No other animal's is like it, with the males being the worst. It's hard to get the scent out of your clothes. Laurel's no cat reason # 74: sometimes they won't even use the cleanest of cat boxes and will just piss on your clothes; real nice. How in the hell was I going to clean this up?*

*It already had dripped down under the hood of my car and affected every single atom of air that came through the vents. With it being almost 90 degrees outside, what choice did I have but to endure it.*

*I make sure, discreetly, when I get out of my car that the smell didn't transfer to my dress. I go in and meet with my long missed friend Jennifer, putting Pepe' far out of my mind. We have such a good time and have more drinks than expected. Pretty soon I'm wasted, emboldened by alcohol and rejuvenated by my visit with Jennifer.*

*It almost doesn't even bother me that I have to sit in a human cat box on my way home. I roll the windows down as the night brings in a refreshing cool air.*

*I pull up to my driveway and there he sits, my feline nemesis, Pepe'. He leers at me when I open my car door, but I don't even care. I feel amazing! As I walk by him to go up the steps he swats at my foot, catching a toe with his claw and drawing blood. "What the hell cat?!"*

## November 22nd, 1980

*I'm not proud of myself and I wish I could blame it on temporary insanity due to blood loss. I went right inside my house, got a pinch of weed, a knife and a can of cat food Iris had bought. If I'm gonna do this, I'll make him feel good first. I sprinkle the herb over the food, put it in this new thing called a Tupperware container and return outside.*

*He looks at me warily, seeing and smelling the container from afar. I sit it down and step away. As soon as he deems me at an appropriate distance, he circles the food bowl. He sniffs at it a couple of times. Then jumps back as if it's going to lunge at him and bite him. Finally, he settles in and starts really chowing down.*

*I creep up behind him and steady the knife. I have to get it right the first time, there won't be a second try. With one swift motion, I grab the scruff of his neck, hold him down, and cut off his tail. I'm afraid the blade won't make it all the way through in one shot; but it does.*

*He yowls in pain and releases from my grip, turning around to attack me. I cover him with a towel and hold him there. He eventually falls silent and still, knowing he's not gonna able to run off.*

*My hands are bloody and I'm delirious from drinking earlier in the day. Iris pulls up in her car. She leaps out and starts running to me, not sure what she's seeing. "Laurel, are you hurt? What happened to your hands?"*

*Upon seeing the cat, her face darkens. I can see flames in her eyes. "That's it! To not prefer animals is one thing but this is totally sick! He's an innocent creature!" Her eyes fill with tears. "Fuck it, I was going to tell you after we paid rent but I'm moving in with Eric. You need to get him to a vet!"*

*By then, Pepe' had disappeared. I knew what I did was messed up. I don't blame her for reacting the way that she did. The mind doesn't work that way when you're drunk though does it? "Fine," I respond, slurring my speech. "Go live with your boyfriend. I'll be just fine here on my own. AND WITH NO PETS!!!" I don't mean it. How far could our friendship possibly progress now though? Sometimes it's best to just let things go, even people.*

### December 1st, 1980

*Eric's truck comes and goes a few times over the days to help move her things. Iris and I don't even say goodbye really. She tries to talk to me; I'm too distracted staring out the window, making sure the cat's gone for good.*

*Right before she leaves, I hear her say, "Fine, bye then. If that cat comes back, just call me and I'll take it home with me." It sounds odd hearing her say the word 'home' and knowing she's not referring to this place. She mutters a, "fucking animal killer," on her way out the door.*

*Eventually, it's time for me to leave the house again. I'm going to go out of town to treat myself to a night out. Maybe I can find a nice man to sweat my frustrations out with; forget the mess about Iris and the cat. A night away is most definitely exactly what I need; and soon.*

## Date Illegible

*I go out and have such a nice time that I decide to spend the night. Know that I went out, had fun, looked for some company, found some company and spent the night. I had a few drinks, not nearly as many as the time before; definitely not enough to excuse my decisions. I wake up feeling dried out and excited to go home. I slip out from the arm atop me and sneak out the front door.*

*When I get home, I can't believe my eyes. Out through my windshield, I see that my entire porch is shredded. It looks like a whole kennel of cats attacked the porch all at once. Their claws eating away at the wood like sharp termites. How the fuck could one cat have done all of this, especially injured? Forget about me being pissed off, this is just getting scary now.*

*This porch was hand built by the man who rented the house's grandfather. Can you imagine how pissed he will be once he sees this? I can't believe it, there's no way this cat isn't intentionally malicious. I have had enough.*

### December 25th, 1980

*I back up my car a little and sit at the end of the driveway, waiting to see if Pepe' will appear. After not too long, he does. He saunters up to the porch, tail stub mangled and yellow with infection. He sharpens his claws a few quick times, almost as if he knows I'm watching.*

*He walks to the middle of the yard and lays there, sunbathing like he owns the place. I put my car into drive and floor it. There's no way this asshole will have the time to get away, and this time I'll be done for good.*

*No more cat shit, I think as I feel the tires go over the bump. No more pissing on my car, I think as I reverse to run over him again. No more         cat.*

*I know it's cold and heartless, but I scoop up his little body with a shovel, put it into a trash bag and throw it in the waste bin. I'm finally done with this whole thing. No one can judge me. The pound would have killed him anyway.*

*His death was quick and though I can't speak for him personally, I would like to think it was         painless.*

### Five empty pages later

*I've made a huge mistake. I don't mean that I'm remorseful for taking a life that was clearly out to get mine. I mean nothing could have ever prepared me for my repercussions. For every day since the day I sent Pepe' to his resting place, a new cat would show up. On the first day there was one and I noticed the trash bin had been knocked over. Then the second day two, and so on from there. I tried shooting them but around the 12th day it became too much. They seemed to be more menacing the larger their group became. Maybe I deserved this.*

### *April 16th, 1981*

*Eventually, I gave up and accepted my consequence of fate. I didn't bother to clear the yard, I put a cat box in every room and even installed a pet door so they could come and go as they pleased. After a while, the numbers stop increasing. However, by then most of the cats had bred, starting a new generation of horror. I keep a punch bowl on the counter filled with food for them and one tub is always filled with water. The other tub takes place of a litter box. Forty-five adult cats, infinite amounts of kittens and still breeding. They clawed at my clothes, my face, my feet especially. They wanted to destroy me and everything I enjoyed for my home. After what I did who could blame them?*

*A long while after it started, he came. Maybe I'm delirious from fumes, maybe I've finally lost my mind, but I swear I see Pepe'. Sitting outside looking in. His tail is gone, his body is misshapen, he has 1.5 ears and an eye that hangs from its socket.*

### February 10th, 1983

*I know that I have a forever pet, a friend who will never leave my side. I have friends of all colors, ages, sizes and fur lengths. Dozens of them, they live with me and I love through them. It's crazy how a slight change in perspective can change everything, isn't it? In my earlier years, I was called Laurel Johnson, but now . . . now they call me . . . the Cat Lady.*

## END OF ENTRIES

I search the pages for the most recent date and find that the last entry was written almost 20 years ago, the pages yellowed but the ink unfaded. The teams come out and do their jobs, none of them much surprised by the sight. I make last minute statements for their reports and leave the scene.

The drive home is half way complete. The light of my phone screen illuminates through the pocket of my pants. I take my phone out and check it. It's a text message from my wife.

*Luna brought a friend home from the store today. We're naming him Whiskas. Please pick up a bag of cat food on your way home.*

As I look in my rear-view mirror, I see a flash of a little yellow glowing eye. It's a black and white clump of fur, with no tail and half an ear. I do a double take to make sure of what I'm seeing, and it's gone.

# Carlton D. Herzog's
## Shopping List

I like to acquire human heads for both decorative and conversational purposes. Nothing says trendsetter better than a set of preserved heads adorning a study. And for dinner conversation, dead heads are the best, since I am guaranteed the last word. Ordinarily, I shop for heads in cemeteries and funeral homes, but every now and then, I feel whimsical, and head for a mall to bag an unsuspecting shopper.

Human hearts, particularly those of newborns and young children, are delicious whether baked, fried, roasted or stewed. Likewise the blood of same for gravies and sauces. I'm getting hungry even as I write.

People who piss me off—for good reason or no reason. On a typical week, I usually bag two, cut out their tongues, and introduce them to the business end of my sledgehammer.

WD-40 to keep the cage hinges from squeaking.

Plastic bags, chains, blankets, paper towels, rubber gloves, bleach, soundproofing panels and other assorted household items.

Latest books on the black arts. My latest acquisition is *How to Turn People Inside Out with Your Mind*.

# The Farmer's Tale
## *Carlton D. Herzog*

This is an excerpt from the diary of Samuel Peeps, 64-116 ac. Michael Ventris discovered the diary while excavating the second level of Telmagordo, the city once known as San Antonio. Originally composed in Texan Cursive B, Ventris painstakingly translated the diary into modern Lallalia for which he won the 2912 Nobel Prize in Linguistics.

The diary is significant in several respects. First, it provides a graphic description of the widespread barbarism, famine and desolation of $26^{th}$ century America, the result of runaway climate change. In those days, people took cannibalism, grave-robbing, revenge killings and murderous marauding gangs to be the norm. Second, it details the early history and social impact of the youth pills we enjoy today. Third, it offers a first-hand account of the rampant birth defects caused by pharmacological pollution of the air and water. Finally, the diary format represents the literary norm during a time when both the internet and publishing houses had ceased to exist, and consequently, would be authors were writing for an audience of one.

# I

The corpses I planted had begun to sprout. About time. I could see them little eyes poking up. Tiny fingers too. Can't eat them though. They're like the eyes on a potato. Give you a bad case of the bubble face. Then you're off to the colony with all the other bubble faces. Where they eat each other.

I seed Old Roy trying to dig them up, so I said "Git!" That dog's a mess. Got three balls all a floppin' and a swingin' twixt them boney legs.

Like everything else in this place, he came out wrong. You got babies born here with flippers and wings and nobody knows why. Maybe it's something in the air; maybe it's in the water, but one thing is for sure, the land is cursed. And if you want to make it come alive you got to bury a dead man in it. And not just any old dead man. Lord knows there's plenty of them about.

No, you got to have a stiff saturated with that stuff they call longevenol. Makes you live longer. It works like this: the longevenol builds up inside you, so when you croak, it mixes in with all your other dying gases. Next thing you know, your body's one big bloated bag of super-fertilizer. And as you rot away, all that fertilizer seeps out your pores to ground.

Now stick that stiff in the deadest land you can find. Toss in some seeds, then just wait. In no time at all, you've got the Garden of Eden at your doorstep. I don't just mean plenty. I mean plenty big as well. Cornstalks as tall as a tree. Potatoes as big as a pig. That sort of thing.

Now where do you suppose longevenol comes from? Well, they make it from babies. Don't ask me how. All I know is Big Pharma sucks the young right out of 'em, puts it in a pill, then sells it to those who can afford it. Mainly city folk. Overseers and the like. Keeps em' going well past a hundred.

That's not the end of the story. Not by a longshot.

Folks tried to get around waiting. They sprinkled and sprayed longevenol on plants, thinking it'd be like fairy dust. Doesn't work. Got to have a human host. What they call an 'incubator.' The brains aren't sure why it happens. Tried doin' it in labs. Didn't work. Maybe it's a miracle. Like Lazarus comin' back from the dead.

Back in the day, was only a few knew about all this. But loose lips sink ships. Now everybody wants a piece of the action. Honest pearlers like me scramble just to find one or two. Some of us—not me—take matters into their own hands. Don't wait for 'em to drop off the vine; harvest 'em while they're still alive. Can you blame them? After all the, Lord helps those what helps theyselves.

It all went south when Big Chain got into the business. Makes sense. They 've got their fingers in everything else. Run the gasoleos and whore-marts. So, they bring their fancy lawyers with their fancy word ways. Next thing you know, folks are signing over the rights to their bodies when they first start taking the stuff.

Them pills be funny. Don't just make you live longer. Turn you white as a sheet they do. Why you're a regular Casper, the friendly ghost. Then there's the eyes. After a hundred years or so, the eyes go all white. Calcify they do. By the time it's all done you've got two jumbo pearls where your eyes used to be. Worth a lot of money on a count of they're so big, and there ain't no more oysters. Or anything else livin' in the sea these days.

But I'm getting ahead of myself. I'm standing there making sure Old Roy don't come sneaking back to dig himself up a treat when I get smacked in the face with the flat end of a shovel. Knocked me out cold, it did. When I woke up, I was lying on my back in an open grave. I look up and see this young fella leaning on my shovel. He asks me, "Do you know who I am?"

I say, "Well sir, I'm no genius, but I reckon you're the fellow that just hit me with that shovel."

He don't answer right away. Instead, he shovels dirt on me then says, "That'd be my pappy you got buried over there. And I aim to bury you alive for killing him."

I can taste blood in my mouth, all sweet and coppery. I start licking inside the hole where my front teeth used to be.

The fella asks me, "Well, ain't you got nothin' to say?"

So, I look up. His hands ain't shakin, and he ain't laughin, so I know he ain't no cannibilly. They do that, you know, 'cause eatin' another man gives you the *kuru*, what they call the laughin' sickness. Eats holes in your brain is what it does.

So calm as can be I say, "I didn't kill your pappy. I found him like that and aimed to take advantage of the situation. Round these parts, law says you find a dead body you can do whatever you want with it so long as you don't leave it lying around. Something about spreading disease."

He gives me a look like I have two heads and says, "You must think I'm an idiot. What man would bury a corpse on his land?"

I said, "You're not from round here are you?"

He said, "I've been shipping with the merchant marine for the past 25 years."

I said, "Well that explains it. Things have changed a lot, 'specially the way we grow crops."

I don't think he heard me, or if he did, he didn't care, 'cause he start shovelin' dirt on top of me again. So, I yelled, "Hold on, pardner. Just hear me out!"

He says, "Make it good, 'cause these are probably your last words."

So, I tell him about longevenol and pearly eyes and fertilizer. He looks at me hard then spits on me and says, "So what! That don't explain how he died. Folks in Resurrection City said you had words with him there a few months back. Makes sense you might hold a grudge and want to kill him."

Now it all made sense. I said, "I was in Resurrection City with my family. We went there to pay our taxes and get counted. Takes a whole day and night by camel. Not a drop of water along the way. Just dust and cracked plains and skulls and dead trees that give no shelter. You can't spit count'a yer mouth's all dried up. A lotta folks die on the way. Buzzards pick 'em clean."

He asked me, "So what happened when you met my pappy?"

"I went to the cannibilly house. Wanted to see what all the fuss was about. Your pappy was in there trading corpses for longevenol. Should have minded my own business but I started asking questions about that business. Thought there might be something there for me. Your pappy got all riled up and had two big old cannibillies named Tashtego and Queequeg toss me out. Heard them names before and said so. But, pardner, I never laid a hand on your pappy."

He said, "That don't make no sense since you buried him here."

I said, "I found him along with two others in Rats Alley. I only knew the one. She'd been a whore. Lived to 132. Looks started to fade round 110, but she whored on. Blind as a bat.

Made a bundle for herself but frittered it away on high livin'."

"The other two were near her, lying on a pile of bones. Don't know what happened there. Don't care. Soon as I found 'em, I cut out those pearly eyes and stuffed them in my pocket. Piled all three in my wheelbarrow and brought them home for a proper burial."

"Some folks just stick 'em in the ground without sayin' any words over them. That ain't right. All folks deserve a wordin'. Course stiffs do reek to high heaven. It's the kinda stink that makes your teeth chatter and hair stand on end. Makes you wish you were dead yourself so you wouldn't have to smell it. Reckon, some folks just can't take standin' over that stink and just want to cover 'em up quick as they can."

"So, you just walked into Rats Alley and stumbled on the three of them?"

"No, my son told me they were there. I don't like to talk about this, but I'm a father like your pappy. Twenty years ago, I had me a son. Wasn't supposed to 'cause the wife was on the pills. But he came out anyway. He had a bat's face and purple skin. And wings. Wife wanted to toss him into the canal. I said we'll give him to the Lady of the Rocks. She'll know what to do. She's the wisest woman in Texas, knows all the situations and intrigues."

"I never asked what she did with him. Twenty years later to the day, I was in Resurrection City, walking the canal bank and counting dead seahorses. I heard a gasp behind me. Then I saw a purple man dragging his slimy belly along the mud. He had wings on his back. He come right up next to me like a great purple slug. Then he stood up. He was an old man with wrinkled udders."

"He said 'I am a sailor home from the sea. I have come to kill my father for giving me away.'"

I knew right away he was looking for me. And I knew that old woman had sold him to Big Pharma. It had sucked the young right out of him and put it in a pill.

I said, "You're too late by a mile. I knew your daddy. Liked to cheat at cards, he did. He tried it with the Hanging Man. Strung him up by his nuts and set him on fire."

He said, 'No man deserves to be burned alive for cheating at cards. But maybe that makes him and me even, since the young in me's been eaten, and he made it happen. I don't want the young they took from me to go a wastin'.' It was then he told me 'bout them three in Rats Alley.

"He said, 'Go on, git. Somebody'll find 'em soon enough.'"

"I asked, 'You kill 'em?' He grinned, 'Maybe I did and maybe I didn't. Maybe I jest watched 'em flicker and go out.' Then he sank into the mud and slithered away. Never saw him again after that."

Now this fella looks at me and rubs his chin. Then he said, "That all sounds a might peculiar."

I said, "That ain't nothin' compared to what I seen at Resurrection City. That place is wrong in so many ways I don't know where to begin. From the outside, it looks like somebody took a real city and flipped it over. Then flipped it back again. There's towers going this way and that way and every way which way except up. Roads going through upside down houses. Round the city gates are mountains of bones. Not white, but brown like the air."

"Things are no better on the inside. Mainly 'cause you got dead folk walking around in broad daylight. Some still in their winding sheets. Preachers say that's cause there ain't no more room in hell. The brains say that the dead have always walked among us. But something in how our eyes work has changed."

"In any case, you gotta watch it. Say two of you go into town. Next thing you know there's a third walking beside you. Just gliding along in a brown hood and mantle. But when you count there's only two. That just ain't right. And they're everywhere. Wouldn't thought Death would have kilt so many."

"Course it ain't just the dead that'll trouble your soul. They got an old sibyl they keep in a cage. Don't know why. Wings fell off long time ago, and she can't sing no more. Just sits there hangin' upside down saying, 'I wants to die.' And them bones I was tellin' you about outside the city? Sometimes the necromancers put on a show with them. Reassemble them, they do and then have them dance and jump around. Some say it's all an optical illusion. But it looked real enough to me."

"Then there's the heart of town where all the deciders work. Folks like the mayor and his overseers. Doctors, lawyers, counters, preachers. Now what do you suppose I saw in front of city hall? Why the last mayor pearlified on a pedestal grinning and a shining and his hands all outstretched like he was a saying 'WELCOME.' Right friendly it was. Pretty too!"

"I learnt the old boy had put it in his will that after he passed on, he wanted to be super-juiced so his whole body got calcified. One fella said they juiced him for two whole weeks before it took. Said mayor ain't the only one. The richer holy rollers been doing it too."

"I had to see for myself, so we went down to the Steeple and went inside, and sure enough there was four of them all pearlified pretty as you please standing around the pulpit. Every now and then the pastor would look down on them and thank them right proper for all they had done money wise for the parish."

"He told everyone there that 'The Lord helps those what help they-selves. If you give enough you can be here too.' And he said, 'You know what that means brothers and sisters? Why that's an ironclad guarantee you're going upstairs and walking through the pearly gates where you'll be greeted by St. Peter himself. Then you'll be pearly everlasting.'"

"I laughed. I told the fella next to me, 'That's some high dollar churching if you ask me.'"

"He laughed and said, 'Well I reckon that's the price if you want to be one of the frozen chosen. If you ask me, dead is dead. No coming back from it no matter how much praying or juicing you do.'"

"I laughed this time and said, 'Don't really matter no how. I've done so much bad in my life that you'd have to butter my hips to get me through them gates, and there ain't enough of that there butter in the whole world enough for that job.' Then we both laughed."

"I could see that the old boy was starting to believe me. So, I asked, "Can I climb out of this here grave?" He nodded and reached out a hand to pull me up. After I got out, we both stood there, side by side. I could see my wife in the window brushing her hair. I could hear the gramophone spinning. 'Give me that old time religion'. The needle cracked the music. She's sweaty and dirty with broken nails. Got crooked teeth and a witch's nose, and smells of vinegar."

Me and that fella both stared at her. I said, "I think the Overseer's been having her. She never forgave me for giving the baby away. And I think he gives her meat too, but she don't share it with me."

Neither one of us moved or said anything. Black clouds gathered above us, clouds as dark as the ones inside my head. The moonlight shone on a ten-legged spider as big as a melon. He had a red cross on his back. He was spinning a box inside four bushes. I could see his fangs dripping with venom and shining like pearls.

Spiders get real busy anchoring their webs before storms. But there's no rain, just dry thunder. I listened for the sound of falling water. But there's no sound other than the locusts and the blowing grass.

As we stood there, I thought about the pearl gas. How it could make a whole field come alive. I wondered what would happen if I buried juicies on Golgotha.

I didn't know what that fella was thinking. Me, I stood there wishing for more juicies. That's my dream. I dream it awake and I dream it at night. It's like a shadow that follows me everywhere. It walks behind me in the morning and in front of me in the afternoon. At night it crawls into bed with me then screws itself into my head. I wonder if it will give me pearls for eyes someday.

Then I thought about my wife, how if I brought her some meat, she would let me lie on top of her again.

That's when that fella said, "Well, I reckon I'll be on my way."

I said, "Good luck to you stranger."

As he turned and walked away, I snatched up the pick and drove it through the back of his head. Sure, he wasn't juiced, but I'm sure he'd grill up just fine for me and the wife. And maybe I could take the leftovers and trade them for some longevenol. That preacher was right, the Lord helps those what helps themselves.

# Richard Raven's
# Shopping List

Flashlight and batteries
First aid kit
Dehydrated food
Canned food
Alcohol stove
Alcohol fuel
Mess kit
Bottled water
Hunting knife
A small metal box with a lid
Salt (a lot of it)
Candles
Chalk

# LEGACY
## *Richard Raven*

Jeremy Cassidy knew it wouldn't have bothered his uncle that so few had shown up to send him on his way. Michael Cassidy had known many people, but he had few, if any real friends. Never married and with no children, Uncle Mike had never had much use for or interest in people beyond his nephew, his last living relative. As he stood at the foot of his uncle's casket, Jeremy glanced in turn at each of the others present at the simple graveside service. Two men from the funeral home, the county Sheriff and one of his deputies, and an aging preacher who claimed he had known Uncle Mike in passing.

Uncle Mike had known a preacher? One that had offered to officiate his service? Would wonders never cease?

The biggest surprise, though, was the presence of the seventh and last person and the only woman who had shown up. There in a manner of speaking, anyway. She stood some distance away from those gathered at the graveside, and there she had remained throughout the service, as if wanting to pay her respects but not wishing to intrude. She didn't look to be much older than Jeremy, himself. Late-teens, early-twenties at most. Not much older, in fact, than the one who had hit and killed Uncle Mike with her car four days before.

Well, Uncle Mike had always said it would likely be one of the young ones that got him. As far as this one at the cemetery, standing beneath the shade of an old oak, with her blonde hair, black dress and dark sunglasses…

*…Uncle Mike has to be rolling in his box right now.*

For his uncle would have easily seen through the young woman. Would have known, as Jeremy knew, that she wasn't there to mourn. As to her true purpose…

…it didn't take a genius to see through her phony façade.

*"They're all the same—and I mean every damned one of them. The spawn of Lilith, herself, especially these younger ones. Sure, they can act like empty-headed idiots when they want to, but don't you believe it, boy. Not even for a second."*

The words were so clear in Jeremy's head that his uncle could have been standing beside him, whispering in his ear. While there was no mystery surrounding the woman's presence, there were a couple of things about her that Jeremy couldn't figure.

First, why the hell did she seem so familiar to him? From the moment he arrived at the cemetery and first noticed her, Jeremy would swear he had seen her somewhere before. Yet, even now, as the service neared its end, Jeremy still couldn't place her.

The second thing, and perhaps the most peculiar of all…why did she seem to know him? It was right there in the smile she had offered him from a distance as he hurried to join the others at the graveside. A shy and hesitant smile that clearly seemed to hint at a past acquaintance. Even now he could almost feel the woman's eyes on the back of his neck. Almost like a caress…

Almost, for Jeremy wasn't fooled by this woman. He had often been fooled, but that had stopped soon after he went to live with Uncle Mike. Her stare and presence was making Jeremy nervous. So nervous that he wished the preacher would hurry the hell up and finish his droning prayer.

*Got to get away from here…not the time or place for this.*

***

The woman remained where she stood as the service concluded and the pitiful few gathered began drifting away. *How sad that only his nephew's left to mourn him…and he looks like he can't wait to get away.* Jeremy seemed anxious, even agitated when the Sheriff approached and reached for his arm as he was attempting to walk past the man in uniform. She watched the exchange between the two, still amazed by how much Jeremy had changed.

Then again, it had been some time since she last saw him. Five years? Lord, had that much time passed since…since that awful night? She was sixteen at the time; as far as she could remember, she and Jeremy were about the same age. Then he was a short, awkward and overweight boy, with a hank of dark hair that he always seemed to be brushing out of his eyes. She couldn't recall that he had ever had a single friend, much less a girlfriend. A loner who kept to himself, avoiding people.

She wondered if that had changed as much as the rest of him. Now he was at least six inches taller, slim and fit in his dark slacks and white button-down shirt, and with nice broad shoulders. His hair, though still a bit longer than most guys wore it, was neat and looked freshly trimmed. *A wonder, really, I even recognized him.*

It didn't appear that he had recognized her.

But maybe, she reflected ruefully, that wasn't entirely right. If she was going to be honest with herself…maybe he had recognized her. When she offered him what she had hoped was a friendly smile of greeting, he had looked…puzzled? Yes, that for sure, but there was something more in his expression. Something in the eyes that fixed on her, then quickly flicked away. Maybe she had misread his reaction—maybe it was because of grief over his loss…but she couldn't get it out of her head that he had seemed to look at her as if she was a monster.

If that was true, he had every right to feel that way—and it wasn't the manner of his uncle's death she was thinking about, either. As it had been since she read in the paper of his uncle's tragic death, it was the memory of that night five years ago, the night of senior graduation, that was running through her mind.

A veritable horde of teenagers gathered with their friends, parties going full tilt all over town and at more secluded spots just beyond the city limits. She was present at one of those more secluded gatherings. She and ten others, including two of her closest girlfriends...and Jeremy. It was Samantha, one of her girlfriends, who had invited him to the party. At first, Jeremy had seemed completely floored, even suspicious, but Samantha had refused to take no for an answer. Back then, Samantha could be very persuasive that way, and she had laid it on thick. Reluctantly, yet clearly hopeful, Jeremy had finally agreed to come.

He was late, the party already going strong. She had begun to think he wasn't going to show. It would have been better if he hadn't shown up but, eventually, he did, and it was soon after that...

As it always had, just thinking about it made her face burn with shame. *How could I have been so stupid to go along with Samantha and the others and do something like that to him? The worst of it was that it was so soon after his parents died, and he'd just gone to live with his uncle. I don't think I'll ever forget the longest day I lived or the look on his face as he stood there, framed in all those flashlights…*

***

"A word, Jeremy, if you have a minute?"

Jeremy suppressed an annoyed sigh at the murmured words from Sheriff Dale Morgan. Jeremy simply wanted to shake off the hand gripping his elbow, but he fought off the impulse, forcing himself to stay calm, while feigning a quizzical look as he regarded the big man in the khaki uniform. Struggled to keep his eyes focused on the man; to keep his gaze from straying to the woman still standing some distance away, still staring at him.

"What can I do for you, Sheriff?" he asked, keeping his voice level.

"A couple of questions is all. Only take a few minutes, if you're up for it."

"Sure, no problem." *Why does she seem so damned familiar?*

*"Boy, I taught you better than that. Just look at her—you know damned well who and what she is."*

"You said the young woman driving the car that hit your Uncle Mike was around twenty-two or twenty-three? Shoulder length dark hair and driving a blue Ford Taurus?"

"Yeah, a blue Taurus, and she had dark hair down to her shoulders," Jeremy replied. "She was young, but I'm only guessing at her age."

"Do you by chance know a young woman named Trish Sanderson?"

Jeremy knew no one by that name; it wasn't even familiar to him. He shook his head, again resisting the urge to glance in the direction of the blonde woman. *Can't let her know that I know, or even suspect...*

The Sheriff said, "I'm not certain there's a connection, but I received a report this morning that a Trish Sanderson has gone missing. Twenty-four, dark shoulder-length hair, and drives a blue Taurus. The last time anyone saw her was about an hour before your Uncle got hit. Now, it may be nothing but a coincidence, but it's a possibility we have to check out. Is there anything else you can tell me about this woman in the Taurus? Maybe a little more detail about how she looked? Maybe something that has come back to you?"

Jeremy shrugged. "Like I said before, I really didn't get a good look at her face. I mean, I was half-way between the house and the road, waiting for Uncle Mike to come back from the mailbox, when the car hit him. All I really remember is this dark-haired woman gets out of the car, stares down at Uncle Mike for a second, then she gets back in the car and takes off like she's racing at the Indy 500."

"Which way did she go?"

"West, away from town."

"I believe you said she was coming from the west, so she turned around, right?"

"Yeah, that's right. She was moving so fast that, by the time I could get to Uncle Mike, she was already out of sight."

The Sheriff nodded, though his eyes remained on Jeremy a long moment before he spoke. "Okay, Jeremy, that's all for now. We'll keep looking for the car and the woman, and if you remember anything—anything at all, no matter what or how insignificant it may seem—give me a call."

"I'll do that." Jeremy, his face void of expression and his eyes narrowed, watched as the Sheriff put on his hat and walked away. Jeremy didn't glance toward the blonde woman, but he could still feel her eyes. He waited until both the Sheriff and his deputy were in their respective cruisers and leaving the cemetery before he headed toward what had been his Uncle Mike's old and faded green Chevy pickup.

That was when he noticed movement in the corner of his eye. His eyes cut toward the woman; she was also moving, her blonde hair flipping about her face in the breeze. Not moving toward him, but on a path that would cut him off before he could reach the pickup. A sudden sense of panic seizied him; it had just occurred to him that, except for the two men standing near the back-hole parked at a respectful distance at the opposite side of the cemetery, he was alone here with this woman. Was she forcing the issue? He could see nothing...*off* about her. Not yet, anyway, but that often made little difference. His throat was bone-dry...hard to swallow.

*"Thanks to that one in the blue car, you're on your own now, boy. Just remember everything I taught you. For now, keep your mind and thoughts guarded."*

Jeremy nodded, his head barely moving, his eyes following the woman's every step. She was close enough that he could see the smile—that phony smile! —playing on her lips. A smile meant to lull and deceive; to beguile and trap. A shiver passed through him. *If I can just stall her. Maybe, somehow, lure her out to the house. Catch her off guard...*

*"You're thinking right, boy. Any advantage is all you can hope for when dealing with their kind. Can't you already smell the brimstone?"*

Jeremy could smell it. Faint but there, wafting to him on the breeze. The same smell that had lingered as Uncle Mike lay broken and bleeding in the dirt alongside the highway, the letters from the mailbox still clutched in his dead hand. *This one...so cleverly disguised in a black dress and dark sunglasses...just like the one that killed Uncle Mike.*

Jeremy moved on resolutely toward the pickup and the woman.

***

She waited until he was only a few feet away and still striding toward the pickup before she said, softly, "Hello there, Jeremy."

He had avoided eye contact with her as he approached, but the sound of her voice stopped him in his tracks. Now he regarded her with a clear and wary light in his eyes. He said nothing for a moment, his narrowed eyes never leaving her.

"You don't remember me, do you?" She was still smiling; still hopeful.

He shook his head slowly, his forehead creasing as if he was concentrating, trying to remember her. She dropped her eyes, her smile fading just a bit.

"I know it won't be a pleasant surprise," she murmured, again looking up at him. "I'm Shawna. Shawna Edwards?"

She was stunned when his eyes went wide and by the sheer horror that washed over his face. Had he put what she and the others had done to him *that* far out of his mind? He abruptly turned away from her, both hands pressed to the sides of his head.

*Oh, God, what was I thinking? This was a* **really** *bad idea.*

"I'm sorry, Jeremy. I shouldn't have come here today." Her face was again hot with shame. "I just wanted to apologize for my part of what happened that night, and to say I'm sorry for your loss. I honestly didn't mean to upset you even more."

He said nothing, his hands still pressed to the sides of his bowed head.

"For what it's worth," she went on, forcing herself, "I was the only one who didn't laugh that night, and I had nothing more to do with any of the others who were there. I was disgusted by all of them, and even more disgusted with myself. Thankfully, because my parents moved that summer and I started at a different school in the fall, I never had to look at any of them again."

He remained silent, but he was now shaking his head as if unable to take in her words. She sighed ruefully and stepped away from him.

"I'll leave you now," she murmured, her eyes wet and brimming.

"Wait." His voice was like the creak of a rusty hinge.

She stopped and looked back at him. He had raised his head, his fingertips now circling his temples as if trying to ease away a persistent ache.

"Haven't thought about that night in a long time." There was still a creak in his voice, only now not as pronounced.

"Jeremy, I truly am sorry for my part of it and for your loss."

"Just a silly prank," he said, his voice almost back to normal. He finally turned to face her again, his hands now at his sides; his face and eyes strangely void of expression. "Not the first time I was on the receiving end of something like that, and it wasn't the last. This is the first time, though, anyone has ever apologized."

Shawna wasn't surprised that none of the others had ever bothered to apologize. She had kept tabs, albeit from a distance, on all the others, and they were all still the same self-absorbed assholes they had always been. Each still quick to condemn and point fingers and laugh at someone else's embarrassment.

"Like I said," she began, but he waved off the rest she intended to say.

"Would you," he said and paused as if unsure of himself. Then, "Would you like to come out to the house and…I don't know…talk for a while?"

The last thing she had expected; she wasn't sure how to respond or if it was the right thing to do. True, she had come here today to try and make amends—to assuage her guilty mind as much as to ease any lingering bad feelings he had—but the way he reacted when she told him who she was left her feeling uncertain, even wary. But if he had felt any anger toward her, she had seen no real indication of it and certainly no sign of it now. If anything, he looked like a young man lost in the pain of his grief. She understood from what she read in the paper that his uncle was a bachelor; that meant Jeremy would probably be going home to an empty house, with only the ghost of memories for company.

How clear did it have to be that he was only reaching out to her? Someone who had shown him a little kindness? If he was anything like the awkward person he was before, and she suspected he was, he probably had no one who even cared what he was going through.

*Why the hell not?* she reasoned. She had the day off from work and no other plans once she left the cemetery. It would likely do them both some good.

"I would like that," she said, her smile returning. Then, deciding it prudent to not get too carried away, added, "But I can only stay a little while."

"That's fine," he said, and he seemed pleased, even relieved.

"So, tell me where you live, and I'll stop on the way and pick up a pizza for us."

"A pizza would be nice," he said and gave her directions.

***

*He's standing in the little spot in the woods, his jeans and underwear down to his knees; the braying and mocking laughter rings in his head like peals of thunder. They have formed a circle around him; he can only stand there, too humiliated to even cover himself. The beams of their flashlights illuminate him and holds him trapped in place like an animal caught in the glare of oncoming headlights. Some of the flashlight beams shine in his face; others are aimed at his flaccid penis. Only seconds before he was erect and throbbing, his heart racing with youthful anticipation. Then the first light hit him, the first laugh reached him. Now, as the laughter rolls on, some of the beams of light shaking with mirth, he forces himself to look down at what lies on the ground near his feet.*

*One of those blow-up sex dolls. The kind with the spread legs and the gaping red hole for a mouth. What he found instead of the breathing female he was expecting. But, in his zeal to take advantage of what he had been promised before the opportunity was yanked away from him, he failed to realize the truth until the beam of the first light shone. Then the voice of the female who talked him into this and made him the promises, calls out to him in a tone of malicious glee.*

*"The only pussy you'll likely ever see, fatty, so fuck her good!"*

*"Get her to give you a blowjob, too!" yells another, a male whose voice he doesn't recognize. There are other voices, other taunts, but none of it registers with him.*

*All he hears is the laughter. He has no idea how long he remains there until his mind finally commands him to leave the place. As he heads back to his uncle's house on foot, the laughter stays in his head, slashing at him like a knife, until, finally, the voice of his uncle rises above the din.*

"I told you what to expect. Why the hell you think I stayed a bachelor? Why, after I was with only one of them, and when I wasn't much older than you are now, I swore never again? Why do you think your father—my own brother! —killed himself and that demon bitch you had for a mother? Why? Because at some point in a bitch's life, some younger than others, she turns into the very fucking demon that possesses her. It happens to all of them, but the young ones are the most susceptible and the most vicious when a demon gets to them. The worst of it is that most everyone—men and women alike—are blind to it. Even preachers and priests, these so-called *'Men of God'* never see it or choose to ignore it—and just look at how many of them have fallen victim in one way or another to a possessed female. But I know the truth, boy—known it most of my life—and if you learn nothing else from me…you'll learn the truth and how to deal with them."

*In time, as his uncle hammers lesson after lesson into his head, he's finally able to free himself of the anger and hatred that fills his chest like congestion. Finally able to block the entire episode completely from his mind.*

*Only now…*

***

…his mind was in turmoil. That blonde-haired bitch—Shawna Edwards, a name he had forgotten and heard rolling so sweetly off her demon tongue—brought it all crashing back to him! The memory of that night was now like something alive inside him, clawing and tearing at him. His head felt like it was going to explode as he pulled off the highway and drove the pickup down the long dirt driveway toward the house.

He piled out of the truck, leaving the engine running and the driver's door ajar. He also left the front door of the house open as he stormed inside. He tore through the house, charging mindlessly into one room after another, opening and slamming doors. His face was awash with fury, his teeth gritted hard enough to snap them off at the gums.

*Damn you, bitch! Damn you back to hell where you belong!*

*"Get a grip, boy. You have a job to do and you can't do it like this."*

That stopped him cold, his fury ebbing slightly. *A job to do…*

Yes, he had a job to do, and he would do it as his uncle had taught him. More than that, he remembered that he also had unfinished business waiting for him, another task that had been interrupted by the funeral, as well as the Sheriff and his damned questions. A chore he couldn't leave for very much longer; further delay would only undo what he had so far managed to accomplish…even as little as it was. It also increased the danger.

*"That's it, boy. Just concentrate on the job at hand—and, remember, that anger you feel is your most potent weapon, so control it. Don't let it control you."*

His face now grim and purposeful, he left the house, crossed the side-yard, his eyes focused straight ahead.

***

At her apartment, Shawna quickly changed into jeans, a sleeveless top, and a pair of comfortable Converse All-Stars, then pulled her blonde hair into a ponytail. She picked up the loaded pizza she had called in, then followed Jeremy's directions out of town and right to a mailbox with the name "Cassidy" printed on the side. It was an old farmhouse with several outbuildings including a barn, all of which had seen better days.

The green pickup she had seen Jeremy driving was parked at a haphazard angle halfway between the house and barn. As she parked near the truck's passenger side, she noticed the driver's-side door was open. *Looks like he was in a real hurry to stop that truck and get out of it.* Only when she switched off her car's engine did she realize that the truck's engine was running. *Now that really is weird.* She got out of her car and looked around.

"Jeremy?" she called, one hand shielding her eyes from the sun.

The only reply was the sound of the truck's engine and the soft sigh of the breeze. She stepped around the back of the truck, her shaded eyes drifting toward the house.

That was when she noticed the front door stood wide open. *Must have really been in a hurry about something.* She called to him a second time and started toward the house.

There was still no answering voice. The wood of the steps groaned under her feet as she climbed to the porch. Still a few feet away from the doorway, she peered through the opening, but all she could see inside were shadows. She moved closer and rapped on the wood of the door frame.

"Jeremy?" called again. When she again received no answer, she stepped into the doorway's open space and poked her head inside. Now, without the brightness of the sun, she had a better view; what she saw left her perplexed.

She would hardly call what had to be the living room a dump. The air smelled fresh, everything looked neat and well cared for; what surprised her was how little there was to see. A pair of sofas, a coffee table in front of each, an old recliner and a couple of end-tables, a single floor lamp…and that was it. No pictures on the walls or other adornments. No whatnots in shelves or even shelves. No books or magazines lying on any of the tables. No DVDs or a player; no remotes or even a TV she could see. As stark and barren as a prison cell and little to suggest the room was used or even occupied most of the time.

*Surely, the rest of the house can't be like this. My God, who doesn't have TV?*

She was staring into the yawing darkness of a hallway, wondering what lay beyond this room, when a noise from outside the house drew her attention. A muffled *thump,* as if something had struck the ground. She frowned. *The barn? Maybe that's where he is and can't hear me calling to him.*

She went out on the porch and looked toward the barn. Just as her gaze fell upon the tall double-doors, one of them opened slightly, as if grasped by the wind's invisible hand, then it banged shut with the same *thump.*

*Well, at least that explains that.* "Jeremy?" she called toward the barn, her voice raised and expectant. She waited but, again, there was no answering reply.

And the lack of response was beginning to make her feel uneasy. Something wasn't right about this…

*Okay, knock it the hell off. He probably just remembered something, some chore that slipped his mind in all the chaos in his life the past several days, that he wanted to take care of before I got here. Since he obviously isn't here in the house, he must be out in the barn or one of the other buildings.* Deciding to check the barn first, she cleared the creaking steps to the ground and started that way.

There was more light in the barn than in the house, sunlight streaming through the hundreds of cracks between the unpainted and warped boards. It was also much warmer in the barn than in the house. The breeze blowing through the cracks made a soft and eerie whistling sound. In the shafts of sunlight swirling dust motes danced in the breeze. Unlike the house, the barn had a heavy and musty smell of disuse and of old hay mingling with the sour stench of grease and motor oil.

There was one additional smell; it was faint but fresh and sharp. She worked at a convenience store and had no problem recognizing this smell.

*Gasoline...*

But where was it coming from? There was nothing she could see among the clutter in the barn that used gasoline. There was the remains of an old green tractor to one side of where she stood. But, as far as she knew, all tractors ran on diesel and there was no smell of diesel in the barn. Her curiosity now aroused, she decided to follow the smell of gasoline.

Her search led her to a far rear corner of the barn. There, beneath a faded gray tarp and completely hidden from view from the barn's double-doors by a stack of old lumber, was what she easily recognized as a car. At the back of the car on the driver's side was a red five-gallon gas can. Protruding from the neck of the gas can was a clear hose, the other end lying on the ground. The ground around the red can and hose reeked of gasoline.

*Siphoning gas from the tank?*

Her face wrapped in a puzzled frown; she was startled when the barn door made the *thump* sound again. She glanced back toward the doors, but the stack of lumber hid it from view. She moved a couple of steps to one side and a yelp of surprise burst from her mouth.

"My God, you scared me!" she declared, her eyes fixed on the figure of Sheriff Dale Morgan. *What is he doing here?*

"Sorry," he said, moving toward her. "And you are?"

"Shawna Edwards. I used to know Jeremy back in school."

"You were the one in the black dress at the cemetery," the Sheriff observed, but he was no longer looking at her, his stare now directed beyond her at the car under the tarp.

"Yes, that was me," Shawna said, stepping aside as the big man strode past her, his face set and grim. She watched curiously as he lifted a flap of the tarp, revealing a smashed headlight on the car's passenger side. The grill was also broken and there was a sizeable dent and crimp in the hood. There was also what looked like splatters of dried blood all over the front of the car's blue finish. Shawna felt her stomach clench in revulsion.

"A Taurus," the Sheriff mouthed, clearly angry. "I told those lazy idiots I have four deputies to search the house and every building, and they reported there was nothing here. I'd bet a month's salary they came no further inside this barn than those doors." He began pulling more of the tarp away, revealing a smashed windshield on the passenger side and even more dried blood. "I knew he was bullshitting me from the start. But I just couldn't put my finger on what was wrong with his story. Not until today when he said the car sped off in the direction it came from. As I suspected, there's no tire marks showing a car turning around in a hurry and speeding away. There's only skid marks of a car stopping."

Shawna was trying without success to follow what he was saying. It crossed her mind that he might in some way be referring to the accident that had killed Jeremy's uncle. *But why would that car be here?*

The Sheriff let go of the tarp and turned to face her. "Where is he?" he asked, his voice hard and level. "Jeremy, I mean."

"I don't know, Sheriff. I've been trying to find him since I got here."

"I would suggest, as I suspect you're in danger, you get the hell away from here," the Sheriff said, pulling a cell phone from a breast pocket of his uniform shirt. "Let me call for some backup, then I'll walk you to your car."

*Danger?* Shawna, her heart beating furiously and still unable to fully grasp this sudden turn of events, could only nod in reply. A penetrating chill was spreading through her; it suddenly didn't feel warm at all in that barn. She had just folded her arms across her chest, hugging herself, the Sheriff's thumb moving across the face of his cell, when…

"What was *that*?" Shawna yelped, startled. The sound was much like the *thump* of the barn door, but this sound had seemed to come from inside the car. The Sheriff had been moving toward her, but the sound had stopped him in his tracks. He glanced back at the car.

"Someone's in there," he breathed, his cell going back into his shirt pocket as he stepped toward the car. "And I bet I know who it is." Then he was pulling at the tarp with renewed purpose. When he had uncovered the back driver's-side door, he reached for the handle. "Locked, damn it," he said, reaching for his nightstick.

There was another *thump* from inside the car, then another.

"*Look out*!" Shawna screamed, pointing at the back passenger side of the car.

Jeremy had appeared like an apparition rising up from out of the barn's dirt floor. His white shirt was dirt-stained, his hair mused and spiked, and there was a look on his face unlike any that Shawna had ever seen before. It was as if she was faced with the devil, himself. It was that monstrous visage, and the old and rusted pick gripped in Jeremy's hands, that had prompted her scream.

Even as she screamed again, Jeremy was darting around the back of the car. The Sheriff let go of his nightstick, stepping quickly away from the car to meet the threat rushing toward him, his other hand reaching for the automatic on his hip.

The Sheriff moved fast, instinctively, his hand closing around the butt of the gun on his hip, the gun sliding free of its holster…

…but Jeremy was faster.

A shriek ripping from his throat that was as maniacal as it was feral, Jeremy swung the pick. There was a horrible rending sound of steel striking flesh and bone, the blow knocking the Sheriff's hat from his head. The red and gory point of the pick burst through the back of his head, a spraying gout of blood splattering the blue car and Jeremy's face and the front of his shirt.

Shawna screamed as she had never screamed before. Unaware of the now frantic *thump, thump, thump* coming from inside the car. Frozen solid, she could only stand there and scream, her terrified eyes locked on Jeremy's bloody face.

Jeremy had let go of the pick, leaving it buried in the Sheriff's head. The big man dropped to the ground like a felled tree, blood quickly pooling around his head. Then Jeremy was bent over the prone figure, reaching for something attached to the man's belt.

It was then that the circuits of Shawna's mind began firing again, sending out urgent signals and triggering dire warnings that sounded in her head like klaxons. She turned to flee, stumbling and running for the double doors. She almost made it outside.

Almost…

She had raised both hands to push open the door through which she had entered when there was a crackling hiss, a searing pain in her lower back, and a jolt so violent that it seemed to set every nerve ending in her body on fire. Her legs simply collapsed under her. Spittle flew from her mouth and her eyes rolled up in their sockets. She lay there with her face in the dirt, jerking spasmodically from head to foot.

***

Standing over her, impassively watching her spasms, the taser still in his right hand, Jeremy was tempted to give her…it…another blast, just to be sure. He quickly decided it would be a waste of juice. He had clearly driven the demon out of this one. No sign of the loathsome and repellent creature remained that he could see, and he judged it would be a while before that monstrosity tried to lay claim to this host again.

Not so with the one bound and gagged in the car, where he had locked it three days ago. The first day, all while the sheriff's deputies were crawling over the place, he had kept the demon and its host in the cellar beneath the house. Finally, once the cops had left and he judged it safe, he had no choice but to move the kicking and thrashing demon to the car. And what a job that was! Time after time he had driven the beast that had killed his uncle out of the bitch driving the car, only to have it come back, even stronger than before, and take control of her again. It was the worst demon Jeremy had ever faced, proving itself more than a match for Uncle Mike. The damn thing had almost escaped him twice, and Jeremy had lost count of all the times it had tried to bite him or use the bitch's fingernails to claw him to bloody shreds.

Well, no more fooling around with simply trying to force it out of her and back into the pit from which it had spawned. There was but one way to deal with this kind of evil. All he could hope for—all he and his Uncle Mike had ever been able to hope for—was that some other foolish bitch didn't throw the door wide open for it. Like the foolish bitch still twitching on the ground, or someone like her.

*Why do they keep doing it? Why do they keep on summoning these damn things when any fool should know better?*

*"Some know exactly what they're doing and don't care. Others, though, know not what they do. They summon innocently or accidentally and, sometimes, they're not even the one who summoned the demon. It can be someone they know, and the demon simply moves from that woman to one that seems like a better host and better able to keep it in this realm. That's what happened to this one—it moved to her from the woman who summoned it by the very darkness of her nature. But, in the end, it really doesn't matter, boy. No matter who did it or why or how it happened, it all amounts to the same thing.*

*"Now, get some rope or some of those strip cuff things the Sheriff has in his car and secure this one before she starts coming to her senses again. Then you can tend to the one over there in the car. Send that abomination back to hell, then deal with this one. But you know what*

*you're facing, right? After killing Meddling Morgan over there, you're running out of time, boy...and there's so much left for you to do."*

*Yeah...so much left to do.*

*"So, send as many of these damned things back to hell as you can, while you can."*

Jeremy stepped to the barn doors, pushed one open, and peeked out. It was easy to spot the Sheriff's cruiser where he had parked it near the paved road.

*"Need to move it back here behind the barn, boy, so it will at least be out of sight. Not for very long, mind you, but maybe long enough to give you some extra time."*

Thinking of the dead Sheriff, a faint smile appeared on Jeremy's lips. *Thought he'd sneak in here on foot and take me by surprise.*

*"Looks like the asshole thought wrong then, doesn't it? Get on with it, boy. Time's wasting, and you don't have a minute of it to waste."*

Jeremy cleared the distance to the Sheriff's cruiser and slid behind the wheel. He parked the squad behind the far side of the barn and, hopefully, out of sight of any vehicles passing along the two-lane. When he climbed out of the car, the two-way radio squawking with chatter from several deputies, Jeremy had a fistful of strip cuffs. It took only a couple of minutes to secure the hands and feet of the one still on the ground and to drag her to one of the barn's support posts. He had nothing with which to gag her, but that didn't matter; he needed this one able to talk. Once he had her bound in a sitting position to the post, her head rolling side to side and lolling forward, he turned toward the blue car, slipping the taser from a back pocket of his slacks.

*Demon...have I ever got a shocking surprise for you.*

***

Shawna never lost consciousness but remained lost and floundering in a drooling stupor as he bound her wrists and ankles, then dragged her to the post. There was still a burning in her back and a horrible tingling sensation rippling up and down her body. She could see, though her vision kept floating in and out of focus, and she could hear. Beyond that, however, nothing seemed to work right. She could plainly hear Jeremy's angry shouts and what sounded like a struggle, both of which seemed to be coming from the blue car. Bound as she was to the post, combined with her inability to force her head to move as she wanted it to, she couldn't see what was going on at the car.

*How could I have been so stupid—again! Please, God...help me...please.*

"Damn you!" Jeremy bellowed. "Not enough that you spread your evil through this bitch, but you make her shit and piss herself? Damned filthy fucking demon!" More of what sounded like a struggle; then there was that awful crackling hiss that made Shawna wince. She heard a muffled scream and the sound of thrashing, then Jeremy said, "Yeah, that took the fight out of you, didn't it? Wish I'd had one of these things long before now."

*Bitch? It's a woman? But why is he keeping her here? And, damn it, what demon is he talking about? Far as I'm concerned, there's only one demon around here!*

Shawna watched as Jeremy dragged a thrashing and writhing figure into her limited line of vision. It was, indeed, a woman. A dark-haired woman and, probably, a very pretty one before she ran afoul of Jeremy. Now, her shorts and blouse and the bare skin of her legs and arms caked with dirt, what had to be her own filth, and what looked like streaks of dried blood, she looked like something that had lived underground until pulled out of its hole. Jeremy was dragging her by the hair with both hands.

Dragging her toward a bare spot in the center of the barn's dirt floor. Shawna hadn't noticed before, but there were four stakes driven into the ground. They looked to her like metal tent stakes.

*Oh, my God...*

Jeremy quickly tied the woman's wrists and ankles to the stakes with lengths of wire. There was no fight in the woman, rendered helpless by the vicious bite of what Shawna had surmised was a taser. Jeremy stared down at the woman, his face a mask of disgust.

"J-Jeremy...p-please," Shawna murmured, her voice quavering.

"Shut up, demon," he spat, still staring at the woman staked to the ground.

"I understand you hate me," Shawna went on, her voice gaining a little strength but still rippling with fear. "I can only imagine what she did to you, but what's the point in making the wrong even worse? Why, Jeremy?"

"***Why***?" he demanded, turning away from the woman and staring at her. "Are you fucking blind? Or just playing your games and pretending not to recognize your own kind?"

"I-I don't u-understand, Jeremy."

"Look at it!" he yelled, pointing at the woman on the ground. "Do you not see the red and evil eyes? The horns sticking out of the side of its head? The claws growing from its fingers and toes? Nothing but a fucking beast like you!"

Shawna forced her eyes from Jeremy and looked at the woman. She, of course, could see none of the things he had described so vehemently. All she saw was a dirty and bloody young woman, gray duct tape across her mouth; her eyes a very pale blue. What would have been beautiful eyes if not for the unspeakable terror that shone in them like the brightest of lights.

"That thing killed my uncle," Jeremy said, his voice now a hitching croak of pain and grief. "The only person on earth who ever thought enough of me to teach me the truth about your kind. Ran him down like a dog and done it deliberately just to get rid of him."

The woman on the ground had locked eyes with Shawna and she was shaking her head emphatically, or as close to it as she could manage. Shawna understood what she was trying to tell her. *An accident...she never meant to do it. But it drove Jeremy over the edge. As if his damned uncle hadn't already done that to him.* She remembered the barren living room, devoid of life itself, and wondered what kind of existence Jeremy and his uncle had shared. Then she wondered how many women the two of them had butchered together.

"But I'll carry on his legacy," Jeremy declared, the vehemence and hatred back in his voice. "As long as I can, anyway…starting with this one. Then you."

Jeremy abruptly stalked out of her line of vision. When he returned, he was carrying the red five-gallon gas can. Shawna, the strength and muscle control only now returning to allow it, began struggling weakly against her bonds.

"For God's sake!" she spluttered as Jeremy doused the woman staked to the ground with gasoline.

"First, you drive the demon out," he said in a monotone, as if repeating words he had probably heard hundreds of times. "If all else fails, you must destroy the host, so the damn thing can't come back to that one." He was now walking away from the woman, leaving a trail of gasoline. "But the damn things always come back. They always find another host." He hurled the gas can away and knelt at the end of the trail. The taser was in his hand.

"Jeremy!" Shawna wailed, but his name was barely out of her mouth when she heard the cracking hiss and saw the taser spark. The trail of gas ignited and streaked toward the bound and helpless woman. Even as Shawna screamed, almost passing out in a dead faint at the sheer horror of it, the loud *WHUMP!* as the woman went up like a fireball filled her ears.

For almost a full minute there was only the sound of the flames, the sizzle of burning flesh, and Shawna's uncontrollable crying and fits of coughing as thick and cloying smoke filled the barn. When she sensed a presence moving toward her, she finally raised her head and stared straight into Jeremy's face as he knelt in front of her. She had never seen such dead eyes as those staring back at her.

"Don't kill me," she pleaded, her voice raw from the smoke.

"Then tell me what I want to know." His voice was as lifeless as his eyes.

"What?" she asked, though she didn't believe for a second that he would spare her no matter what she said or did.

Jeremy told her what he wanted to know; a level of fear she would have thought impossible after what she had so far seen and endured washed through her. "Go to hell!" she spat with all the contempt she could muster. "I'll never tell you *that*!"

Jeremy smiled…and it was a gruesome thing to see. "Oh, I'm betting you will," he drawled, producing a large folding knife from a pocket of his slacks. He opened the blade; it locked in place with a click. "Might take a little persuasion…but you'll tell me."

*****

The bitch screamed and thrashed, holding out for almost fifteen minutes. Precious minutes he could ill-afford to waste on her. But, in the end, he got from her what he needed to know. He left her secured to the post, her head lolled to one side. Her face and arms were streaked with small thin cuts and the blood that had seeped from them. The front of her sleeveless top and her jeans and the ground around her was soaked with her urine and the blood from the final and killing slash to her throat.

Strangely, the demon that had inhabited her, never tried to return. Obviously, it had deemed this host not worth fighting to keep.

Leaving her there, he went into the house and cleaned up and changed clothes. Then he left the old farmhouse, doubting he would ever see it again. The pickup's engine had died at some point. Probably ran out of gas, as there wasn't much in the tank to begin with. The keys were in the ignition of the car parked near the truck; in the passenger seat was a pizza box. A pizza? It made absolutely no sense to him that the damned demon inhabiting the bitch would have her bring a pizza. He didn't even like pizza! The smell of it was nauseating. He got in the car, threw the box and its stinking contents out, started the engine, and drove into town.

He arrived in a quiet residential area and parked the car on the street at what seemed a discrete distance from a particular house and driveway. And there he waited almost two hours. Finally, darkness beginning to spread its blanket and a sickle moon rising in front of him, an SUV pulled into the driveway he was watching. A smile spread across his face.

Two kids spilled out of the SUV, followed by the woman driving it. The kids, both boys who looked to Jeremy to be around five or six and bore a striking resemblance to the woman, were running toward the house. Jeremy wasn't surprised she had kids that old. She had been nothing but a slut in school. Rumor had it that she had made it with every member of the football and basketball teams. The woman was shouting at the boys not to run, but they ignored her.

Jeremy had no interest in the boys. Neither probably had any idea what they had been riding with or realized the favor he was doing for them. They would someday, though, if they were lucky. The only thing Jeremy hated about it was neither would probably ever known who had done them the favor.

He slipped out of the car and approached the house along the street as unobtrusively as possible. The woman had disappeared into the house, two grocery bags in her arms, but he figured she would be back. He was right.

He stepped from behind the SUV as the woman leaned into vehicle through one of the back doors. Not as pretty as he remembered her, and she was heavier now. Not that it mattered. All that mattered was that the demon was in her. He was close enough to sense the evil it reeked like a stench. The same evil presence he had sensed from that Shawna bitch.

*Back to the one who summoned you in the first place.*

Strangely, though, the demon never seemed to suspect his presence.

He hit her in the small of the back with the taser. The woman convulsed with a grunt and went limp. Then, both hands pressed to her broad ass, he shoved and pushed her bulk into the back seat and quietly closed the door.

"Who's the fat one now, Samantha?" he murmured. He hurried around to the driver's side and climbed behind the wheel. He would secure the bitch's hands and feet with some of the strip cuffs in his back pocket once he was away from the house. After that…

*Before I'm done with you, I'll not only drive out the demon that possesses your rotten soul…but I'll make you regret everything you did to me a thousand times over.*

*Serena Daniels'*
*Shopping List*

*Oreo Easter eggs*
*Stuffed Burgers*
*Chips Ahoy Easter Eggs*
*Reese's Easter Eggs*
*Chocolate Bunnies*
*French Fries*
*Honey Buns*
*Sour Keys*
*Oranges*
*Whole Wheat Bagels*
*As much chocolate as can fit in cart*

# The Huntress and Her Beast
## *Serena Daniels*

The city streets were quiet; the heavy summer rain that had been plaguing the citizens for hours had finally let up, but puddles were still prevalent everywhere and eerily reflected the streetlamps that littered the roads. It was difficult to move around without splashing in a puddle and making noise, yet somehow she was able to.

The woman was dressed in a tight leather one piece suit with stiletto heels—thin enough to be used as knives if necessary. She had long blonde hair that fell loosely around her shoulders and bounced just the littlest bit as she walked carefully and quietly along her merry way. Her brown, almond shaped eyes were narrowed in concentration as she looked about, trying to find her target; all the while she felt her pet breathing down the back of her neck.

It wasn't threatening, it never was and she had no fear of him, even from the very beginning, when he had been assigned to her. She didn't mind having an unusual sidekick like him, despite his odd appearance, as she was the only one who could see him (at least until it was too late for her prey), she enjoyed the company on the hunt and the perks that came with a job well done.

She still had her orders though, the fun could wait, and she was becoming antsy and bored; she was told that her target walked along this particular avenue every night after they got off from work. Routines; such a hazard for those targeted for assassination.

She stopped her walking and hid in a nearby alley that cast a large shadow where she couldn't be seen. Out of the corner of her eye she saw that her companion shuffled over beside her, it's claws clicking on both the street and screeching against the nearby brick wall.

The noise that was made caused her to feel quite glad that he was invisible to targets as his large footsteps alone were loud enough to frighten away people from miles around, not to mention his quirks such as clawing invisible lines along the walls of their hiding places regardless of whether or not it was a building that served as their permanent residence or along alley walls—like at the moment.

She suppressed a sigh; it was just a territorial thing among his kind; the feeling to mark places that he'd been in such a way, and it was almost constant enough to be considered a form of OCD.

It seemed as if letting him mark her wasn't nearly enough to curb his instincts...maybe she wasn't fucking him often enough? Twice a night just doesn't seem to satisfy her...or him for that matter, maybe.

Footsteps echoed in her ears, halting her sexy thoughts and pulled her back into the present, her far-above superior hearing picking them up easily now that they were in range. High heeled steps and certainly belonging to her target as there was no one else out on this particular avenue this late. Admittedly sometimes it was overwhelming and made it difficult for her to tell the distance between her and the target, since her powers were still so new to her.

Not wanting to risk poking her body out if she misjudged the distance, she closed her eyes and popped her soul free from herself and made her way through the street, following the sound of the target's steps until she had come upon her, and just as she had finished mentally calculating when the woman would fall into her trap, the slutty dressed woman stopped and looked around fearfully before she turned and walked off in a different direction.

*'What the fuck?!'* She cursed as she allowed her soul to follow the woman a little while longer and nearly cursed aloud that the target was getting further and further away from her location. She was losing her chance!

*'Guess I have no choice,'* she sighed as she took out one of the most secret weapons she had, something that took years of practice for some but had come to her quite easily; a technique that only could be pulled out in the

most dire of situations—but she had no choice if she wanted to get the job done tonight.

Taking a deep breath, she forced her soul to speed up and lunge at the target. For a second, all she could see was a silvery figure of a woman charging toward her. Her target didn't have time to scream before she'd shoved a hand into her chest and squeezed.

Mary somewhat enjoyed the target's quiet croaks. She squeezed harder and harder until the woman's eyes no longer showed any signs of life, then she dropped her to the ground with a loud thump.

Now for disposal; the slightly harder part— something else that typically required a soul projection.

Clasping her hands together and then half opening them with her palms facing the corpse, she unleashed a beam of light that hit the body, causing it to transport back to headquarters for inspection, making sure this was indeed her target and not just a look-a-like. If it was, in fact, her target than she would be able to enjoy a well earned rest. If not...well a whole lot of damage control was needed.

She was suddenly feeling drained now, and quickly dragged her soul back before she collapsed against the wall.

Tor reached out for her in concern, holding her up. This was an open street rather than a private residence, or she would have teleported the target to her so that Tor and herself could have had some fun, but it was too risky doing such a thing in public where someone could stumble upon the scene itself and attempt to interfere.

She was getting a headache now just thinking about it. She needed release, and judging by the way that Tor was raking his claws against her neck, so did he—and she was more than willing to give it to him—she could deal with headquarters later. Now she just wanted to get back to her hideaway and feel Tor's scaly body against hers...

#

Later, she was still awake as Tor snored next to her. She'd only had enough energy to do him once and she knew he was not content as he'd huffed angrily when she'd commanded him to go to sleep.

She sighed at the thought of how much making up she had to do with him for the next little while.

She slid out of bed naked, and stood by the window that was covered in thick black curtains, keeping out the sunlight and anyone trying to look in. She parted them just a little and looked out at the night sky. There was a new moon and the street lamps were the only light available.

The a/c in her room was cranked to maximum and her nipples were starting to chap but her cunt was drying off. She sighed again at the sensations—it had been a long time since she hadn't felt horny when she was in Tor's presence. She must be more tired than she thought, despite her mind racing with thoughts of her overall mission.

*'I have to try and get some sleep,'* she thought as she walked back toward the bed and plopped down, knowing that Tor wouldn't wake up—it would take a large scale natural disaster for him to even stir.

Despite the coolness of the room, she didn't get under the sheets like she normally would, they just felt restricting and she couldn't sleep that way unless it was Tor restricting her, curling around her, but that was an entirely different feeling altogether.

Forcing her eyes closed, she tried to clear her mind, but adrenaline was still coursing through her veins from tonight's kill—only one of many since her journey began five years ago...

#

*It had all started with those strange dreams when she was just fifteen; of places and of killing people in different time periods so far back that there was no way that she could have ever lived them. She also dreamt of dark rooms with lit candles, strange rituals and people being trained to kill.*

*Most people would have been horrified at having such dark content in their dreams night after night, but she had felt no shame or disgust; in fact, her dream self seemed to have sensed that these were people who had deserved to be killed. She had felt a strong sense of justice because terrible people were getting what they deserved.*

*However, admittedly she felt off kilter the first time she saw a "companion" through her dream eyes and later on she had began seeing the ones who had belonged to her "dream self"; but she had never felt afraid, not once. Her true appreciation came about when she began having the...spicier dreams of her body being used by the companions freely or even watching the other characters be used. It made her lust feel hungry, famished even and her need to seek out the reason behind her dreams awakened but didn't know where to start.*

*But she didn't have to do any work as it turned out, they came to her. It had been so surreal at first, being a freshly turned eighteen year old girl that was living in a fleabag motel. It was all she could afford after her parents had kicked her out for not being "normal enough". She didn't care though, she'd always hated them and was glad to not have to live under the same roof as them.*

*The arrival of the dream companions to her room was admittedly fruitful as she'd had concerns as to what she was going to do for money—she certainly didn't want to live in the disgusting hotel any longer and if she'd had to endure one more solicitation whenever she went outside for ice...there would have been a bloodbath guaranteed. Sometimes she wondered if they had sensed her thoughts and had decided to intervene before she had wasted her potential and ended up in the slammer as a result.*

*At first she had been leery of them when she'd been told that they were waiting for her to reach maturity—until they had mentioned the dreams. . .then she had become intrigued. Truthfully their story sounded a little out there. Then again having similar recurring dreams about strange creatures and killing people was also a little out there. And so she had listened.*

*She had been a member of their organization all of her lives...because their members were reincarnated over and over again to serve their higher purpose; the companions were the same way, they were attached to the same human every incarnation and instinctively came to them when their humans' memories began to awaken through their dreams.*

*They had explained to her that their purpose was to continue to punish particularly bad individuals (the foulest weren't supposed to slip through the cracks, but some managed to do so anyway, sometimes more than once). They were to chase them down and eliminate them and hope that the jailors would be able to keep them locked up permanently.*

*Despite how honest they seemed to be, she couldn't help but believe they were holding back quite a bit. The first and only question she had asked—how they found each reincarnated assassin—had been met with a vague answer that she hadn't understood about oracles. She had a feeling that she wasn't supposed to ask questions and so she had stopped there as she had no desire to annoy them.*

*They too had asked only one question: would she join them? It had been easy to say yes, not just for her beliefs but also because she had nothing else to do (although she had also been dying to meet her companion for life). They had warned once she came with them, she was not allowed to leave, that this was a lifetime contract but she hadn't worried, she just wanted some excitement.*

*She'd had few possessions—her laptop, a couple of small electronics, some clothes and a few trinkets—so packing didn't take long.*

*Then things had gotten strange when instead of using the door like before, they had asked her to close her eyes. There had been no sensation of anything and when she was told she could open them, she was in the candlelit foyer of the headquarters. Magic became the answer for anything that happened around the headquarters that she couldn't explain.*

*She was then shown her temporary rooms and had been given the night off so that she could be rested and fresh for training the next morning.*

*And damn if it hadn't been hard and gruelling. She hadn't been what you'd call athletic so she had to work really hard in order to unlock her full potential. But she refused to give up because each slow day was still one step closer to achieving her true destiny. And she'd been impatient to meet her companion.*

*It had taken her two years—two fucking years—of silent impatience until she had finally been paired up with Tor, and even then it was for more training rather than her first mission because they needed to learn how to work together. By that time she was just anxious to get to the killing!*

*But she never complained, fearful they would kill her or erase her memory and kick her out if she so much as made a peep about where she wanted to stick their training regiment and rules. Suck it up and stick it out, became her mantra and this sweet gig was her reward; killing for justice, the optional apartment outside of headquarters and of course, her very own fucktoy to use when she wished. Yes, life was good now.*

She woke up just as the sun was going down to the feeling of Tor raking a claw against her inner thigh. She'd barely noticed falling asleep but was feeling more refreshed now. About to part her legs, she felt it—that tingle in the air indicating she and Tor were needed at headquarters.

Tor showed his displeasure by removing his claw and flopping back onto the bed with a monstrous groan, his huge bulk causing the bed to shake.

"C'mon, Tor. Let's go see what they want," she groaned as she rose from the bed groggily.

He gave another angry groan and hopped from the bed.

"Don't do that," she hissed as she began getting dressed. "Just because this apartment is full of our people doesn't mean that they won't come up here to complain about the ceiling falling down!"

His whimper was much like a puppy dog's as he hung his head low.

She finished dressing and with a heavy sigh stomped over to Tor, wrenching him up by the arm. "Get up, you asshole."

That seemed to rouse him a little, as he turned his head towards her.

"The sooner we get this done the sooner we can get back to bed, okay?"

This finally did the trick. He gave an annoyed groan as she let go of his arm and began walking away. He followed as she went to the kitchen area where she opened a nearby door to reveal a closet full of clothing on hangers. She pushed the clothes apart in each direction so that the back wall was revealed.

Despite the shadow covering the back wall, her well trained eyes could see the faint symbol that was inked there. Reaching for the top shelf with practiced ease, she removed a small octagonal box and opened it, dipping her fingers into the blue powder. She pinched a few grains and tossed it at the symbol. She and Tor are engulfed in a bright light before they disappear into the air.

"What a croc of shit!" she muttered to Tor after they had fully reappeared sometime later. Her mood was darker than a starless sky and his was no better, perhaps even worse than this morning.

Despite being distracted by her ire, her eyes didn't miss the sheet of paper that had been shoved under the door, and she groaned inwardly.

She stomped over and picked it, promptly crumpling it into a ball after reading it. Her asswipe neighbor from downstairs was complaining again about Tor's tantrum from earlier.

Clutching the paper ball, she sprinted over to him and threw it angrily in his face, causing him hiss annoyingly.

"This is your fault," she seethed. "You should learn to control your temper!" She didn't need more shit on top of the pile of shit the council had already given her. She'd been looking forward to having some time off, but learning she was scheduled on a new mission had soured her mood entirely.

It was for another assassination, assigned to someone else just last night. However it had all gone wrong when the target had gotten the drop on the lousy assassin and now their organization was down by one. They had to expend the energy to find more reborn that were of proper age, which meant she had extra work to do.

She ignored Tor's distressed noises as she stalked upstairs and began packing for a longer trip since surveillance had to begin all over again since the target most likely knew that they were after him. She feared this was going to be her most difficult assignment yet.

This was the life that she had chosen for herself and she had said yes because she had a feeling saying no wasn't an option. *That stupid, dead fuck*—but the council *had* promised extra time off if she completed the assignment.

"C'mon, Tor," she muttered. "Let's get this show on the road."

#

*'Even during my longest surveillances, I never thought I would be this bored, I was apparently mistaken, this is the worst ever!'* She looked through her binoculars at the man below. After two weeks, she was starting to go a little crazy at not being able to take action yet. In case the target changed his routine around, her superiors had advised surveillance be at least this long.

They had given her the dead assassin's notes and she had read them while journeying to her destination, memorizing the target's routine. There had been no way to tell whether or not he would change things up, so here she sat.

She had been right...and wrong. The fortnight had been a waste of time because the fool hadn't changed his routine one iota. He was either a moron, or just arrogant enough to think that no one else would be sent after him. She was betting it was the latter.

Oh but he was mistaken—more and more assassins would be sent after him even if he kept killing them. He was a soul that should never have escaped punishment. The bad souls were numbered like ants, as were the souls of the assassins.

*'At least he's only killed one—his last,'* Mary vowed as she lowered the binoculars. This had gone on long enough and judging by Tor's restless movements near her, he felt the same way.

She smirked; this was going to be fun...

#

Harold James walked as if he hadn't taken out a man trying to kill him a fortnight ago. he felt no fear, he left no evidence to connect him to the crime and even if he were questioned, he could either play ignorance or the victim card— whichever was needed. He was surprised that he'd heard nothing in the news about the discovery of a body in that location, but he brushed it off.

He didn't care. He knew that he was too clever to be taken down by mere police. *Hell, even the assassin after me was no match.*

Or so he thought right up until he felt a hard fist hit the back of his head. Still conscious but dizzy, he felt dizzy, he was picked up and placed on a rough shoulder. That was the last thing he remembered before the blackness overtook him.

#

"Wakey, wakey!" She chimed gleefully to her passed out captive, slapping him silly in order to wake him.

With a confused groan as he opened his eyes. He tried to speak but the tape across his mouth only muffled his attempt. He narrowed his eyes at her.

"You know why I'm here don't you? Not that it matters," she continued before he could attempt at a response. "Your stunt has cost me a huge amount of vacation time and I plan to make you pay it. I won't be gentle in killing you and I won't be concerned with time either; I am going to take this very slowly and enjoy it..."

To her delight, his angry muffles turned into whimpers when she cut his clothes off, knicking him a couple of times in the process. She gave him a reason to scream when she ordered Tor to rip off his eyelids should he close them—she really wanted him to see this.

She was cold in her feelings about killing—she didn't enjoy it but she didn't hate it either. Normally she made it quick, but she was prone to exceptions once in a while, especially when she was pissed off. She began to feel some satisfaction when she started cutting off his toes.

#

*'Okay, I feel a little better,'* she admitted to herself as she admired the pieces of him that

were strewn about the chair she had previously tied him to.

Truthfully Tor had done most of the work. She'd only taken off a few digits and gave him a few—okay, several—cuts before she had felt Tor's impatience and allowed him to vent his own frustrations.

She was somewhat surprised at how restrained he'd been, chopping the man up. He had gone slowly enough for it to be painful. Yes, she would certainly reward him for this...

She heaved a small sigh as she now had a bloody mess to teleport back to headquarters. But at least she finally earned that damned time off and personal pleasures with Tor...

## Duane Bradley's
## Shopping List

Bottled Water
Electric Kettle
Instant Noodles
Umbrella
Waterproof Boots
Copy of "Mandarin For Dummies"

# Desert Grave
## *Duane Bradley*

*4:02 pm*

Gonzalez shot the first kidnapper in the head, then spun around to check his danger area. Sure enough, a second man was behind the door, a Beretta in his fist. As the gun came up, Gonzalez put two in his chest, and the man spread out across the floor.

He nodded to McKenzie, Williams and Harding, then began up the stairs.

A volley of shots stitched the wall next to his head, causing Gonzalez to duck and roll clear. He brought up the M4 carbine just as the man fired again, but the dumb bastard held the gun sideways, the way people did in movies, and the shots went wild.

Gonzalez shot him in the face.

Getting to his feet, Gonzalez climbed the steps, emerging in a corridor just as two men came barrelling out of the main bedroom. The M4 barked once, cutting them down, and Gonzalez stepped into the room.

The girl was in her late teens, twenty at a push. She was tied to the bed, a gag across a mouth, and as she struggled against her restraints, Gonzalez wondered what the hell he'd walked into.

They were there to recover Professor Brian O'Rourke, an Army scientist. Microbiology or some shit. This girl wasn't part of the equation.

A distraction, maybe?

Removing his knife, Gonzalez pressed the blade against her cheek and said, "Make a sound and I'll kill you."

Her eyes darted to the left and Gonzalez turned, too late.

A man filled the doorway, a Beretta M9 in his hands, and at that range he couldn't miss. Gonzalez went for the M4 when the man's head exploded.

The man flopped like a rag doll and Williams walked in, grinning at Gonzalez, who nodded but didn't say anything.

Harding entered the room.

"Who's the chick?" he asked.

"Don't know," Gonzalez said. "How about you two get acquainted while I look for O'Rourke?"

"O'Rourke's in the cellar. McKenzie's got him. He ain't gonna be modelling for GQ anytime soon, but he'll live."

"Get him up here," Gonzalez barked.

As Harding left, Williams nodded at the girl. "What about her?"

Gonzalez handed him the knife. "Knock yourself out."

O'Rourke was a big guy, maybe six-four, but it was all fat and he moved like he had a stick up his ass. He was bleeding from a cut above his right eye and they must've knocked him around some because he looked dazed. Harding helped him to the couch, and he sat.

"We'll handle introductions later," Gonzalez said. "And you'll have to excuse me if I sound curt, but time is a factor. First things first: who's the girl?"

"Girl?" O'Rourke asked.

Dazed, Gonzalez thought.

"Girl?" O'Rourke repeated again, looking across at the bed. He tried to rise but stumbled and landed on his hands and knees. Harding and McKenzie helped him up.

As Williams removed the last of the restraints, O'Rourke looked up. "Don't."

Leaping off the bed, the girl launched herself at Williams. Three fingers disappeared into the soft flesh of his throat and then hastily withdrew, blood spurting from the wound as he spiralled backwards.

She went with him as he fell, slamming into Gonzalez and knocking him off his feet. By the time he recovered, the girl had McKenzie pinned against the floor and was sinking her teeth into the flesh of his cheek.

Gonzalez kicked her in the ribs. She weighed ninety pounds dripping wet and flew across the hardwood floor but before he could follow through, a hand touched his shoulder and he turned to see Williams behind him, only this didn't look like the man he'd known a few moments earlier.

Fists bent into claws, a crazed expression smeared across his face, Williams grabbed him by the collar and pushed him against the wall, his mouth descending towards Gonzalez's throat. Gonzalez kicked him between the legs and hit him across the face, but Williams came at him again, so Gonzalez flattened his palm and struck him beneath the nose, sending bone splinters into his brain.

Williams flopped to the ground and lay still.

Gonzalez looked and saw the girl on Harding's back, her hands wrapped around his face. There were scratch marks down one cheek and he was trying to shake her off, but no soap.

Gonzalez reached for the M4 when McKenzie sprung at him, one clawed hand reaching for his face. Gonzalez blocked the hand and head butted the other man in the face, then as McKenzie staggered backwards, Gonzalez brought up the carbine and fired.

McKenzie's face disappeared in a red mist and Gonzalez turned, bringing up the rifle just as the girl rode Harding to the floor. Breaking free, she sprinted towards the doorway.

Gonzalez emptied the clip, thirty 5.56mm slugs making kindling of the door a split second too late. By the time he crossed the threshold and fed in a new clip, the girl was running out the front door.

"Did they scratch you?" O'Rourke asked.

Gonzalez shook his head.

"That's how it moves from person to person, you know. All it takes is a scratch."

Gonzalez stared at Harding crying and bleeding on the floor. Aside from some cuts to his face, he appeared unharmed.

Gonzalez started to say something, but O'Rourke held up a hand. They were quiet for a spell.

A few moments later, Harding quit crying and looked around. Seeing Gonzalez, the kid hissed and got to his feet. Fingers bent into claws, he launched himself at his former colleague.

Gonzalez shot him in the head.

"The girl's name is Morjana," O'Rourke said. "She's been injected with a virus that shuts down everything except basic functions while simultaneously delivering a jolt to the central nervous system. Simply put, it turns people into rabid animals."

Gonzalez said nothing.

"The Army decided wars aren't won by bombs but by micro-organisms. The carrier moves from place to place, passing on the virus and destabilizing the local population."

Gonzalez stared at the dead kidnapper, face down in the doorway. "They were going to use your virus against you."

O'Rourke nodded.

"For profit?"

"For the hell of it."

Gonzalez thought for a moment.

"What's the nearest town?" he said.

*6:12pm*

Until the stranger tore out her manager's throat, Luna figured it was another quiet evening in Westlake Falls.

While Mr. Fallon sat on his ass, staffing the ticket stand, Luna scurried between taking tickets at the door and operating the closet-sized booth laughingly called a refreshment centre. Later, she'd have to start the movie, which these days meant flipping an on-off switch.

While she multi-tasked, Mr Fallon drummed his fingers, served the occasional teenager and listened to whatever was on the radio. It was standard MOR pap, which didn't surprise her because that was this desert town in a nutshell: *bland, bland, bland.* Soft rock and shitty summer blockbusters.

The rush died down, and Mr Fallon sang along to the radio while Luna went to the projection booth. When she returned, he was shouting at a girl banging on the other side of the glass, telling her don't do that, goddamn it, you're gonna leave streaks.

Leaving the booth, Mr Fallon tried shooing the girl out the door, which was when she grabbed him by the hair, pulled him forward and bit a chunk out of his neck.

Luna turned and ran.

Racing into the bar, she closed and locked the door. Something thumped against the wood, eager to get inside, but the thick door wouldn't budge.

The thumping ceased a moment later, and Luna put her ear to the door. Easing it open, she peered out and, seeing nothing, began up the stairs.

There was no sign of the girl at the concession stand, but Mr. Fallon was on his feet, a hand pressed against his throat. The hand came away bloody, but the wound no longer bled and Luna thought that wasn't right, no way, when her boss lunged at her.

She'd run various scenarios where she punched out her manager, but summoning up the strength to do it still surprised her. It turned out to be fun, so after the first blow she gave him a couple more and then ducked into the theater.

The crowd was on its feet and turning away from the girl, who'd hooked a teenager by the shoulders and was sinking her teeth into his throat. Luna watched people jump over seats and over each other, making a frenzied assault on the fire exit, but didn't see Mr. Fallon come up behind her.

She wasn't ready for him, and as their bodies collided, the pair of them went backwards over the seats and crashed in the narrow aisle. Mr. Fallon was considerably broader, and as his girth wedged between chairs, Luna got to her feet and kicked him in the face a few more times.

Running down the aisle, she joined the throng as it surged out into the night.


*6:45pm*

Sheriff Monica Keene's first hint that this Monday evening wouldn't be typical came when the station called her at home to pass on multiple reports of a strange young woman whose lack of suitable attire—she wore what appeared to be a hospitable gown—hadn't exactly gone unnoticed by Westlake Falls' considerable population of elderly white men.

Somewhat less amusing was the news that this young lady had followed up her assault on good taste with an actual assault, perpetrated against the owner of the local fleapit. As Keene absorbed this, someone appeared at her window and hammered on the glass, startling her.

Keene looked and saw the fleapit's projectionist, Lily or Lana or something, and decided that inviting her inside would be a step forward.

When she opened his door, though, Lily or Lana—no wait, her name was *Luna*—started babbling so Keene held up a hand and said, "Slow it down. Who's chasing who?"

"Some woman just attacked Mr. Fallon."

"Did you call an ambulance?"

She hadn't, so Keene put the call through, then grabbed her keys.

"If you're going out there," Luna said, "shouldn't you have a gun?"

"Gun's at the station."

"You don't keep one at home?"

"Do you?"

"I'm not a cop."

"When I'm home," Keene said, "neither am I."

When Keene entered the station fifteen minutes later, Deputy Philip Straker looked up and said, "There's trouble."

"I'm on it."

Unlocking her desk, Keene removed a Glock .22

"That all you got, Chief?" Luna said.

"Fifteen rounds per clip isn't what I'd call travelling light. And for the record, I'm not the Chief, I'm the Sheriff."

"What's the difference?"

"A Sheriff's sworn to serve and protect a smaller population, which is exactly what I intend to do. Straker, you're riding shotgun. And, uh…Lily, right?"

"*Luna.*"

"Luna, I want to keep your eyes and ears open. You see anything weird, just holler."


*7:01pm*

Keene went in through the fire escape and emerged in an empty theater, the movie still playing.

"I'd better switch that off," Luna said.

They made a beeline for the projection booth, and Straker looked around the dark theater.

"Say it," Keene demanded. "Say what you're thinking."

Straker exhaled.

"Mary Celeste," he said.

Luna raised the lights and killed the movie, leaving the room silent. When she returned, her footsteps sounded on the hardwood floor.

"You know who you guys remind me of?" she said. "John Wayne and Dean Martin in *Rio Bravo*. Ever see that movie?"

Keene shook her head. "I'm not too good on films."

"John Wayne's a small-town Sheriff, and he's got this bad guy in custody whose brother wants to break him out. So he enlists Dean Martin to help him, except Martin's a drunk-"

Keene held up a hand, silencing her.

"Later," she said.

They returned to the car. Keene was fishing for the keys when Straker elbowed her in the ribs.

She looked and saw a dozen people, maybe more, moving towards them.

Mainly young, and mostly male, they crowded around a young woman who stood straddling the central reservation, her expression blank.

"Time to go," Straker said.

As the engine roared, the girl jumped onto the hood. She went with them as the cruiser reversed down the street, then as Keene braked, she flew into the windshield, her head starring the glass.

While Keene made a three-point turn, the girl scrambled across the roof, reached down and shattered the driver's window. Hitting the gas too hard, Keene sent the cruiser up the sidewalk and into the wall, the impact throwing the girl to the ground.

While the girl got to her feet, Straker stepped out and kicked her in the face. She dove at him and they went down in a tangle of arms and legs, Straker's weapon skittering across the asphalt. As he hit the ground, dazed, the girl seized his head and her mouth descended towards his neck.

Straker lashed out, hitting the girl beneath the jaw and snapping her head back. She rolled over and Straker broke free, getting to his feet and recovering his weapon.

He was straightening up when one of the teenagers ran at him.

Keene shot the kid in the head.

Her back towards Straker, with Luna between them, Keene raised the .22 at the mob as the remaining teenagers spread out. They began circling, then moved in and Keene opened fire.

Several bodies fell. Keene kept firing until she saw the girl get to her feet, then she broke away and put the Glock to the girl's head, looking up as headlights approached.

A Ranger Special Operations Vehicle slammed into the crowd, flipping bodies like bowling pins before fishtailing to a halt.

There was a man behind the wheel. "Get in," he said.

As Luna climbed on board, Keene reloaded. The girl grabbed her shoulder, so Keene elbowed her in the throat.

Straker followed Keene onto the Ranger, but before the driver could accelerate, the girl grabbed the rear gate. As she pulled herself up, Keene kicked her in the face. She flew backwards through a plate glass window, causing an alarm to wail.

Glancing over his shoulder, the stranger looked at Keene and asked, "You the Sheriff?"

She nodded. "Who're you?"

"Name's Gonzalez. Your station nearby?"

"Yeah, but-"

"Good. We'll hole up there."

"*Hole up*? Against what?"

"A goddamn siege," Gonzalez said.

*7:59pm*

Gonzalez laid four guns on the table: two Glocks, a Sig Sauer and a Beretta ARX-160.

"I admire your spirit," Keene said, "but this thing took out your team who, I'm sure, were some very tough hombres. I'm just a small town Sheriff. What're our chances?"

Gonzalez said nothing.

"Can't argue with a confident man," Luna said.

Gonzalez looked through the blinds.

They were at least two dozen people out there, which meant they were outnumbered six to one.

"Where's your armoury?" he said.

"I told you," Keene said. "I'm a small town Sheriff."

"Got a basement?"

"Sorry."

Bodies appeared at the windows. Glass shattered.

"Enough chatter," Gonzalez said. "Let's do this."

Gonzalez stood up and let rip with the Beretta, shredding the first wave of bodies that burst through. Behind him, Straker and Keene fired into the surging crowd. The air grew thick with smoke.

More glass shattered. As several bodies strained to get inside, the door came off its hinges. Gonzalez turned and fired, several .223 Remington slugs turning their bodies into mincemeat.

"What's the plan when we start running low on ammo?" Straker asked.

"Fuck everything and run," Gonzalez said. "Why?"

"We're running low on ammo."

Gonzalez stood up, firing until the Beretta emptied, then pumped the underslung grenade launcher.

"Go to the Ranger," he said. "Take the girl."

"What about you two?" Straker questioned.

Keene sighed, "Do as the man says, Phil."

As they rose, Gonzalez fired off two grenades to cover them, then threw the empty weapon aside and unholstered a Walther P38.

"You out?"

"Yep," Keene said.

"How about it? Butch and Sundance?"

"I don't even know what that means."

"Man, you didn't see *Butch Cassidy*?"

"Never did."

More bodies piled into the room.

"Means we come out fighting. You know, in a blaze of glory."

"We kill everything and walk away?"

"It's a little more complicated than that."

When a woman lunged towards him, Gonzalez shot her in the chest. Two more assailants took her place. He shot the first one in the head, then ducked and rolled as the second one reached for him, coming up beside the thing and pumping a round into its face.

As more bodies closed in on them, Gonzalez let rip, decimating the group until two remained standing. Smiling, he raised the Beretta and-

*Empty.*

The Ranger smashed through the doorway, slamming into the group and hurling them across the room. One of them, a teenage boy, struggled to his feet, so Keene brought a fire extinguisher down on his head.

"Small town Sheriff, huh?" Gonzalez said.

Keene shrugged.

As Straker reversed into the street, Morjana lunged towards them, grabbing the shotgun door. She was dragged a hundred yards, then clambered up on top of the vehicle.

As she did so, Straker nudged the brakes and swerved, sending her flying over his head. Morjana landed on the hood and perched there, staring at them.

Straker tapped the brakes again, and she slithered across the hood. Another quick nudge, and the girl went over the edge. As she clung to the front grille, Straker accelerated.

Keene gripped the wheel. "Jump," she said.

Straker said nothing. Grabbing Luna, he hurled himself into the night.

The Ranger swung right, leaving the road and heading into the desert. Keene stared across at Gonzalez and said, "*Jump*, you stupid motherfucker."

He did.

Landing among creosote bushes, he looked up just as the Ranger slammed into a tree and exploded.

Pinned against the tree, Morjana howled as flames washed over her body. When the screams died, she flopped across the Ranger's hood.

A hundred yards away, Keene stood up, brushed herself off and walked over.

"Small town Sheriff," Gonzalez said.

"So was John Wayne."

"I thought you weren't good on films."

"No, but I've heard of John Wayne. He's got this bad guy in custody whose brother wants to break him out. So he turns to Dean Martin, but Martin's a drunk-"

"*Rio Bravo*," Gonzalez said, and nodded. "Come on. It's a long walk back into town."

*Joanna Koch's*
*Shopping List*

French Burgundy
Onion
Celery
Carrot
Garlic
Black peppercorns
Chicken, backbone removed, cut into 8 pieces
Olive oil
Pancetta
Flour
Shallots
Thyme
Parsley
Bay leaves
Chicken broth
Butter
Crimini
Shiitake
Pearl onions

# For the Angels, Unseen
### *Joanna Koch*

Mack didn't expect Stu's call, started the evening with very different plans. She tucked the rose gold angel necklace under her clip tie and cranked the thermostat down before she hit the road. It was going to be a hot one.

Margaret McElhaney—Mack for short—grew up in Canyon Holler and had always been treated like an outsider. To make things worse, perimenopause was really kicking her ass. But no one knew about that. The uniform was her disguise. Security work suited Mack just fine. She knew all the blind spots on the cameras, the hours and habits of the staff, and the decent folks versus the predators. The big outlet mall had its fair share, like any public place. Old, they stalked alone. Young, they ran in packs.

*Like wild dogs*, Mack thought as she pulled her truck into the parking lot. Sodium lamps switched on, signaling the onset of night.

The pack was restless. Jake was missing. He was gone less than a day, but it was the kind of news that travels fast in a small town. Especially a town where parts of other boys had turned up scattered around the forest reserve months after each disappearance.

"Hey, Mack, how they hanging?"

"Pete Spears, do you want me to call your mother and tell her about that mouth?"

"What, are you saying it isn't true?"

Avery Washington clutched his chest behind Pete. "Don't break my heart, Mack. You know I need me a sugar daddy as pretty as you."

Mack looked above the boys' heads and scanned the mall corridors. "You kids keeping out of trouble tonight?"

"Sure," Pete said. "Hey, can you show me your gun?"

"You know the answer to that."

"Don't hurt to ask. Come on, pretty please?"

Avery said, "I'll show you mine if you show me yours."

There was a wave of laughter and Pete backed off. Mack waited for the swarm to disperse but they hovered. "Go on," Mack said. "Get a move on."

Avery said, "Miss McElhaney, we kind of wondered if you heard anything about Jake yet? Like from the cops?"

Mack shook her head. "Doesn't work that way, boys. I report to them. They don't report to me."

"Fuck it," Pete said. "Jake's just run off. There's no way he'd let some fag take him down."

Wildlife destroyed most of the remains, but there was enough evidence left to suggest sexual torture. Mack was on the outskirts of the investigation, questioned extensively as the last to see some of the victims alive. She tried to glean more from the detectives, even shared some secrets she knew about people in town. Investigators only told her the man responsible would expose himself by his own escalation if they didn't catch him first.

Mack thought: *That's true. Men get caught by their cocks.*

She asked point blank why they weren't looking for a woman. The older detective rambled about hormones and evolution. The younger one quoted statistics. Mack asked how they knew anything if they only studied people who got caught. The detectives chuckled and said she was right, theirs was an inexact science. They'd thanked her for her time and said to call them if she noticed anything unusual at the mall.

Mack patted Avery's shoulder. The boy looked pretty upset. "I guess I know about as much as anybody around here. Let's hope Pete's right."

### 

Mack drove home fast. The winding switchbacks were second nature. She sped around each pothole and blind curve while half her mind daydreamed. She couldn't wait to get home. Even when she wasn't in a hurry, she made the hour and fifteen drive in about forty-five.

Any other woman living out in the middle of nowhere was labeled crazy in town. Mack got a free pass. It came with the uniform and with the gun. No one worried about Mack.

No one asked if she was okay, either. For most of her life that worked in her favor. Lately, though, she'd been feeling more and more alone.

Any day now, Jake's mom would be on the news. It was a wonder she'd ever had Jake. She used to tease Mack until eighth grade when Mack found her in the bathroom with a finger down her throat. Mack pulled a paper towel from the white metal dispenser, dabbed away the yellow slime clinging to the other girl's hair, and held it back. "Go on. I got you."

The name calling stopped, but Jake's mom abandoned their friendship next year when she started dating boys. Mack had always been different, and Jake's mom was one of the prettiest girls in class, destined to be a trophy wife.

Mack didn't blame her. Lots of women didn't know how to stand in their own power.

As she drove, Mack thought about special times when she wasn't lonely, even when she was alone. Tonight was going to be one of those special nights.

She'd strip off the uniform and emerge reborn, a fully fleshed woman. The cool air would feel good on her hot skin. She'd walk around without the restriction of a robe or a tampon. Lately it seemed like she never stopped bleeding, but there was no problem with making a mess in the basement. That's what it was designed for.

### ###

A piece of the boy slid down her leg like a blood clot. The tension in her belly loosened and bloomed from her vagina. More pieces fell as she carved. Slimy trails descended like snails between her legs. Lukewarm chunks clung to her skin, and then slipped down in his quick blood.

There was no odor of ammonia. The boy was fresh. The smell of his shit was clean, like rice. Mack didn't give him time to be scared, didn't want to deal with the tainted diarrhea smell of shock. She let him sink against the wall until he slumped on the floor. She smoothed his crumpled body and stretched him out. Her cervix ached. She sank onto him. He was still hard. The cock ring helped. Her muscles tugged at his last drop of life.

Mack liked the way the thick head leaked as it hit her cervix and mixed with her own blood. Christ, would she never stop bleeding? Hot flashes weren't flashes. They were endless fires. An internal demon tended them day and night. Mack pounded Jake's cock against her cervix, ache equaling ache, pain releasing pain, fire turning to water and the salt of her sweat baptizing the dead boy's destroyed face.

It was impossible that his cock was still hard, and yet it was. Mack had the crazy thought she might get pregnant with the dead boy's baby. It would be a miracle. Her vaginal canal swelled and crushed his cock when she thought about it and she rode him fast. Then she went slow, and then fast again. Whatever she liked. As long as she liked.

Most of Mack's play had been in stripping the face. It oozed, expressionless. The eyes were punctured and unfit to judge. Mack licked at the holes in his cheeks. She'd left his tongue surrounded by exposed teeth. The unveiled flesh yielded to her. It tasted like rotten chocolate; its melting gristle punctuated by loose cartilage hanging from the nasal orifice. Mack found it accommodating and moist.

Done with the bloodied cock, she moved up and rubbed her clit against the teeth and textures of the liquid face. That's when her phone started playing *Magic Bus* and she knew Stu was calling in, and she had no choice except to answer.

### 

Dammit, dammit dammit. Different types of worlds needed to be kept separate. It wasn't right for them to get mixed up like they'd done tonight.

Mack shook the bad feeling off at home as she went through the ritual of stripping away her uniform and allowing her body to expand. The wings of a guardian angel grew from her shoulders and her hips. Like black curtains, they allowed her to pass above and below the law, in the shadows and the set changes that were hidden between the scenes of everyday life.

Mack knew a predator when she saw one. She did good work in the world. She understood right and wrong on a higher level than most people. Jake was one less man making innocent women live under someone else's thumb.

She headed downstairs happily to finish what she'd started earlier that night.

### 

Mack scanned the basement for a quick visual and then clicked off the light. Her mind ran an instant replay of entering the house. Nothing was out of place, except Jake wasn't where she'd left him.

There was more blood than before on the epoxy floor. Some animal? How did it get in? Mack moved with her back to the wall. She went slow and stopped to listen between steps. When she was close enough to see the garden level patio doors beneath the outside deck, she spotted a slender triangle at the bottom of the blinds where moonlight came in. The air conditioning hummed on and the blinds clacked. Mack held her breath. Cool air bathed the room. Slower, closer, Mack gained enough ground to spot an object wedged at the base of the blinds. It was the boy. His fingertips almost touched the glass.

"Jake?"

The air conditioning stopped. The blinds quit chattering. Mack held her breath.

Jake's still skin in the moonlight undulated with the muscular beauty of a swimmer. Movement seemed implicit. The line of his spine led her eyes to the cleft of his ass. He was pristine except for a defecation stain. Mack had never killed a man by stabbing him in the back.

And she hadn't killed Jake, although she'd treated him like a corpse. Weird thing was, his response made her think he liked it.

She nudged his ass with her foot and stepped back.

Nothing. She took hold of his ankles. The body felt cool, but with her internal thermostat running high, it was hard to judge. The boy was heavy, and she had to tug a few steps and then catch her breath. When he was far enough from the window, Mack made a wide berth around his torso and went to secure the patio doors. That's when she heard him whine.

It wasn't much of a cry. Almost a squeak. Mack felt a flash of fondness for Jake, remembering the tiny field mice she'd caught as a child. Their tufts of gray fur, translucent white bellies, wiggling claws. She'd kept a collection of tails until her mother found them and threw them out.

Mack turned Jake face up without a fight. He was heavy, compliant. She took his left hand. He was a southpaw catcher.

"Jake, listen. If you can hear me, I want you to squeeze my hand."

Not much, but it was there. A change in pressure between her forefinger and thumb.

"Good boy."

His throat muscles moved, partially exposed. Another whine, almost inaudible, escaped his frayed face. Mack placed a gentle hand on his chest. With her other hand she traced a path down to his cock. It was soft until she touched it. It lifted and pulsed. The heart under her hand fluttered to life. Mack was a priestess raising a man from the dead, an angel with the power to reverse her own dark spell of annihilation.

She was burning and bleeding inside. She mounted and swallowed his shaft after stroking it stiff. Each thrust engorged it more and made the mouse squeak. His paws clawed the air. She clasped them together and used the knuckles to rub her clit.

Mack's slick muscles milked him. Jake thrust back. She was the holy guardian angel. No man could resist her wrath. The wings inside covered her eyes and made everything go black. He was going to come, whether he wanted to or not. Something broke open inside, and she felt him burst, weak and hot.

He wilted inside her after he came. Her cunt grew clammy. She expelled the used cock. The blackness around her sparkled, and Mack squinted through the stars to find Jake's ruined face. Fluids pooled and scabbed in cavities between ligament and dented bone. A pink bubble formed where the nasal passage was exposed. The bubble inflated and deflated like a slow motion shot. Mack watched it expand and contract until it popped.

For once Mack felt warm instead of hot. Her body was made of cream and she was ready to mold the boy like a wax doll.

She pushed his knees back and probed into his handsome ass. Her finger felt resistance. She wasn't used to live flesh. It gripped her and released more of the smell of his insides. She massaged in and out, going deeper with each stroke. She hit some kind of barrier and fought until there was a sort of snap. Internal lubrication gushed with a rush of strong odor, and the next finger went in easy, as did the next. The mouse made more noises. It wanted her whole fist.

Whether it was empty or full was entirely her choice.

The once beautiful boy was a puppet on her arm. Mack luxuriated in how shiny and rich it was inside. How it gave up its juices and slid around her powerful hand much longer than any dead thing had before.

It stayed alive for a long time. Mack didn't cut it apart until it stopped all its squeaking and started to bruise where its body pressed the floor.

### 

The floral dress was an awkward uniform, ill-fitting, with no place to carry a firearm. Mack felt foolish swathed in an excess of fabric. She didn't have the right shoes, so hand-me-downs had to do. Mack trudged from her red truck up the dirt driveway to the wake. She was pleased to see Jake's mom was up and about.

"Come here."

The other woman greeted her with open arms. Mack accepted her embrace.

They rocked for a few moments, and then Jake's mom held Mack away to look in her eyes. Pain seemed to weigh down her slender frame.

"It's hard for you now," Mack said. "It won't always be this way. Everything happens for a reason."

The grieving mother tucked a lock of hair behind Mack's ear. "You're sweet to say so. But you don't understand. He was my flesh and blood."

"I know what he was."

"If you had children of your own." Jake's mom touched the rose gold angel necklace exposed by Mack's dress. "So pretty. I always thought you were so pretty when you tried."

Mack grasped the other woman's wrist and moved her hand away.

Jake's mom quivered from her bitten lips to her emaciated thighs. Mack thought the woman might collapse, but she held firm. The angel was a secret, and she had no right to touch it. The woman wavered in Mack's fist.

"My boy, my sweet baby boy. What they did to him..."

Her head wagged in denial. Her mouth continued working without making any words.

A bevy of friends pulled Jake's mom away and eyed Mack. Their suspicions faded when they tallied the lack of threat. Lousy flowered dress, thrift shop shoes, farmer's tan.

Mack didn't understand these women, Jake's mom least of all.

She filled her plate from the spread of covered dishes, aware she was different. Better. Always had been. Mack wasn't afraid of power. Blood poured out between her legs. The smell of blood had started her crusade. Now the bleeding had stopped.

It was the crazy miracle she'd envisioned.

Mack knew it was going to be a girl. She felt it in the warm soft center of her belly. She saw it in her dreams. Mack smiled with quiet joy as she foresaw a future when all would bear witness to the virgin birth of a secret power, and when predators would fall beneath the wrath of a new generation's holy guardian angel.

# Michael Byrne's
# Shopping List

Wholegrain pasta
Tomatoes
Skimmed milk
Duct tape.
Washing powder
Rye bread.
Quicklime.
Iceberg lettuce.
Toothpaste.
Hemp rope.
Toilet paper.
Cheddar Cheese.
Dozen eggs (Free Range)
"How to Pick Locks" by Anonymous.
Granola cereal.
Shower gel.
"Practicing the Left Hand Path…the Right Way." by Aloysius Hobbe.
A Twix.

# Routine
## *Michael Byrne*

He's christened him the 'Wise Man'. A commuter Dr Alex Pinner sees every day on the train to London. Every day. Without fail. Same seat, same station. Rodent-like hair sprouting from pale Anglo-Saxon jowls with wire glasses masking green eyes. This could be Merlin, he thinks, disguised as best a fey creature a thousand years old could. Cord trousers and a tweed waistcoat a decade or so out of date. He wonders, Dr Alex Pinner, a consultant psychiatrist at Hollow Hill Hospital, why the Wise Man should still have to get up of a morning and travel to work when he is clearly past retirement age. Had he not saved for his future? A young tearaway perhaps now making up for lost time? Or was the reason more benevolent? Volunteering in a day centre for homeless children? Or nursing abandoned kittens to health before seeing them off, tear in eye, to their forever homes all across London? Or maybe he was a paedophile. Or a John off to see his favourite girl—wasting his pension on what little comfort he could derive from feeling close to someone, even for just half an hour.

The Wise Man shifts in his seat and Alex realises he is staring at him, a thing he often does. Neither seem to mind, however, and Alex takes his time to turn his eyes away back to his laptop and his paperwork locked within. Five more stops come and go, the ratio of people injected and ejected staying unbalanced. At the sixth stop the Wise Man stands silently, slips past the gaggle of people and exits as the doors seal the remainders in. Alex can barely see him leave behind the denim clad buttocks of an overweight man, but he is comforted by the repetition of his exiting all the same. The Wise Man's reliable pattern now part of his own routine, synchronising two strangers into a cosmic sequential tapestry.

Dr Alex Pinner himself maintains a regimented routine. Daily he is up at 5am to jog around the emerald plains of Surrey, deposited as he is in a three-bedroom detached with his wife, Margot—an editing executive for an advertising firm. After his jog is complete, when his chiselled muscles glisten with sweat and he feels as confident as the male models in Margot's adverts, Alex returns home and showers. He then sits with his wife of ten years for breakfast. Her cheeks flushed from her own morning exercise. Raven hair tied back hiding its symmetrical shape and precisely even bangs, looking like a helmet worn ready for battle in the realm of advertising. Breakfast consists of fruit, protein smoothies and black coffee with filtered water from the pearl white monolith fridge that dominates the kitchen. Natural light from the multitude of windows cascading onto shimmering surfaces making the room feel like a greenhouse. Or ant farm. After breakfast; shower, dress for work, a kiss to one another then for Alex a short drive to the station before boarding a train into the city. Post work Alex goes to the gym near Hollow Hill Hospital. Continues to maintain his pristine figure. Returns home for around seven pm. Eats a light, well-presented evening meal before then focusing his attention on Margot if she is free to be focused on. They will watch a film together, discuss work and irritations of the day and enjoy a small glass of wine each that sometimes leads into two. Occasionally they even fuck. Though this is pre planned as well. Clothes are arranged, scents wafted, lubricants prepared. Pills checked. There are three bedrooms in Alex and Margot's detached house. There is no rush to fill them.

This day, a Thursday in May, had started no differently to the countless Thursdays that had come before it and that Alex had presumed would come after. He entered Hollow Hill Hospital, consulted at ward round, spoke to patients with manufactured empathy and aloof authority. Responded to calls, emails and letters and wrote up cases before heading to the gym from which he would then head home. But as Alex finishes grunting and straining in front of a wall long mirror his phone begins to vibrate, stored as it is, in his locker. Post shower, towel taut around his waist Alex notices the missed call. It is from work. He takes his time to answer, dressing first.

"Dr Pinner?" Alex recognises the voice as Angie, the Matron of Bondi ward. He mumbles a response and she continues. "We've just had word from the police. They're bringing Nigel Innes back in." her voice raises as if the statement were a question.

"I see…" he says waiting for more information.

"It's not good. They're saying he's killed someone."

Alex's mind goes blank except for a singular flashback from four weeks ago. In the cavernous space of his memory he sees himself sat alone at a table, a spotlight on him from the heavens that shows him signing the discharge papers of one Mr. Nigel Innes.

## 2

By the end of his two week stay, Alex Pinner had considered Nigel a malingerer. He had arrived with no particular fanfare or spectacle. Was calm and co-operative throughout assessment, took medication as and when prescribed, did not get involved with other patients and often times would be found in his room reading. His only reason for being there,

Alex found, was that quite suddenly he had left his ten-year job as a librarian in a small municipal library to wander the streets of London and sleep in a cardboard box despite owning outright a house in Epping. When asked why, he had said because his neighbour was not real. Alex had asked him in what way and Nigel's response was vague and inconsistent. Was he manufactured? No, was the response. So he was human? No, was the response. An alien then, demonic creature? None of the above. In the fortnight Nigel was there, no answer of any substance found its way out of his mouth, and notes on his progress were scant. Then, as his section came close to expiry, it emerged that Nigel Innes was not taking his medication after all when a nurse found him in the bathroom, fingers down his throat ready to flush out his anti-psychotics. At the same time, information dripped into the hospital from external agencies that Nigel had not so much left his job but had been suspended for following a woman, a regular patron in fact, around the library, as evidenced by the CCTV.

It was clear Nigel Innes was unusual, but Alex could see no evidence as to how this was a result of mental illness. As such he recommended discharge. Nigel was given the option of staying informally until arrangements were made to get him home, but he left the same day, as quietly and unobtrusively as he arrived. A ghost hidden behind the mania of the other patients. Had he not signed his discharge sheet they may never have known he'd left.

This past recollection continues to swirl around Alex as he re-enters Hollow Hill, the thoughts of enjoying his evening meal dying in the face of the reality of staying late at work. Thinking of the unassuming Nigel Innes with blood on his hands. Blood that could easily pass to him. He was right to discharge him, Alex assures himself—swiping his ID badge to access Bondi ward. There was no evidence he would harm anyone. The courts loved an oblation on which to pin the blame however, and Alex knows he will be it if he wasn't careful.

Bondi ward; ten rooms connected by a large communal area painted in bright but tired primary colours and adorned with positive but exhausted affirming quotations. The night staff greet him and Angie approaches, an older woman, tall and naturally nimble, her dark skin still fresh despite the demands of work and family. Surrounded by an invisible mist of authority.

"We've put him in room ten." she says, placing notes into Alex's hand.

"How is he?"

Angie shrugs, "He's…Nigel. Quiet, calm— we've placed him in restraints as a precaution but honestly he doesn't seem to be agitated or aroused at all."

Alex reads the notes from handover, scans through the fluff and rhetoric to find that from police custody a mental health professional concluded he was detainable. How the police had been called to a possible attempted break in followed by numerous calls of suspicious persons in the same area. How they had walked up to Nigel's house and knocked loudly and finally, when checking the perimeter, found him sat in the garden, tired from exerting himself. His arms covered in blood and gore up the elbows, a streak across his forehead where he had wiped his moistened brow. His neighbour supine on the grass next to him. Mouth open wide. Chest even wider. The report failing to mention one of the officers' sudden urge to vomit.

"Yes," Alex says letting the image sink in "let's keep him restrained for now."

They enter Nigel's room together. His eyes are closed but he is not asleep and slowly he opens them, a small smile of recognition appearing on his face. He has been medicated intravenously as a precaution, Alex noting the cannula still affixed to Nigel's right arm.

"Hello again." Nigel's voice is without emotion or inflection. Alex ponders if this is put on.

"How are you feeling, Nigel?" Alex asks as he continues to scan the notes.

"Fine. A little tired," his response.

"Yes, that will be the medication, I'm afraid."

Nigel shakes his head, "I was tired before that. Been a busy day." Alex recreates the crime scene mentally. Slowly he sits on a chair next to the bed. Near Nigel's feet. Near the door which Angie guards in case the restraints fail by an act of some unholy deity.

"My God, Nigel, whatever possessed you to do such a thing?" The concern is genuine. Nigel fidgets in his bed, stretches a little while he constructs an answer.

"I was looking for something," he says. Alex wonders if he's deliberately being evasive and so asks him outright.

"No." Nigel says and then after a silence that would seem to contradict his one word answer, "It's just that I'm not sure you'd understand without evidence."

"I take it that means you didn't find what you were looking for?"

Nigel nods.

"But you knew it was inside your neighbour so you had to kill them to get it?"

Nigel now shakes his head and sighs. "Yes but he wasn't alive to begin with, was he? So how could I have killed him?"

"You might not have thought so, Nigel, but he *was* alive. He had a name, a family…"

Agitation stirs the still waters of Nigel's presentation. "Yes, yes. All the trappings of being alive, sure. A job. A house. But he wasn't alive. Not like you and I. He was different."

"Explain to me how."

"This would have been a lot easier if I'd found some proof." Nigel appears to say to himself, like a scientist dictating notes midway through an experiment. "They're cunning, I'll give them that."

Alex looks to Angie who returns the stare before he refocuses on the man ahead of him in restraints.

"Let's go back to the beginning." Alex probes deeper. "You first came here because you said your neighbour wasn't real."

Nigel nods.

"What first made you think this?"

Nigel deliberates for a moment. "He was trying too hard to be normal."

Alex's face is one of confusion. Nigel takes the hint.

"His life was too perfect. He had the perfect car. The flawless house. Faultless hair even. But what did he do exactly to get these things? Where had he come from to fill this void of monotony that was missing in the world? I'd speak to him and he'd say he worked in finance. Could never explain what that meant. I'd greet him of a morning. Same time every day for ten years. It would be the same response. "Nice weather," "Terrible weather," "How's it going?" and so on. Triviality for a decade. And then one day, while I waited in for a parcel, I watched him leave his house dead on eight as usual. I watched him walk to his car, the alarm switching off with a flash of headlights. And then he turns. Turns to face where I should have been standing to greet him."

Nigel goes silent for a moment.

""How's it going? Nice Weather we're having!""

"There was no one there?" Alex asks and Nigel nods.

"Very odd—as if he didn't even realise he was talking to himself. A week later I was off with a cold. Sure enough each morning same thing. A greeting to the aether. Then I noticed his car."

"What about it?" Alex asks and Nigel tries to sit up in his bed, alert if sluggish from the drugs.

"Eight in the morning he sets off to work in his blue BMW. The elusive world of finance awaiting. Nine AM looking out of the window I happen to see a car drive past; a blue BMW. Home early. But he just drives past. Ten rushes by and the same thing happens. Eleven, twelve, one, two, three, four, five. Clockwork. Then I begin to worry. Does he know I know something? That I'm watching him? So Monday I begin the routine again. Leave the same time he does, approach the end of my garden wait for a confrontation or complaint, but instead?"

Alex predicts the answer, "Hi How's it going?"

Nigel nods. "Exactly."

"Is it just your neighbour you saw doing this?" Angie asks as Alex scribbles some notes, and Nigel shakes his head once more.

"No, I've seen people at work too."

"The woman you were following?" Alex again predicts accurately.

"Ten am arrival, same bookshelf, stand fifteen minutes, select same book, read twenty minutes. Sit down ten…repeat variations on a theme." Nigel looks down, remorseful almost.

"If only I could have found some evidence then I wouldn't sound as crazy as I do. Instead I look like another lunatic killer."

"So you admit you're a killer?" Alex looks for a nerve to bow like a violin string but finds none.

"…A figure of speech."

Alex begins to notice his head throbbing from all the content. How, they will ask, could he have let someone so purely unwell out into the world with no treatment plan? No follow up? No regard will be given to his previous presentation. The focus will be on the here and now. Rubbing his eyes, he gets up to leave but Nigel interjects.

"Inquiline. From the Latin *Inquilinus*." Nigel says and Alex turns to him. "Look it up, it's happening all around us."

Alex closes the door and speaks in hushed tones to Angie, declares that the patient is clearly suffering from paranoid delusions and that despite his calm exterior there is penchant for violence as brutally demonstrated from his attack on his neighbour. Angie agrees to keep him sedated and restrained for now. It is past nine and Alex feels the walls of the ward closing in on him, he needs to get home. Before he does, curiosity pulls him to a nearby PC and he searches the internet.

INQUILINE: *noun Zoology.*

An animal exploiting the living space of another, e.g. an insect that lays its eggs in a gall produced by another. From the Latin *Inquilinus* meaning Lodger or Tenant.

# 3.

Alex did not usually let the ravings of his patients interfere with his commute. But then this was the first time in a short but successful career that one had gutted a fellow human. This within weeks of him writing a report to suggest he was simply trying to obfuscate from his infatuation with a woman at work. He knew that the mental health professional who visited Nigel in custody did the right thing in sectioning him again and that Nigel Innes was clearly very disturbed. Yet he couldn't help but feel that if he were to see that colleague anytime soon, he would punch the fucker right in the mouth.

Alex sighs. Looks down at his phone. There are no texts from Margot. He has written one for her. An apology of sorts. An explanation of why he is home late. Of the horrors of his day. Of fear of what is to come. He has not sent it. Staring at himself through the funhouse mirror of the train window he considers if he wrote the text for himself. Hoping that somehow this state of the art device would suddenly evolve to possess AI, and would reassure him everything would be alright. It did nothing of the sort.

What did he mean, Alex wonders. What cryptic world view is hidden by the word "inquiline"?

Once birthed from a tunnel and with full signal, Alex looks again at the word's meaning on his phone. "Exploiting the living space of another." Did Nigel believe that his neighbour was another species perhaps? And if so, how was it exploiting the space it inhabited? Alex scrolls past synonyms and articles relating to parasites and insects. Of Gall Wasps who, with almost unearthly design, deposit their eggs with those of other wasps. Unseen. Unnoticed.

Alex conjures a wasp version of Nigel Innes; a rundown scraggy-haired wasp; the cloying smell of sweat clinging to him as he desperately tries to convince other wasps that the pupating larvae are not their own but of an invasive species.

As he reaches his car Alex thinks of Nigel Innes's victim and the randomness of such a vicious attack. Considered an outsider by an outsider. Victimised for being faultless and predictable. Careful to separate the visual and auditory hallucinations from Nigel's expositions he finds himself empathising with the neighbour. He too is successful, he thinks firstly. He too drives a BMW. But it is when he arrives home that the real thought he was supressing climbs to the surface. He too is unexciting and regimented.

Alex undresses in the dark as he realises this, careful not to wake Margot who is making quiet nasal utterances in her sleep. He lies there a moment, feeling awkward in his own skin before turning to Margot and kissing her. Gentle at first but then harder, more sensual. She stirs in frustrated half sleep. Asks him what he's doing. He answers with a tender hand sliding under the covers. She complains of work in the morning but he whimpers, innocently, but demanding also. Slowly Margot begins to enjoy herself, taking the lead as she often does. Alex lies back and smiles. A routine is being broken. They rarely ever screw on Thursdays. But it's not enough, he thinks as she kisses his navel. The bedroom suddenly feeling stale and clinical, Alex takes her hand and guides her to the kitchen. He lifts her onto the kitchen worktop. It is a cliché, he knows, but one he has never practiced before and so he is satisfied both in the experience and the spontaneity though over excitement means the coitus is short-lived.

Margot adjusts herself and pours a glass of water while Alex sits silently at the kitchen table. She asks if he's coming to bed.

"In a minute." He responds. Only then is he asked if everything is okay, but he chooses not to say anything. Margot returns to her torpor, still irritable at the lack of sleep she will now have. Alex makes to follow but the thought of breaking the routine further still haunts him and so he takes a glass and bottle of wine and heads to the living room though he knows already the glass is just for show. The TV glows putrid greens and yellows into the dark room and he tries to pay attention to the pointlessness of it all. But exhaustion and alcohol wrestle him into submission and he slips into a deep drunken slumber at two-thirty.

4

It is the black dreamless sleep of an inebriated mind. Alcohol and late hours at work combining forces to weigh Alex down for longer than he anticipates. Away from his bedroom it is not his alarm that stirs him but a sheet of natural light intruding past the blinds and onto his face. A mask of sunrays over his eyes. He wakes and stretches, taking his time like a man on holiday until he realises that it is past nine and this is a workday. And that a murderer sits in a forensic mental health ward he has duty over. Knowing his presence will already be missed he none the less grasps onto some glimmer of hope that he can still arrive in a reasonable time. His morning jog and breakfast schedule kyboshed, a slim slice of sourdough bread and glass of orange juice a poor fuel for the day ahead. Margot is nowhere to be seen, her side of the bed neatly returned to order, bowls and cutlery cleaned and returned to their stoic sentry in the cupboard. It was almost like living alone, Alex thinks as he slams the front door closed and enters his car. Almost like living with the ghostly presence of a partner no longer around. Was Margot the spirit in this scenario, he wonders or was it himself, removed as he was from a pattern of behaviour they had perfected for years.

Attempting to park the car is futile, his usual selection of spots by the station all taken due to his tardiness. A congestion of vehicles runs down the narrow tract of road and it is a good three-minute walk to the station from where he finally embarks on foot, running now to catch a train he had otherwise timed proficiently for.

Alex sits catching his breath in a manner as to not draw attention to himself. No loud gasps or exertions. In through the nose, out through the nose. Finding a seat is easy, the morning exodus is already dying down. Strange to see a different set of faces, he thinks. Strange that this commute exists for people not in a blind panic to get to work before nine. Like existing outside of time, he muses. Stranger still then, when scanning the array of human oddities before him, that Alex Pinner's eyes fall upon the Wise Man. Sat as ever in his usual seat, staring blankly as ever in his general direction. What odds must it be? Alex asks himself internally, that we should both be late on the same day. Alex thinks on Nigel Innes, scares himself slightly when he remembers the videos he watched of the gall wasp. Metallic ovipositors pulsating as they eagerly pierce the gooey flesh of fruit. The gooey flesh of other larvae.

He reaches for his phone through a force of habit, but it is not in his jacket pocket and Alex realises he has left it at home, where it rings off and becomes bloated from voicemails. The victims' family's solicitor. The head psychiatrist of the hospital. The police. All are trying to inform him of the most recent events in relation to Nigel Innes.


The vultures are already circling Hollow Hill when Alex arrives, checking microphones and camera equipment. Taking notes and phone calls. Despite leaving his phone at home he takes this swarm of journalists as the clear omen of doom it portents to, yet secretly prays that it is not in relation to him. He slips past, a rat in a viper pit, the congregated staring at him hungrily but unsure if he is their intended prey. He shows his ID card subtly to reception and is let through the airlock, making his way to Bondi ward, where on arrival he is confronted by Angie, a few health staff, and Lorraine Symons; Chief Executive of the Hospital. He is not surprised that Angie's demeanour is much more sympathetic then that of Lorraine Symons. Behind them all are two unknowns. Plain suits and ties, hiding any humanity they may otherwise present unclothed.

"Where have you been?" Lorraine asks in a predictable farrago of concern and annoyance. Alex explains his absence, says he stayed late when he heard his patient had returned after the incident, overslept. But he is distracted by the unknowns who chatter amongst themselves by Nigel Innes' door.

"Sorry but what exactly is going on?" he asks.

"We tried calling you-" Angie interjects then Lorraine bulldozes into the fray

"It's about Nigel."

"My phone…I left it at home—what about Nigel, what's happened?"

"That we are yet to figure out." Lorraine's voice is ice.

"Alex, Nigel is dead. He was found this morning." Angie says putting Alex out his misery.

Alex reels slightly, smirks in the face of such absurdity.

"Dead? But he was in restraints. He was sedated."

"They're not sure yet how. Cardiac arrest perhaps." Angie takes a deep breath, "But they're not ruling out accidental overdose by staff."

"Which, as you can imagine, puts us in a very serious situation." Alex tries to focus on Loraine as she speaks but the information is difficult to process. Why did he drink so much wine last night?

"Angie tells me the patient was calm and lucid. Was there a reason you felt he needed to be restrained and administered sedatives?"

The trial begins, Alex thinks to himself, feeling the woodpile building below his feet. But he won't go timidly.

"Well considering he had just ripped his neighbour apart, I thought it best not to let him roam around the ward."

"Staff are trained to physically restrain patients are they not, Angie?"

Angie stutters, "Well yes but the risk-"

"I'm only thinking about what the tribunal will say." Lorraine looks over her shoulder at the unknowns, "And the courts."

Police, Alex realises. Of course that's who they are. Their prized possession now eternally silent. No answers will they be able to give the grieving relatives or the voyeuristic mob. They too will want to pin the blame on someone.

"They would like to speak to you, naturally," Lorraine puffs her chest out, "after which I think it's probably best you head home while we figure out what to do."

Already Alex feels the eyes of patient and staff alike scour him for answers he does not have. The medical chart was checked and double checked. If the medication wasn't given as prescribed, then it's the staffs fault surely. Alex makes a note to repeat this mantra to himself until he believes it to be so. How sure was he that he checked the dosages? Was he remembering accurately that he left proper instructions to staff, or simply overlapping past memories of doing this to create a reassuring fantasy?

Lorraine excuses herself to talk to the officers in an effort to introduce them to Alex who wanders over to the reinforced window, peering down at the TV vans and cameras. Angie moves aside him silently.

"It was on the news this morning," she says.

"I didn't see it." He rubs his temple.

"Lucky you managed to get through that crowd."

Alex chuckles, "I'm not famous. Not yet anyway."

"Give it a week." Angie adds and they both smile.

There is a polite cough behind them, and Alex turns to see the detectives standing before him, ready for an audience.

<u>5</u>

Alex uses a back entrance to make his escape. There is still no suggestion that the reporters gathering outside have any idea of his identity or even if they are concerned about his part in the tragedy that has unfolded, but

Lorraine Symons does not want to take any chances. And neither do the detectives. He thanks the caretaker for giving him his freedom via a fire door, fresh air hitting his exhausted face without remorse. Walking to the station he thinks on the detectives' questions. He had been with them for an hour or more. Apprehensive at first, but calming when the line of questioning seemed less focused on if he had been negligent and more on what, if anything Nigel had said regarding motives.

"Did he say why he killed him?" The first had said, adjusting his tie. The eldest of the two, he'd smelt of abrasive aftershave. Square jawed and dark haired, parted to the side. Alex had answered without hesitation. Told them of Nigel's belief that his neighbour was unnatural in some vague sense. Taking note as he spoke of the intense stare from both, thin smiles painted on skin that needed to see more sun. Their clothing, he had noted, also seemed slightly too big for their frames. Not so big as to look like clowns in a circus, but enough, on close proximity, to wonder if they both went to the same inept tailor.

The youngest then took over questioning.

"Did you believe him when he said his neighbour wasn't real?"

"What?" Alex had shook his head. "Of course not."

"Err, I think what we mean is," the eldest interjected, "is that did you think Mr. Innes was being honest with you about his motives or was covering up?" The youngest then nodded. That's exactly what he had meant. He was bald with thin eyebrows covering dots for eyes, his appearance conjuring images of terminal illness in Alex's mind.

Alex had admitted that he did believe that Nigel was genuine, that for whatever reason, Nigel believed his neighbour to be somehow not natural and had taken it upon himself to prove this in the most monstrous way imaginable. But then was quick to add, Nigel did not present as such on first admission so as not to destroy his own reputation and incriminate himself.

"And you believed him?" the youngest asked again. Alex was confused by the question but the eldest dismissed the need to answer with a wave of his hand.

"Did you read his diary?" The eldest had spoken again while correcting his tie before looking at the youngest who flicked his fingers repetitively against the palm of his right hand.

"I didn't know he had a diary."

"It's online," the youngest had said with overflowing enthusiasm but again was cut off by the eldest. Their relationship, their demeanour, was it actually as unusual as Alex thought, or was he overtired from the last eighteen hours? But the more he attempted to shake the feeling the more he focused solely on their mannerisms and the more Nigel's delusions ran wild in his imagination. Every ninety seconds the youngest would flick his fingers on his palm as before. The eldest would readjust his tie after each question and sigh and nod after every answer. Suddenly he found himself asking to see their badges and they presented them as they did when they first met without issue.

"Are you okay?" the eldest had asked, and the tie was slightly repositioned as ever.

"I, err. I'm just tired. As you can imagine it's been a pretty stressful morning."

"We can imagine," the youngest had repeated.

Alex had stared at him and he in turn returned the favour, smiling but distant. He looked down and saw that the note pad in front of the youngest was empty.

They let him go. Said they'd probably need to speak to him again. Details were swapped.

Before he left the room, Alex had turned to them both. "Do you have any thoughts on Nigel's death? I mean are you treating it as suspicious?"

The detectives had looked at each other briefly before the eldest answered. "We'll be looking into it."

"Dr. Pinner," the youngest chirped, "Please don't look at Mr. Innes Diary. The online one. Please."


The air is, while uncaring, still helpful in clearing the fog from Alex's mind as he reaches the train platform. Helping him focus on objective reality. He had heard anecdotes, while studying, of psychiatrists going crazy from exposure to the mad and maybe this was his moment to become an addition to the urban legend. The train arrives and Alex stands his ground while others alight from it en masse. Confirmation bias, he reassures himself as he sits down. He was looking for patterns and thus he found them. He smiles to himself, recycling his medical training that acts as a mental wall to the bellicose thoughts. Apophenia, he thinks to himself; abnormal meaningfulness. The fact that he can identify what he is doing is a relieving indicator that he is not going crazy. Alex reassures himself further by noting that if he looked around the train now, seeking only those wearing glasses, he would be certain that the entire world was losing twenty twenty vision. And so he looks up and scans the other commuters, smiles at the number he counts wearing all manner of spectacles. Then freezes, scans back and holds, dumbfounded. There he is. A different seat on a different train but appearance identical to every day he has ever seen him. Sat the end of the carriage alone. It is the Wise Man.

<u>6</u>

Alex knows what he is doing is beyond reason and yet he can't help himself. Unsure if he is trying to prove Nigel right or wrong and how he will feel from either outcome. It's been an hour and the Wise Man still has not noticed Alex Pinner following him, Alex keeping a cautious distance, feeling the cold sweat of guilt jolt through him at every casual glance directed his way from passers-by. Feeling as if somehow they know he is stalking an old man through the streets. He reflects on the notion of getting caught, how he would explain his preoccupation with a man going about his business to the authorities. So far he had watched him from across two aisles in a chemist, the Wise Man contemplating on a purchase before, with steadfast movement, he grabs his chosen prize and takes it to the self-checkout. Alex examines the aisle to see it containing a smorgasbord of denture cleaners. The ordinariness of it almost brings him to his senses, but Alex persists. From the chemist, the Wise Man walks against the current of pedestrians on the busy street and Alex struggles to maintain his view of him, twice excusing himself to people he knocks into who hardly pay any attention. Suddenly a sharp right and the Wise Man descends a pallid stairwell in a narrow alley, grey with soot and grime from the city's air. Alex sprints a little to make up the space between them, at first thinking he has lost him, a pit of anxiety opening up in his stomach. It soon rescinds though, as Alex catches sight again. The Wise Man has entered a coffee shop, his back to the large window allowing Alex a perfect view of his specimen. The chase simmers here for an hour, Alex buying a coffee and sitting in view of his prey who sits alone with a newspaper and tall clear glass of hot water with a tea bag diffusing within. Alex wonders what looking natural actually looks like, begins to worry that he is obvious somehow, but when he tries to take a sip of the coffee in front of him, he only panics himself. That in the split second his attention is elsewhere, the Wise Man could cast some silent conjuration and spirit himself away. He tries then instead, to sip the coffee without averting his eyes and is successful but for the odd dribble which he wipes. The slowing of the chase gives Alex time to think again on the absurdity of his actions, but he can't help feeling a little exhilarated also. Wondering how many people did a similar thing every day. Selecting random strangers to follow and observe for some form of morbid fulfilment. Pathological people no doubt. He lifts his coffee once more but as he does the Wise Man rises sharply, as if a pin has been placed on his seat. The suddenness nearly makes Alex drop his beverage. With a purpose only Alex notices, the Wise Man exits, his tea half drunk, the speed of his departure so unexpected that Alex struggles to shuffle his way out of the booth he has settled in. And so the game begins again, this time going with the herd back toward the underground station, boarding a train heading west towards the suburbs and Alex's home. The carriage is silent as they travel and Alex becomes more lackadaisical with his espionage, staring straight ahead at the Wise Man, trying to pick up on any visual twitches or repetitive movements but all he does is blow his nose with a vibrantly coloured handkerchief that matches his waistcoat in a garish sort of way. Soon the train halts at Alex's usual spot. The point to end this is here but he is unwavering. The doors close as quickly as they opened, sealing him into his mission.

Ten minutes later the Wise Man alights at a leafy station basking in sunlight. He walks deeper and deeper into the small hamlet that the station caters for. A pretty place, Alex notes, serene and clearly occupied by the wealthy judging by the detached houses and Mercedes' on silent guard outside them. He had not considered the Wise Man being of such fiscal stature but given his dress sense perhaps he was a retired man of the arts. It was reassuring, Alex thinks, as the Wise Man turns into a small garden that leads to a quaint thatched cottage, to see this figure he has obsessed over for the past two hours return to a normal suburban environment. He could now return home himself to get some much needed rest before seeking some legal guidance on the situation at work. Alex turns to walk away, giving the Wise Man one last casual glance as he enters his house. But the Wise Man does not enter. He simply stands there, occupying the hinterland between his home and the garden. Alex tries to see if he is looking at something. His phone perhaps. But there is nothing in the Wise Man's hand except the plastic bag from the chemist he visited. A fear grips Alex and he steps out from a small crop of trees, steeling himself to approach the Wise Man, but as he moves closer, the Wise Man pivots on his heels and as if reset, begins to walk away from the cottage back through the garden and toward Alex. He freezes, the excuses he has for his borderline criminal behaviour are pathetic and so as the Wise Man reaches him his only defence is a garbled mesh of syllables. But the Wise Man takes no notice, does not even stop to process Alex's presence. Merely continues back through the hamlet and toward station once again. Alex takes a moment before turning to follow suit. The route back is uneventful save a brief stop at a rubbish bin which the Wise Man casually drops his plastic bag and denture cleaner into. When Alex reaches the same bin, he lifts its lid to inspect it. He shudders. It is filled to the brim with denture cleaner and plastic bags from the chemist.

Another hour with the Wise Man and Alex begins to familiarise the pattern, the mental wall of objective reality he had created now well and truly shattered. It is all truly uncanny. The same streets, the same chemist, the same coffee shop, the same sudden surge of energy before heading back to the cottage to stand there momentarily before heading back again to repeat. There was more to the Wise Man's movements for sure, more labyrinthine rambles through a square mile radius and sometimes the pattern of the walk varied. But it was always the same streets and always with the same stops.

Day begins to make way to evening, the sun drowning slowly into the horizon of skyscrapers. Alex confident enough now to not pursue the Wise Man so closely, knowing he will catch up with him without much effort. Instead he focuses on the chemist's staff and the coffee shop's baristas. Asks them if they know him and if he has patronised their stores for some time. But the answers are empty to the point of being unbearable. Most do not know who he is talking about and those that do only have a vague recollection of seeing him in the past week or two. They are unstirred by Alex's impassioned elucidation of how many times he has watched the Wise Man come and go this past evening. His irritation now mixing with his desire for an explanation, Alex decides there is only one course of action.

He has been waiting at the Wise Man's cottage for an hour. He had thought his timing was near perfect but the delay in his arrival had proven otherwise. Despite the sunny day it has turned into a blustery night. A light rain causing the sharp smell of ozone to permeate the air. Alex stands in darkness, the shadow of the cottage obscuring him from the streetlamps. He holds his arms tight across his chest to keep the warmth in. He knows how he looks but he no longer cares and as the Wise Man finally begins to make his way to his home and through his garden Alex emerges, his face glassy from rainwater. The Wise Man stops in his tracks, looks Alex up and down and then smiles.

"Do I know you?"

Alex scoffs, "You've seen me around. I've certainly seen you."

The Wise Man nods, moves out of the way but Alex counters.

"Can I help you?" the Wise Man is calm which scares and angers Alex equally.

"What's in the bag?" Alex asks, a shivering finger pointing at the chemist bag.

"Oh just some-"

"Denture cleaner, yes I know." Alex snaps "What was wrong with the other five you bought today?"

The Wise Man tilts his head "The other five?"

"By the looks of things, you've had at least thirty bags worth."

The Wise Man pauses, looks at his bag and smiles, "I'm sorry I don't know what you're referring to."

Alex's finger now points at the Wise Man's round nose. "Don't play coy, I've watched you all fucking day go in and out of the same shops. In and out of the same café. In and out in and out like a…a…like I don't know what. But I want to know." He composes himself, "So…tell me…what exactly is going on?"

The Wise Man's voice quivers. "Honestly, I don't know what you're talking about, but you are beginning to scare me."

The implication of Alex being the threat stirs even more animosity. Even more determination to get to the bottom of this. His finger now points to the cottage.

"If I scare you then take your key and go home. Go on, open up and call the police."

The Wise Man shifts his weight but does not move. Alex smiles.

"Exactly. You won't because you can't go in there." His confidence boiling over, he pushes the Wise Man aside. "I, however, can."

The Wise Man protests, grabs Alex by the shoulder. A scuffle erupts. Petty in its appearance but both parties sincere in their determination. Both seem at a stalemate until Alex lets fly a hard elbow which hits the Wise Man in the gut. He collapses to the ground. Alex moves to the front door, reaches for the handle but stops. He is distracted by the whimpering of the Wise Man. Realisation sets in that he has just assaulted an old man. Possibly one that suffers from OCD. Alex approaches the Wise Man, begins to reach out to reassure him but the whimper turns quickly into a low-pitched moan before spasms ripple through his body. Alex grabs him as convulsions turn into a full seizure, reaching for a mobile phone that he remembers with profanity is still at home. He thinks in a panic, worrying three deaths may be on his conscience now, and reaches into the Wise Man's waistcoat to check in case he has a phone. As he does so, the seizure stops and Alex worries he is too late, the coldness of the body making him think that he has already passed. But as he moves his hand away it is grabbed by the Wise Man tightly round the wrist. His eyes flick open and he stares at Alex before beginning to snigger. Alex asks if he is okay, but the response is more bemusement, now evolved into a full-blown belly laugh. Alex squirms in the grip of the Wise Man, eventually prying himself free with enough force that he falls backwards. The Wise Man closes the gap between them, still laughing and Alex begins to walk away. Slowly at first but with increasing speed as confusion makes way for sheer terror. Before long he is running, the laughter from the Wise Man fading in the distance. A train is at the station and Alex tumbles into the carriage as its doors close. His fear does not subside until he reaches home where he sits curled in a ball in pitch blackness, the sound of the Wise Man's laugh echoing through his mind.

Slowly he gathers enough courage to collect his misplaced phone from the sofa. It is low on battery but still usable, dozens of missed calls and text notifications cluttering the top of the screen. He types Nigel Innes' name in hope of finding his blog or diary, but all he discovers are search results that lead to a URL that has been deleted. By whom he dreads to think. His phone blinks out of life, its battery dead and he is left to process the day. Alex pictures the Wise Man still laughing at the entrance of his cottage. At Alex's failed attempts to expose what was happening. Deciding to forego his previous nickname for the old man, Alex settles on something now more appropriate. He christens him the Trickster.

<u>7</u>

Three months have passed. Three months since Nigel was found dead. Since Alex Pinner had been suspended from work. Since he had confronted the Trickster. His time waiting for the tribunal and the trial of the facts spent either at home trying to piece together what resonances of Nigel's blog remained online and returning to his commute, following others in the absence of the Trickster who now seemingly had disappeared. But his stalking of new subjects yields no results. And online the only thing found are short paragraphs of example text below links that lead to *404 page not found*. Paragraphs that spoke confusingly of Hell or extra-terrestrial experiments. Flying wildly from one topic to the other though never enough of the script was shown to create a coherent context. Thus with stimuli waning, Alex began to think on more pertinent matters. Sought professional legal help for the trial and tribunal, paid large sums to experts in medical law and was rewarded unceremoniously with a clear of any wrongdoing. Nigel Innes was not presenting as psychotic at the time of his first admission and there was no way of knowing he would go out and kill someone. As for Nigel Innes' death, a review of policy and procedure was called for, and a few heads rolled. Front line staff that could be easily replaced. Nigel Innes had no family so there was no risk of compensation. In short Alex had been removed from the pyre.

But normalcy was still far from him. He had not been to the gym in twelve weeks, his perfect body bulging slightly with imperfect fat and weakening muscle. If Margot had noticed or objected, she had kept it to herself. Indeed they had spent little time together despite Alex's abundance of it. The three months allowing the notion that he was in a loveless relationship to germinate.

But now exonerated, it is only a matter of time before he is called back to work, to earn money again to pay for organic food, for his perfect house and to repair his eroding body. Purpose begins to take shape in his mind again and he slips quickly back into his routine, ready for his return to the real world. To celebrate, he sits with Margot at the kitchen table for dinner, a meal he has prepared. She congratulates him on his rebounding strength of body and mind. And after a few glasses of wine reminds him that this is their usual date night, so they retire to the bedroom early. Alex wakes at the usual time for his morning jog with Margot already up and dressing for her exercise regime. He bends forward to escape the bed, but its softness and warmth entraps him. He's got used to the laid back existence and the thought of returning to the laborious formula of before is tiring in itself. One last lie in, he concludes, before tomorrow, getting back on track with complete conviction. His eyes droop as he drifts off, explaining himself to Margot who does not respond.

He sleeps deeper than he intends, waking an hour later. Stretching his body in an effort to push the sleep from him he notes his urgent need to urinate and so heads to the bathroom. Once relieved, Alex staggers down the stairs toward the kitchen, hearing Margot preparing breakfast. There is the faint sound of conversation and he wonders who could be calling her at such an hour. Yet when Alex turns into the kitchen he sees Margot stood looking out of the window, her mobile phone on the table a few feet away. She is distracted and takes a moment to notice his presence.

"Everything alright?" Alex asks and she responds matter-of-factly. Why shouldn't it be?

"Who were you talking to?" Alex sits down while watching her, carefully pouring a glass of fresh orange juice. But Margot does not know how to respond. She was not talking to anyone.

Alex processes her response and concludes: "I must have been hearing things." And returns his attention to breakfast. Margot laughs and moves the conversation to light meaninglessness to which Alex responds in kind until she makes her way to the hallway and onward to work, stopping only to kiss Alex goodbye. He returns the affection, then holds her close. Longer than normal until she starts to squirm.

"Stay with me today?" Alex pleads. She strokes his hair while prying herself from him. Repeats that she has to go to work. Alex nods and gives up his wife, watching her leave the room. And then, as the front door clicks back into place, he is up from the table, racing to the bedroom for his car keys and shoes.

It's been about an hour now, the time it normally takes Margot to arrive at work. At least that's what Alex had always thought. But instead of arriving at her employment he has followed her down one random road after another, snaking her way through residential streets in what feels like a hexagonal pattern on repeat. Though there are tears welling in Alex's eyes it is not of any sense of loss or betrayal, not completely anyway. Rather a sense of validation and fear. He considered the idea that Margot was having an affair and that she was aware of him following her and so was leading him on a merry dance to spite him. Despite himself, he found that the notion disappointed him. Such a pedestrian circumstance flying in the face of his discoveries.

Margot turns onto a roundabout as she has done ten times already today, Alex not far behind, instinct taking over his driving, he knows that she will take the third exit back toward home before starting the journey all over again. But this time is different. This time quite suddenly she takes the first exit and off onto the duel carriageway. Alex careers across two lanes to pursue, an accident barely missed. His departure hailed with a cacophony of car horns.

The carriageway leads into the main artery of a motorway and Alex continues his pursuit until after about twenty minutes Margot signals to turn off into a junction. Alex easily replicates the move. From there it is a main road followed by smaller and smaller ones until finally Alex finds he and Margot are the only vehicles on a country lane, surrounded by green hedges that obscure the horizon, closing him in. He begins to fear an ambush but from who or what he cannot say. Then Margot turns with the road and out of view for a moment until Alex reaches the same corner though he does not need to pursue any further. Margot has stopped and Alex stares dumbfounded.

Ahead of him a small bullring road, mud as opposed to tarmac. There Margot sits idling in her car staring out into the fields around her. But she is not alone. Alex exits his car and walks toward her, the last of several cars all doing the exact same thing. All parked in the same direction and all with one occupant staring dead ahead in the middle distance. Young, old, man, woman all manner and variety of person are presented. They take no notice of Alex as he walks amongst them, still donned in pyjamas and dressing gown, peering into their cars, half crazed. Eventually his courage builds to knock on one of the passenger windows but there is no response from the man inside. A dark-skinned youth with short cropped hair and well-cut suit. And so, Alex turns to Margot, kneeling at her window and talking softly to her.

"Margot, it's me. What's going on?" He wonders if he is heard at all and so tries to open the door, but it is locked.

"Margot!" he shouts now but there is still nothing. "Margot, what the hell is happening here?"

An engine bursts into life at the front of the herd, and the others follow suit. As the convoy rolls out, Alex shouts and bangs on Margot's window, but it is useless. At the end of the road the convoy separates, the congregated presumably returning to wherever they came from. Alex stands in the middle of the turning as he watches Margot, the last in the group, return to the country road and drive out of view.

## 8

It is four pm and Alex Pinner has returned to the Trickster's cottage. There is no response when he knocks at the door and peering through the window reveals nothing but a dark void. Repercussions have no weight now and so Alex takes a rock from the garden and smashes it against the window. It takes some effort, the first three times the rock simply bouncing back onto the ground. But eventually it shatters and as it does so a warm gust of air bellows from within.

The fact that Alex cuts himself on the shards of glass is irrelevant to him. He is more concerned with the contents of the building or rather the lack thereof. The house is empty. A rational part of his mind fails to convince him that the Trickster may have simply moved to a new house. If the last few months had taught him anything it was that the simplest explanation rarely held up to scrutiny anymore. The desolate nature of the cottage's innards make it easier for Alex to focus on the warm wind emanating from within, the only thing of any notice. And so he follows it, rolling as it does out from the hallway and kitchen where, next to a gas cooker, a door whistles from the gap at its base. Alex opens it and the wind becomes a blast, a comfortable warmth as opposed to stifling, but definitely getting warmer as he descends the stairs into the cellar.

Empty wine bottles collect cobwebs and dust which sway in the wind. Alex continues to follow, extricating a wooden crate from the source of the wind to reveal a tunnel seemingly dug by hand into the soft gravel. It is around a foot in diameter and descends sharply into darkness. Alex takes a moment to think about his next course of action. He could simply walk away. Have a normal life and return to work. Maintain the status quo and keep up the routine. It dawns on him then that a part of this routine would be Margot and he realises then that there is nothing normal to return to, no life to reclaim before this revelation. There is no debate in the matter any longer. Alex crawls headlong into the hole.

The tunnel soon becomes larger, allowing Alex to crouch and then walk fully upright while the soil changes from the gravel near its entrance to a softer more clay like substance. The surrounding temperature is constant, becoming more humid the further Alex travels. Until at last he reaches what appears to be a central point, a vibrant white light casting a central chamber in illumination, revealing countless tunnels all surrounding a circular chasm that from its centre, emanates a dull industrial hum.

It is almost too much for Alex to contemplate and he wonders how many of the tunnels he can see lead to homes of people he knows. Was Margot always the way he witnessed her today or had she been replaced? Was there a tunnel under his home? Or Nigel Innes' neighbour? Even Nigel himself?

He could not be sure of anything or anyone now, except of course himself. Throughout this whole ordeal he concludes, unaware of the presence behind him, his own faculties have prevailed.

He is not mad, Alex realises, as a blow from behind brings him to his knees. He is not mad, and neither was Nigel Innes. Alex Pinner had been right to release him. He smiles before fading out of consciousness. His integrity and his sanity remaining intact to the very end.

## Clark Roberts'
## Shopping List

4-6 pound braided fishing line
Cheap spinner lures
2 dozen crawlers
Aberdeen hooks
Mosquito dope
Fishing forceps
Dynamite (in case the spinners or nightcrawlers aren't effective)
1 package of chocolate Zinger cake snacks
Pint of The Fat Trout Scotch Whisky

# Craftsmanship for Food
## *Clark Roberts*

*ood God,* Gary Jennings thought as he hustled to his car, *I can't get away from this place fast enough.* He'd spent an extra hour at the dealership crunching numbers, trying to persuade a customer into one of the new cars displayed in the front lot.

It was written on the woman's face when they shook hands that she would be buying elsewhere.

If only he could sell his writing, just get a foot in the door in the publishing business, maybe life wouldn't seem so unbearable. Maybe the ball would get rolling for him. Even if he never made it big-time, so what? He could keep working jobs he didn't care about. He'd been doing it his whole life. If published, he'd be able to celebrate accomplishing the one goal in life he was bent on becoming reality.

Of course the possibility of striking gold lingered in the stretches of his mind. That would be the life. Novels, cocktail parties, and women. Heck, with a flourishing career as a novelist he might even find a woman suitable for marriage.

He glanced at the clock—six-thirty. Of course he was in a pissy mood. He'd wasted an extra hour at work, an hour he could've spent drumming his mind for magical words and phrases.

As he turned onto the expressway ramp, he noticed a man dressed in rags with a sign propped against his legs. Scrawled and colored in with dark marker, the crude yet bold penmanship read, *Craftsmanship for food.* Jennings had seen the man there yesterday, slumped on his ass in the same tired posture with the same sleepy face.

This time, when Jennings passed the man, they made eye contact. Jennings instantly felt downright deplorable for the pity-party he always threw for himself over his job and not being able to achieve some otherworldly goal. At least he'd always had a steady income.

On impulse, Jennings slowed the car down, pulling over to the side as a couple commuters sped past. He wasn't sure how many days the bum would be out there in the heat begging for work, but Jennings knew he couldn't just drive by ignoring him every day. After all, the man was a real life representation of the types of characters Jennings so desperately tried to portray in his stories. Besides, Jennings liked how the sign was written.

*Craftsmanship for food.*

At least it didn't read, *Will work for food.* That phrase was so tired, so overused, so banal.

*Craftsmanship for food.*

The phrase was tight, to the point, and about as original as a sign begging for a handout could be.

Jennings waited as another car hummed past; he then backed up to the stranger. The stranger idly watched as Jennings leaned over while thrusting open the passenger side door.

The stranger hid any excitement or gratitude behind a poker face.

"Come on, hop in," Jennings invited. He took off his sunglasses and flashed a huge grin. "I think I can help you."

"What do you have in mind?" the stranger asked.

"Umm, I don't know really, but I'm sure I can find some kind of work for you to do. Clean my apartment maybe."

The stranger coiled his face in disgust. "You people are all the same. Read the sign again, Asshole. *Craftsmanship for food.* It doesn't say I need charity, or that I want to be a pet monkey."

"Come on, man. I'm just trying to help you out."

"Yeah, and maybe when I'm done changing your toilet paper roll, I can clean your ass too, but that would mean wiping away that shit eating grin." The stranger's face dared Jennings to make another offer.

"Sorry," Jennings mumbled, more than a little bewildered. "I didn't mean anything by saying...anything." Mentally, Jennings kicked himself for sounding so stupid.

"Piss off!"

That was tight and to the point, not very original, but definitely concise.

Jennings opened his mouth to say something but found he was lost for words. He swung the door shut and drove home.

***

Jennings cried himself to sleep that night. Not over the confrontation with the man, but because nothing had gone right with the story he was currently drafting. He'd studied the first few pages, analyzing them, trying to pinpoint why exactly the pieces weren't fitting snuggly together with the tale he was trying to weave. After only a half-hour he pushed away from the computer screen cursing and throwing papers. Nothing could be done to save the story. It was doomed, sentenced to the half-finished, half-imagined vault of his mind.

He broke down in the shower, curling himself into a knot of limbs while the water pelted his bare skin. This was how professional authors behaved—wasn't it?

Yes, of course people with artistic minds behaved in this manner—didn't they?

Or did they go so far as to bleed their stories out?

Eventually, still passing tears, he got out of the shower and went to bed naked and wet.

***

He traipsed through work the next day, meddling only with the customers he knew had already been helped and avoiding those with questioning faces.

The times he did talk to a customer, he used a surplus of adjectives, big fifty-cent words without knowing their full meaning. Alabaster. Albescent. Using this type of vocabulary on a daily basis would strengthen his writing. An insane thought, still, he'd arrived at the conclusion that this very well might be the last method of self-training to help his cause.

Another day droned by, and Jennings made no sales. Mr. Johnson called him into the back office at the end of the day. Johnson told him he'd better get his act together—*a salesman is supposed to sell.*

*Writers are supposed to write,* Jennings thought, but bit his tongue and complacently nodded.

On the way home he stopped at a fast food joint to pick up dinner. There was no time to cook at home. All attention had to be given to the craft.

*Craftsmanship for food!*

Jennings prayed the bum would be at the onramp again today, hopefully looking shabbier, hungrier than the day before and more willing to bargain.

Yes, the man was there.

He was standing instead of sitting, as if expecting Jennings's arrival. The sign was propped against his shins. Jennings didn't drive by him but wheeled his car in frantically. The man stood stock still, looking down curiously at the nose of the car only inches away from his legs. Jennings rolled down his window.

"Hey!"

"Hello, Asshole," the stranger said.

"Get in the car. I've got an offer you can't refuse."

Now he sounded like a salesman.

Amazingly, the bum did not retort. He simply folded the cardboard sign in half before dropping into Jennings's car.

"Listen," Jennings said, pulling the car back onto the ramp. He ignored the honking from the traffic behind him. "I'm trying to become a published writer. I like your style. I don't know why you live the way you do, but you seem intelligent, and more than anything I like your style." He cursed himself for sounding so redundant. "Your sign, I mean. I like the style of phrase there. *Craftsmanship for food.* That style...that...that voice. I really like it. I like the style of that voice you used on the sign."

"Get to the point, Asshole."

Jennings cleared his throat. "I want you to edit my writing. I'm not sure why I think you'll be able to do it, but there's just something about you I can't describe, can't quite put into words. I guess it's the style of that sign. I can just hear a voice when I read it. It's got—oh I don't know what it is—*style* man. Style is the best I can do."

"I think we can come to some kind of agreement."

"Great!" Jennings said. "This might work out just great. By the way, I really am sorry about yesterday. I certainly didn't mean to insult you in any way. What's your name anyhow?" Jennings freed a hand from the steering wheel and extended it out.

"Jennings," the bum said. "Gary Jennings and I'm a cannibal."

The man leaned over to spit on the floor as if this were a practiced custom after shaking hands.

They rode to the apartment in mostly silence.

The stranger sat with a smug smile covered by his wildly unkempt beard. Humming, the bum twiddled his thumbs.

***

"I don't know what's going on here, but your name can't be Gary Jennings. I mean, *I'm* Gary Jennings." Jennings stood in bafflement as the stranger strode into his apartment not bothering to remove his dirt-caked shoes.

Paying no attention to Jennings, the man headed straight to the kitchen, pulled a glass out of the cupboard, and drew water from the tap. He took a long drink, gulping nearly half the glass down in one giant swallow. Jennings feared the man might actually eat the glass.

Why had he let this man into his home? Why had he even bothered to try and help the man? Had he heard the man correctly when he'd said he was a cannibal?

The man went right past Jennings to sit on the couch. He propped his feet onto Jennings's hand-me-down coffee table and flicked on the television. A cold sweat broke out on the back of Jennings's neck. His hands began to shake. He had to show some authority here. He couldn't allow a stranger—a bum of all things—to act like he owned the place.

"Hey buddy," Jennings intoned while trying to sound authoritative; yet his voice rattled with nerves.

"What, Asshole?" The stranger turned; his expression frozen as a winter gravesite.

"First of all, quit calling me an asshole."

"Asshole! Asshole! Asshole!"

"Get out of here!" Jennings roared. He pointed towards the door as if sending an impudent child to bed without dinner. "Leave! Leave at once!"

"Is that really the best you can express yourself?" The man stood. He placed a sympathetic hand on Jennings's shoulder. "No wonder you can't get published, Asshole."

The man strode away taking his invasion of the apartment even farther.

*Call the cops,* Jennings thought. *They'll come and throw this piece of shit out, probably haul him off to jail. Cops enjoy kicking this kind of person around.*

Then Jennings heard the familiar sound of his computer booting up. He ran for the spare bedroom where he attempted to write every night.

The stranger was sitting in front of the monitor, looking as patient as a nesting turtle.

The stranger canted his head to the side to spit on the floor.

"Don't do that. Stop spitting all over the place," Jennings pleaded.

The stranger spit again. "Shut up, Asshole."

"Who the heck do you think you are?"

"Jennings. Gary Jennings, and I'm a cannibal."

"You're not Gary Jennings! I'm Gary Jennings! You're nothing but a bum!"

The stranger's hand clicked on the mouse. The word processor opened on screen. He began diligently typing. There was deftness in the manner the man's fingers worked, gliding over the keys, barely pressing on them. He never once glanced down at his hands. From time to time he would pause to spit. The current of anger in Jennings ceased as he watched with his mouth agape.

"Listen up, Asshole." Typing at a mind-boggling pace, the man's attention didn't stray from the screen. "This is how it's going to work. I write. You leave. Jesus, Asshole, don't you know the first thing about this craft? It isn't easy. You have to let a man write in peace. Now go fix some dinner. I haven't fed in nights."

The man was a lunatic, an absolute lunatic. Jennings couldn't imagine why on Earth he'd thought to help out this bum. He'd let a total stranger into his home. He'd let the man invade his life.

"Didn't you hear me, Asshole? Believe it or not, I can get extremely agitated. I suggest you find me something to eat."

Now the man did stop to look up at Jennings. He grinned. For the first time Jennings noticed that every single tooth came to a point, as if they'd been sharpened with a steel file.

Jennings stepped out of the room shutting the door behind him. He went to the kitchen to cook a dinner.

Spaghetti.

*** 

"Here it is, Asshole." The stranger plopped a thick bundle of papers onto the kitchen table. "Your first story that will get published. I'll send it out tomorrow. You should probably read it just so you know the basic plot if any editors have questions."

The man sat down and heaped a large portion of noodles on a plate. He smothered them in a thin sauce with meatballs.

Jennings picked up the manuscript. Judging by its thickness it was about fifty pages deep. Jennings's name and address were at the top of the first page. The title read *Running with Rabid Dogs*. The corners were marred with dirt where the stranger had handled them.

"You got all this done in under two hours?" Jennings asked, digging a red pen from a drawer.

"Yes. You can put the pen down. It doesn't need editing." The stranger stabbed a meatball and took it right off the knife with his mouth. He chewed and then spat it out. "I thought we had a deal."

"Huh?" Jennings looked up from the story.

"Our deal. *Craftsmanship for food.* Remember? I'm a cannibal." Red sauce dripped down the man's beard, and of course, Jennings remembered. "Maybe I'll take your story back. How would you like that?"

"No!" Jennings cradled the pages to his chest. "Please don't do that."

In a flash the knife was an inch away from Jennings's eye, the point of it promising unrelenting pain.

"Tomorrow night you feed me better, or else I start finding my own meal around this place. I won't have to search far."

"Yes," Jennings trembled.

"Yes, what?"

"Yes, sir."

The knife dropped away from Jennings's sight. The fear was so strong he thought he might retch over the table.

"Good. Go ahead and read your story. It's good."

It was good, better than good. The man was some kind of deity of the craft. Just two pages into the story Jennings found himself enthralled by the simplicity of the writing as words and phrases coalesced drawing out perfect sentences, perfect paragraphs. He was too deep into the story to feel any jealousy towards the man sitting next to him. The action of the story was fast, happening in flashes. The dialogue minimal but absolutely essential and effective. There was just the perfect amount of imagery, painting a background to allow the reader to fill in the details with his or her own experiences.

Emotionally it packed a punch; there was love and love lost, pain and sorrow, and in the end, a hint of redemption as the protagonist's soul bled out, whether to heaven or a dark nothing was left for the reader to contemplate.

Jennings was lost to reality. He finished reading in what seemed five minutes, but when he shook his attention from the imaginary world, the clock on the wall indicated an hour had passed.

The seat next to him was empty. The shower was running.

After the shower turned off the stranger stayed in the bathroom for an impossibly long time. When he came out, he was naked and clean-shaven. The resemblance was undeniable—the muscle-build, the facial features, even the birthmark on the man's back shoulder. How had Jennings not before recognized this man as his doppelganger?

"What did you shave with?" It was all Jennings could think to ask.

"My razor of course. I keep it in the medicine cabinet."

"That's mine!"

The stranger smiled, a second time flashing his predatory teeth. "Your story, it's good isn't it?"

"Yes."

"I'm glad you like it. No small market publishing, it deserves much more. Goodnight, Asshole."

The stranger spit on the floor once more and left the room.

Jennings ran to his bedroom, but the stranger was already in bed with the light off.

"I never said you could sleep in my room."

"The story, Asshole. Your first published piece. Go sleep on the couch."

Jennings glared flatly. When the man in his bed ignored him and rolled over, Jennings headed for the couch. The apartment seemed dark and cold.

Jennings stayed awake most of the night listening to his own thoughts. Maybe fame wasn't so far out of reach after all. The story really was that good. It was early morning when he finally nodded off.

***

Someone was shaking him.

"Wake up, Asshole."

Jennings rose out of sleep, his joints complaining and cracking from the awkward, strained positioning he'd been forced into from the restraints of the couch.

Jennings realized he'd never set an alarm clock. He popped his eyes alert and gasped, "What time is it?!"

He'd overslept. For sure Mr. Johnson was going to fire him.

"Relax," the man said. He was dressed in Jennings's best suit. "I still have over an hour before I have to be at the dealership. I'm just getting an early start because I'll be hitchhiking. You're going to need the car today. Remember, I want a solid meal tonight."

"Wait," Jennings said. "I just have one question."

"What?"

"Young or old?"

"Doesn't matter, just make it human." The stranger held up the manuscript. "I'll mail this out today."

He walked out the door, smiling.

To Jennings, it was like watching a happier version of himself leave.

***

Could he do this?

Why not?

He'd already committed murder. The wound on the old man's head had finally stopped bleeding so profusely. If Jennings shifted the neck in the right position more blood would seep out, but it wasn't as messy as he thought it would be. He'd used a hammer, only meaning to knock the man out before toting him home to slice away a muscle or two that would make a good slab of meat. If the man's consciousness came around, the plan was to simply crack him in the head a second time. Then he was going to ditch the old man in a side-alley and make an anonymous call to 911.

Instead, the old man had expelled the weakest, most haunting groan Jennings had ever heard and died in the backseat of the car.

So he'd killed an old man.

Fine.

Could he actually carve him up to cook the meat?

The flesh came away from the bone considerably easier than he'd anticipated. He didn't worry about the blood spilling. The kitchen floor was linoleum, easy to mop up with a little time and elbow grease.

Maybe the meat of a human was actually palatable.

Maybe it was like chicken.

When he was done butchering the legs, he decided to try a thigh for himself. He melted some butter and slapped a slab of meat in the frying pan.

The meat sizzled; juices jumped. A sweet aroma wafted about the apartment.

It didn't taste like chicken, but with some added spices, it was good.

***

When the stranger came home, he told Jennings all about his day. He'd sold three cars and Jack Johnson, not Mr. Johnson, had thought that was just exceptional.

"By the way, I emailed out a copy of the manuscript today. We should be getting an acceptance letter in about three weeks." He said this mildly with the slightest overtone of confidence. He spit on the floor. "We can expect a check for at least five-hundred. Smells good in here, almost like veal. You must've tried some. I like my meat pretty rare. Did you eat it rare?"

"Medium."

"That's fine," the stranger said. "but you're losing all the juices by cooking it that long. I'm going to bang out some more pages. The old noggin is just crammed with ideas. Fry me up some back straps. You did butcher out the back straps didn't you?

"I did."

"Great. Don't overdo mine and hold off on the spices."

Jennings unwrapped a cut of meat he'd stored in the freezer. It was amazing how fast it had frozen. He unthawed it in the microwave.

Jennings cooked the meat along with a baked potato as a side.

The stranger ate dinner without complaint.

***

Gary Jennings woke up the following day feeling fresh, ready to make some more sales. He was silent on his way to the shower so not to wake up his roommate sleeping on the couch. He shaved using *his* razor, pissed in *his* toilet, and brushed his teeth with *his* toothbrush. He took the time to make sure his shirt was tucked in just right and the knot of his tie was nice and snug.

*Have to look sharp to make sales.*

He would let Asshole sleep in today.

Gary Jennings found the couch unoccupied. He wasn't all that surprised as it had been a rough couple of days for Asshole.

There was a note on the end table.

*Dear Mr. Jennings,*

*What happened to me? I killed a man yesterday, an old man. Then I cooked him. I ate part of another human! And—oh God—I liked it.*

*I don't deserve my life. I'm gone. Please don't worry or look for me. Good luck with your future*

*in writing. I killed an old man. Don't look for me.*

There was no signature at the end of the letter, only a damp spot, as if spitting was the perfect closure.

A whistle on his lips, Gary Jennings strolled out of *his* apartment.

*Please don't worry or look for me.*

That part of the letter was almost funny. In time, Asshole would be fine. He just had to learn what it meant to be a starving artist. He'd figure it out eventually.

Once Asshole reached a point where he'd eat almost anything—well, then he'd have some real stories to tell.

# Sergio "ente per ente" PALUMBO's
## Shopping List

Water and other secret peculiar herbs
Smell of roses and some wildflowers
Juice from a legendary fruit
Faeries' remains
Add blood at will…

## Love Perfume

*Sergio "ente per ente" PALUMBO*
*edited by Michele DUTCHER*

There was a wondrous smell of roses and other wildflowers that morning, as the thirty-year-old man named Helweg walked along the arched pathway that crossed through the wooded area. The sun shone high in the sky, there were only a few clouds to the east and all was going well, as usual.

The landscape on the outskirts of town was primarily agricultural, characterized by forests, pastures and meadows, as was the wide garden full of trees and local plants that he attended to every day. There was a lot of work to do but working hard had never made him dejected or worried. There were many tasks the young man needed to accomplish today, and he knew very well how to do them to his best ability.

Things were going along peacefully in Odense during that period, as a matter of fact. Since Denmark had become a constitutional monarchy on June 5th, 1849, a two-chamber parliament had been established and, even though the defeat of 1864 had left deep marks on the Danish national identity, the country had set all the steps in motion to follow a policy of neutrality in Europe. Being one of the oldest cities of Denmark, Odense's name referred to the ancient god of the indigenous Norse mythology, and was the second-largest city in the present-day country.

The city lay close to Odense Fjord on the Odense River, a 25-foot deep canal, dug from 1796 to 1806, that led to the town's harbor from the fjord. The city's main railway station, built in 1865, connected the urban area with Sweden and mainland Europe, thanks to the grand and reliable modern steam ferries that also serviced the two main Danish islands. After being the first town in the entire country to get modern water and gas works in 1853, many industries had quickly started to appear, thus spreading the residential areas south of the river. Iron and metals, textiles, food and beverages had soon become central elements of the city's commercial life.

The city's landmarks were well known: like *Sankt Knuds Kirke* originally dating from 1081–1093; Our Lady's Church, built in the 13th century and restored in 1851–1852; the Odense Palace, built by King Frederick IV, who died there in 1730; and also *Fyns Kunstmuseum* that first opened its doors in 1885—just one year ago—which already held a wide range of works primarily by famous Danish artists. The city had been the birthplace of Hans Christian

Andersen, one of the most famous writers of plays, travelogues, novels, and poems worldwide, who had passed away only 11 years before.

However, all those attractions were very far away from the wide garden of the noteworthy Lauenburg mansion where Helweg worked nowadays. As a matter of fact, all the main cafés and restaurants in town offered excellent cuisine, with fresh produce that was bought directly from a local farmers market, but these were also very distant from his place of employment.

Generally considering itself to be a somewhat forgotten part of the country, in reality, the old city was positioned on Denmark's 'garden island'—as that stretch of land was commonly called. It was packed full of manor houses and castles dating back more than 1000 years, in some cases, and the many well preserved buildings gave you a good glimpse about how life in Odense was lived during the Middle Ages—which was really considerable and made people immediately figure out how beautiful and pleasing the whole region appeared.

Together with the soil composition, the climatic factors were rather variable within Denmark and had an influence on the distribution of plants. Generally the western parts of the country had an Atlantic climate and the eastern parts a Continental one. The common flowers that grew around were *Conostylis Aculeata*, Tassle Flower, Red Helleborine and Danish Orchids. While the famous decorations used as gifts usually were Red Clovers and Roses.

The huge, expensive stone mansion of Mr. Oluf Lauenburg, who was the old proprietor of that place, had been built in 1642 and was endowed with a wondrous yellowish columned porch facing the courtyard - which was typical of such aged rural though costly houses. The garden was within the boundary of the outside of the building, and covered about 15 acres, making it a remarkable feature in a neighborhood whose common lot size was usually measured in feet. Upon its completion, the place had been occupied by many rich farmers before becoming the house of a wealthy merchant. Eventually, having been passed on to many other owners, another rich man, who many said had been born in Norway, showed interest in this pleasant property, turning it into his residence in the late 1800s. He was the one still living there.

The garden itself was really remarkable, full of plants and many trees, even though some portions seemed to be a bit dark and secluded from the main paths that intertwined in the middle of it, given that wide leaves didn't allow the sunlight to reach the ground for most of the day. There were also several kinds of wondrous flowers inside and that meant there was a lot of work to do, of course... Every single flower necessitated its own special care, and that required enough of his time to fill its needs, clearly. For example, he spent several minutes every day attending to the *Conostylis aculeata*, a tufted perennial plant species: it was able to grow between 2 and 20 inches high and produced yellow flowers between August and November in the species' native range. Other than that, a great number of subspecies were recognized, and they all needed the right amount of attention. Other herbaceous plants known as *pualele* required even more care, but he never let some other urgency in the garden prevent him from properly attending to them as well.

Many would consider his job a sort of slow, stupid or regrettable activity that no true man would ever think of choosing for himself, of course. But Helweg didn't think so. On the contrary, it required strength, stubbornness, experience and intelligence. His job allowed him to make a comfortable living and he also liked it, which wasn't exactly what other workers might say about their occupations. As the 1880s had seen the culmination of emigration abroad, he still considered himself a pretty lucky man as he had decided to remain in his own country and he had also found a good job, as his abilities as gardener were well known around town.

Day in and day out things went well though a bit slow, and nothing seemed to change, which was good. As a matter of fact, his love life was almost non-existent, and it didn't appear that it would change any time soon—in spite of what he hoped for in his heart. That part of his life wasn't what he was fondest of, indeed, but there was very little he could do about it. He didn't know if his lack of a love life was because he simply didn't appear attractive to women or if it was because of his character, perhaps. After all, he was tall, still young, fair-haired and well-muscled, with two deep green eyes—a typical Nordic type of man, even though not too handsome, in his case…

However, all of his good qualities hadn't proved to be enough; at least it hadn't so far. That was why, after his duties were done, he spent his nights in a corner of a local pub drinking beer and sipping wine—even though he didn't stay too long before getting home to sleep, as he had to wake up early every morning to start gardening again. But he didn't complain too much about all that, despite his worries and a sort of sadness he felt in his heart, of course.

*And then one evening everything changed.* It was an unexpected occurrence and it happened only by chance.

It all started that day the old man who owned the mansion asked the gardener to cut back a few plants that stood in the farthest part of the garden, as the proprietor had told him that he had noticed too many leaves on the ground the night before. It was already early evening and the young man didn't usually remain in the garden so late, but he didn't want to disappoint the owner, anyway, as he relied very much on his appreciation for his livelihood. So, he hurriedly headed for that point and started to remove the remaining leaves and cleaning the small area.

And it was at that moment, when he had completed all the cuts planned, that Helweg spotted something unusual. *Or, at least, he thought he spotted something.*

Next to a curved branch on a young pine tree he noticed a long, moving line. There seemed to be many strange tiny insects in the line, which was not that uncommon after all, but what really left him speechless was the fact that ***they weren't insects at all***. Not, by any means. They all flew in the line and were of all shapes and sizes—tall and short, fat and skinny, so there was really no clear classification among them. Different types of creatures moving together quickly, that was pretty unusual in itself he thought, but they had an even weirder feature: they all looked like tiny humans, more or less, with pointed ears, peculiar deep eyes and delicate though thin traits. Those creatures were really unbelievable! *How was it possible*?

Beyond that, they all wore different jackets: some had on green ones, while others were adorned with red apparel, but most of their clothes were grayish. Nothing appeared to be able to stop their advancing line, as far as he saw, and the man thought he had also heard some laughing and chatting as they kept moving forward while flying in the air.

Still uncertain about what he was seeing, the young man asked himself if these were really those mischievous legendary beings known for playing practical jokes on mortals. While Helweg was considering the various, incredible options, all of a sudden the scene itself ended and all of them immediately disappeared. It was exactly as if those creatures had never been there in reality! ***How wondrous all that had been***…

Helweg was still thoughtful and a little shocked while he walked back to the exit of the garden. He was sure he had not had anything alcoholic to drink that day, *at least not yet*. He would probably have taken all those unanswered questions home with him, not thinking about them until he got home—if he hadn't seen the characteristic graying hair outlining the rough traits of the old proprietor of the mansion. He was standing outside his house and the gardener had thought it better to approach him out of courtesy, in order to take his leave.

"Hello," the old man waved to him, with those dark-chestnut pupils looking towards the gardener. He was endowed with oversized ears, mostly due to his noteworthy age, along with a big, curved hairy nose that made an outstanding display on his hard, wrinkled face. Being much taller than Helweg, although he already was about 80-years-old, his build looked massive. People living around those parts considered him to be a lonely, strange individual who owned a renowned mansion—even though he liked to keep to himself, not frequently going into town. "Did you already complete your job? Great, thanks for your kindness, indeed…"

"Yes, Mr. Lauenburg, all is done, as you requested." The young gardener paused briefly, as if he had something else to say but seemed to be unable to express it in plain words now. "Well, there is another thing…"

"Alright, tell me…did you notice some trees in bad shape or something else that you'll need to do?" the old man asked him with a smirk.

"There's something I would like to ask you, Mr. Lauenburg," Helweg whispered.

"Yes, of course," the other replied. "Just tell me what's the matter?"

"Well, it's only a notion, but I got a very strange impression this evening, before leaving the garden…"

"*That being?*"

"Actually, maybe I was mistaken, certainly I didn't see everything perfectly…" the young man added quickly, as if he really couldn't find the courage to reveal what was on his mind. Then, he eventually decided to go on.

The deep eyes of the old man were staring at him and he was displaying a curious look on his worn-out face.

"I, yes, how can I say this…" the gardener spoke finally. "I think I saw some strange little beings, maybe they were fairies…"

The other didn't appear to be very surprised, which made Helweg even more perplexed. "Good boy, about time! I thought I was the only one around who could see them."

"So, you have also seen them before?" the young man replied in a warm tone.

"Yes, many, many times."

"But…how can this be? I mean, fairies are creatures of legends, *they are not real…*"

"Oh, they are more real you could ever imagine, be sure…" the old proprietor retorted. "Just have a look at the more isolated paths of the garden during the hours before the sun goes down over the course of the next days and you'll see!"

Helweg looked uncertain about what to say.

"Especially in the evening they dare move around, when the flowers are still open, and humans have the chance to see them. It's at that time that you can spot those little creatures in great abundance, my dear gardener…" Lauenburg convincingly nodded.

If he hadn't been told that by the proprietor of the mansion—and if he hadn't seen it for himself—he would never have believed that in this garden, a continuous procession of creatures the size and color of green and grey insects with short wings could really be true. They moved along the more secluded paths of the wooded area right next to the building! And that fact repeated itself more and more during the following days, when the man kept watching and examining the place, much to his growing bewilderment, certainly.

After all the young man saw, many questions were on his worried mind, and he approached the proprietor again one morning to find out more, to be informed about the true nature of those beings. The other man began speaking in a clear voice. "I'll tell you something more about them, if you'd like—since I've learned quite a bit after I discovered them myself. A fairy (sometimes known as a fae) is a supernatural creature that is said to be found only in the legends or mythology of many different cultures. There are many definitions of what constitutes a fairy: usually it appears as a tiny magical creature like a goblin, and at other times it is described as a specific type of being with short wings."

Helweg kept listening to the experienced Lauenburg in silence as the other continued explaining.

"There are many scholars who think the fairy originated in Italy, where they were known as '*Fatae*', stemming from a *Latin* term. They then supposedly traveled to France where their name was corrupted to 'fees' and then to Britain where they were known by means of a word which the population eventually changed into 'faeries'. But they all are wrong, as they originally belonged to the ancient Celtic tradition before all the others and their tales come from oral recounts before they were transmitted into writing. Those beings truly have been around a lot longer than everyone expects, and they look very much like humans at least in shape, even though not in size..."

The gardener opened his eyes wide, being all ears.

"The Norse versions of the fairies were a consequence of the first assaults on the old Viking ships, starting in the early Middle Ages when they began to approach the coastlines of Ireland, Scotland, England and Wales in order to plunder or search for new valuable territories. After those bloody landings, some of those creatures became curious about such newcomers, and they followed those bearded warriors back to their peculiar ships and found themselves at sea before they could ever try to return to their forested areas. So, they traveled along with them until those humans got back to the villages of the Norse countries they had left to go searching for prey and riches, and there they finally settled down. After all, there were many woods, mountains and isolated places in those new cold lands where they could live without ever meeting men again. So things went. The various Elves and the *Dísir* that exist now in the northern traditions are the names that some of those little beings were given from the local people who had never seen anything like that before and that occasionally started stumbling into them at times."

The old proprietor stopped his speech just for a moment, and then added whispering, "But, there's something even more important, and much more useful that a man can get from those little creatures. Maybe, it's a secret that would be of interest to you. First of all, you must find some rare flowers, then you also have to capture one of those little beings; otherwise you will not have what you need for your purposes…"

"What do you mean?" a perplexed Helweg asked the other.

"Alright, I'm going to tell you," he said "Just listen to me…"

And so the young gardener listened closely. He attentively kept staring at the old man and heard in silence what the landowner was revealing to him. Being surprised and uncertain, at first, he finally considered that he had, at least, to see it for himself, according to every sentence he was told.

"Just have a try, Helweg, and then you tell me if I'm right…I think that this is something that you could really find interesting and might please you. I'm already old and I can't turn to such things anymore, but about you...*who knows*?"

The gardener didn't reply. Yes, indeed, that was true, it could be really important to him! Maybe he had only to follow the older man's instructions, and then discover the results for himself. There was no other way of knowing if it would work.

***

Hilkka aappeared to be pleasantly surprised when he invited her into the garden that night, after he had introduced himself and said he wanted to speak with her. In reality, he didn't have much hope when he did so, while walking near her at a small Danish winery called Wessels—a so called *bodega*, with the peculiar taste of an authentic tavern. In that pub, old locals and young hipsters, too, usually sat side by side enjoying cheap beer and bitters. Helweg had never had a lot of luck with his pick-up lines, but he really wanted to test the substance that the proprietor of the mansion had told him to prepare.

The girl's name—Hilkka—came from an old fairy tale, and she really looked wondrous and fantastic to him, so he was already enticed and attracted to her as soon as he saw her sitting in a darkened corner of the venue. There was a vintage, cozy atmosphere in the establishment, which was mixed with the modern and youthful, the walls having been painted in light colors. The wooden bar served traditional

Danish food morning, noon and night—even though it was a place where you could hang out, especially for a nightcap, into the wee small hours of the morning.

Anyway, it seemed that things had started going downhill since the beginning, given the nasty look she had shot his way as his eyes had turned to her beautiful sky blue irises. But things had immediately improved after he had come nearer and the redolence of the perfume he had previously put on his heavy shirt reached her senses. From that moment on, the young woman had begun stroking her own long blonde curls more and more, while her lips frequently opened into a wide warm smile that was inviting Helweg to stay and talk with her. Of course, this pleased the man more and more and made him sure that he had chosen the right move when he had dared to give the potion a try.

She looked around as he led her along the stunning path, full of trees and plants, through the garden where the man usually worked during the day, but he was also nervous, confused and a little afraid. There was no reason to think like that, he told himself, as the substance was functioning perfectly so far, and the night was heading the right direction, undoubtedly, even exceeding expectations...

She excused Helweg for a couple of minutes as he moved away from her briefly, so he could reach the table where he had left the rest of that perfume, in order to sprinkle some more fairy dust on his clothes. He lied to her that he was alright when she asked what he was so concerned about. The fact was that he didn't want to waste any more time during such a wonderful moment, so he simply had to have more confidence about it all. Adding more of that perfume couldn't be inappropriate, after all. Better too much than too little, he considered. *A faint heart, they said, never wins a fair lady* so he persevered, even though he wasn't completely sure that such an old proverb could apply to him, but it didn't matter really.

Probably some other woman would show interest in him or love him eventually—even though most of them had turned him down. However, if they weren't too hesitant, that perfume might simply spin them to be more attracted to him, to be more uninhibited and to open their hearts more freely. After all, if Hilkka could only see his true feelings or know who he really was, she would like him sincerely—*or at least that was what the man told himself.* However, he was probably deceiving himself by thinking that, and swindling her using that secret trick, certainly.

When they were finally alone with each other, his heart almost missed a beat and his mind went blank as never before. Then, she simply went ahead—probably because of that magical redolence that aroused her will, and her mouth brushed against his. Their lips immediately met, and a long passionate kiss followed. Then the two became more and more involved with each other. As their tongues investigated the deep, distant corners of each other's mouths, they became increasingly immersed more and more in their feelings of the moment, and soon things went even better. Hilkka's soft and very capable pale hands expertly unbuttoned the man's shirt, and then she reached round and unclasped his trousers. In return, Helweg started undressing the beautiful slender woman and quickly got wicked as he saw that her breasts had become an easy target for his warm exploring fingers.

After they had extraordinary sex, which had been a very rare occurrence for the man so far, some moments of rest followed, in silence. Their bodies remained on the ground, lying exhausted under the tall trees and the many plants that filled the place and encircled that part of the path in the garden. The dark sky over their heads seemed to be alive thanks to the brilliance of the Milky Way and the gusts of the soft wind of the night that were touching them very gently now.

While the moments went by, Helweg reminded himself of how all that had become finally possible. He well remembered the words of the old proprietor that had told him that day *'First of all, you should capture one of those little beings, otherwise you will not have what you need for your purposes, **that is a fairy's blood**...'* And so the young man had acted accordingly, two days ago.

Imprisoning one of those little winged-beings that resembled a small human-like creature hadn't proven to be a simple task; as such prey wasn't an easy target at all. But if he was able to catch a mouse, he could certainly catch a little fairy, undoubtedly, even if such a creature was able to fly away and was very fast.

In fact, he had accomplished it, thanks to the useful suggestions that Mr. Lauenburg had given him, in the end. And then, you had to get the proper ingredients to make that love perfume he had on his mind since the old man had told him how to create it. The procedure was pretty simple really: you needed those brilliant rare flowers, then you had to put the body of the captured little fairy into a sort of metal lemon squeezer designed to extract juice from fruit that Lauenburg had previously provided him with; and then add the pulp of the unlucky little creature, **along with its blood**— once it was ready—running it through a filter, adding water and other peculiar herbs, in order to attain the desired perfume.

There was no better or more powerful love potion in the entire world, according to the proprietor of the mansion. No woman could resist it or defend herself against such a preparation. And that was exactly what Helweg needed to solve his love problems.

∗∗∗

"I see you are more satisfied and happier today…" Lauenburg had told the gardener the next day, as he met him outside the courtyard of his house.

"I am, really," the other had replied with a smile. "And I owe it all to you, Mr. Lauenburg. If it hadn't been for you, I would never have achieved such happiness…"

"Pleasure is something appropriate for young people like you. How was she?"

"Wondrous, beautiful and passionate. And I plan to meet other local young women over the course of the next few days…"

"Well done, my dear boy, well done!" the old man stated. "Now I'll leave you to work in peace." That being said he moved away in order to go to the entrance of his mansion.

While slowly walking, Oluf Lauenburg thought that everything was going exactly as planned. He reminded himself of the fact that in the past Christian authors had thought that such tiny creatures might be servants of the Devil, and had said that the fairies were actually demons. However, this view was no longer widely shared, and most common people didn't believe it anymore. In reality the local fairies were really cruel devils to beings like him, because the owner of the estate was **a troll** in disguise and trolls had always been hated and attacked by fairies. This had begun far back in history when those beings had first come to the ancient lands where they had been living freely in the forest and in the mountains, occasionally preying upon men and their cattle during the previous ages. So, the trolls and the fairies were natural enemies, of course, and the magical powers they possessed could deeply harm them, even though the fae appeared tiny and weak in comparison with trolls, certainly.

That young man, Helweg, was a gentle soul, and also very good at his job, so the owner had immediately known that he could be of great help to himself as soon as he had first seen him. By living among humans, he had learned how to deal with men and what really motivated them, so he was certain that the gardener might prove very useful if he only explained to him how to take advantage of those fairies by capturing and killing them in the proper way, getting that invaluable substance out of them.

Actually, the members of Mankind had always found their methods to fight against such creatures since the oldest times—the same as they had done when opposing trolls like him, as a matter of fact. The use of iron had turned out to be perfect to hit and wound those magical little beings. Of course, such metal was also harmful to the monsters like him, which was why he himself couldn't turn to it in order to get rid of those fairies…In the ancient ages, the fact that such winged beings were capable of using magical powers against trolls had made the confrontation uneven and unfair in most cases, unfortunately. That was the reason for turning to such a common man at present: he would completely wipe out all of those little creatures for him, doing him a great favor, even though the final goal was meant to remain unbeknownst to Helweg, certainly!

The estate's owner had departed from the lonely snowy northern ranges he was born in many centuries ago, and had started living next to the villages and the towns humans had built all over the country they had created with the passing of the years. The more men moved on to conquer and control new lands, the more those areas became populated, without trees and food, which was just unbearable to creatures like him, so there had been no other way. The ones in his species who hadn't done so or had fought against humans had been killed, as men were far larger in number than the trolls had ever been. Then, Lauenburg had long been forced to get accustomed to human traditions and he had also decided to follow their common way of life, and in doing so he had also thought it was better if he continually removed the greater part of his thick downy hair in order to look more like a man.

The troll had never killed again a citizen or a peasant in the vicinity in order to feed himself, even though it hadn't proven to be easy at first, but he had to restrain himself if he wanted to pretend to be one of those humans and not give rise to suspicions, anyway. Helweg himself looked very tasty to him, ***and his pulsating blood would surely result a very pleasing ingredient for seasoning his carcass***, but the service the young man did for him was much more useful than any enjoyment Lauenburg could ever get out of him if he devoured his succulent body…

Well, he still attacked and ate some sheep or some pigs at times, but he made his best not to be spotted by anyone around, as that was a behavior he was simply unable to get rid of once and for all, you know. The main courses and the food humans commonly prepared and liked were so warm, without blood and sadly so plain—that he needed some much tastier things occasionally to please his mouth and to be more satisfied, certainly.

While moving along, Lauenburg considered that it was funny to think that trolls in many Norse sagas were frequently reputed to be the troubled dead, to be wrestled with or otherwise laid to rest. *Actually, he was still in good health, and he really wished himself the best of luck to live much longer, for several centuries, as only the smartest ones of his species usually did.*

# James H Longmore's
# Shopping List

Soft taco fixins
Rat poison
Large tarp (black/extra heavy-duty)
Hacksaw
Secateurs
Shovel
Flashlight
'D' size batteries

# Bartholomew's Tallboy
## *James H Longmore*

There were rabbit turds all around the front of the tallboy again. They reminded Bartholomew a little of the liquorice torpedoes his grandfather brought over from his frequent trips to London; rounded, black stumpy things that left a decidedly bitter aftertaste in the mouth. Bartholomew had never much cared for that particular candy, although even at the tender age of nine, he was mature enough to know not to say anything to Grandpa Denis, and he'd gleefully pop the multi-coloured sweets in his mouth, one at a time, suck the sugary coating from them, and then discretely spit out the foul tasting, inky black interiors into one of Mom's all too numerous houseplants.

Funny how no one seemed to notice that the *ficus* plants always seemed to thrive and send out countless new shoots following one of Grandpa's visits.

Bartholomew struggled from his bed. It was still early – way too early for a Sunday morning – but his curiosity simply couldn't wait any longer. He stepped gingerly over and around the scattered clusters of droppings – the very last thing he wanted was smooshed rabbit crap between his bare toes – and followed the trail that led quite obviously towards the tallboy.

A peculiar piece of furniture for a pre-teen's bedroom, the tallboy was a battered old thing a good five feet in height and sporting a half dozen warped drawers – three of which were impossible to open, and each one adorned with its original pair of fine, brass handles that rattled when Bartholomew brushed by them. The tallboy had been hewn from oak or maple or some such, back in the bad old days when slavery had been a popular thing; Mom had literally *swooned* over it in the Galveston antiques center and begged Dad to buy it for her.

Unfortunately for Bartholomew, his brother, Benny, had thrown in his *I'm two years older* trump card and had flatly refused to have the thing in his bedroom. He'd actually claimed it was most likely haunted – or at the very least, possessed by evil demons or something similarly hellish.

And so, the antique tallboy had made itself at home in Bartholomew's bedroom, as if the space in there was not already limited as it was.

Dad had promised he'd move it out into his and Mom's room just as soon as he'd done restoring the tatty old thing to its former glory.

That, unfortunately, had been three years ago. Dad had long since moved on to his next Big Project, which was the restoration of a '76 DeLorean that Bartholomew knew full well would never make it out of the twin garage under its own steam, let alone fly out courtesy of *Mr. Fusion.*

"Curious," Bartholomew muttered beneath his breath – he'd recently discovered *Alice* and figured this was a conundrum worthy of Carroll himself – as he tiptoed over to the tallboy, and narrowly dodged a particularly dense clump of rabbit droppings that were difficult to see against the dark brown pile of his carpet.

What made the appearance of rabbit poop – for the fourth morning in a row, no less – all the more confusing for Bartholomew, was that he did not own, nor had he ever owned, a rabbit. And, even if he had, Mom would never have allowed such a creature in the house; she would have condemned the poor thing to a life outside in the brutal Texas heat, and to the mercy of the fire ants whose dirt mounds popped up with alarming frequency all over Dad's precious back lawn. Bartholomew had not said anything to his folks – Mom would just freak out and call in the exterminators and he'd have to share Benny's room for a few days until the poisonous stink died down – he just cleaned up the poops every morning and flushed them down the toilet.

The trail of rabbit droppings wove a seemingly random, yet distinct pattern around Bartholomew's bed. That left him in no doubt at all that whatever had left them had been frolicking around his bed while he slept. The thought sent shivers up and down Bartholomew's spine; what if they'd clambered up onto him in the night and watched him sleep?

What disgusted Bartholomew even more than that, though, was he'd read somewhere rabbits – not rodents, as the common misconception goes, but actually *lagomorphs* – were coprophagic; this meant they ate their own poop. Sure, it was part of the wonder of nature and all of that, and they needed to consume the droppings – white upon their first go around – in order to give their gut bacteria a second chance at digesting all the pesky cellulose that dominated the rabbit's diet, but the very thought of them eating crap next to his sleeping body made Bartholomew want to barf.

As Bartholomew studied the trail, his eyes took him, inevitably, back towards that tallboy. It was fairly obvious the rabbits were heading that way in the night. Therefore, to Bartholomew, it was a sensible conclusion the creatures had actually come from there in the first place.

Which led to yet more riddles. How on earth were they getting around the bulky piece of antique furniture? And just *where* were they coming from?

He'd looked in each of the drawers, of course, or at least those he had managed to get to open. Of the others, Bartholomew had done his level best to prise them open, only to have been cruelly thwarted by Old Father Time and a not inconsiderable amount of damp wood.

Not one to be deterred, Bartholomew jarred open the very bottom drawer and plucked out the jemmy he'd hidden there the evening before. He'd purloined the thing from Dad's overly organized tool chest on wheels that lived in the garage next to the half-dismantled DeLorean.

Setting his determined sights upon the jammed-shut middle drawer of the tallboy – and taking great care not to step in any of the rabbit turds that lay about his feet like some weird kid's discarded marbles – Bartholomew eased the thin edge of the jemmy between the drawer and its warped surrounding, and tiny splinters flaked away to float gently to the carpet. Bartholomew had figured it best to start in the middle; the bottom drawers he'd managed to open had revealed nothing but a few dried-up old mouse turds he figured had been there since well before the Civil War, and the crumbly remnants of the paper drawer linings that had no doubt been there even longer. He reckoned rabbits weren't much at climbing, and since the bottom two drawers had revealed no clue as to the creature's origins, the center drawer seemed like the best place to continue.

Slowly, surely, the jemmy made its way into the small gap it had dug into the hair-thin space between drawer and frame, and provided Bartholomew just the slightest bit of leverage. As gently as he could – Mom would throw a fit if she saw her precious piece of history damaged – Bartholomew gave the jemmy a little weight and was encouraged to see the drawer shift slightly in its housing. Another pull on the cold steel, then another, and the drawer struggled outwards on its corroded old runners with a wet, grating sound.

"Awesome!" Bartholomew allowed himself a little self-congratulation, but remembered to keep his voice down lest he awake his folks and arouse suspicions. Laying the jemmy on the floor, Bartholomew wiggled the tallboy's drawer side to side. He jiggled it out an inch at a time until it jutted as far out as it could go; Bartholomew thought it resembled a huge, wooden tongue poking rudely out at him. Then, gripping the drawer tightly by both sides, Bartholomew gave the thing a sharp yank. He coughed loudly as he did so to disguise the low, scraping growl the warped wood let out as the drawer reluctantly popped from its frame.

Carried by the force of his pulling and the sheer weight of the solid wood drawer, Bartholomew staggered backwards – there was no such thing as *Ikea* flat-pack and laminate back in the good ol' days – and only stopped when the back of his legs hit the soft edge of the bed. Bartholomew sat down hard. The mattress cushioned his descent and the drawer remained clamped between his hands; its wood felt desiccated, yet *sweaty* all at the same time.

And then he saw it.

There.

In his bedroom wall, behind the tallboy.

There was a hole.

Bartholomew rested the drawer carefully on his bed. He wrinkled his nose at the fact that he'd stepped on a couple of bunny poops on his backwards trip between tallboy and bed, and they'd squished themselves to the ball of his left foot like a pair of tiny, black pancakes. He flicked them away with a finger and returned his attention to the large, ragged hole in the drywall, which glowered at him from within the framework of the tallboy.

Beyond the wall, Bartholomew's bedroom shared solid brick with the garage – he'd often hear Dad tinkering and swearing late at night as he worked with growing disinterest on his once-beloved car – and yet there was no sign of that. There was just a thick, murky blackness that seemed to *ooze* around the periphery of the sinister-looking hole.

Studying the hole, Bartholomew figured he'd be able to squeeze through it, should he decide to do so, although just the thought of venturing into the inky darkness beyond made his blood run cold. He also noticed – but chose to ignore the fact – there were no signs of mess; no crumbled-up fragments of drywall, no shreds of the hideously patterned wallpaper his mother had foisted upon him, nothing so much as a splinter of the timber frame that propped up the interior walls of the house. It was as if the hole had been carefully, meticulously dug out from the other side.

Bartholomew stood up from the comfort of his bed and leaned hard against the side of the tallboy. The antique stood firm and refused to budge; the solidness of its old, old wood was impossible to shift given Bartholomew's slight frame. He dug his heels into the carpet, pressed his back squarely against the clammy side of the tallboy, and with an audible grunt, he gave the thing a hearty shove.

It moved.

Just a fraction, but it moved.

"What are you doing in there, Bart?" a muffled voice came through the bedroom door. It was accompanied by Benny's insistent knocking.

"Nothing," Bartholomew hissed. His brother was nothing if not unsubtle, and he was bound to awaken their parents. "Leave me alone."

"Wanna come ride bikes, Bart?" Benny's ready-to-break voice was amplified by the thin wood of Bartholomew's bedroom door.

Bartholomew gritted his teeth to suppress his annoyance. As if attempting to move the damned tallboy wasn't difficult enough, the added annoyance of an older brother constantly desperate to hang out with him was the last thing he needed right now. It crossed Bartholomew's mind to let Benny in, have him add his slightly bulkier weight to the job at hand, but then he'd have to explain why he was attempting to shift the tallboy, *and* show him the mysterious hole that lurked behind it. And besides, Bartholomew *hated* that Benny called him Bart now; it grated on his nerves to be saddled with the same moniker as that spiky-haired loser kid on the cartoon. Some days, Bartholomew actually missed the days his brother used to call him *Squirt*.

"No, I'm still sleeping," Bartholomew whispered as loudly as he dared.

"No, you're not," Benny replied. "If you were, you wouldn't be talking to me." The kid's reasoning was infallible.

"I'm *trying* to sleep," Bartholomew said, "and you're not helping."

There was a pause as Benny no doubt processed his little brother's logic and made the decision to give up – poor Benny had never been the brightest button on the shirt, which was probably how come he'd used to bully Bartholomew mercilessly, back before…

And there was the strangest thing.

Of late, Benny *always* wanted to hang out with Bartholomew, be it riding their bikes around the subdivision until old Mrs. Stanislavski across the street shouted at them to quit and go play in their own yard, tearing up a storm on the PS4, playing Monopoly up in the rickety old treehouse Dad had built before the DeLorean had taken up all of his free time, staying up all night watching old horror movies – the list was seemingly endless. It was all such a far cry from the days when Benny would greet his brother with a solid thump to the bicep or a vicious kick to the shin, or when he'd sneak into his room at night just to drop a loud, rancid fart in Bartholomew's face as he slept. In short, Benny had been a complete little bastard to his younger brother right up until the magic show.

It had been the occasion of Bartholomew's ninth birthday party, a little over two months ago, and Mom and Dad had booked the Great

Suprendo – some cheap, hack magician with a sinister, waxed moustache and the faint reek of stale alcohol about him. He'd performed all of the usual kid's party standards – endless colored handkerchiefs from the billowing sleeves of his oversized cloak, shiny quarters pulled from the ears of Bartholomew and his friends, a rabbit from a top hat, and a couple of doves from the inside of his pants. The birds had flown away the second they tasted freedom, and had disappeared over the rooftops with a look of relief on their little faces.

For his finale, the Great Suprendo had produced a large, black box adorned with glittery stars and lightning flashes that appeared a tad faded and long past its best. The magician revealed the box with a great flourish, whipping away the large, black cloth that had covered it throughout the duration of his act, and Bartholomew thought that it reminded him of an upright coffin.

"I need one volunteer," the Great Suprendo had announced with a smile that Bartholomew guessed hadn't meant to look quite so ominous. He threw open the door to the box to reveal its black interior. "Perhaps the birthday boy?" He smiled down at Bartholomew, and all attention fell in his direction.

Bartholomew shook his head *no*. There was absolutely no way he was getting in that box, birthday boy or otherwise.

"S'up, Squirt, you a pussy or something?" Benny had taunted him with wicked delight in his voice.

"Benjamin!" Mom chastised her eldest with arms folded tight across her ample chest to emphasise her displeasure.

"Sorry, Mom," Benny replied, although he was not one iota sorry at all; he'd learned the power of the p-word just recently at school and had been dying to give it an airing.

"How about you, then, young man?" Suprendo pointed a long, bony finger at Benny. "How's about I make you disappear?"

Benny was up like a shot with that broad, shit-eating grin spread all across his face. He was thrilled to show up his stupid little brother at his own birthday party.

"Make some noise for the young gentleman." The magician incited the small crowd of entranced youngsters, all of whom clapped enthusiastically and cheered for Benny.

The Great Suprendo had Benny step inside the magic box, and to Bartholomew, his brother seemed so incredibly *small* within its grimy, matte black interior. Benny grinned across at his little brother as the magician spun the box around on its little wheels and tapped at its back and sides with his magic wand to *prove* there were no secret trapdoors. He then tip-tapped on the interior to show that there were no false walls or secret compartments either.

"As you can see, there is no possible means of escape," Suprendo's spiel spilled from his mouth as well-rehearsed patter. "Only by magic…"

With that, the magician had slammed the black box's door shut with a flourish, and the entire framework of the thing rattled its protest.

"And now, I need you all to say the magic word with me!" He waved his wand in the air next to the tired old magic box.

*"Abracadabra!"* the little kids shouted out.

"Louder!"

*"ABRACADABRA!"* they screamed at the very tops of their little lungs.

There came a loud bang and a puff of white magic smoke that looked like a baby cloud and had an unpleasant, acrid tang to it, which made all the kids' eyes stream.

A pause.

Suprendo – obviously well-versed in holding the rapture of a young audience – allowed the smoke to clear in silence before throwing open the magic box's door to reveal an interior that was decidedly devoid of Benny.

The little kids erupted in a cacophony of cheers and clapping and raucous whistling – none more so than Bartholomew, who was perhaps a little *too* delighted to see his older brother gone, even if for only a short period of time.

The Great Suprendo spun the box around again. Its casters squeaked loudly. He tapped on all of the plywood walls – inside and out – with his long wand. He made an exaggerated show of studying the inside of the box and then gave his audience that universal arms-wide, *where could he be?* gesture.

"Should I bring him back?" Suprendo asked. He appeared surprised at the lackadaisical response from the kids, none of whom were particularly enamoured with their friend's older brother. "I think I should," Suprendo added, somewhat thrown by the shrugs and pulled faces. He slammed the magic box's door closed once more, spun it around three times, and tapped the side loudly with his wand.

*"Returnilliamus!"* he shouted. The Harry Potter fans in his audience beamed with delight as he flung open the door.

Benny wasn't there.

Bartholomew's mouth dropped open as Suprendo peered inside the magic box and darted about its periphery with an exaggerated look of concern upon his pinched face; it simply did not occur to Bartholomew that this could well be all part of the act.

Suprendo closed the box's door once more, spun it around, and gave it a hearty thump with the wand.

*Bang!*

White magic smoke drifted out across the backyard, mercifully above the heads of the kids this time. Suprendo had them all yell out *Returnilliamus!* as loud as they possibly could, on the pretext that perhaps it hadn't been said loud enough the first time, and thus whipping them all up into an excited frenzy.

"Ta-da!" Suprendo threw open the door to the magic box and pointed his wand inside.

The little kids gasped, none more so than Bartholomew, who, despite his intense dislike of his brother, was beginning to worry.

The box, of course, remained noticeably Benny-less.

The magician made another huge show of looking around the outside of the box, even going so far as to step inside the thing to rap his knuckles upon its inner walls and crouching down to peer through the thin gap at its base – as if Benny could somehow be hiding in a space less than an inch high.

It was difficult for Bartholomew to discern if the look of consternation etched upon Suprendo's face was genuine or not – the guy was clearly one heck of an actor – and the man was just about to close the door to the magic box for the third time when –

"I'm here!"

All the kids turned around with looks of relief upon their shiny, tear-streaked little faces. And there was Benny, standing at the entrance to the treehouse with that dumb-ass grin on his face. "Hey there, Bart!" he called down to his brother with an enthusiastic wave that actually appeared genuine.

And that was pretty much that.

The Great Suprendo earned himself some uproarious applause and a sincere promise from Bartholomew's folks that they would recommend him to all of their friends, *and* give him a mention in the family Xmas newsletter. Benny had clambered down from the treehouse and stuffed his face with birthday cake while the magician packed away his props into a shabby, old black van and disappeared off into the sunset with a surprisingly relieved look on his face.

Of course, everyone wanted to know how Benny had so inexplicably reappeared in the treehouse, but he said he was sworn to secrecy – the magician's code or something – and his lips remained sealed despite the constant cajoling throughout the remainder of Bartholomew's birthday party.

In the days that followed, Bartholomew thought Benny seemed somehow *different*. He'd quit calling him *Squirt*, for starters, and had taken to hanging out with him – he even afforded his little brother a go or two on the Grand Theft Auto game that Mom and Dad didn't know he had – he seemed altogether more considerate and, well, *nice*.

Bartholomew couldn't help but wonder at just what Benny had experienced during the Great Suprendo's illusion that had made him realise just what an absolute shit he'd been to date and mend his ways.

After a while, the fact Benny wasn't quite the same had begun to bug Bartholomew, but when he mentioned it to Mom and Dad, they told him not to be so silly – although he got the impression they saw it too.

*"Hey, Squirt!"*

Bartholomew jumped. The disembodied voice sounded dulled, as if it was coming through a thick cascade of cotton balls. "Go away, Benny," Bartholomew whispered loudly, "I told you, I don't want to ride –"

Bartholomew happened to glance through his bedroom window. A movement caught his eye. Benny rode by on his burgundy *Schwinn*, the playing card he'd jammed in the spokes of the front wheel making a god-awful sound – like the staccato fire of a distant machine gun; there really was no wonder that Mrs. Stanislavski was forever on the kid's case.

*"I'm in here!"*

The voice again. A little louder this time.

Bartholomew looked around, even though he knew he was completely alone in his bedroom, just in case. He squinted at the hole that glowered at him through the exposed innards of the tallboy and cocked his head to one side with a quizzical expression on his face.

"Benny?" he said. "Is that you?" A dumb question, Bartholomew thought to himself, considering the fact his brother was outside kicking up a ruckus on that damn bike of his.

*"Who else would it be, doofus?"* the intangible voice replied, *"Pope Gregory the Third?"*

Bartholomew jumped back as if the tallboy itself had addressed him. Benny had picked up the Pope Gregory line from some show they'd caught on *BBC America* last fall, and it had been a firm favorite ever since. "B-but, you're outside." Bartholomew tried his very best to hide the quiver in his voice.

*"No I'm not, you moron."* Benny's trademark impatience just shone through. *"You gotta help me get out of here, Squirt. They won't let me leave."*

"Where are you?" Bartholomew asked. "They?"

*"I'm in the damn hole, you idiot."* The voice's patience was evaporating. *"And yeah,* They. *I'm not supposed to leave. But I can't stay in here – that's why I dug the stupid hole."*

Bartholomew sat down heavily on his bed and began to wonder if he was actually dreaming all of this. Benny was quite clearly outside, and not in any kind of hole – although he might just end up in one if the cranky old Polish lady across the street caught hold of him – yet Bartholomew was *positive* it was his brother's voice being rude to him from the inky blackness behind the tallboy. "Are you sure it's you, Benny?" He gave his arm a good old pinch to wake himself up. "Ouch!"

*"Of course I'm sure, you Muppet."* There really was no limit to the names Benny loved to call his little brother. *"And quit pinching yourself; you're already awake."*

A knock on the door. Bartholomew all but jumped out of his skin.

"Time to get up!" Mom's voice trilled. "Busy day today!"

"Okay, Mom," Bartholomew groaned, although he *was* grateful to hear her voice; it made for a welcome change from the ghostly one he was conversing with. "I'll be down in two." The rote line escaped his lips without him realizing it, as it did every Sunday morning she woke him early so they could do the family rounds of all the open houses in the district.

Not that they were interested in moving anytime soon. Mom just enjoyed nosing around other people's homes for décor ideas to emulate. It was a hobby that over the years had resulted in her own house resembling an eclectic hotchpotch of wildly differing design ideas. The whole place looked like a sorry amalgam of half-assed efforts from one of those home makeover shows that Mom cluttered up the DVR with.

Still, at least he and Benny got to eat well from the nibbles the real estate agents invariably laid on – if they were lucky they'd hit a full finger buffet or two, and on the odd occasion, sneak a sip at the cheap Champagne that was fairly ubiquitous at such events.

"I gotta go," Bartholomew said to the hole in the wall. He began jiggling the drawer back into its slot in the tallboy and made a mental note to be sure to pick up the rabbit droppings before exiting the room.

*"Open house Sunday?"* the voice said with the slight hint of humor to its tone. *"Now there's one thing I haven't missed."*

"I'll be back later." Bartholomew had begun to feel rather silly talking to a hole in the wall at what he was increasingly convinced was a figment of his own imagination. "We can see about getting you out from…" a white, fluffy shape bobbed by the hole. Bartholomew slammed the drawer shut, and in an instant obscured the pink-eyed rabbit that peeped at him through the dark hole behind the tallboy.

*"Bye, Squirt."* The voice sounded to Bartholomew like it was a thousand miles away.

Outside, Benny rode by on his bike. He offered up a cheery wave to his little brother and sported a warm grin on his face that was shiny and flushed with exertion.

Bartholomew managed a half-smile and waved back.

***

It was already dark when they returned. Mom and Dad had insisted they catch a movie on the way home. Bartholomew hadn't really been in the mood, having felt distracted all day, and the movie had been something unnecessarily loud with dinosaurs in it. Dad had loved dinosaurs since before he was Bartholomew's age and naturally assumed his sons would too. Benny seemed to enjoy the whole cacophonous mess, but ever since Bartholomew had learned dinosaurs were really nothing more than oversized birds, his enthusiasm for the things had waned somewhat.

Bartholomew excused himself the minute they got in. He told his folks he'd eaten way too much popcorn at the theater and didn't have room for the Mac 'n' Cheese Mom was cooking up. Truth was, his stomach was all knotted up at the thought of his bedroom, the tallboy, and the menacing black hole he'd discovered behind it.

The bedroom carpet was mercifully devoid of rabbit poop, but still Bartholomew skirted ever so carefully around the tallboy, as if it were something altogether alien. It looked to be the same tatty piece of furniture he'd left that morning, but somehow it *felt* different to Bartholomew – perhaps knowing what it concealed, and the strange voice that sounded ever so much like Benny was simply creating the illusion in his mind?

Bartholomew waited until everyone was asleep. He kept himself awake by reading through the stack of old comic books he kept stashed beneath his bed. And, as soon as he figured everyone else in the house was asleep, he eased the bottom three drawers from the tallboy to once more expose the dreaded hole, which looked just like a gaping, toothless maw in the half-light of his bedside lamp.

"Hello?" Bartholomew whispered at the hole.

Nothing.

He dropped to his hands and knees and crawled into the framework of the tallboy, taking extra care not to crack his head on the support struts that held the entire thing together. He'd rescued his thin flashlight – a birthday gift from his brother, oddly enough – from the detritus beneath the bed, and was grateful he'd forgotten all about the thing; its AA batteries were still fully functional.

Nearing the hole, Bartholomew clicked on the flashlight and shone the thin, strangled beam directly ahead. The hole swallowed up the light, stopping it dead in its tracks just three or four inches into the gloomy interior. Undeterred, Bartholomew ventured onwards until his fringe brushed against the torn drywall at the top of the hole.

He peered into the darkness. "Hello?" he said again.

A dull, shuffling noise echoed out through the dark. It sounded like tiny feet scampering about on a thick pile carpet. Lots and lots of tiny, pattering feet.

Bartholomew gulped down a deep breath as curiosity outweighed his terror of the lightless void that confronted him. He stuck his head into the hole.

The sun was setting. It was a corpulent, swollen blob of dirty orange on the horizon of the landscape that stretched out beyond the hole; its dying light painted the sky and fat, fluffy clouds a gaudy, smudged salmon color.

Bartholomew pulled his head out from the hole, scuffing an ear on the crumbly drywall. It flaked off onto his neck in miniscule flecks of plaster, like sloughed skin.

From the outside, the hole was a foreboding, lightless void, yet on the inside, Bartholomew had found it almost inviting; a picturesque landscape much like those on the dusty, antique cookie tins Mom had dotted strategically around her kitchen in an attempt to create that authentic farmhouse feel she'd seen on the TV shows.

He slipped the flashlight into his pocket and poked his head into the hole once again. This time he felt a soupcon braver with knowing he wasn't about to crawl into nothingness.

A warm, not entirely unpleasant breeze caressed Bartholomew's face as he shuffled through the hole behind the tallboy, almost as if it was welcoming him to the strange and secret land that dwelled behind the wall. It took a little wriggling and writhing – whomever had gouged the hole in the drywall had little concept of perspective, that much was for certain – but soon Bartholomew found himself somewhere entirely new. He plopped a foot or so down onto a patch of soft, springy grass.

*"Pssttt, over here!"* the now all-too familiar voice called out.

Bartholomew looked around, and was not at all surprised to see his brother sitting upon a car-sized rock just a few strides away from the hole, which from this side appeared to have been gouged out of the moist, peaty dirt of a gently rolling hillside.

"Benny?"

"Hey, Squirt." Benny hopped from the rock and sauntered over to Bartholomew, hands thrust deep in his pockets and that stupid scowl across his dirty chops. "How ya been doing?" Benny delivered a swift kick to his little brother's left shin. The resulting sound was a muted *clunk.*

*"Oww!"* Bartholomew protested. He rubbed the sharp pain away with one hand and propped himself up against the hillside with the other; the grass felt damp and *fleshy* against his palm.

"Missed me?" Benny said with a grin.

"No – err, I mean, yeah, no, I mean –" Bartholomew really had no idea as to what he was meant to say here; *I couldn't miss you because you've been there all along?*

"Walk with me," Benny said. He stepped off the grass and onto a narrow pathway that wound its way as far into the distance as Bartholomew could see. Benny's feet sank a half inch or so into the path, and upon closer inspection, Bartholomew saw it was made entirely of glitter. Tiny puffs of the stuff kicked up around the heels of his grubby high-tops like motes of twinkling dust.

"Where are we going?" Bartholomew asked as he tagged along behind his brother; his mind swam with a bazillion other questions.

"Somewhere." Benny was his usual obtuse self. "Over there." He waved an arm in the general direction of a low escarpment away in the distance and the untidy jumble of large, angular boxes in its shadow.

They walked along in silence, Bartholomew fascinated by the glitter that wafted up and frolicked around his feet, as Benny stalked along the twisting pathway with his shoulders hunched and chin pressed to his chest. A trio of rabbits scampered by. Their tiny eyes twinkled as their noses twitched in Bartholomew's direction. A small flock of birds flew overhead. They were as white as the rabbits, and so low Bartholomew heard the soft *swoosh* of their wings.

"*He* sent me here with that dumb box," Benny finally broke the silence as they neared the mess of boxes and were close enough for Bartholomew to see they were, in fact, small dens. They'd been constructed from cobbled-together boards, which were adorned with tiny stars, crescent moons, and long swirls of silver paint that denoted the tails of innumerable comets. "One minute I was inside and he was doing his crummy magic stuff, the next I was –"

They stopped at the periphery of the small shanty town of battered wooden buildings. There were hundreds, thousands even – each one pretty much the size of Dad's tool shed – clinging to the rolling hillocks beneath the sharp face of the escarpment. The makeshift buildings were arranged in clusters of a dozen or so, each one facing a central bonfire that licked the dusk sky with tall, yellow flames.

"To keep the damn tigers away." Benny said. He studied his brother's face as

Bartholomew stared blankly into the closest fire. "The white ones are the worse."

"Tigers?" Bartholomew winced at the word and peered into the gloom between the rickety buildings. "There's tigers here?"

"Yup," Benny replied with a smug grin. He seemed delighted by his younger sibling's discomfort. "They help keep the rabbit population down, I guess, but they sometimes eat people, too."

"Hi, Benny!" a trill voice called out through the gloom. The boys turned their heads and saw a leggy, statuesque blonde making her way out of one of the buildings. She was so tall she had to stoop her head low to manoeuver out of the squat doorway.

"Oh, hey, Patricia." Benny returned the greeting with a smile.

"Who's your friend?" Patricia made her way towards them. The sequins on her white, low cut leotard glinted orange in the firelight. She bent over to tend to a spit roast at the periphery of the fire – a sorry looking line of small birds and skinned, decapitated rabbits skewered on a long, pointed stick – and Bartholomew feared her not inconsiderable bosoms may pop out.

"He's not my friend," Benny growled, "he's my little brother."

"Well, I'm pleased to meet you, Little Brother," Patricia greeted Bartholomew. "You got a name, sonny?"

"Bartholomew, Miss."

"Welcome to…" Patricia paused as she absently twirled the roasting carcasses on the spit, some of which were turning a worrisome shade of charcoal black on one side. "…*here.*"

From one of the other huts, a small, stocky shape appeared. Bartholomew tried his very best not to stare as a chubby midget waddled over to Patricia, slipped an arm around her bare shoulder and planted a loving kiss on her cheek.

"They prefer to be called *little people,*" Benny said, staring into the fire. "There's lots of *them* here, too."

"Are you reading my mind?" Bartholomew asked, somewhat perturbed.

"Nah," Benny said. The shit-eating grin spread across his chops. "You're just that predictable, Squirt."

The boys wandered away from the fire and the acrid stink of burring meat, and over to one of the small huts. As they walked, more people emerged from their rough-and-ready homes; a bizarre collection of pretty young ladies all scantily clad in shiny one-piece outfits, short dresses split to the thigh and emblazoned with stars and strange symbols, a sad-faced old man in a cape and top hat, a couple more *little people*, a small, bewildered looking girl, a middle aged man wearing a bedraggled business suit that had once no doubt looked rather sharp, and a young woman dressed up in a too-tight lycra mini skirt and matching crop top and teetering about in vertiginous heels – like she was all ready for a wild night out on the town.

"This one's mine," Benny grunted. As he eased the door to his shack open, its hinges let out a high-pitched squeak. "Don't touch anything."

Bartholomew followed his brother in to the candle-lit gloom, and Benny closed the door behind them.

"What is this place?" Bartholomew's voice was soaked up by the black-painted interior. "Benny?"

Benny sighed, as he always did when Bartholomew asked what he considered to be a dumb question – which was *every* question he asked. "It's where we come," he said.

"We?"

"Did you get even more stupid while I was gone?" Benny huffed.

Bartholomew shrugged his shoulders. "Didn't know you were gone."

"Figures," Benny sighed. "I guess you prefer the all-new Benny, eh?"

Bartholomew imagined he caught a flicker of sadness in his brother's eyes, and kind of hoped Benny couldn't read the reply in his.

"Everyone here has been disappeared," Benny told him.

"Disappeared?"

"If you're gonna repeat everything I say, I'm not going to bother," Benny snapped. "Just sit down, keep your stupid mouth shut, and listen."

Bartholomew looked around for somewhere to sit, but all he could see was a long, coffin-shaped box at one side of the room. It appeared to be his brother's bed. The cabinet was one of those illusionists use to saw their glamorous assistants in half, and came complete with a slot in the center for the saw. Bartholomew half-expected to see the inside coated with old, dried blood.

In the end, he opted to sit on the floor.

"Did you ever wonder where things go when magicians make them vanish?" Benny continued, pacing the short distance to the end of his shack.

Bartholomew shook his head; he honestly hadn't.

"Well, it's here," Benny told him. "Everything that's ever been disappeared comes here." A grunt. "Handkerchiefs, rabbits, birds, silver dollars – there's plenty of those here, but nowhere to spend them – cell phones, a lot of underwear for some reason, elephants, even the Statue of Liberty, all thanks to David Copperfield; nobody here talks to him much." Benny gave a derisory snort that made him seem far older than his tender years.

"And people?" Bartholomew forgot his brother's instruction and broke his silence.

"And people," Benny said, "lots and lots of people. There's an entire studio audience a couple of subdivisions down. And there's magicians everywhere – those who learned about this place the hard way. It all happens so fast – one minute you're in the magic box, the next…"

"But – you came back."

"Obviously, I didn't," Benny snarled. "Otherwise I wouldn't still be in here, would I, you idiot?"

Bartholomew shrugged his shoulders once more. It seemed an appropriate response.

"I was *replaced*, just like all the others," Benny explained. "Everything that vanishes is replaced and the *replacement* is sent back." He lifted a large flap of canvass – upon which was written, in large, fancy letters *The Mysterious…* – at the end of his shack; it acted as a glassless window. "They make everything over there."

Bartholomew stared through the hole in his brother's new home, and out at a sinister trio of tall, soot-stained chimneys that dominated the distant skyline. They towered over a vast, windowless building that sprawled as far as the eye could see, and reached high up into the orangey-pink sky like three grotesque, grasping fingers; each one barfed out thick, black clouds of smoke. Bartholomew shuddered. The chimneys reminded him of the one he'd seen at the crematorium when they'd gone to say goodbye to Grandma.

"I don't know how, or how they do it so quickly, but that's what happens." There was a distinct tone of terrified awe in Benny's voice.

Bartholomew didn't want to look at the chimneys anymore, or at the inky plumes that billowed from their gaping tips, yet somehow they were less disturbing than what dominated the undulating, glittery landscape in front of them. There, tilted at a crazy angle, stood Lady Liberty herself, and behind her, the Eiffel Tower, a huge cruise ship tipped on its side, and what appeared to be half of the Golden Gate Bridge embedded into the hillside.

Copperfield again.

Much to Bartholomew's relief, Benny closed the canvas on the macabre tableau and plunged the shack once more into gloomy half-light. "Hungry?" Benny asked.

"Sure," Bartholomew replied, although he wasn't really, having stuffed his face at the rather splendid open house buffets. "What ya got?"

"Mostly rabbits," Benny told him with a grimace. "They're stringy, but okay once you get used to them. There's birds, too, when we can catch them – mostly doves, but sometimes we get lucky and one of the assistants bag a parrot – and loads of fruit, you'd be surprised how many amateurs practice magic with fruit." Benny's mouth curled up at one corner. What was meant to be a wry smile came across as a twisted sneer. "I do miss fries, though. Nobody ever seems to work with potatoes." He looked sad. "You've gotta get me out of here, Bart."

Bartholomew was taken aback, not just with his brother's sudden change of tack – he was beginning to think Benny liked this weird, twisted take on Narnia – but because this was the first time in forever his sibling had *asked* for his help rather than ordering him about. "Why don't you just climb out through the hole?" he asked the obvious question.

Benny squatted down beside him and rested a hand upon his shoulder. It felt heavy there, like a clammy lead weight. "Because *They* don't like people to leave. Not when they've already made the replacement."

"They?"

"Don't ask. Let's just say They make the white tigers look like pussies." With a wistful expression on his grubby face, Benny sighed.

"I've been working on that hole since I got here – always at night when They are not around. I've been lucky so far it's not been found yet."

Bartholomew eyed his brother with suspicion; trust had never really been their thing. "Why do you need me, Benny?" His voice trembled.

"Because of the other me on the other side. I'm gonna need your help getting him in here to replace me – there can't be two Bennies out there. And They won't come looking for me if they think I never left." Bartholomew was forced to agree with him on one point – one Benny was quite enough.

"And besides, if They come after us when we make a run for it, I can run faster than you."

And that was Benny to a tee, always the douche.

They waited until everyone had eaten their fill of burnt rabbit meat, mangoes, and oranges around the bonfire – no use waiting for it to grow dark, because it never did in that odd land of perpetual sunset, not ever – and Bartholomew, belly stuffed, even managed to doze off into a light and fitful sleep. He dreamt of glitter and tall, blonde women, of sinister-looking magicians in inky black coats, and angry, white tigers skulking between ramshackle villages that spread as far into the distance as one could imagine. And, round and round in his young, sleeping mind, went the impossible conundrum – as much as he considered returning the brother he despised home the *right thing* to do, New Benny was certainly a vast improvement on the original, and certainly didn't deserve to be banished to this dreadful place through no fault of his own.

"Bart!" Benny's loud whisper snuck into Bartholomew's dream. "Wake up, Squirt!" More insistent this time, and accompanied by a hard thump to Bartholomew's arm.

"*Ow!* Benny!" Bartholomew grumbled. He sat up slowly on the floor of his brother's shack and rubbed at the throbbing pain in his bicep. "Will you quit doing that?!"

"It's time to go." Benny prodded at his brother's leg with his foot. "Now."

They snuck from the hut in single file. Bartholomew followed closely behind his brother, the pair of them were all eyes and ears, ever vigilant, even Bartholomew had no idea precisely what to look out for, other than tigers.

The tiny corner of the village Benny had called home for eight weeks and more was encased in an eerie silence. The soft, pinkish glow of the sun that never quite set cast grim shadows about the place, and created bloated pockets of darkness where dark, unimaginable things could lurk. Bartholomew was not sorry to be leaving, although he was kind of dreading getting his brother back home, and the dilemma that would present.

The hillside was in sight, just around a sharp bend in the glitter path, when Benny stopped dead in his tracks. He cocked his head to one side and his darting eyes scanned the stained horizon. "We'd better run now." His voice was worryingly calm.

"Why?" Bartholomew asked, unable to see – or hear – anything untoward. There was nothing so far as he could tell, except that unnatural landscape, the imposing chimneys with their tireless puffing of black, swirling smoke, and not a sound to be heard above the faintest rustling of the tall grass.

Benny didn't reply. Instead, he turned on his heels and pelted away down the loose pathway as fast as his legs could carry him. And in the time it took for Bartholomew to register his brother had left him high and dry, in the periphery of his vision, he'd spotted a dark shape slithering through the grass – the grass itself not so much being parted, but *moving* out of the way.

*I can run faster than you.*

Bartholomew's legs finally took the hint and he set off after his brother, feet pounding at the thick layer of glitter that clung to his shoes as if it was doing its very best to slow him down. "Benny!" His voice was absorbed by the thick, oppressive air as his sibling was already well on his way to the hole in the hillside.

Benny was already halfway through the hole when Bartholomew caught up. His ass and legs were stuck out of the hillside as if it were eating him. He appeared to be stuck, as the hole was not quite wide enough to accommodate the width of his hips. Benny dug his heels into the slick grass and squishy dirt in order to gain sufficient purchase to force himself through. "Push me!" he called out to Bartholomew. Some sixth sense had informed him his little brother had finally made it. "*They're* coming; you're gonna have to push!" His voice sounded distant, dulled by the hillside, and Bartholomew wondered if Benny's head was poking out into his bedroom through the tallboy on the other side.

Bartholomew eyed his brother's butt. He didn't really want to go anywhere near the thing; memories of the foul thing dispensing a copious number of rank, strident farts into his face over the years had given him an ingrained aversion. Behind him, the rustling noise increased its intensity, and although he really didn't want to, Bartholomew simply couldn't help himself. He turned around, and the sight that greeted him knocked the wind from his lungs as surely as one of Benny's best gut-punches.

Rising up from the pink-painted grass, and slithering along the peculiar, glittery path, there came a whole host of dark gray hands – an easy couple of dozen or so, with still more advancing behind them – every one the size of a small child. The hands were affixed to impossibly long, naked arms that snaked all the way back towards that foreboding factory and its chimneys in the distance. The arms had the sickly, putrescent pallor of the long-dead; they were ridged, bobbled with fat, pulsing veins and lumpy warts, and had an unmistakably serpentine appearance. But, it was the fingers that held the most terror for Bartholomew – long, spindly, and skeletal, with nails that were jagged, as if freshly gnawed, and at the very tip of each, there was a gold-rimmed, unblinking, glinting eye.

Needing no further encouragement, Bartholomew dropped to his knees and pushed at Benny's butt with every ounce of strength he possessed.

No matter how hard Bartholomew shoved at it, Benny's fat ass refused to budge. He either hadn't dug the hole big enough, or…

*It was closing up.*

The malevolent hands – *They* – slunk ever closer, and Bartholomew was sure he could hear them whispering to each other in some low, burbling language that sounded horribly malicious.

Something touched his ankle.

Bartholomew squealed out loud. Although he refused to look, he just *knew* one of those awful hands was curling its twisted, gnarled fingers around him, and its hideously reptilian eyes were studying his leg with evil intent.

Adrenalin surged through Bartholomew's body and brought with it a panicked burst of strength. One massive heave at Benny's butt, combined with his brother's scrabbling feet, provided the leverage to propel him through the hole. Tiny puffs of drywall dust wafted out from the hole in the hillside, which looked as menacingly black from this side as it had from behind the tallboy.

The hand tugged at Bartholomew's ankle. He felt himself slip backwards an inch or so. More of the hands reached out for him; grasping, clawing, intent on preventing his escape, and evermore determined to hold him hostage in that terrible twilight land.

*"Benny!"* Bartholomew screamed as he threw himself towards the hole, which he was now certain beyond a doubt was shrinking. He

thrust his head into the darkness as yet more of those cold, clammy fingers curled themselves around his ankle and began to tug.

It was impossibly dark inside the hole, and with no sign of the other side, let alone the comforting sight of his bedroom. Bartholomew began to panic and kicked out against the vile things that pulled at him. He wriggled his small frame through the shrinking hole one painful inch at a time, with his entire lower half at the mercy of *They*.

Slowly, surely, Bartholomew edged backwards as the myriad grasping hands got their way. Unable to help himself, Bartholomew began to cry as the spreading terror squeezed at his guts and the acidic tang of bile stung the back of his throat. He groped around in the darkness, desperately trying to gain purchase on the sides of the preternatural tunnel, but his scrabbling fingertips met with nothing but cool smoothness. *They* pulled at his legs once more, and Bartholomew slid even further backwards, and thoughts of spending the rest of his life living in a tiny wooden hut and being stalked by white tigers flooded his young mind.

"Here!" a voice from way, way ahead of him called out. Bartholomew squinted through his tears; his eyes barely able to focus upon the odd, pink shape floating towards him through the dark. *"Squirt!?"* Benny's voice drifted through the gloom, and Bartholomew saw the pink shape had fingers.

Bartholomew grabbed at his brother's hand. Relief washed through him as their fingers locked and Benny pulled hard. Bartholomew's knuckles popped loudly, like firecrackers, in the blackness.

Not to be deterred, the otherworldly hands yanked hard on Bartholomew's legs, and his body strained in the middle as they engaged in a macabre tug-o-war with Benny. It crossed Bartholomew's mind he may well be pulled entirely in half, and the gruesome part of his little kid's brain wondered what that would feel like, if he would actually get to see his guts before he died, and if it would be preferable to living in the strange world of disappeared stuff and those hideous, grasping hands.

Benny's disembodied hand pulled once more and caught the otherworldly hands by surprise. Bartholomew felt himself slip from their grasp, and his shoes and socks shed from his feet like a lizard's sloughed skin; ragged nails scratched at his flesh like myriad tiny, snaggled teeth.

Bartholomew plopped through the hole on the other side – scraping the top of his head along the interior framework of the tallboy as he went – on top of his brother.

"Thank you," he gasped. His tear-filled eyes brimmed with gratitude and his nose bubbled with clear snot.

Benny shrugged and grunted as he extricated himself from both Bartholomew and the furniture. "I needed you to get *him* in here," he said by means of explanation.

One of the hands snaked through the hole. Its grotesque fingers waved about in the air, and its sinister little eyes at their tips glowered at the brothers, those tiny black pupils at their center oozing with undisguised hate.

Benny grabbed one of the drawers that lay discarded on the bedroom floor. He shoved it into the tallboy and slammed it shut, forcing the hand to retreat with haste on its slithering arm.

Bartholomew followed suit. He slid the next drawer into place. Benny was close behind with the third – and final – drawer. From behind the tallboy, there came insistent thumping and scrabbling of fingernails on ancient wood.

"Go get him, Bart!" Benny ordered. "Now!"

Bartholomew stared at his brother, puzzled.

"*Him* – the other me!" Benny yelled in Bartholomew's face. "And hurry up, before all this wakes up Mom and Dad!"

The tallboy drawers jerked forwards, sliding uneasily on their runners, as They pushed and thumped from behind. Benny pressed his back against the front of the tallboy to slam the drawers back into place, but the rough shoving from the other side grew ever stronger and they inched outwards once more. "Move it, you pussy!" Benny squealed at his brother. His panicking face was flushed red and dampened with a slick sheen of fear-sweat.

Bartholomew dashed from his bedroom and across the landing to Benny's room – the room whose door actually bore a sign, handwritten in red Sharpie, which read 'STAY OUT SQUIRT!' Ignoring the sign for the first time in his young life, Bartholomew barged in to where his brother – his new brother – was sound asleep.

Benny was rapidly fighting a losing battle against the evil hands that thumped and pushed and scrabbled against the back of the tallboy, as slowly but surely, they forced its drawers outwards in spite of his valiant efforts. Benny dug his feet hard into the thin pile of the carpet, and forced every ounce of his weight and strength against those drawers. But, one by one, the hands pushed them out of the tallboy.

*"Oh no,"* Benny gasped when Bartholomew led him into the bedroom and he saw his other self fighting against the tallboy. "What have you done, Bartholomew?" he fixed his brother with an accusatory stare.

"I'm sorry," Bartholomew replied, and really, really meant it. Even so, he closed his bedroom door, so that New Benny couldn't escape.

All half-dozen of the tallboy's drawers shot outwards in one clattering heap and took Benny with them. He landed in an ungainly mess adjacent to Bartholomew's bed, along with the drawers. From the hole behind the tallboy, a grasping quartet of those dreadful hands snaked out into the bedroom. They paused as their beady little eyes fixed upon both versions of Benny with a look of puzzlement.

Bartholomew grabbed hold of his replica brother's arm and pulled him towards the tallboy. New Benny gave only a token resistance. He had a sad look of resignation on his face. "You don't have to do this, Bart," he said, "*They* don't care which Benny they take back with them."

"Don't listen to him!" Benny barked as he heaved aside the tallboy drawers that lay across his legs. He scrabbled to his feet. "He's an impostor!" He then stood nose to nose with his counterpart, lip curled in that Benny sneer he'd perfected over the years, as the two Bennies seemed frozen in time.

Bartholomew's mind raced. Memories of the tumultuous dream he'd had on the floor of that grotty little shack in that strange world were still painfully raw; the uncertainty of the *best thing to do* was tearing him up inside. It would certainly be better to banish Old Benny to the eternal dusk, but would that be fair on the original version of his brother, even though he was a complete and utter shit? How could he be sure New Benny was actually human, and not some robot replica, or some slimy plant thing like he'd seen in *Invasion of the Body Snatchers*? And if either were true, did he really care?

Bartholomew took a deep breath, took one short step towards his brothers and gave one of them a hearty shove towards the tallboy.

Benny screamed as the hands grabbed him and their golden eyeballs pressed hard against his body as they yanked him towards the ink-black hole in the drywall. Yanked clean off his feet, he flew backwards through the framework of the tallboy with his arms and legs flailing against the old, dry wood and his head *thunking* loudly on its insides. As the hands dragged Benny through the shrinking hole with sickening ease, his body bent double as he was forced through it. His spine snapped with a stomach-churning *crack*. Benny's eyes met with his little brother's one last time; they were crammed full of pain and the sheer hurt of betrayal. His mouth spread wide open in one last, silent scream.

And then Benny was gone.

The hole closed itself up with a rude haste. The wall knitted together like dry, flaky flesh, until nothing more remained than a thin, gray scar on the faded wallpaper.

"Thanks, Squirt." Benny delivered a swift kick to his little brother's shin. The dull *clunk* split the room's silence.

"S'ok." Bartholomew rubbed away the sharp throbbing in his leg as he stood barefoot amongst the rabbit turds on his carpet.

"Wanna go see if we can't go piss off old Mrs. S in the morning?" Benny asked. "Or are you too much of a *pussy*?"

Bartholomew offered up a wan smile and a nod, and couldn't help but wonder if he'd made the right decision after all.

# Bill Evans'
# Shopping List

A few romaine lettuce leafs
Small pack of Chia seeds
Light salad dressing
Diet soda
One medium sized ox

# A Fair
## *Bill Evans*

### (part one)

The hotel marquis prominently displayed *PSYCHIC FAIR, Today from 9-5*.

I entered the lobby and couldn't help but be impressed. The waiting area was well staffed. The lined tables contained clipboards with sign-up sheets and descriptions of each of the numerous psychic readers. This was all easy to understand and user-friendly. At the end of one of the tables was a sign-up sheet for "Ghost Hunters…Exploring Paranormal Activity; 4:30 pm." I hurriedly scribbled my name on the form.

Upon entering the packed house at the "Ghost Hunters" break out room some fifteen minutes before start time, I surveilled the nervous and excited crowd. I saw an opening and squeezed in next to a cute middle-aged woman dressed in frilly "witchy" black garments. We immediately connected and started talking excitedly about what was to come.

The next hour was riveting. Two gregarious men who were carpenters by day and ghost hunters by night, gave an engaging presentation regarding how they explore a location with presumed paranormal activity. They pulled out and demonstrated divining rods, tachometers, and all kinds of gadgets and gizmos. We were captivated.

"I want to hunt ghosts someday," my new female buddy whispered to me.

"No thanks, not me. I'm not messing with this stuff."

"Chicken," she teased.


In short order, the most amazing thing happened. The ghost hunters displayed a contraption that looked like a police walkie-talkie. This 2-way radio transmitted the language of your choice into "ghost speak". If the entity responded, one could hear the reply deciphered into the language selected.

"Let's try this to see if there are any spirits lurking around," suggested one of the ghost hunters. He had a wide beaming grin on his face. He ceremoniously held the walkie-talkie up about six inches from his mouth and engaged the device. "Hello, is anyone there? Will you talk to us? Is anyone there?"

No response.

The other ghost hunter tried his hand at contacting an entity. He too met with no success.

Some guy from the crowd then brashly predicted he'd have success at contact and volunteered to try. He got up in front of the crowd and was introduced as the Reverend…something or other. The ghost hunters explained to the crowd that he had been on paranormal investigations with them in the past. He was quite experienced in matters such as this. I recognized him as one of the psychic readers on the clipboard. He was tall and heavyset; about 35 years old with dark hair and two days of stubble on his face. This reverend was wearing some kind of astrological floor-length vest. The first thing to be noticed about him was that he was loud and cocky.

"Hey is anyone there? Where are you? Hey…I'm talking to you," he began abruptly after wresting the communication device from the ghost hunter. This inquiry was met with silence.

The smirking grandstanding Reverend turned then to face the captivated audience. He reminded me of one of those carnival barkers of long ago. He enjoyed reveling in this self-absorbed pompous display of reckless behavior. Meanwhile my intuitions were screaming at me that something was horribly amiss.

A silence fell over the crowd as the Reverend put his hand up to quiet everybody.

With the other hand, he again placed the walkie-talkie to his mouth, primed to scold any entity within earshot.

"A fair."

The muffled words emanated from the small handheld gadget in the Reverend's hand. The startled Reverend leapt off his feet and almost dropped the device. Most of the crowd nearly fell out of their seats. The suppressed sound was heard clearly enough. There was no inflection in the voice, and the words were robotic. Nevertheless, we all heard it.

"A fair."

(part two)

"Ahhh...our ghost had an affair. Naughty, naughty ghost."

The Reverend spoke these words in mocking admonishment. It was met with quiet annoyance...at least from me. The Reverend had recovered his sense of false bravado and was in full taunting mode again.

"Tell us about this affair. Are you a cheater? Come on, fess up. It'll do the soul good. Are you there, ghost? Hello? Answer me, you adulterer. I know you're there. Answer me."

The Reverend continued to chastise the entity in this snide one-sided dialogue. From time to time, he would turn and grin at the audience. Finally, I decided that I'd had enough.

Boldly standing up, I cleared my throat to stop all of this nonsensical frivolity.

"Hey, everybody, wait a minute," I shouted. The room fell into a hush. "Think about it. Where are we? We *are* at a fair. We are at a psychic fair…*A FAIR!*"

The silence was deafening. Even the Reverend just stood there with his mouth agape.

One of the ghost hunters decided to break the uncomfortable silence.

"Oh my, folks. It's true. That confirms it. There is indeed a bona fide presence here with us."

With that, he took the walkie-talkie device from the stunned Reverend. He tried his hand at communicating.

"Hello and welcome. Will you speak to us? My name is Bill. What is your name?"

The entity would not respond. For the next fifteen minutes or so, many others including the Reverend took turns trying to communicate with the entity; but to no avail. The consensus was that the entity had decided to leave the premises.

I knew better.

At the behest of my friend, I wrestled the device away from the group and took it over to a quiet corner of the room. My female friend followed. When we were out of earshot of the others, she eagerly took the device from me and engaged it to speak.

"If you are there and care to communicate, I would welcome it," she said softly.

I audibly concurred.

"I understand if you choose not to communicate," she continued. "Please accept my apology on behalf of our group if we've offended you. I am truly sorry."

"Me too," I chimed in.

"Please go in peace and be safe in your travels," she continued.

Nice touch I thought.

We turned to rejoin the group. I led the way while my friend trailed closely behind.

Suddenly I heard her shriek in pain. She had dropped the walkie-talkie device on the ground with a sickening thud and held her hand up to show me. It was blistered as if having been badly burned. Muffled chanting could be heard from the fallen device.

"Give me your hand…quickly," I urged my friend.

She shakily extended the injured hand toward me as I reached into my inside coat pocket. After uncorking the vile of holy water, I held her firmly and doused the injury with the sanctified water. The scarring and wounds began to heal almost immediately.

"Please go over with the others…for your own safety."

"But…but…what are you going to do?"

"I've got a demon to deal with," I replied coldly.


(part three)


I returned to the walkie-talkie communication device. I dared not touch it. It laid there where it had been dropped and was squawking like an old transistor radio not quite properly tuned to a clear channel.

It suddenly became very cold in the area. I knew the ramifications.

"Demon…name yourself," I impulsively commanded.

There was silence. The device then began incoherently squawking again.

"Demon, I command you in the name of Jesus Christ, to name yourself."

"You are no exorcist, arrogant one," a high-pitched unholy voice said shrilly from the communication device. "You have no authority to place such demands upon me."

"I have the authority of…"

"Silence, John Kane," the voice hissed. "I have been sent here to issue you one final warning. Your meddlesome ways have become an annoyance. You are but an insect and will be squashed if you persist. We are everywhere. We hear what you are saying. We know what you are doing. Your futile efforts against us are useless. Abandon all hope. Abandon your delusional dreams. We will prevail and reign supreme. Beware the might of the indomitable, Morax."

Morax? Now that was a name from the past. I thought I had disposed of that demon some years ago. I was perplexed, but I'd have to address the Morax thing later. I had a demon to deal with now.

"Go back from whence you came. And you can tell your boss, Morax, I'd be happy to skewer him again if he dares cross paths with me. Give him that message, low-level vermin from Hades." I paused for a moment. There was no response from the demon. Was he stalling? I decided to act.

"I now grow weary of this conversation. Be gone spawn from Hell!"

I reached into my side pocket and retrieved the small bottle of holy water. After ceremoniously raising the vile and making the sign of the cross, I doused the walkie-talkie with the sacred liquid. It began to smoke. The shrill voice grew faint as the demon shouted multiple obscenities. The threats soon subsided. The room began to warm. The demonic spirit had departed—for now.

I safely retrieved and returned the communication device to the startled owners, and then walked over to my shaken friend.

"I'm sorry you had to experience that. You're safe now."

"Will that demon come back to terrorize me again?" my lady friend asked with an unsteady voice.

"They won't bother you again—unless you are with me. It is best we part company." I bowed gallantly. "Farewell, my friend."

"May I ask your name, kind sir?" she requested.

"Kane… John Kane."

"Oh my," she said gasping. "The…the famous demon hunter?"

I just calmly walked away.

I slowly shuffled out the side entrance and towards my vehicle. As I began to open the front car door, I heard a shout and saw the two ghost hunters racing toward me.

"Hey, we apologize," one of them said breathlessly.

Then the other chirped in. "We didn't know the great John Kane was in our presence. Why didn't you say something?"

I stood in silence.

"Anyhow," the first one said. "We were told to show you this."

"*Who* told you?" I interjected. They were reluctant to say more. They both began to shake.

"Never mind," I said in resignation. It wasn't important; at least at the moment. "Show me what you have there."

I was shown a photo of a bride and groom grinning broadly. They were a happily married couple whom had just recently completed their vows. Lurking and peering closely over the shoulder of the groom was the clear image of a *hag*. I had never seen the pure essence of hideousness and evil depicted more graphically. The best Hollywood make-up artist could have never replicated the image before me. It made my blood run cold.

"You are here for a reason, Mr. Kane. Of that, we are certain. We need your expertise and guidance. You are our last hope. Are you going to join us? Are you in?"

# Larry Griffin's
# Shopping List

Milk
Bread
Cereal - Special K
Rice
Beer
Garlic
Tiny crosses
Wooden boards
Nails
Hammer
Night-vision goggles
Box of ammo

# The Day I Met the Monster
### *Larry Griffin*

## I

The night the Eternity Killer came, Aidan Peterson did what he'd been doing for some time, and covered himself in blankets like a cocoon, wrapping them all around his entire body and even his head. It was early November, and the house—with its big old structure—was cold. It was almost like the house was breathing, Aidan thought, and it felt, always, fairly chilly inside in the winter, even with a fire in the hearth downstairs. The cocoon of blankets was just a way to fight the cold, and it made Aidan, at age seven, feel like a resourceful hunter, braving the winter and carving out shelter in some dead bison like some of his frontier heroes from the books did.

And he was just so close to sleep that night, when the sounds began.

First it was a creaking of the stairs, those old wooden things from the beginning of the century. It was definitely footsteps. There was an unusual cadence to them. Aidan figured his father, heavy with sleep and not his usual self, was getting a mug of tea, as he often did at odd, nubile hours. Aidan, unfazed, was almost off to sleep. But there was something in the footsteps that made him think it was an intruder, something that tickled at even his young subconscious as distinctly wrong.

The first door opened was his own. He didn't know what specifically tipped him off, maybe just the footsteps, but he didn't move at all, didn't even exhale. There was a hollow, ragged sound of breathing from the intruder. Aidan wondered if he was coming inside. But he didn't. He seemed to believe Aidan's illusion, that no one was in the room. The intruder closed his door.

There were footsteps, then, big and lumbering and slow, down the upstairs hall.

But then there was the sound of another door opening—Aidan had always had good hearing. It was yet another thing that always made him feel like a hunter, out in the Alaskan wilds, searching for poachers, when he played out in the family's formidable farmland yard.

He heard the door open and then the surprised, startled cries of his parents. First his mother, high and brief, then his father's lower voice saying something, threatening something.

Aidan thought this was confirmation. So it was for sure an intruder.

He listened and felt his soul clench up as the screams started. He thought maybe he should go and do something, but his whole body felt frozen up.

After a few minutes, the footsteps appeared again. Ragged and uneven and lumbering, they pounded on the hollow upstairs floor. His sister's room was at the other end of the stairs. This ignited a kind of flame in him: he had to save Cornelia.

She was 14, and she always told him what a pain he was, when he'd come and bug her while she was getting ready to go out with her friends. They only ever went to the Main Street Diner, a few miles into town. He didn't know what she always needed to prepare so much for.

But as he got out of bed, bare feet hitting the wood floor, he knew he had to ensure she could do that all again.

He grabbed the first thing he could find in his dark room, a wooden sword, bought last year at a market of oddities in the big city. It was his prized possession in the summer afternoons, used for marathons of sparring with the neighbor boys and their homemade ones. Then, as time was of the essence, he began his trek down the hall. His feet felt cold on the floor and he could see the door at the end of the hall, cracked open now, wide enough for a large, lumbering intruder to fit through.

On the way, he passed his parents' door, left carelessly open. It was dark in there, but the moonlight illuminated their lifeless forms. He held back tears. He wanted to stay here and cry, but he had to keep going...

But when he got to the end of the hall, the small scream of his sister Cornelia, a high and thin sound, had already been snuffed out like a flame. And the man was exiting the room.

He was at least seven feet tall, it seemed to Aidan's child mind. He wore all black and his skin was as pale and milky as a corpse's. What was most striking were his eyes; a complete and total whiteness, an absence of color, and yet there was somehow inexplicably feeling in them. It was an odd vengeful thing, something prideful and vain, without any humility. He looked then like a satisfied man, well-off, done with a sizeable meal. He looked down at Aidan and grinned huge block-like tombstone-shaped teeth. Then he was kneeling down. He put a hand on Aidan's shoulder and his fingers were ice-cold.

"I'm leaving now," he said, in a voice that was like an icy branch scraping on a window in January. "I've filled myself. And I can see in you that you won't disappoint me in the future. This will be fun."

And then, as if he had exited on a stage in one of the plays down at the opera house in town, the man in black was gone. Aidan was standing alone in his empty house, truly alone, the last one alive.

The Sheriff's men would come soon. They would look in the rooms and determine that the deaths of the Peterson family were unlike most others. Each member of the Peterson family had been laid out on their backs and their hearts ripped clean from their body, precise, as if a surgeon had done the work.

Though one deputy told the news that he wouldn't have wanted to be under the scalpel of a surgeon like that.

The killings were never solved. Aidan Peterson would be sent to live with his grandparents, in the city. New York City, to be exact, where he'd be enrolled in school and live out the rest of his childhood. He would gradually return to something appropriating normalcy, though his grandparents saw a hollowness in him. There were schoolbooks and friends, movies they went to on the weekends at the downtown theater with its red curtains, its buttery popcorn smell, hockey and soccer played in the streets between bouts of school and various meals. It was an unremarkable childhood on paper.

But there was always another side. Aidan got into the habit of reading the New York Times often, picking it up whenever his grandfather was done. His grandfather was a habitual reader, a constant devourer of information, who read the paper to see what was going on in Vietnam or in the president's shady dealings.

Aidan read it for a different reason.

He was scouring the crime stories, looking for any morsel or detail that could point him to the man all in black. With his tombstone teeth and ice-scraping voice.

Whether he knew it or not, Aidan Peterson had found a life's purpose even at a young age. He would track down the man and exact his revenge.

# II

In 1974, Aidan Peterson was accepted to the Medill School of Journalism. He'd wanted to be a writer for years, having delved deep into classic literature as well as modern pulp fiction in high school. His grandfather, an unimaginative stickler with no room for fancy in his life, didn't know why he spent his days cooped up in the towering old library at the end of the block, leafing through copies of Vonnegut, Jack Vance and Ray Bradbury novels, but Aidan was entranced.

It was also the newspaper, which had become a ritual for him as much as his grandfather, as it had been since he was a child and had first moved in. After his grandfather read the paper, Aidan would pick it up and scour it for any mention of a kill like that which had happened to his family. Any mention of the pale man in black. There had never been any that he'd found. But in those early days of hunger and restlessness, he'd gained an appreciation for the news. He was fascinated with the whole process, and the idea of reaching that many people with just words on paper stayed with him.

And so he was at the Chicago School of Journalism, 19 years old. He felt a renewed sense of purpose. For years now he'd been defeated. There was no way to catch the monster if he was saddled by teenage norms, stuck in a house with no real rights. This country, he thought, didn't let kids do anything. Because of that, he'd felt he had lost sight for years of his goal of finding the Eternity Killer, or the Monster, whichever name he felt like at the time for the black-clad entity that had snatched his entire family up as if they'd never existed.

Now he could correct all of it.

He began to take his classes, learning the mechanics of writing a news story and taking his first steps into the world, an infant again. He wrote his grandparents often. They were doing well, and life was moving along. Aidan periodically thought that it was so absurd how his entire family had died so long ago, and everything just went back to normal; that most people didn't know or care that such an upheaval of a child's life had occurred.

So he'd work to shed some light.

The first new break in the Eternity Killer case for Aidan came in 1975 when a crime report came out that two people, husband and wife, had been found dead in their uptown Chicago flat, no mysterious cause of entry, no sign of anyone who'd have motive to kill them. The newspaper was vague on how they had died. All it said was that they'd been killed violently.

Aidan knew he had to find out more.

He took the subway train down to the street where their apartment was listed. It was a cold dreary November day and the skies were slate-grey with no sign of blue anywhere. The apartment was the top-most one of a tall 12-story brick building, the color of rust. Aidan had to go through a lobby to get there, and the lobby was dull and drab. The desk manager looked at Aidan with uninterested eyes. Aidan explained why he was there, and the manager said he was free to go up to the hallway and look around, but if they heard he was pestering any residents, they reserved the right to kick him out.

That was fine with Aidan. He took the elevator all the way up, felt his heart pounding the entire ride. Intrinsically, he knew this was the first step. The first link in a chain.

The hallway was carpeted in beige and had small square windows at either end. The wallpaper was patterned in lazy brown-yellow flowers. He walked on shaky legs and found the door he wanted, 101. It was taped off all in yellow and had a threatening vibe about it, something still and cold and dead. He reached out to touch the door, just to see if there was any connection there. But before he could touch it, a loud bang sounded. He jumped, startled, realizing he'd almost been in a dream-like state.

A tall, dark-haired woman had exited her apartment and was standing there with a little Yorkie terrier. She looked at him with some apprehension, and of course; everyone here must be haunted by what happened, he thought. Trauma was rife in the air.

"Can I help you?" she asked.

"Uh, well, I'm just a journalist," Aidan said. "Just came to check out the apartment. To see what it's like, you know."

She let out a dark chuckle. "Not much to see. Just a closed door. Unless, like, you're super fascinated by closed doors." She had an impish, mischievous quality. Perhaps it was the smile across her elfin face, like she knew something secretive and it amused her.

Aidan decided to take a shot, the manager downstairs be damned. "Were you here when... you know, when it happened?"

She nodded. "I mean, it was kind of hard not to be. It was like, four in the morning when it happened?"

Aidan nodded. He'd taken out his pad and pen and was writing. The woman's dog was straining the leash, trying to scamper off down the hall. She grinned apologetically.

"Here, come on," she said. "Walk with me. I'll tell you the whole thing."

Then the two of them were walking outside in the chilly Chicago air while the Yorkie terrier pawed and explored the ground. Her name was Octavia and the dog's name was Spencer. She had been lying awake with insomnia when the killing happened, and she knew because it had not gone quietly. She heard the door slam open and then a struggle, some shouts... and this had paralyzed her. She laid there in bed and listened to them scream, that nice couple across the way. Ben and Gina Rathbone, she said, had been their names. After about thirty minutes she found her movement again, pulled on a jacket and ventured out on shaky legs into the hall.

By then everyone was coming out. They stared at the gaping open door, which itself was disturbing, simply for the fact that it shouldn't have been that way. It was like a perversion, already.

The cops were on their way, but the residents of the top floor were restlessly curious. They had to know, and plus, what if someone were still alive in there and needed help?

Graham had a gun, so he volunteered to go in, just to take a look. Ruthie from down the hall told him not to mess with anything, because the cops didn't like when people messed up evidence. He went in with his gun out, everything about him confident and rigid. Everyone watched with bated breath. He was all of them. They were living vicariously and if something happened to him, it would happen to all of them.

It was a small apartment, as they all were, and a few minutes later Graham emerged looking as white as a corpse. They rushed to him, but he pushed through the crowd, bent over and vomited up everything he'd eaten that day. He kept his back to them, shivering, and by the time he had composed himself, the police were coming.

Aidan listened to Octavia's recounting with wide eyes. "So what did it end up being?" he asked. "What'd he see?"

"I heard later, from a friend of his," she said. "Apparently, Ben and Gina's hearts had just been... ripped out of their bodies. It sounded gruesome."

That was all Aidan needed.

"So he's fed again," he said.

She asked him what he was talking about, and he asked if she really wanted to know. When he became convinced that she was serious, he told her to come with him to the diner down the road that he'd passed on his way in. Together they got coffee and he told her his story, told her of the Eternity Killer and his deadly precision and the way he'd taken Aidan's family so many years ago.

Octavia was to be his confidant and partner in the search for the Eternity Killer. She was a curious soul who thought differently from most around her. Her insomnia kept her up and she was happy to have something to whittle away the time, so she set about looking up obscure crime stories at the library on her free afternoons, looking for any similar murders as far back as she could go. From this endeavor she brought back five killings from across the country, from the early 1900s, that could've been the work of the Eternity Killer. All in the dead of night. All families, at least a husband and wife, sometimes children. All with their hearts torn clean from their body.

She told him one afternoon sitting in her apartment, tea brewing, that she'd always felt like she was drifting alone, without a purpose, and only found a semblance of one when she was filling her brain with knowledge.

"I'm in it," she said. "I'm like a dog with a bone when I get on something's tracks. I can't quit."

"Well, that's good, right?" he asked, letting out a small chuckle.

"I guess," she said. "I think I get fixated, though. Like, one time in school, I got this project to look up some stuff about dinosaurs. I spent so much time in that library I forgot to eat. I came back with more stuff than the teacher could grade. She told me 'Octavia, your passion is great but unwieldy, and I don't know what to do with all of it.'"

"Yeah, but what do teachers even know?" Aidan asked.

She was pouring their tea into Christmas mugs, emblazoned with Santa Clauses and jingle bells and reds and whites. "A lot, I'd hope," she said.

He said, "Well, still. You really helped me out. I just feel dumb I didn't find a lot of those ones you found. I was only looking at current news. Trying to find where he was going next."

She sat down across from him on the couch, a grin on her face again. "Oh, it's okay," she said. "It's just 'cause I'm a lot better than you in every way."

"Oh, hush," he said.

So the two of them, sitting in Octavia's apartment over tea, began to work out a tentative pattern. They determined that for whatever reason, the Eternity Killer struck about every ten years, give or take, and always in different parts of the country. The only pattern seemed to be that the victims were married and lived together.

"There seems to be no indication of how he finds them," Octavia said to him one day as they sat in her apartment, just doors down from where the most recent murder had happened. "Like, does he know them? That doesn't seem possible."

"He must have money," Aidan said. "Either that or he's comfortable just bumming it and sleeping outside. I don't know, though."

"It's all so random," she said.

"I've often wondered if it's even one killer," Aidan said. "Like maybe I'm just crazy, right? Maybe there's a bunch of guys doing it and we're off-base here. I mean, he'd have to be in his 80s if he were still doing it now."

"It feels like just the one," Octavia said. "Like, are there that many people who rip out hearts? That's no country I'd want to live in."

"I know," he said.

"The cases are all too similar," she said.

They had all their pictures laid out on Octavia's table, from the ones taken at the most recent crime scene just two doors down to the oldest they'd found, on a farm in 1901, a distinguished farmer and county businessman and his wife eaten in the night, savaged more brutally than the others. Octavia's theory was that the killer had refined his technique over time, leading to the surgical precision with which he'd carried out his recent crimes.

But no one had ever caught this killer. No one, to their knowledge, had put the crimes together. They were random and disparate points on a map of the years. And why wouldn't they be? Aidan realized the gravity of what they were proposing. The sheer insanity and breadth of this.

"It's like, is he a vampire or something like that?" Octavia asked him near the end of that brainstorming session, as the sun was growing scarce and burning red as it sank, the air taking on a chillier disposition. "Are vampires real? Is that what we're saying here?"

"I've asked myself that a lot," Aidan said. "He's definitely something."

"Even so, it's not like a real vampire would have to be exactly like the ones we know about, from fiction and stuff," she said. "That's just something somebody wrote. We wrap our minds around the stories. But it could be some other kind of way."

Aidan said, "Yeah, but they were written that way for a reason, you know? It's all just so odd."

"Well, let's ask him, then," she said. Her eyes were gleaming with something radical.

"How's that?"

"We'll find him, and we'll ask him," she said. "I'm sure it'll be enlightening."

Aidan chuckled, but then said, "I don't think you want to meet this guy. I think you want to stay far away."

They were watching TV on the couch later, just an old Agatha Christie program, when a thought occurred to Aidan. It was a weird seed that, for some reason, had not come to him until they had splayed the pictures everywhere and looked at that first case, of the farmer who lived in a place so much like his own.

"My father was well-known locally, too," he said. "He was going to be Sheriff. They were all almost sure of it. He had the most support in the race and had been a cop for my whole life."

"Hmm?" Octavia asked. She was leaning forward now.

He said, "That first guy, he was a local politician of some sort. Town council or whatever, back then. My dad was a Sheriff. Both real well-known figures in their community. Nobody who lived there long enough wouldn't have known my dad."

Octavia was nodding, seeing where he was going.

"What did Ben do?" he asked her. She shrugged.

"But Gina, she was running for school board," Octavia said. "She was at all the council meetings, talking about better pay and all of that. She was very outspoken."

"I guess with better pay, she'd have been able to move out of this place," Aidan said.

"Hey, don't be mean," she said. "I like it here. It's cozy."

"I'll give you that," Aidan said. She smiled at him.

"So what are we going with?" she asked him. "That he's... what? Killing the most well known people he can find?"

"It seems more plausible than any other theory we've got," Aidan said. "Not that that's saying much."

She nodded. "Let's run with it."

Aidan wrote about the Eternity Killer for the finals of his Investigative Journalism class that year. He compiled everything he and Octavia had found and wrote it up in what he felt was the most compelling manner he could. Then he went back and wrote up, from his own first-person, the account of the deaths of his own family, now almost 20 years in the past but still so fresh to him. He could still hear the creaking of the boards under his feet. He could see the Eternity Killer's tombstone teeth and milky-white skin. All of this, he wrote up in the night, shivering with a mug of whiskey next to his typewriter. All of it he turned in the next day with a kind of tautness about him, a nervousness of exposing this private part of himself to the world...

He got the paper back two days later. The grade was a C-. The instructor had written: *compelling tale, but I fail to see any concrete evidence that the killings are related.* Aidan felt his heart sink a little. But then, he hadn't really expected anything else.

He got coffee with Octavia sometimes after that, as things slowed down, the two of them talking less and less about the killer each time.

She was a student at the local community college and hoped one day to be a marine biologist. For that, she wanted to move down to Florida, maybe the Keys, eventually.

"I just always wanted to do it," she said. "Ever since I was a kid and my aunt would take me to the aquarium, and I'd see all the fish and the little corals and things. It's a whole, wide universe down there. A whole ecosystem going on and they don't know we're looking. It's so interesting to me, Aidan."

"I can see that," he said. "It must be enticing. Like some sort of escape."

"Well, it's not really that for me," she said. "It's the exploration. I like that idea. Of just, like, finding somewhere totally new. Of discovering things. When I was a kid, my dad wouldn't let me go outside barely ever. Said it was too dangerous."

"Well, he was probably right," Aidan said, smirking at her.

"Oh, shut up," she said.

They would go to the movies sometimes, seeing Dog Day Afternoon and Jaws. In Jaws, Octavia jumped at the scariest moments and unconsciously gripped Aidan's arm tight, squeezing him for comfort. She'd look at him afterwards and tell him she was sorry if she hurt him, and he told her it was no big deal.

Meanwhile, Aidan had begun interning at the Chicago Tribune. He was just writing up obituaries and advertisements, not yet allowed into the pilot's seat of the newsroom. But he relished the experience. He watched the mechanics of it, with the reporters rushing in and out of the building. The chaos of deadline time was always a thrill, editors walking briskly past and snatching stories out of typewriters whether they were finished or not.

But there was always that other part of him, silent and deadly like a sleeper agent, that listened for clues of the Eternity Killer. The Associated Press, with its bevy of stories from all over the world, was an asset. He read them quickly each day and scanned for mysterious murders. Most of the time, it was nothing. So it went. Time became a long grind. The understanding he had with Octavia was clear, though: at the next sighting of the Eternity Killer, they'd spring into action and investigate immediately.

To Aidan's surprise, it didn't take long for him to strike again. It happened the following February in a small town called Idlehorn, just south of the border line between Illinois and Missouri. The mayor of the town, Kenneth Jackson, had been found with his wife of 30 years, the both of them dead, throats slashed in the night. It was far enough south that no one else placed the connection with the murders of Ben and Gina Rathbone in Chicago.

Aidan didn't know how, but the murders had lit up something in him, an extra sense, that told him this was the Killer. He and Octavia took off as soon as they could, driving six hours and stopping at road-side diners for quick grub. He was apprehensive about taking her with him, so soon when the Killer could still be in that totally unknown small area. But she was tenacious, and she kept looking at him with the expectation of something else happening. She wanted this. So he took her along.

"Are we sure it's him?" she was asking as they began their drive. "Their hearts weren't taken—this time, the throats were slashed."

"Must be how he's gone undetected," Aidan said. "He switches up the murders. That's how nobody's ever put this together. But it's still two prominent, powerful people. Still in a remote location like a lot of the older ones."

"It could just be a random murder," Octavia said.

"Maybe. But I've just got a feeling."

By dawn they'd reached Idlehorn. It was a small town, one street, with rows of small businesses: a barber shop, a realtor, an Irish pub. Aidan guessed it'd take 10 minutes to canvass the whole of the place.

Kenneth Jackson's house was out of the way of the main road, but only by a few blocks. A large two-story structure with a fenced-off yard, it was the color of clay and had Spanish-style roof tiles and a wide veranda and a man-made pool. They'd made the most of their small, rural setting. But all their riches had not saved them from demise, Aidan thought. They were equal to the impoverished single-room trailers down the street in that regard.

Jackson's home was guarded and blocked off by cops now. They wouldn't speak to Aidan, but the place was near enough to the gas station, just at the corner of the block.

It was a small independent chain that seemed to have so far defied the big names swallowing it. Inside there were yellowing tiles, rows of snacks and freezers full of sugary carbonated drinks. The cashier was a skinny old man with a walrus mustache, gazing bored at them, seemingly able to see through them.

Aidan asked him if he'd seen a man in dark clothes with very pale skin. The cashier said he had, the previous day. He called the man a "creepy looking guy" and said he'd know him anywhere. At this, Aidan cast a knowing glance at Octavia, an I-told-you-so, and she rolled her eyes.

Aidan asked if he could see the security video from the previous day, and the cashier looked skeptical.

"What, you with the cops?" he asked.

"No," Aidan said. "A journalist." At this, the cashier scoffed. But Aidan slipped him $20. Then he and Octavia were escorted back to the little room in the back with its metal fold-out chairs and shelves full of cleaning supplies, where a desk with a VCR was set up and the camera tapes were sitting. They were handed the one from the previous day, when, that morning, the man in black had come in.

Aidan held his breath and waited for him to appear. It felt like preparing to see some long-lost relative, gone in war, for the first time in years.

Then he was there. He looked as Aidan remembered him, tall and gaunt, all in black like a character in a Gothic fairytale. He didn't look at the camera, but Aidan remembered his eyes as if it had been only yesterday, those crystal-white orbs.

Octavia, next to him, saw the man and knew for the first time how Aidan had become obsessed with finding him. He was a man who it would be hard not to hate.

They asked around every place in town with the man's description, energized now. About half of the places they tried yielded no results. The local hotel, sadly, had not seen him. Aidan said it made sense, since he wouldn't stay so close to the scene of a crime. No one had seen him at the auto repair, nor had the law clerks seen him. But the grocery store said he'd been there, buying milk and crackers. A cart boy said he'd seen the man leaving in a beat up, rust-colored Chevy, heading off in the wintry cold like a lone sentinel. The cart boy said he would recognize the man in black anywhere.

On the road out of town, they were surrounded for a time by snow-covered plains, fields of endless white, with the sky a mix of grey and white.

"It feels like we're inside a snowglobe," Aidan said.

"It's beautiful," Octavia said, able to forget for a moment their grim mission.

"Yeah," Aidan said. "Back when I was a kid, it always looked like this. I would just look out the window and get spellbound."

"I bet it was nice," Octavia said, but then she remembered that all of this was likely reminding him of his long-lost family, and so she switched the topic to herself. "I mean, I never had that. My family dragged me to

Florida for the winters. I would be in shorts and a T-shirt. Felt like summer."

"That sounds nice about now," Aidan said. "After we're done here, we should do that. Go to a beach somewhere. Hell, we could use it."

She smiled. "You might just be a genius," she said.

What eventually stopped them was the sight of the rusted Chevy, parked on the side of the road, off-kilter. There were woods in the far distance now. The town wasn't visible behind them anymore.

"Shit," Aidan said. "Is that...?"

"I think it is," Octavia said.

They pulled over. He got his gun from the duffel bag in the back seat that had stored his clothes. A little black Glock, which he'd obtained specifically for this occasion.

Then he and Octavia were walking through the snowy plains. The air was cold but still. Octavia had her hands jammed in her coat and she tried to hide her shivering. They were at the edge of the woods, then, staring at this great primordial chasm, the natural world. Aidan looked back at her and asked if she was ready. She said she was as ready as she'd ever be.

Under the cover of the tall trees, it seemed that it was now difficult to tell what time it was. The shadows covered everything thoroughly. Aidan was on the lookout for any movement. In the cold, it seemed that even the animals were unmoving, so Aidan figured any movement would much more likely be his target here...

They came to the circle with the fire burning after about twenty minutes walking. There was a duffel bag on the ground. Aidan inched close to it and found it full of supplies; a water bottle, a ring of dozens of keys, a hotel key.

"It's him," Aidan said. "Unless there's two people hiding out here."

"What should we do?" Octavia asked.

"We wait," Aidan said. "We make ourselves inconspicuous."

He had the gun out in front of him. Every muscle in him felt tense and on-fire, like even his primal sense was afraid.

Then there were the crunching footsteps, branches breaking underneath boots, approaching from the east of them. And then, before they even had time to say another word, he was there. He stood about six-foot-three, and clad all in black, exactly the same as Aidan remembered him in dreams, periodically since he was a child. His skin was blanched, pale white, and his hair was the color of gunmetal. The eyes were the strangest. Octavia had heard Aidan describe them, but up close, they truly were like misty crystal balls, a kind of white alien to the Earth.

And his eyes, if it was possible, set upon Aidan specifically and had a gleam of recognition now.

"So you've come back," he said, his voice like a hollow whisper, scratchy and hoarse.

Aidan didn't say anything, for there were no words and there was no more time for words. He put the gun in front of him and fired, not even thinking. The Eternity Killer's eyes widened, the smirk leaving his face, and he lunged far enough to the side that the bullet didn't hit his head as Aidan intended. Instead, it grazed his arm.

Then the Eternity Killer, caught off guard maybe for the first time in his long life, just began to run. There were no more words.

Aidan and Octavia began to chase him. Pure adrenaline surging, they ran through the woods. The cold no longer fazed them. He was a large black shape fleeing, a wounded beast. There was no more sound but the ragged breathing of all three of them and the crunching of twigs and ice beneath their boots. Aidan cast periodic, brief glances back at Octavia, who was slower than he, but keeping up consistently. But the Eternity Killer, on his long legs, was running too fast for them to catch. Aidan strained. He would end this now...

There was the oddest thought, just a brief snippet, really, as he ran. He wondered what he'd do with his life once this was done. For the first time he realized he didn't have a plan after the Eternity Killer was gone, and that struck him as so damned strange.

It was just a momentary thought. But it was enough for him not to notice the root jutting up from the ground, tangled and twisted and thick. His foot collided with it and he was sent tumbling. His view was of the sky and ground alternating, and he came to a stop with his whole body aching, lying on his back. Octavia was looking down at him, kneeling with him, asking if he was okay. He told her he was.

But then the Eternity Killer was there. He was looking down at them now.

"You failed again," he said. "You tried so hard and yet you failed."

It was at that point that Aidan realized he was missing the gun. Then the Eternity Killer was holding it up. "Looking for this?" he asked.

"If you're gonna shoot me, just get it over with," Aidan said. "You might as well. I don't think I know what to do anymore."

The Eternity Killer, who in some ways was his oldest and most meaningful relationship, smiled in a way that could've been father-like if not for the ghastly countenance, for his tombstone teeth and those devil-eyes. "I can't kill you yet, Aidan," he said. "We're still having so much fun."

He shook his head. "What?"

But the Eternity Killer dropped the gun. He instead turned his eyes to Octavia, kneeling with Aidan. He reached out and touched her shoulder. Something changed in her eyes. It was like a new shade came over them, one that was more complacent and obedient. Drugged out, Aidan thought. He was reaching for her, but she was already going. She was standing up with the Eternity Killer. She had a kind of pleading look about her, but it was like he'd hypnotized her, and she wouldn't just move away. Aidan pushed himself to his feet.

"Give her back," he said. "Just let her go. Your fight's with me."

"Seems like she's part of it, though," the Eternity Killer said. "I don't think she understands. So I'll show her."

Then, as Aidan lunged forward, hands out to try and save Octavia, she and the Eternity Killer were gone. Just like that, gone, as if he were a magician, pulling a disappearing trick. There was no residue left, no proof that they'd been there at all.

He was alone in the cold. He could see his breath coming out in puffs of white smoke.

# III

She was found three days later, walking along the side of the highway in Chicago at sunrise. The lights were all coming on and there were only a few stragglers on the road, coming home from night shift jobs. They saw her zombie-like, walking on the road with a slow gait and dead eyes. The sight of her was ghastly and unnatural, and although no one who passed her considered themselves a stingy or miserly soul, they felt the clenching in their gut that warned them of danger and the unknown. And so they passed her by, went to work and comforted themselves by thinking I'm sure someone else will help her.

But finally, a man slowed and rolled his windows down, tried to ask her where she was going. She turned and looked at him as if she were just waking from a long, restless sleep.

"Where am I?" she asked.

He told her to get in the car. When she did, he saw her up close, saw that her hair was mussed as if it'd been windblown for hours, and while there were no physical wounds he could see, she looked as traumatized as anyone the man had seen, eyes all hollow, everything about her looking far away. By pure coincidence, the man was a clinical doctor and worked in a small walk-in place in the heart of downtown, helping the poorer segments of the city. And she looked some kind of way, for sure.

She didn't say a word the whole ride down the bridge, into town and into the underground garage that served as parking for the clinic. He had to help her out of the car, guiding her gently by the hand and upper arm into the clinic with its bright lights and abundant white cloth, and she fortunately came willingly. Digging through her belongings, he found her name on a driver's license: Octavia Jones. And there was a list of contacts written on a small, folded piece of paper.

Aidan Peterson found her sitting, dazed, in a small room at the clinic. He had been set adrift since that day in the snow, left alone. He'd looked for her everywhere. Cutting his classes, he'd driven the circumference of the small town and the surrounding areas until his gas was low and his eyes were tired. He couldn't see hide nor hair of the Eternity Killer, Octavia or even the beat-up old Chevy. They had all vanished like a magician's trick. He'd wondered if he were actually just insane.

Defeated, he had returned home to sleep, but felt even as if this were a betrayal. He had continued his search the next day, driving around the perimeter area and talking to locals. No one had seen them. The Eternity Killer had overplayed his hand and now, after this, would never do so again. He was upping his game.

Then, on the third day, he got the call that she'd been picked up on the side of the road. His heart stopped in his chest and he went to her immediately.

He could see that something in her had changed fundamentally, and she might as well have been a new person now. Her eyes were colder and further away, and her attitude was reserved in the manner of a soul in utter shock, like a war veteran, Aidan thought. He recalled the ones who came back over from Vietnam. He'd had to interview a few of them for his Intro class that first year, and they, too, had seemed the same; like someone had reached in with a spoon and scooped all their insides out.

He sat with her a few moments. She said she was hungry. He told her okay, they'd get some food, and he took her hand as if she were a child and they left the clinic. They walked a few blocks, with the traffic sounds in their ears and the pollution smell about everything, reminding Aidan exactly where they were, until they found a McDonalds. They sat in the window and ate. Aidan attempted to tell her some of what had been going on at school, wanting to try and return things to a sense of normalcy. But normal might be out the window forever, he thought. She listened to what he said without any particular investment. Her brain was simply somewhere else.

He did not bring up the Eternity Killer. Not now. That would be a gap to bridge later, if she ever came down from where she was. He didn't know what it would do to her now; that was the problem.

They were walking to his car, parked in the garage, under the giant cement frame of the place, no sunlight at all. She stopped in place, looked up at the shadowy ceiling of the garage, and spoke in a voice that was small and eerily calm, surprising in how it resonated in the massive cavern in which they stood.

"He took me to a dark place," she said. "It wasn't like anywhere I've ever seen on Earth. It was all dark everywhere and sometimes he allowed me to see the Earth, though only the worst parts. People getting sick. Murders in alleys. He told me, through all this, that it was all people were and he was better than that because he could live longer and see more. Whispering in my ear that I didn't have anything to live for because this was all we were. Then he'd take me back to that dark place and it felt like I was never going to get out. I felt like I'd die there. Like I was there decades."

"It's only been three days," Aidan said, reaching out and touching her shoulder. It was meant to be a comforting gesture, but she withdrew from his touch as if he'd burned her.

"He told me I'd never get back," she said. "Told me I was in my new home, and that he'd breed me to be his follower, his acolyte."

"But you are back," Aidan said. "Come on. Let's just go. Let's get you home."

She got close to him and put her hands on his collar. "He's not done with you yet. He talked about you a lot," she said.

"Okay, now..."

"He's not going to give you up," she said, her voice rising in urgency. "He'll want you to chase him forever. As long as you can."

He was softly ushering her to the car, surprised at the revulsion now welling up in him, the fear like water from a struck fire hydrant, springing unpredictably. He didn't want to hear this. Since her disappearance, he supposed he'd not thought much of the Eternity Killer, his bogeyman of years. He'd only been focused on saving Octavia. Now she was back and channeling his words to Aidan. It felt like an odd betrayal, a scar upon his conscience. Everything was perverted now. He felt a squirming uncomfortable feeling, a black snake in his gut.

She got into the car after that with little fanfare. Apparently, the Eternity Killer's message had been delivered well enough.

Octavia would stay with him, sleeping in his room while he took the couch. Her family made frantic calls, her father in particular very angry, inquiring what had happened. Aidan lied and told them he didn't know. He said he'd been walking with her in the woods one day. The both of them chatting about poetry when she disappeared. He said he'd just lost track of time. Octavia's father called him a fucking idiot; said he should be ashamed. He hung up. There was no word on whether they were making the trek over from their native Manhattan.

But after two more days Octavia began to exhibit signs of her old self again, her normal self. She was more responsive and conversational. Aidan would sit with her in the mornings, the both of them eating toast and eggs he'd made, and they conversed about the future. She'd missed a few days of school, but it was not beyond repair. She said she eventually hoped to go back.

"You can any time you want," he told her.

A look of apprehension came over her. "Not yet," she said. "I still haven't gotten the sludge out of me."

She would make comments like this frequently, alluding to an unclean presence about her, but she never elaborated. He went to work and tried not to worry.

It became the new normal for a short time, and Aidan felt that he was living in a bizarre alternate world. Everything had changed. At his job, he went through the motions, writing meaningless things about local calendar events and government meetings. None of it seemed substantial. Instead it seemed to all be ephemeral and cloudlike, human constructs to stave off the inevitable oblivion and darkness. He began to feel like he was on the outside of a smudged, darkened window, looking in at everything and wondering how it had all gotten so fucked up.

He came home one night and found her sitting with her legs curled under her on the balcony. The air with the wind was down in the 30s and she only wore a nightgown with a thin coat. Her legs, pale and milky-colored, were visibly bare underneath her. Aidan spoke and saw his breath before him, translucent fog. "Jesus," he said. "You want to come inside?"

"No, I think I like it out here," she said.

"It's fucking freezing," he said.

She shrugged. "The world's cold sometimes. Regularly, in fact."

"Yeah," he said, trying to smile and put on the sarcastic air they used to share. "That's why we invented inside."

But she didn't respond; just kept staring out at the horizon.

He sighed and sat down with her, back against the wall, knees jutting up. They were facing outward on the balcony, out at the city. And it truly was something, wasn't it? Rows and rows of lights, vertically up and down, seemed to stretch on for miles; an ocean of lights. In the sky, planes came and went, leaving trails of smoke. And there was a whole world beyond all of this, but they could not see it. The buildings were too tall and had entrapped them in this man-made maze.

As if reading his mind, Octavia said, "We just choose to trap ourselves here in the city. 'Cause it's got what we need, you know? We could say to hell with the rest of the world if we had no shame."

"Yeah, I guess," Aidan said, rubbing his own arms – he was cold, and he was wearing three layers. He wondered how Octavia was able to stand this weather.

"But it feels isolating now," Octavia said. "I dunno. I just... since I got back, I've just felt so alien here, like nothing at all makes any sense. I feel like I just got dropped back into the same world I had, but yet everything's strange and unfriendly now. And I look at myself in the mirror and I hate everything about what I see. And I look at the world and it looks like everything's got sharp teeth and can eat me if I go too far, so I just stay here, but even then I'm thinking that I'm just a damn burden to you. And none of it makes sense. But I can feel the cold, so I stay."

Aidan just looked at her. "Hey, I just want to help you. I feel like it's my fault you got taken."

She shrugged. "Who's to say whose fault it was? Probably his, more than anything we did. It was just inevitable, I feel like."

"Still," Aidan said.

"You've been so one-track minded about this Eternity Killer," she said. "I wonder what you'll do when he's gone. How will you deal?"

He opened his mouth to speak and then remembered his brief, fleeting thought as he tripped in the snow, wondering what his life would become. It seemed uncanny that these words were coming out of Octavia's mouth, but then, some part of him, the part that felt they'd been one foot in another world that day in the snow, was unsurprised.

She was looking at him like she could see through him and there was a glassiness to her eyes. He saw there was something missing in her now. She wasn't as she had been, and he'd seen this when she first got back, but now he saw that it was permanent, that there was no going back from this. She had been irrevocably changed, and that filled Aidan with a cold kind of darkness inside. The hollowing again. It kept coming back to that scooped-out feeling.

Then the phone inside was ringing. Aidan got up and walked in, answered it. It was her father calling for her, and he beckoned her to come inside, which she did. She spoke, as if putting on a disguise, sounding like she used to. It filled Aidan with a kind of nostalgia, a heaviness of the heart so thorough and weighty he wanted to cry.

"No, Dad," she was saying, her light, chirpy voice like the one he remembered. "No, I'm fine. Just enjoying a night at home."

He listened to them for a few minutes. The smile on her face was as bright and generous as the one she'd had when he first met her, but when she hung up the phone it evaporated like mist after rain on a hot summer day.

# IV

There were no sightings of the Eternity Killer again for years. It seemed to Aidan that he'd made himself scarce on purpose, wising up to his shortcomings. And he also detected a whiff that this was simply the next level of the game. Now the hunt would be harder.

He tried to remain dedicated to his job. He needed to make a living, after all. The stories came and went, as journalism was an ephemeral thing, never staying in place. Aidan chased his stories the same way he'd chased the Eternity Killer. He rose through the ranks. Eventually he was known as a quality writer and people came to him with stories and tips and confidential things. It was a job, a mechanical thing.

He dated here and there, women who were attractive and career-minded, and for whom dating was a pastime, a brief respite from their busy lives. None of them turned into lasting relationships. Mostly just dinners and movies, a cold and clinical line of nights.

Octavia had long since left his care. After that night on the patio, she seemed to get better. By the end of that week she was talking about moving out, and then was actually doing it that Sunday. She looked at Aidan with something like a mental camera, taking in everything about him and his apartment. Then she was gone, just out in the world, and Aidan found himself rehearsing what he'd have to say if she was found hit by a car somewhere, in her daze of the recent weeks.

But that didn't end up happening.

From time to time he'd see her, and they tried to keep their conversations focused on other things, an unspoken agreement having been made to shy away from talk of the Eternity Killer or what happened that winter in the woods, those three lost days. They saw movies in the evenings and got coffee and omelets on weekends at a select few diners they both enjoyed. They became aware of politics, and their conversations became animated again, words crackling, their opinions flying and sometimes colliding. It felt like before again, and Aidan wanted to keep it that way; preserve it like a museum exhibit.

But then there was the article that came over the wire, a big story from overseas. It happened now and again, usually for political strife and trade deals. This one was something grislier. A murder, it happened, of an Egyptian diplomat. That previous day he had returned from a trip to China, and had been found that morning, heart cut out, a gaping hole in his chest, his face a frozen mask of horror. The local police were stunned, the article said. They had no clue what they were dealing with.

Aidan felt a long-dormant thing stirring in him. His mind immediately, without any qualification, went to the amount of money in his savings. A ticket to Egypt was... how much? He decided he'd figure it all out.

He told his boss he needed to take a few days off. Family troubles, he said. His boss looked at him skeptically, and Aidan briefly thought that it was obvious why this man was a reporter; he could not stop questioning the world.

As he walked out of the building, Aidan Peterson felt driven and purposeful, much like a journalist himself.

He met with Octavia that night, back in her own apartment now, a high rise 10 stories up. She'd told him before that it felt good being here, so far above the world. The lights were dim and the night pitch-black outside. To Aidan, it felt like the both of them were completely alone, which was a rare feeling in general.

They started out beating around the bush; her telling him she had an interview that Friday with a specialized marine biology school program down in Florida. She said she felt good about it and that it was nice to be moving along with life.

"There is something to be said for it," Aidan said.

"I'll be out on a boat all day," she said.

"Don't forget your sunscreen," he advised. There was something restless twitching in him. She saw it, too. She asked what was going on with him.

And so he took a breath and told her he was going to hunt down the Eternity Killer. They spoke of him only rarely now, just in passing, with Aidan feeling like his talking of the old devil would only trigger something in Octavia and bring her back to her odd otherness of when she'd first been found. But now there was no getting around it.

She listened and, when he finished, looked at him with pleading eyes.

"I wouldn't go," she said.

"I know," Aidan said.

"But you," she said, "you're not like me, are you? You'll chase this thing forever. It's more important to you than anything."

"You've known that for years," he said.

"Yeah," she said, crossing her arms underneath her bosom, pacing the room. She wasn't meeting his eyes anymore. "But then things happened. Now I just can't... you know, I can't get with it anymore. And I'm sorry."

"I'm not asking you to," he said. "But I wanted you to know what's happening."

"What for?"

He realized he didn't have a good answer. He said, "Because you're important to me," because it was his only answer. She looked like it didn't satisfy her, these words. Outside, orange lamp-lights flickered, and he became conscious again of the isolation. It felt like everything had more weight up here.

The plane ride was the loneliest Aidan had ever felt; leaning against the window and watching the ocean sail beneath them. All of them up there in that giant machination, all for different reasons traveling to the oldest hub of recorded civilization, and yet all so close together. Aidan thought it bizarre. He slept for a little while, and woke to the sun, bright and pale, gleaming through the window; an unwelcome wake-up call. Hostesses were going around with trays of pre-packaged breakfasts; bananas and muffins and cups of coffee or juice. The other passengers were waking as well, all with the murmurs and rustlings of the recently conscious, trying to reassess themselves in the world.

Egypt was a place of sandy colors and tall, cluttered buildings, not unlike the middle-class and poor apartments he'd seen in Chicago for years, save for their sunnier colors. The sun was inescapable, and the skies were bleached baby-blue and cloudless. He got to his hotel room in the mid-morning, a small space with a trim bed and a night-table. The window looked out on the city, but in the far distance he could see the sands. He showered and then read for a little while, to level out his mind.

Then, as the sun was sinking and casting its red-orange rays across the city, he left the hotel and started his quest. He asked everyone he could about the Eternity Killer, describing him in detail and hoping he hadn't drastically changed his looks. But he knew he hadn't. The concierge at the hotel hadn't seen him; nor had two cabbies he flagged down.

But he began to have more luck when he came to the bar, a large warehouse-sized space with wooden, rickety tables spread out like a country-western concert space in America and a high oak bar with a stern-faced man serving beer behind it. Aidan sat at this bar and he spoke to anyone who could speak English even mildly well. A few of them told him they had no clue what he was talking about, had not seen the man at all. But then there was the squat little man with his grey walrus-stache, who said he lived in a slum-like apartment on the outskirts of town, and had a neighbor who'd complained of seeing the tall man in black coming and going at odd hours, making noise and making it hard for her to sleep.

Aidan's eyes were wide and he was suddenly very awake. He asked the little man if he could take him there. The little man said it'd cost him, and Aidan paid up.

Five minutes later he was in the little man's Jeep, and they were rumbling down the old streets, the engine struggling. They came to a ramshackle structure, barely standing and which would've been knocked down with even slightly harsh storm-winds. It was the color of mud and the doors looked to be paper-thin. The old man grunted as he got out of the Jeep and Aidan followed. They walked up a set of stairs constructed of stone, and then were knocking on one of the flimsy doors, which seemed to rattle and vibrate with every point of contact. Finally, a tiny old woman, wrinkled face and hair the color of snow, answered the door. She stared curiously at Aidan. Then she directed her attention to the old man and spoke in her native tongue, presumably inquiring who this white man on her doorstep was. They exchanged words, and then the old man said to Aidan: "She'll tell you what you want to know. But you can't tell anyone it came from her. She wants to be completely anonymous."

"That's a fine deal," Aidan said.

And so he was invited into her apartment. It was a little place with a large bookshelf and two ancient, soft chairs and a loveseat cluttered around a tiny antique glass coffee-table. Here they sat. The old woman spoke and the man translated.

"He started sleeping here a week ago," the man translated for his neighbor. "On the upper second floor at the far end of the balcony. He would walk with these big heavy boots at around 1 a.m. all the time, going who knows where. This isn't a sleazy kind of place. We aren't some hovel for druggies or prostitutes. But he seemed to be into something. He was so loud and seemed to come and go all the time. Finally, I confronted him. I went out and shouted at him to stop making such a racket, that we were trying to sleep. He looked at me with such a fierce glance. A horrific look. It was like something out of a terrible movie. I had never felt such a piercing cold. He didn't say a word, though. Just kept walking."

"Is he still living here now?" Aidan asked.

The old woman shrugged, said something short, and the man translated her words: "I haven't seen him today."

Outside the dusk had fallen and the night firmly set in. The old woman made them all tea and they had the radio on, where commentators chattered away in a language Aidan couldn't understand.

Then, as they sipped their tea, the footsteps began to ring out on the ceiling. Aidan instantly saw why it had been a concern; the footsteps were loud and raucous and made the whole little apartment shake. They sounded like thunderclaps and pots and pans, both together somehow, right outside the door. The old woman sat frozen, not afraid so much as resigned. The man, though, had a look of horror about him, eyes wide as saucers.

"Haven't you heard this before?" Aidan whispered, unsure why he was whispering; it wasn't like they were in a library. But the feeling persisted; that he didn't want to attract undue attention.

"I'm a heavy sleeper usually," the man said.

Then there was the sound of a door creaking open, rusted hinges straining, and then the door slamming shut. Aidan thought it a marvel that this building still stood upright.

He got to his feet. There was still a little bit of tea in his cup, cooling now. He didn't have the will to finish, and felt at that moment like he didn't need even one bit of food or drink, his entire being focused elsewhere...

"I'm going to go see him," Aidan said. The man nodded solemnly, the kind of look about him as if he were nodding at a man about to attend his own funeral. The woman spoke in English for the first time that night: "Be safe."

Up the rickety stairs he went, the crisp air nipping at him. To the west of him he could see the man-made constructs growing more sparse, giving way to the desert. Eventually it would all be that; just miles of sand. Somewhere out there were monuments too old to comprehend. Like from some different universe.

The door at the edge of the second floor, right at the corner, spoke something ominous to him. There was nothing particularly different on a mechanical level; it just radiated some kind of negative aura, and Aidan felt the kind of superstition that had haunted man since consciousness was born screaming in the void of the primitive Earth, the old ape-brain rearing up and superseding everything he'd evolved into since his childhood.

But still he went. He stood there with his hand raised up ready to knock on the door. Like he would just do this; just knock on the door like a Jehovah's Witness, and he felt like laughing at that thought...

But then the door flew open and the Eternity Killer stood there already. Like he'd just been waiting. He looked grim as the grave already, gaunter and older somehow, though Aidan could not place a definitive way that he looked older. His face twisted into a sick grin when he saw Aidan.

"My old friend, at last," he said, in that same branch-on-glass voice that sent a chill down Aidan's spine.

"We aren't friends," Aidan said in response, and then lunged forward, punching the Eternity Killer in the side of the head and sending him crashing into the door frame. The tall gaunt man in black reeled back, standing up on shaky legs, wiping blood from his face, though it was an odd pitch-black color, nothing like human blood.

"The fuck are you?" Aidan asked.

But the Eternity Killer did not answer. Instead he lunged forward and grappled with Aidan. The two of them wrestled there, the Killer's hands, clawed and sharp, digging into Aidan's flesh, drawing blood. The fresh cuts felt cold in the night and the blood dripped to the ground. He cried out as the Killer clawed his cheek, ribbons of flesh coming loose. Aidan felt a surge of power through him then. He shoved the Killer back and then began pummeling him with his fists and his feet, feeling an adrenaline through him like a drug now. He hit and kicked until his veins burned, and it occurred to him that this was what he'd craved, really. He didn't want some easy kill with a gun. What mattered was confronting his family's murderer with nothing but the body he was born with. The primal violence. The kill by the most honest and natural means...

The Eternity Killer was clawing and trying to fight back, but he was losing. Aidan had cornered him there on the balcony. He kept hitting, kept kicking. There was a small smattering of people out now, sleepy-eyed, watching with some mixture of awe and skeptical disbelief. Could they really be seeing this, they wondered.

The Eternity Killer looked at him with something like mischief in his white hollow eyes, however that was possible. He said, "Not here," and Aidan heard it like a whisper.

And then the Killer leapt over the balcony, and he was a flying black shape in the Egyptian night, a spectre in the winds...

There were audible gasps. Aidan was running down the stairs. In his peripheral vision he could see the Killer fleeing into the wilds beyond them, away from civilization.

As his feet hit the ground, Aidan shouted at everyone to get back in their houses, it wasn't safe, although he didn't know if there was any danger left and didn't know if anyone could understand him. He could see the Killer as a disappearing blot in the dark, heading for the abandoned warehouses and the worse slums, and beyond that the wilderness, God's country, or what could be appropriately called that. And so he followed.

The stars were brighter out in the country, even more so than in the heart of the city. It was all new to Aidan, for back in the States light pollution so often obscured the stars. He ran with no concern for his body, running on pure adrenaline, a machine. The tall husks of buildings he passed looked like giant corpses here. The weeds protruded from the ground like tufts of rotting black hair. There was a stench from somewhere, but he couldn't place it as anything he'd smelled before. It was warm and foul, something left in the sun too long.

It was a few blocks more, now with only barely-held-together apartment buildings, holes rotted through plaster and rain-stained walls, before he realized how silent it was out here. It hadn't been a metropolis back at the apartment they'd started at, but there had been the tangible presence of humanity there. Here, even that was long gone. Everything gave the aura of the absence of life, like an ancient civilization to be found by explorers, all the broken-down structures like a mirror opposite of the historic pyramids and such that tourists came to this country for.

In retrospect, Aidan realized he'd let his guard down here, to indulge this thought.

He didn't hear the slight footsteps of the Killer behind him, now having modified his approach from the thunderous uncaring steps he'd terrified residents of the apartment complex with.

And he only barely registered the sound of the wind as the long arm of the Killer, holding a shard of glass, came down. Aidan moved just an inch, detecting the threat, but the glass cut into his shoulder. He cried out. Went to his knees. Turned around to the face of the Killer, bruised and battered now after their scuffle, face a mask of rage uncharacteristic to him.

Sensing danger now, Aidan's instincts kicked in.

He rolled onto his back and took a breath, and then kicked upwards with both feet as hard as he could. He caught the Killer in the gut and sent him reeling backwards. Then the Killer was on the ground and Aidan got to his feet. He spotted the glass shard and grabbed it, and then he was kneeling over the Eternity Killer, knee to his gut, holding him down. The glass shard was close to his face.

"Tell me who you are," Aidan said. "Tell me what you are."

The Eternity Killer giggled; a high and inhuman sound. "That's what this is, huh? That's all you've come here to learn? Is your curiosity so important to you?"

"Fuck are you saying?" Aidan asked.

"You don't really care about who I am," the Killer said. "You're here because I've made you. You are the product of everything I've wrought, and I did it for fun, to see what it'd do to you. I get bored like that."

"You're speaking in fucking riddles," Aidan said, and brought the glass shard down, impaling the Killer through the upper shoulder. The Killer let out a high scream, the pain of a being not of the world. Black colorless blood spurted up and splashed Aidan's face and torso. He didn't notice. "Tell me what the hell you are," he said.

"I'm everything and nothing," the Eternity Killer said. "I can't die. I was born in the stars and I've been alive since close to the dawn of time. Came down like a comet and I haven't been able to leave. I feed on the hearts because it's nourishing. They keep me alive."

"Maybe you should die," Aidan said.

"Don't know if I can," the Killer said.

"You can try," Aidan said.

He raised his arm and brought the glass shard down again, this time straight into the Killer's left eye, that white orb, now punctured as the Killer screamed and screamed. The blood spurted up again, black chilling slime, as well as white goop from his eye. It covered Aidan like he'd been rolling in the muck in a pigsty. The Killer was gasping and wheezing now, a hole in his face. Aidan could see the universe through that hole. But he could feel the Killer's life force slipping away. Movement stopping and pulse slowing...

Then it was just Aidan alone. He was in the weeds and surrounded by buildings abandoned for decades, and the Egyptian stars above him shined down on him in judgment. After a few moments of quiet he got up and walked back towards civilization, leaving the body there.

## V

Aidan returned back to his hotel and realized it was past 1 a.m., the night a strange parallel world, everything feeling out of sorts. He looked at what had transpired, out there in the country, and could not fathom how it had happened. It was the work of another mind. Perhaps some kind of strange ambrosia or alchemy, he thought. But it had not been his mind, not him as a person.

He washed his face in the sink and took off all of his clothes, so soaked in the unidentifiable pitch-black blood of the Killer. They were the last remnants of what had happened. After a shower he clothed himself again anew and threw his soiled clothes in the dumpster outside the hotel, watching the bag sink into the cavern of the bin like evidence of a crime to the bottom of an ocean. Then he returned to his room and slept so easily that it was as if sleep had been right at his door.

He slept for a few hours, waking with a dry mouth and an aching head, like a hangover or a slight cold was coming on. The sun shone in and downstairs, everything was normal, and no one looked twice at him. He found this comforting in an odd, electrifying way – could he have gotten away with murder? It lent him more certainty that the whole thing had just been some kind of strange surreality, that it hadn't really happened in the real world. Not in the way that normal things happened, anyway.

Boarding the plane, the feeling of slight queasiness, that sick feeling, persisted. He laid his head back and as the plane glided over the ocean he slept some more. Egypt was fading behind him. Soon he'd go back to his job in America, which seemed bizarre to him now, the construct of men, something utterly temporary and which would be gone very soon in the grand scheme.

In his head, visions swirled. He thought of an infinite blanket of stars against a cosmic blackness. Then there were ages of man, rising and falling in rapid speed; towers built and civilizations forged, but how flimsy? They were gone within seconds, only for new ones to rise and fall in equal celerity. He was seeing it all. It all seemed so transparently temporary.

In the morning, once he had landed and slept in his own apartment, the sick, queasy cold feeling was gone. In fact, Aidan felt better than he had in months – certainly better than before he'd gone to Egypt. He woke and looked out the window at the cloudless sky and felt the cool air blowing in. He made a cup of steaming bold coffee and drank it while sitting on his porch, leafing through the day's newspaper. There was no feeling of haste anymore. He went to work and felt at sync with himself and with the universe. It was an odd and rare feeling.

Octavia called him that same evening, and they arranged to meet for coffee the following day after work. They met in their old spot, a diner, and sat in the corner booth where they could maintain the illusion of privacy. The waitress poured their coffee and they waited patiently for her to retreat to the main area of the place. Then Octavia, leaning in, asked what really happened over there, as she'd only gotten a very short version over the phone previously.

And so Aidan, leaning in as well, with a cockiness and assuredness that he'd never had before, told her what had transpired, feeling his head back in that cold, quiet Egyptian night, feeling the thrust of his arm holding the glass shard, stabbing, stabbing...

When he finished his telling, she sat back and her eyes were wide. "Wow."

"I know," he said.

"That's... uh, a lot," she said.

"He's gone, though," Aidan said. "You don't have to worry about him anymore."

She nodded, but she did not seem as elated as Aidan had expected. She wouldn't look at him, again like that last night in her apartment, when it had felt like just the two of them were the last people alive.

He asked her what was wrong. His coffee was getting cold, but he didn't care. The bravado in him was seeping away as sure as though a hole had been blown in him.

Eventually, after she sipped her coffee a few more times, Octavia spoke up: "I'm just not sure I like what it's done to you."

"To me?"

"Yes. You have a different aura about you."

"Aura?"

"It's just... I don't know how to describe this," she said, putting a hand to her forehead as if she felt a headache coming on. "You seem like you're actually happy that you've killed someone. Not that it's him specifically, but that you were able to stab someone so many times. You sounded like that excited you."

He reached out and was touching her hands, covering them with one of his. It just felt right. "It's just about the Eternity Killer, Octavia," he said. "It was only him. Maybe you don't get it.

But I've been waiting for this for... hell, my whole life, really."

She nodded. After a few more beats, another sip of coffee, she said: "I guess I am real glad he's dead."

At this he grinned. He called the waitress over, and asked her to refill his coffee, which she did.

They spent more time together over the coming months, as winter bled into the blustery spring, with its fast and awkward awakening almost like a puberty of Mother Nature, and then into the long and rolling folds of summer.

They would drive to the coast in late June. There was no stated change in what they were to one another, but the feeling was there as sure as seasons shifting. They drove through a storm in the upper East coast, but came through it in time for the coastal New York sky, bleeding colors, all red and orange and yellow like a painter's palette.

The cabin they'd found, from a friend of a friend of his and negotiated over the phone, was way out of the way from the tourist spots. It was all weeds and grass and solitude out there, and in the evenings they could stand on the beach and feel like it went on for infinity, just for them. There were occasional cars speeding by on the highway too fast, and every now and then sporadic bursts of noise from kids playing volleyball sounded. But for the most part, the quiet was like a glass dome that shielded them from the rest of the outside world.

The innards of the cabin were all wood and there was no electricity. At night they'd sit by the fireplace and talk, the both of them bundled in blankets. If they were quiet, they'd hear fireflies and the sounds of the world from which they were now separate, meshing into a kind of frantic buzzing. And they were glad for the reprieve.

They would wake beside each other in the mornings and lazily drift through the days. They became friends with the local restaurant owners and coffee shop baristas. They took to dining and drinking often, gaining a bit of weight and trying to burn it off on their long walks, hand in hand, down the beach. It was a lazy time. They each called work and said they'd be back later and later. Might as well just go the long mile, use up all their vacation time, was their logic.

On the beach one evening, the both of them lay on their sides and alternately looked at each other and at the shimmering sun reflected in the water. Octavia said, "It seems like we earned this, doesn't it?"

"How do you mean?" he asked.

"Like, we worked so hard to get here. We spent years hunting the Eternity Killer. You went all the way across the ocean..."

At this, there was a brief gleam of remembrance. He realized he had not thought of the Eternity Killer in some time, not since before they'd left Chicago. It was, strangely, as if the memory had been wiped clean from him. But now it came back in spots and snippets, and he felt a weird hot burn in his throat rising up like vomit.

"And I'm this close to being done with my degree," she said. She was sitting up now, elbows on her knees, eyes on the ocean. "I'll be out there in a boat. Studying who knows what. It feels pretty good, and I can't always say so."

Then she noticed he wasn't looking at her or with her. Instead he had turned to the side, was clutching his throat.

"What's wrong?" she asked.

"Nothing," he said, reaching over to their basket for the water bottle he'd brought. "Just parched, is all." He took off the cap and drank liberally, the water spilling onto his chin, down to his chest.

That night Aidan snapped awake. He felt something in him. That burning feeling again, except now it was spreading to his whole body. Slow, though, like water released incrementally from a tap. Everything was hot and sweaty, and he got out of bed, needing fresh air more than anything else. Casting a look back to make sure he hadn't woken Octavia. But she slept on, undisturbed.

He walked barefoot out of the house and down onto the beach. The sand was cold and soft against his feet and the water was lively, lapping on the sand, bursting up in little spurts against the endless night sky. Aidan felt a weakness about him then, related perhaps to the heat, and he sank to his knees in the sand. The moon was full and brighter than Aidan had maybe ever seen it, to the point where he wondered if this was some once-in-a-lifetime super-moon event and he'd simply missed the memo. They hadn't been keeping up with the news, after all.

But the burning persisted. He wondered if it was some weird cancer. Maybe something he'd brought back from Egypt. It seemed like he was always reading about that sort of thing from explorers and travelers.

It didn't feel like anything of Earth, though.

Instead, he began to hear a soft voice, whispering something like ice scraping on a window. He could not make out the words. They seemed to be some sort of incantation; muttered in a quick and monotonous way, and in that voice that seemed so familiar to him. Yet he'd forgotten for what felt like months now. He didn't know how that was possible.

The moon seemed to stare into him, as if it had a giant eye somewhere. Whatever it was, Aidan could feel a kind of probing of the soul. He looked down at his hands and arms and was surprised at how pale they looked in this light. He knew on some level it was the moon doing it, but he thought there was something genuinely different about his looks. Pushing himself up from the sand, he ran inside.

The mirror was dark in the night and he didn't want to wake Octavia. So he just stood there and stared at himself in that night reflection, seeing the same sallow, long face and big eyes he'd always had, but why did he look so pale, and why were his eyes so damned bright? The voice echoed in his head, cold and sharp, a ghost that would not leave.

Over breakfast the next day, the both of them sitting at a rooftop cafe that offered a view of the ocean, he told her what had transpired the previous night. When he finished, she'd clapped a hand over her mouth in shock.

"Oh, jeez," she said. "Do you want to get to a doctor? I think you should."

"I don't know," Aidan said. "It's weird. It's not like any sickness I ever had before."

"Well, all the more reason," she was saying.

"I want to see how it goes," he said. "Let's not ruin this yet. We only got a few days left."

She rolled her eyes. "Typical man," she said. "You'd rather fall over and die than ask for help."

"Hey now, you know I'd never let it get that far," he said. He could feel guilt rising, though; he knew he hadn't told her everything. So he took a breath and then decided to just say it. If he was wrong, they could laugh about it later, he figured. "I think I've missed something, though. I guess I was afraid to say it."

She looked at him suspiciously. "Well, that's ominous..."

"I think I'm becoming the Eternity Killer," Aidan said.

"What?"

"Yeah," he said. "I think his blood got in me when I killed him, and I think it's turning me into him. Like something passed on. We were always wondering how he lived so long, right? Maybe it was never just the one. Maybe it was different guys throughout decades."

"Well, that's... crazy, you know," she said, but her voice had no conviction.

She sat silent and just looked at him, studying his face for any sign that he was kidding. Seeing none, she was transported back to that awful three day stretch of nothing, when she'd been tortured by the Eternity Killer, kept in that vast black space. It made her feel small and then she wasn't hungry anymore. She looked at Aidan, seeing the ghastly serious mask of his face, and then said, "We're going to the doctor."

So Aidan sat on a doctor's table, feeling childish again, like when his mother used to drag him there for every cold, every itch. Though his real fear wasn't that he'd be diagnosed – rather, the opposite; that no one would be able to tell what was wrong and that he would continue to undergo metamorphosis. That he wasn't crazy. Soon, then, he'd be unrecognizable, if his worst fears were correct.

The doctor, stern and businesslike, went through the whole process of giving Aidan a physical, testing his temperature and blood pressure, and then taking a sample of his blood, telling him they would have results back in a matter of days.

And Aidan walked out of there with his poker face on, afraid inside, the creeping realization that he had gone beyond the world of the humans.

The notice came in the mail at the end of the week. By that time, they'd left the beach and were back at their jobs in the city. Aidan opened the letter with trembling hands, the culmination of a week of waiting, clammy hands and restless sleep. The impulse to just look away, to pace the apartment until he collected himself. But that was futile. He'd never really be ready. Instead he took a breath and read through the test.

Once he was done, he put in the call to Octavia, feeling jittery, like he'd drank down a big cup of coffee.

"Well?" she asked.

"I, uh... I'm perfectly healthy," he said. "It's better than the last time I did this. I'm apparently perfectly healthy."

"Well, that's great!" she said, sounding somehow elated but apprehensive at the same time, multitudes in her voice. "I mean, isn't it?"

"I don't know," Aidan said. "I've woken up in a cold sweat a few times this week, same as when we were in the cabin. It's hard to get back to sleep then. I feel like I'm invincible and that I can live forever, and the whole universe seems wide open to me. Like I could literally just rip open the sky, go anywhere."

Octavia was silent as she considered this. The phone seemed so empty then, as did Aidan's house, and the temptation to leave was growing.

They spent a weekend together after that that felt very much like an extended eulogy, though Octavia would not hear of that, would not entertain the thought. She said it was just because they'd been working hard. Aidan had noticed his skin paling, even despite the amount of times he took walks in the summer sun. He had noticed his diminishing appetite. There was a different kind of craving in him, though it was vague. He was afraid to find out what exactly would quench him these days.

Octavia pretended not to notice. She had a whole itinerary planned. They went to a favorite restaurant for dinner, gorging on salmon and wine even though Aidan didn't feel hungry or thirsty, and then caught a late movie, where Aidan found it in him to laugh unabashedly. Then they walked in the park under the moon. There were few others around, and the sounds of traffic even seemed far away.

"If I go, you'll be alright?" he asked. He wasn't looking at her. The shadows were a benefit here. He didn't think he could stand to see her face right then.

"If you... go?" she asked.

"Just tell me you'll be alright," he said. "I want to know you'll be able to move on, you know. That this isn't making you too sad or anything."

They had stopped now, standing face to face now, finally, by the shimmering black lake. It was cold outside but they barely felt it. She wore a pouting, petulant face now.

"What is it?" he asked.

"What should I even say?" she asked, her voice all trembling, afraid and yet defiant, sad and yet full of rage. "That I'll be fine now that you've monopolized my interest, my time? I got into this with you, what, seven years ago now? Because I was curious. Because you were fun and we had a good time. And now, I guess, we're something else, maybe. We're still having fun and I've invested myself, you know? And now, what, you might leave and I just have to nod and say okay, and just go along? You treat me like I'm some accessory. Some kind of side piece. Fuck that, Aidan. I told you not to go over to Egypt. I told you."

He looked at her with multitudes in his eyes. She just stood there and stared him down. Her anger was like a wildfire, and he couldn't find anything to say that would be satisfactory. He could feel the weight of what he'd done. They walked home together, but they were not really together in any other sense but that. It felt now like they were on disparate planets and the connection between them had been severed. For him, it had happened like a lifetime ago, as he could see eternity, and this moment, the present one, felt so damned small now.

In the dark and quiet of his bedroom, she slept. They had spoken barely five words to each other after his botched attempt at saving things in the park, and she told him she was tired, flopping down on the bed and losing consciousness almost immediately. Aidan undressed and lay beside her for a little while, the lights off and the moon shining through. It was always the moon now, Aidan thought; an odd season for sure. It always spoke to him – he could hear that little voice whispering to him that he'd been wrong his whole life. That the Eternity Killer had never just been one man. It had always been a passed down job, inherited from one unfortunate wandering damned soul to the next, and it had chosen him. The fever was giving way to an odd, queasy enlightenment. The way forward seemed almost simple now.

Lying there on his back, Aidan felt a heightening of all his senses. He could hear everything, it seemed. Down on the ground, five stories below, a dog barked, his owner likely tired, rubbing his eyes. A taxicab passed, lightly playing an old Beatles classic. A homeless man shuffled aimlessly through the street, his battered shoes scraping pavement. Aidan didn't know why any of it was important. Everything now seemed like exactly what it was, and nothing more. He felt that he now saw the reality of things.

But with this came another thing, a craving. He felt it more deeply and intensely than any hunger he'd ever felt. It seemed to hollow him out, gutting him, and he knew there was only one thing that could ever satiate him.

Rising on his elbow, he looked at Octavia sleeping next to him. In that moment, he could hear both their hearts beating, thump thump, not quite in sync. It was louder than he had ever heard a heartbeat, and he knew if he stayed there, he'd give into the impulse that was now drilling at his skull, a begging louder than any proper civilized human one.

So he got out of bed delicately, pulled on pants and a shirt and a jacket and shoes, and he left his own apartment. The time on his watch said it was just after 1 a.m.

Outside, the cold air nipped at him. The guy with the dog that he'd heard was gone. But he could still see the homeless man, now a block and a half up, moving at the lackadaisical pace of a man with nowhere to go. Aidan considered him, could hear his heart beating in the same lazy manner. The thirst was too strong now. He felt parched. In the future, he told himself he wouldn't do this in any way close to his apartment or where anyone knew him. He began to follow the homeless man. In step, they walked through the night.

# W. T. Paterson's
# Shopping List

Wet food for my demon cats
Advil for when my demon cats discover there's food in the bag
Paper towels for when my demon cats rip open the food and goes ham
Ice cream for me, because I've earned it.

# Heart of Darkness
## *W. T. Paterson*

They had drugged and taken the girl in broad daylight putting her in the backseat of their black Lincoln town car as a church bell counted off the hours marking another life a world away.

At the black site, their car was hidden deep inside of a parking garage overgrowing with weeds and tall grass. Around them were abandoned industrial parks and dried up ponds that at one time had served as a peaceful view of solitude for employees on lunch.

Through the front doors and down to the basement level were a handful of nearly empty cement rooms. One had a single metal chair bolted to the floor. The far side had a small dogs eye view. The neighboring room could have passed as an operating station in an ER with a table, tools, and a myriad of coma inducing drugs. A separate area had a plush couch with overstuffed pillows and an enormous TV. Beside it was a stove, a fully stocked refrigerator, and a portable cooler.

The girl was waking up and starting to struggle, so they chloroform ragged her until she went limp. The man who called himself Mr. Water carried her over his shoulder into the empty cement room with the stainless steel chair. He bound her hands behind the back and tied a red bandana around her face. The man who called himself Mr. Fire watched casually from the doorway, silhouetted as though only his shadow self existed.

"Coffee?" Fire asked walking over to a Keurig machine and loading it with a K cup.

"I'm all set," Water replied kicking off his shoes and flopping onto the couch after he closed the heavy steel door.

"You sure? America runs on Dunkin," Fire said.

"Any Coke?"

Fire opened up the refrigerator and moved around some cold cuts, condiments and beer to find the last can.

"Ice?"

They both laughed really hard at this. There was enough ice in their black site to sink three Titanics.

"It never gets old," Water said, catching the can and cracking it open. "You want first watch, or do you want me to take it?"

"By all means," Fire said, "keep your feet up. I'll jostle you awake when I'm feeling ready for my shoes to come off." He blew on his coffee and winked. Taking a slow sip, he walked out of the room and into the cell where their hostage was tied to her chair. She was awake and sweating. The bandana inside of her mouth was slowly inching out. "You can scream all you want, darling, but no one will hear you except for us and if we're being quite frank, I'd rather not have a headache while I read."

"Please sir, just let me go. I won't tell anyone! I wouldn't even know what to tell them."

"My dear, you are worth far too much money to simply let go. And if I may, your rhetorical appeal could use some work. Most of these girls make…bargains…to at least be untied. You haven't given me any incentive, and so I must decline. But the sentiment is not lost!"

Fire took a sip of his coffee. The light from the doorway illuminated the girl in the chair whose eyes were puffy from crying and shoulders shaking from shock.

"My name is Katrín! I'm only 15 years old, 16 next month!" she whimpered, "I'm not a virgin, I know how to do things! We can make a…bargain."

"You're fiery, I'll give you that but there shall be no sexual favors. Besides, you're too young for my tastes. Too young even for my associate."

Katrín went wide-eyed.

"Have you sold your soul to the Devil and this is punishment?"

"The Devil?!" Fire laughed, nearly spilling his coffee. "My darling, if only you would be alive long enough to realize that the Devil and God are just human constructs to explain away an unexplainable world. What you call evil is nothing more than a fable created to keep the poor from starving at night. There is no such thing."

He blew her a kiss and closed the door, immersing Katrín in total darkness. She cried out a few times, but the thick cement walls did little for her efforts.

Fire found a chair in Mr. Vertigo's surgery room and opened up the book he was reading. But then the noises began.

They were small tremors in the wall and then a deep guttural laugh that seemed both eerily distant and alarmingly present. Had Mr. Vertigo come early?

The more he listened, the more Fire thought someone else had arrived. A male voice was coming from the room where Katrín was bound, and Water was asleep on the couch with a muted game of soccer playing on the big screen.

Fire put down his paperback and creaked open the door to the cement hostage cell. Katrín was staring at him and drooling white foam from her mouth. Her skin had taken on a greenish hue and looked like it had started to crack open. Puss was boiling through a sore on her neck and her hair was dripping with oil.

"What's this?" he asked sternly and turned on the single Edison bulb above the girl's chair. When he did, he saw the walls etched with inverted crosses, 666's and the phrase Never Bow.

The light bulb started glowing hot and when he looked, the glass began filling with a thick red liquid.

"I cast this room into shadow with the blood of the children I will never have," Katrín said, though it wasn't her voice. It was far more sinister.

A group of mice ran out from under the chair and fled towards the open door where Mr. Fire was standing. A flock of birds flew by the windows so low to the ground that Fire watched them crash into the glass of the dogs eye view and break their wings.

"Oh my…" Fire said and closed the door. The room temperature had dropped 40 degrees and he could see his breath. The moment the door clicked shut, it violently swung open and pulled him headfirst into the cell. He landed hard on his shoulder and somersaulted onto his knees. "This could be a problem," he muttered before standing up and brushing the collected dust off of his pants.

He walked out of the room and shut the door again, this time without any issues. Mr. Water was stirring with a yawn and reaching for his Coke.

"What's that noise?" he asked in wide mouthed syllables, squinting at the TV.

"I don't mean to raise any unnecessary alarms, but there's a bit of a situation."

Water shot upright.

"As in…"

"As in the girl we took is acting possessed."

"Like…demonically possessed?" Water's face twisted with skepticism.

"What I'm saying is that she is acting possessed among other...oddities. I was hoping that you could be ready to take an earlier watch before she destroys herself and the whole operation becomes worthless."

Water nodded and then looked at the TV. The score was tied, 2-2. What was at the front of his mind was something far greater than soccer, it was the sign that he had been asking for ever since that day 10 years ago. He clicked the TV off and stared off into the dark screen where the reflected image of Fire was walking back towards the room.

"I'll do what I can," he said watching his partner's reflection pull a rolling chair into the holding cell, which was somehow glowing red. Then he caught the distorted blackened reflection of himself sitting forward with his head in his hands.

Mr. Fire rolled the chair into the holding cell and sat down in front of Katrín. She was smiling, her face breaking out into pulsing boils.

"I know you think this whole demon routine is supposed to scare me, make me realize my own humanity, and somehow find God – but it won't."

The possessed girl laughed and leaned forward in her chair.

"I do like a challenge."

"Wonderful," Fire said, clapping his hands together like a realtor who had just sold a home, "then let's start with the basics. Did you know that there has never been a documented – or even reported – case of an atheist being possessed by the devil?"

"Is that the case, Lucas?" she said using his real name. "Well, I guess everything that happens is thoroughly documented and nothing is ever left out."

"Your sarcasm is biting. Are you certain that it isn't one of the seven deadly sins?"

"Pride is, Lucas, or Mr. Fire, or whatever stupid name you think you'll get away with," she snarled delightfully.

"Pride is an emotion, and I stick to the facts. For instance, I didn't look at the walls before I tied you up. All this Devil worship mumbo jumbo could have been here long before I noticed it. Fact: I've never once replaced that light bulb. The temperature drop could be due to the run down ventilation systems here in this building. But these are things I do not know and cannot prove, and what I do not know is plentiful and therefore does not concern me. What does spark my fascination is that you look to me the same way I'd imagine a girl in a possessed girl in a movie would. It's a bit much, wouldn't you say?"

"Perhaps this says more about you than it does me."

Something in the room smelled like burning. A few flies buzzed in and out of the shadows. It was getting colder and colder in the room and Mr. Fire had to unclench his stomach to keep from visibly shivering.

"Believe in what you want, but we both know the truth. Evil recognizes evil."

"Ha!" Fire laughed, genuinely amused, "Darling, even with this whole charade I can say with certainty that such concepts are of human design. Evil is only classified as those things which stand to oppose our moral beliefs or way of life. Good is a concept that simply aligns with them. We say, 'Do not murder!' and if someone does, we execute them. We say, 'Love thy neighbor,' and then go to war with people who don't love us back."

"If there is no good or evil, then what is there?" Katrín asked.

"Survival. Does the wolf eating the rabbit think of itself as a murderous monster? Do doves believe they are truly the symbol for peace? Or are these human labels we put on non-human things to make ourselves feel better about the ultimate truth of our existence?"

"That you are flawed bags of meat and bone," the girl laughed.

"That we are a cancer. We are a plague on this earth. Did you know that there have been five extinction events since this planet has been created? Five, my demon girl, five. Do you mean to tell me that God got it wrong all of those times until humans came around? We are not the end game. We are a sickness that the earth needs to purge. It is not out of good or evil, it is out of necessity."

Fire sat back in his chair and rubbed his arms. He could feel the goose bumps through his dress shirt.

"Perhaps your problem is that you think of Good and Evil—of God and Satan—as human constructs as well. Perhaps their true power and meaning elude you."

Katrín shook in her chair. The screws bolting the metal chair into the ground were starting to unscrew. Another swarm of flies darted out of the darkness buzzing like a crooked symphony. The silhouettes of dead and broken birds lined the small windows.

"If there is a greater power that is in control, then even you must admit that this is all part of the plan. Me being who I am, you being who you are. If there is not, then I guess my survival does hinge upon my selfish need to get done for my own survival. Either way, I cannot be swayed. I know you like to think that the Devil is real, or that a demon possesses you, but I don't believe that. I think you're a fine little actress who is too smart to be living in a bad neighborhood. You called me Lucas, but that is not my name…"

"Only because you find names to also be of human construct," she smiled. It stopped him cold because it was true. For years, he was known as Lucas before shedding his former self to take on the alias of Mr. Fire. All it took was a proposition, a way to leave his stale life behind. A life with a mortgage, a job crunching numbers, a bank account, and a disturbing lack of purpose. That night in the bar when Mrs. Light slipped him the envelope with the ultrasound. The way she said more money than you can dream and licked his ear.

Lucas accepted, went home and had passionate sex with his wife. Then he kissed his sleeping son on the forehead and never showed up for work at the accounting firm again. His family didn't ask questions when he disappeared for days at a time because whatever worries his wife and son felt, they went away when he returned. His wife stopped calling him Lucas, and only referred to him as My Love.

"Do you know why you're here?" Fire asked, snapping out of his trance. "Show me the power you claim to have that our rabid human minds cannot comprehend."

Katrín didn't hesitate.

"You kidnap people and harvest their organs for rich people. Sometimes they are dying, sometimes their children are dying, but for the right price you find people like my vessel, this girl, and have a doctor slice us open and take what they need. You've never been caught because those same rich people can pay to make sure others turn a blind eye to your crimes."

"This is true," Mr. Fire said. "But I still do not believe in God. The end game for all living things forever remains the same: death. The end game for a rock is simply to remain a rock. I still have emotions, I still feel love, I still feel fright, but I am not a slave to them. And for that reason alone, little girl, you do not scare me. Nor do I believe that you are actually possessed."

Katrín popped both of her shoulders out of their sockets and freed her hands. Her tongue had turned blue and serpent like. The metal screws holding the chair in place popped out and the girl fell forward, spun, and bridged onto her palms. With her stomach pointed upwards and head nearly scraping the ground, she crab-walked towards Mr. Fire. Fire stood up quickly and kicked in a panic. His shoe landed on the girl's face and she dropped.

"So much for supernatural power," he said, and tied her back to the chair. He twisted the screws in place with his fingers. Something in his mind clicked. "She's been here before. What are the odds?" he laughed.

For some reason the image of the ultrasound flashed into his mind. It was the first infant he had ever taken, ripped from an open window in a family's one story farmhouse. The payout was a quarter of a million dollars. He didn't care why the financers didn't want to adopt, didn't care if the child was a fetish fantasy, or anything else for that matter. Mr. Fire took his money, went home, and played Uno with his wife and son until daybreak without a care in the world.

"How'd it go?" Mr. Water asked, sipping his room temperature Coke.

"All mind games," Fire said opening up the fridge and taking out a beer. "She's smart."

"Organs are still intact?"

"As long as we keep her alive and talking until Mr. Vertigo comes, we'll collect our cash and go home."

Water nodded lucidly; a bit concerned about spending time with anyone who believed themselves to be possessed. In the back of his mind he could not let go of the idea that his faith being tested was part of God's plan. Maybe the falling out was meant to happen so it would lead him here, to this girl, who needed to be exorcised by a man who needed God, and a God who needed this man.

He pushed open the heavy door and saw the girl sitting there, face turning ashen and open sores oozing. It was hardly the same girl he dragged into the back of the car.

But maybe that was the reason for all of this to begin with. Chloroform could cause severe allergic reactions and they had dosed her twice. Who's to say that this wasn't a horrific side-effect?

Water watched her and she began watching him. His composure and understanding eyes had never truly left, even after abandoning his virtues. When other targets had begged and pleaded for their lives, Mr. Water still looked upon them with forgiveness.

"If it is true and you have taken this young girl, prove it. Don't give me that Exorcist line about your displays of power being too vulgar for my human eyes. The fact is, you can either do it – or you can't."

Katrín grinned. Then she opened her mouth letting a dead and decaying mouse fall out. It hit the ground with an airy thump. Water felt the back of his neck swell with heat and his throat start to pulse. He ran out of the room and over to the sink near the refrigerator splashing his face with cool water. Fire was nowhere to be seen, but a loud cough from the bathroom gave away his whereabouts.

The back of his hairline was damp, so was his brow. He filled a glass with water and guzzled it down. An idea emerged.

A moment later he stormed back into the holding cell with a full glass.

"Creature, this is holy water. May you burn in the land of fire from which you came," he said, and doused the girl. To his utter surprise, she shrieked in pain and began smoking. Her skin began to boil and sizzle.

"A man of GOD?!" the girl said in a twisted voice that should not have been hers.

"You are a liar. You are a coward. But above all, you are not real. This was tap water, so though I do not understand why you reacted the way you did, I can only imagine that it is because you believed so strongly that it would. You are not possessed; you simply believe you are."

"Is that not the nature of God?" the girl asked, panting in her chair still bound at the wrists and ankles. "What is belief if not the idea that greater things can happen than what currently surround us?"

That was a line from one of his sermons, word for word. This was back when he still ran a parish, before he left the church. This was during a time when the Church still held respect. His parish knew Mr. Water as Timothy Sullivan then, or Father Sullivan. He had never once laid hands on a child, nor approached them with anything but respect and care. Still, when the scandals broke across the nation and were making national headlines, allegations against Sullivan arose too. He denied the claims calling them 'preposterous' and 'wildly inaccurate' but the damage had been done. His name had been forever tainted and he was run out of town when death threats written on bricks were thrown through his window. After reaching out to Cardinals and the Archdiocese with not luck (all of their time and effort had gone into shuffling around the guilty parties), he was unsure where to turn. No church would take him, and no community seemed to look past the headlines.

Shunned and cast aside, Sullivan left the church. Years later the stories were recanted and proven false, but the damage was irreparable. The former priest had begun to think of God as a silly nothing who would not step in to help a faithful and devoted servant during a time of great need. If there was a God, He would not let these things happen. And so if there was no God, there was no reason to preach love and acceptance. There were no more reasons to stay abstinent. He partook in what he used to call 'sins of the flesh' only to find that they made him feel alive with something new.

"You fuck like the world is ending," a hooker named Bootsy said, lighting a cigarette in their motel bed. "You dying or something?"

"The path to self-destruction begins the day we are born," he answered, staring at himself in the mirror. He left $40 in cash on the dresser and left with his shirt still unbuttoned and untucked.

He remembered that night specifically because when he went to a bar, he had a chance encounter with Mr. Fire and Mrs. Light. A man lost had been found.

Over the next six years, he confirmed his theory that people live and people die, and God didn't care how it happened.

Now in this room, all of that felt childish and secondary. He looked at the girl who recognized in him something that he could barely recognize in himself: hope.

"Are you going to save me, Father?" she asked, her voice now sounding more like the scared girl they had taken.

"I'm damned if I do, and damned if I don't," he said. "Say I do nothing, and they cut you open. Say your organs have turned black. What then? Say I take the demon out of you and they still cut you open. You're dead."

"You focus only on the ending, Father. What if you focused on the unknown?" the girl chuckled, the mischievous grin smearing her face. "What if something happens that you could not predict, and it saves you?"

Water went silent again. It was like this girl – this creature – was reading his mind. Yet, why would a demon ask to be exorcised? Why would it want to save the life of this young girl? It wasn't making sense.

"Well, demon, by your own logic you are an agent of good. You tempt me to save the life of an innocent girl, which means you believe that I can. If you took over this girl but really don't want to be in her, why do you not just leave? You would not need my help."

"Perhaps I want to keep this girl alive because she is actually more important to you than you know. Perhaps only a man of God would understand."

A swarm of flies began circling Katrín's head. The dead and decaying mouse at her feet was dragged off into the corner of the room by a bigger mouse. The etchings in the walls were starting to bleed.

"If you imply she is my daughter, she is too old," Water said.

"Think bigger."

"Antichrist? Then it's better that she dies."

"Bigger," the girl grinned.

"Second coming? Then God will save her."

"Bigger."

Water thought for a moment about what could be bigger. What was he missing?

Then all at once it hit him. He dashed out of the room and into the kitchen area where Mr. Fire was laying out on the couch.

"Everything okay?" Fire askcd, already on his second beer.

"We need to let her go. We can't let her die," Water panted.

"What? I just got confirmation that Vertigo is going to be here in five minutes. We are not losing our payday."

"The girl has cancer."

Fire froze.

"So what? That doesn't concern us. We did our job so those rich bastards can get their organs."

"It's not that simple," Water said, his voice becoming more commanding than it had been in years. "Say Vertigo comes and takes what he needs. We burn the body, no traces back to us. Except for one huge detail...the people who receive the organs will get cancer and die and if they have the money to pull jobs like this, they sure as hell have money to go after Mrs. Light. Do you think she'll take a black market fall? Who do you really think this will all fall back on?"

Mr. Fire was visibly irritated. He was chewing on his bottom lip so aggressively that it started to puncture.

"We don't know that," he said, "you're letting her demon act get into your head because she knows it will. These are all just games."

A door clicked open, and heavy, calculated footsteps echoed through the cement rooms. A man in a long black trench coat carrying a leather briefcase appeared. His dark round sunglasses covering only his eyes and the hat on his head made him look otherworldly. He gave them a slight nod, and then walked into the room where Katrín was bound.

Though neither said it out loud, both had the exact same thought at the exact same time. Were they going to find Vertigo dead in that room with his neck snapped and facing the complete opposite way? Or had they just watched too many Hollywood movies? Had their eyes finally showed them the guilt of their minds?

As they peaked through the door, they found Vertigo slowly pulling a needle out of the girl's neck. He was cradling her head gently and Katrín's eyelids were fluttering. She had no more cracked skin or boils, and the red light had turned to soft yellow – the natural ambiance of the Edison bulb.

Vertigo motioned for the two to carry the unconscious girl into his operating room. The two untied the straps and lifted her body into the next room. Once on the table, they again strapped her down while the man in black hooked her up to anesthesia.

He took off his hat and placed a surgical mask over his nose and mouth. He opened the briefcase full of tools to cut through bone and sever organ tissue.

After putting on his black gloves, he went to work slicing. A machine tracked the vitals of Katrín. It beeped in time with her heart. Both Fire and Water stayed inside watching, which was something neither typically did. It didn't seem to bother the man who quickly and expertly made incisions and pulled out organs. They were guided into airtight bags and placed into coolers of ice.

"Does she have cancer anywhere?" Fire softly asked.

"Her heart might. You can see the black," Vertigo answered in a thick German accent pointing to spots. "But they pay me to take, not to test."

Water couldn't stop looking at the girl's face. She looked so serene, even as the very things that gave her life were stripped from her. However given long enough, these same things would have taken life from her too.

Then, Veritgo quickly cut out the heart and the machine beside them let out a long, singular sigh. She was gone, officially and absolutely. The man pulled the plug from the monitor and the sound stopped. He pulled off his blood-slicked gloves and put them into another plastic baggie. He then placed them into his suitcase along with his freshly cleaned equipment.

He handed two envelopes to the men, both brimming with money. Vertigo put his hat back on and left without saying anything else.

Just like that both he and Katrín were gone, disappearing into their respective unknowns.

Fire wrapped the body in cellophane from the neck down and heaved it to the old incinerator.

Water sprayed down the cement floor with a power washer, and then doused it with ammonia. When he was done, he sat down on the couch and stared off into the blank television.

"Hey!" Fire suddenly called from the other room. Water got up and hobbled over.

Fire was pointing to a body that was melting away. Everything was hissing in the flames except for the face, which was turned outwards with both blue eyes open. They watched as the heat moved the face into a twisted smile before melting it from the bone. For that split second, she was looking at the men again – possessing them forever.

Fire closed the furnace and walked to the main room without a word. Water did the same. They collected their things and didn't bother to count the money. However much it was, it was enough.

As they walked out of the abandoned warehouse to their car in the parking lot, Water spoke.

"*Ex mundis igne factus est,*" he said.

"The world is made of fire," his partner said, knowing the Latin phrase well. "*Ex mundis aqua factus est,* also."

Water half-heartedly smiled and got into the passenger seat lost deep in thought.

"If evil exists, are we it?" he asked, staring into the dashboard.

"People are like the ocean," Fire began, sitting in the driver's seat. "The deeper we look, the darker it gets and the more hideous the creatures that dwell. However, just because they are not aesthetically pleasing does not make them bad. They simply survive and adapt under the conditions that they were born into. It is us, the humans, who deny and suppress the idea that these things should ever surface. Whether we admit to it or not, they exist and are a part of our world. And that is what matters."

He twisted the ignition and the car hummed on. It idled in the overgrown parking garage while both men looked out silently over the setting sun.

*Ian Bain's*
*Shopping List*

Coffee
Chick peas
Peppers
Beer
Tofu
Chips
Frozen za
Broc
Onions
Cold brew coffee

# One Last Dip in the Lake
## *Ian Bain*

In a lake that is no longer there, on a day no living beings can recall, a teenage boy floated, free and wet in a cosmos of peace.

The boy had never felt free anywhere else. He was chubby; a fat-ass in the words of his schoolmates, and often the voice inside his head. But in the water, it didn't matter. He didn't have to wear baggy clothes to hide his boy bosoms, he didn't have to make up excuses to get out of exercise so that his belly wouldn't jiggle, he didn't constantly worry about his ass-crack hanging out or about splitting open the only pair of pants from the Wal Mart that he could actually fit into.

No.

In the water, no one could see him, and he could float, and dive down, and explore the sandy bottom of the lake with no intrusion. No fish would laugh at him and call him "fatso," or "lard-ass," or "bitch-tits". Though he was mindful of what might lurk beneath the sands. But that was no cause for concern, he simply swam above the ground all the way into and out of shore, avoiding taking more than two steps on the loose bottom.

On this day, the boy had swum out farther than he usually would on his own. Maybe if he had been with his mom or his older brothers, but he was twelve for Christ sakes! He could swim out as far as he wanted to! He'd swam 5 kilometres only two months prior in the swim teams swim-a-thon, surely, he could handle a couple hundred metres out from shore. And on this lake, the bottom stayed at a depth barely deeper than the boy could stand for almost a full kilometre from shore.

Close enough that he could see the light brown sandy beach, but far enough away that he couldn't make out a single particular face, the boy decided he was far enough. He floated, feeling the warm sun on his face and the cold water underneath him. He performed somersaults, and loop-de-loop, and dolphin dives, skimming the surface of the lake bottom, coming up, jumping out of the water, and repeating.

Always the boy swam with goggles. This prevented his brothers from making fun of him for having pink eye when he returned home with swollen and red eyes. But more than that, the pieces of plastic lined with foam cushioning allowed the boy to fully enjoy his underwater fortress of solitude. Holding his breath for upwards of a minute at a time, the boy would pass low over the lake bottom, imagining himself a diver; and underwater archaeologist; an elder god, newly awakened, flying low above the cities of men. Oh, the things he could discover.

A rock! Pointed and ebony-black with sharp white lines cutting through the middle. An arrowhead? Why not? The boy let his fingers hover around the rock, like he was feeling it. Imagining the thing felt cold and smooth and sharp, but never daring to touch it. What if it truly was sharp, sharp enough to cut him? Would he make it back to shore before he bled out? Or what if something were underneath the rock? What if something called the rock its roof? Worst of all, what if the rock was a something else? What if the rock was simply the head of a very stealthy snapping turtle? There'd be no escaping a snapping turtle in the water, it'd have the home field advantage, even up against the best diver-underwater archaeologist-elder god.

Awkwardly and abandoning his usual aquatic grace, the boy breeches the lake surface, taking in deep gasps of air. Imagining all the terrible possibilities of the rock had shot up his heart rate, decreasing the efficiency of his blood's use of oxygen. Head above water, the boy could tell himself he was being ridiculous. He smiled, and watched the other people enjoying the lake. He watched what he assumed to be shapes of sunbathers, the boats zooming around the deeper sections of the lake, the kite boarders and sea-doers and pontooners and tubers. Taking three long stokes—to escape the black rock, whatever it was—the boy descended to the bottom once more.

The boy always stayed away from the real thick patches of weeds, the ones that seemed to search for legs and necks to grab hold of, the kind the boy pictured his dead and drowned body caught up in often. But it was impossible to completely escape the serpentine arms of vegetation. It wasn't uncommon for the boy to exit the lake with weed around his shoulder or his neck or his ankles. The lake bottom which he so lovingly searched contained many smaller weeds that you couldn't see on the surface. You couldn't even tell they were there until you were above them or entangled in them.

Some of the underwater weeds did not grow vertical and tall, some grew wide a thick. Some looked lush and soft while others looked spiky and allergy-inducing. Some where an even darker brown than the lake floor, while some weeds were almost Snow White. But then some weeds…some weeds called to the boy, confounded him, drew him in and confused him with their very existence. On the day of the boy's last swim, he saw such a weed.

A fish! Was the boy's first thought, and what a fish it would have been. If what the boy saw had been a fish's tail, Jonah himself would have been running for shore. But the way the thing moved with the slight current told him this was not a fish, not a creature at all. The closer the boy got, the more he was sure the thing was just dead grass, dead grass at least two feet long.

The boy swam closer, the weed wasn't green or brown, it was gray. This unnatural plant colour told the boy it must be dead; dead or dying, yes. Continuing to swim around the peculiar dead plant, before he could make another guess, the boy saw its face.

Thin-skinned, eyeless and toothless, lipless and earless, the weed was not a weed at all, but the hair on the head of some long dead poor soul.

The boy gasped at the head, caught in a pose of a horrid scream, so much so that the boy swore he could almost hear the head screaming. As he gasped, the boy began to choke, but he could not bring himself to return to the surface. Was he afraid of the thing coming after him? Or was he simply so intrigued by the lake's mummy that he could not move? It didn't matter, wouldn't matter for long.

You hear things at the bottom of the lake. The boy often thought he heard people calling his name, but it was faint and discernible as far off sounds carried through the liquid medium. What he heard on that day was clear and penetrated his brain as if the speaker's tongue were driven deep into his ear-canal. "Youuuuu," the voice called out to him. He heard it, but the skull's face did not move. Was he losing his mind? Or was the voice coming…from behind him?

"Youuuuu," he heard again. As he spun around, the boy saw not one, but hundreds more skulls, all with the same weed-like hair, reaching for the lake's surface as if the follicles were trying to pull their dead owners to safety.

Now the boy did return to the surface, paddling front crawl as fast as his arms would allow him while not letting his face back into the water, lest he see more of the amphibious creatures below.

Fifty metres later, and making no noticeable progress back to shore, the boy stopped to tread water and think.

There's no way they were speaking, thought the boy, no way! That's…impossible. They probably weren't even real heads, just weeds and rocks, just my overactive imagination. Oh God, my 'overactive imagination'? That's something mom would say.

But what if they are real? The boy pondered, his head looking around to see if anyone else was around.

And if they are? They're dead, they died because they're stuck down here. Either they are just heads, cut off in some sort of mass tragedy, or they are the buried victims of what will surely turn out to be the world's greatest serial killer. And I could be the one to discover them…

After catching his breath, the boy resolved to return to the underwater heads. If not for the fame of discovery, he could at least receive closure to ensure he was able to avoid the inevitable terrible nightmares of aquatic zombies.

He swam head-up to where he thought he found the rotting heads and dove. The boy had to remind himself to open his eyes when he got to the bottom, as he'd subconsciously shut his eyes while submerging.

At the bottom of the lake…the heads had all disappeared. But the lake bottom was not bare, now, spiny, boney weeds reached up from the sand, and appeared to continue far above the surface of the lake. Confused, the boy surfaced.

The sun had gone, hid behind clouds. The happy boaters were screaming and fleeing for shore. The kite-boarders had fallen from their instruments and paddled as hard as they could, many getting run over by the chaotic mass of boats all headed away from where the boy had been swimming. The sunbathers were holding phones and cameras towards the boy's position, though the smarter ones were already heading for their cars, scooping up their children and leaving their beach accessories behind. Finally, the boy looked up. The weed-haired skulls, now looking all the rottener from exposure to air, their skin no longer held in lessened gravity, had begun falling from their faces. On what the boy had originally thought to be spiked weeds, but what were revealed to be impossibly long spinal columns, the skull had risen ten, twenty, thirty feet above the lake. What the boy thought had been hundreds of heads had turned out to be thousands, tens of thousands, and uncountable number of skulls moving in serpent-fashion above the chaotic lake-exodus. A zombie-headed hydra, whose body still lay somewhere beneath the bottom of the lake, began to strike.

It seemed the spinal column necks had no end-range. They went for those on shore first, confident they would still have time to pick off the people still trying to make it to shore. The loose-flesh heads dropped their lower jaws, having no use for them, the rotten appendages fell splashing into the water below. Instead of tongue, great spikes became visible underneath the skulls' upper jaws, and when the horrid heads got within ten metres of their victims, they let lose the barbed stingers.

The boy watched as what he assumed was a mother, in a full-piece bathing suit, running to her car with her baby in arms, took one of the black spikes to the base of her skull. The woman went limp so fast, the boy couldn't believe she'd ever really been alive. The bundle in her arms dropped to the paved parking lot and the boy swore he could hear the splat all the way from his position in the lake.

A man in a speedboat, cranking the engine to full speed, took a black spear to the same place as the unlucky mother. He was dragged backwards like a fish who met the sharp end of a harpoon gun, and the boat carrying his family continued onwards, concussing a kite boarder who'd begun the long and pointless swim back to shore. The kite-boarder's suffering was short-lived, however, as the boat's motor followed the hull's cranial head pummeling and tore his brains apart to unrecognizable pieces in the blink of an eye.

The skulls were smart in their initial targets, they took the operators of boats, the drivers of cars, sending the related parties on course for horrible crashes. Though if they survived, the demonic heads were sure to pick up the survivors.

One boat, almost big enough to be called a yacht, pulled a couple of young girls behind on a big round raft. They had been screaming before the skulls rose above the lake, but when the skeletal abomination awoke, their screams changed to a much more esophagus-tearing tone. When one of the skull heads hit the driver of the almost-yacht, his instantly dead body hit the steering wheel before being ranked from the boat, flying backwards and disappearing under the surface. The almost-yacht turned hard to the left, narrowly missing a head-on collision with another boat. After breathing a sigh of relief, the oncoming boaters were clothes-lined by the rope attached to the sisters' raft. Their heads cracked on the boat's floor, but they didn't feel a thing. The force of the rope had snapped their necks, killing them instantly.

The girls onboard the raft weren't able to hold on as their boat continued to spin in angry circles, and eventually they had to let go of the raft's handholds. The bigger sister skidded atop the surface of the water towards the boy. He ducked as she continued over his head, narrowly missing his own decapitation. The smaller sister was flung high, towards a small island on the lake. Her mid back hit a cedar tree growing on the island, and the small girl split in two, her two halves flung into the bushes of the island.

The bigger girl from the raft, still wearing her life jacket, dog-paddled towards the boy. The girl cried and tried to talk to the boy but between her sobs and snot and choking on water, she was unintelligible. The boy let the girl grab on to him, and though she was the bigger of the two sisters, he still outweighed her by a solid hundred pounds. In her frantic state she was keeping herself above water by pushing down on the boy. The boy's swimming skill and flabby buoyancy allowed them both to keep their heads above water.

As more and more people were cut down and dragged to the bottom of the lake, the old skulls floated to the surface. Whatever the spines were attached to, the boy thought, it no longer needed the old heads, it had new ones.

"What is going on?" The girl asked, the boy was unable to respond.

"Why aren't they attacking us?" The girl cried to the boy.

"Because," he responded in a horrifyingly calm tone, "we're out here in the middle of the lake without a boat. They can save us 'til last."

## <u>Other HellBound Books Titles</u>
## <u>Available at: www.hellboundbookspublishing.com</u>

### The Toilet Zone
### RESTROOM READING AT ITS MOST FRIGHTENING!

Compiled and edited by the grand master of 80's schlock horror, Bret McCormick, each one of this collection of 32 terrifying tales is just the perfect length for a visit to the smallest room....

At the very boundaries of human imagination dwells one single, solitary place of solitude, of peace and quiet, a place in which your regular human being spends, on average, 10 to 15 minutes - at least once every single day of their lives.

Now, consider a typical, everyday reading speed of 200 to 250 words per minute - that means your average visitor has the time to read between 2,500 to 4,000 words, which makes each and every one of these 32 tales of terror - from some of the best contemporary independent authors - within this anthology of horror the perfect, meticulously calculated length. Dare you take a walk to the small room from where inky shadows creep out to smother the light and solitude's siren call beckons you?

Dare you take a quiet, lonely walk into… The Toilet Zone

## ROAD KILL: TEXAS HORROR BY TEXAS WRITERS - VOL 3

Everything is bigger in Texas - including the horror!

A Piney woods meth dealer clones Adolph Hitler. A nightmare exorcist meets an inexorable fined. An eyeball collector gets collected. The apparition of a lynching victim tracks down his executioners. A Texas lawman is undone by shades of his past. A Baphomet recruits converts as a local summer camp. The tales of the baker's dozen who appear in this anthology demonstrate why everything is scarier in Texas…
Including tales of terror from
Jeremy Hepler
Madison Estes
Bret McCormick
James H Longmore
ER Bills
Shawna Borman

And many more...

## Schlock! Horror!

An anthology of short stories based upon/inspired by and in loving homage to all of those great gorefest movies and books of the 1980's (not necessarily base in that era, although some do ride that wave of nostalgia!), the golden age when horror well and truly came kicking, screaming and spraying blood, gore & body parts out from the shadows...

This exemplary 80's themed/inspired tales of terror has been adjudicated and compiled by one Mr Bret McCormick, himself a writer, producer and director of many a schlock classic, including *Bio-Tech Warrior, Time Tracers, The Abomination, Ozone: The Attack of the Redneck Mutants* and the inimitable *Repligator*.

Featuring stories from: Todd Sullivan, Timothy C Hobbs, Mark Thomas, Andrew Post, James B. Pepe, Thomas Vaughn, Edward Karpp, Jaap Boekestein, Lisa Alfano, L. C. Holt, John Adam Gosham, Brandon Cracraft, M. Earl Smith, Sarah Cannavo, James Gardner, Bret McCormick, and James H. Longmore.

## Graveyard Girls

*Female authors + Horror = something spectacularly terrifying!*

A delicious collection of horrific tales and darkest poetry from the cream of the crop, all lovingly compiled by the incomparable Gerri R Gray! Nestling between the covers of this formidable tome are twenty-five of the very best lady authors writing on the horror scene today! These tales of terror are guaranteed to chill your very soul and awaken you in the dead of the night with fear-sweat clinging to your every pore and your heart pounding hard and heavy in your labored breast…

Featuring superlative horror from: Xtina Marie, M. W. Brown, Rebecca Kolodziej, Anya Lee, Barbara Jacobson, Gerri R. Gray, Christina Bergling, Julia Benally, Olga Werby, Kelly Glover, Lee Franklin, Linda M. Crate, Vanessa Hawkins, P. Alanna Roethle, J Snow, Evelyn Eve, Serena Daniels, S. E. Davis, Sam Hill, J. C. Raye, Donna J. W. Munro, R. J. Murray, C. Bailey-Bacchus, Varonica Chaney, Marian Finch (Lady Marian).

## The Devil's Hour

A new and altogether awesome anthology of all things horror!

Seventeen spine-chilling tales of the darkest terror, most unpleasant people, and slithering monsters that lurk beneath the bed and in the blackest of shadows…

## An Unholy Trinity

## 3 TERRIFYING NOVELLAS, 3 SUPERLATIVE AUTHORS, 1 BIG, FAT, JUICY BOOK!

ENÛMA ELIŠ (When on High) – Terry Grimwood. The Babylonian Creation story is a tale of monsters and cataclysmic wars. An epic saga dominated by the gods Tiamat and Mardak, bitter rivals who battle for supremacy over the unformed universe. It is a story replete with Minotaurs and scorpion men, dragons and monstrous blood-sucking demons.

A myth, a fantasy...

But when a traumatized ex-soldier rescues a young woman, washed up and barely alive on the shore of a sleepy Englîsh seaside town, the fragile borders between myth and reality begin to crumble and gods and their legions wake from their long-slumber.

THE REMNANT - C. Bailey-Bacchus

When fifteen-year-old Bianca Baker is blinded by rage and hatred, her inner demons take control and turn an ordinary school trip into a horrific tragedy. Witnesses to her violent act, succumb to Bianca's aggression and agree to say events were a terrible accident. Sixteen years later, those involved find the past clawing its way from the shadows to haunt them, and this time there is no way it will stay buried.

ALICE IN HORRORLAND - Vanessa Hawkins
Alice is an 11 year old orphan living within the veins of industrial England. When she meets a mysterious gentleman with the power to turn into a white rabbit, she finds herself tumbling down a manhole into Horrorland. Here the creatures are strange and uncanny, lost in a revolution of madness. Drug addicted Caterpillars, grinning cats and homicidal Mad Hatters gambol around Alice like blood-drunk mosquitoes. However, at the center of it all is the Queen of Hearts: said to have given up her own a long time ago…
Horrorland used to be so wonderful… Can Alice make it so again?

**A HellBound Books LLC
Publication**

http://www.hellboundbookspublishing.com

**Printed in the United States of America**